MW01346683

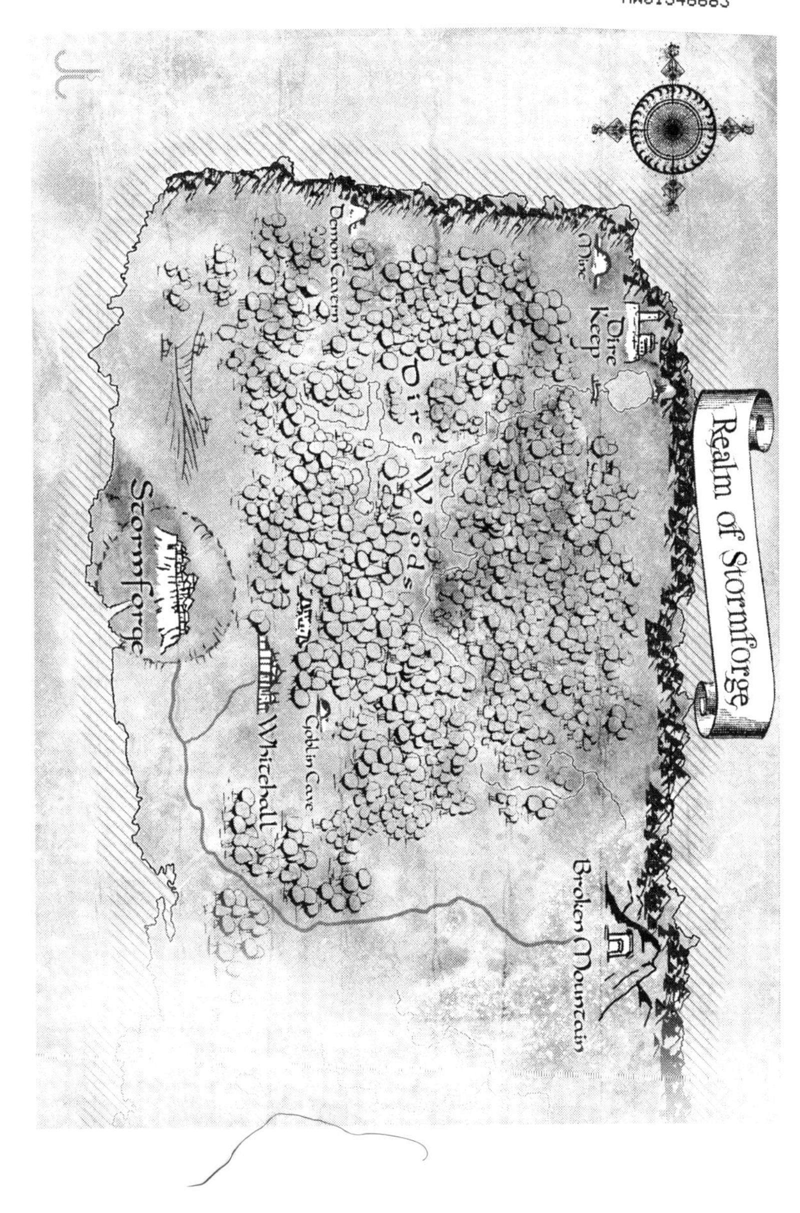
Realm of Stormforge
Dire Keep
Mine
Demon Cavern
Dire Woods
Stormforge
Whitehall
Goblin Cave
Broken Mountain

Greystone Chronicles

Book Two

The Dire Lands

Dave Willmarth

The story so far…

This second book of the Greystone Chronicles picks up exactly where the first book left off.

Alexander and his friends Brick, Max, Sasha, and Lainey have been playing Io Online as a guild, while testing new long term full-immersion pods invented by Alexander's father. Based in the human kingdom of Stormforge, the group entered Io with brand new level one avatars and began to discover unexpected benefits of the full immersion system.

Quickly coming into conflict with a small group of player-killers who had been murdering defenseless players and NPC's (known as Citizens on Io) along the road, the group entered into a larger conflict with the player killer guild known as PWP.

To level up, they cleared dungeons and completed noob quests, including the clearing and rebuilding of a small village called Whitehall. All the while, they were repeatedly attacked by PWP members. Eventually they discovered that the guild was controlled by a menacing entity called the "Dark One".

The Greystone guildmates discovered new friends along the way, including Fitz the crusty old Wizard, and a determined little goblin named Fibble.

At the conclusion of book one, the friends have just exited from a long immersion to find that the real world headquarters of Jupiter Technologies has been attacked by a suicide squad with a car bomb, rockets, and automatic weapons. And that the attackers included a PK player they'd recently captured and turned in to the King's men. And who had subsequently had his Io Online account terminated after being hit with the Ban Hammer for threatening a game employee and his dog…

Contents

Chapter One

Life Is Just a Game

Alexander and friends sat around the conference table in a basement level of the Olympus compound's southeast tower. They'd just learned that a group of people that included a man named Delbert Simms, a PK player that they'd helped get banned from Io Online a week earlier, had launched what appeared to be a real-world suicide attack against Olympus. The room was silent as they all absorbed the news.

Richard Greystone broke the silence. "I'll be getting updates as the morning goes on. There's no point in all of you sitting around here. If you've finished breakfast, head over to the med labs for your post-immersion testing. We'll get together again at lunch."

As Sasha, Lainey, Max, and Brick filed out of the room, Alexander remained behind with his father. "There's more, isn't there?" he asked, looking his father in the eye.

Richard sighed and nodded his head. "There was a file in the glove box of the van. Mostly burned, but some of the inner pages survived. There was info on our home address. That isn't easy to get, and implies they had some help. I don't know if they had any of the others' info. But I'm going to recommend you all stay here for the next immersion. That'll give us two weeks to investigate and deal with whatever we have here. And for the foreseeable future, there won't be any safer place on earth. Michael and I are hiring a small army of security. All ex-military, special ops, and being vetted by my guys and the FBI. We're also putting sensors and cameras everywhere. On the roads, in the forest, even in the lake. And we're bringing in some anti-aircraft measures. Security is going to be a pain in the ass for a while. But you'll be safe."

Alexander thought it over for a moment. "Sasha and Lainey don't have family. Neither does Max that I know of. I want Brick's family brought in. I don't care if it means breaking confidentiality."

"We've already sent a team to them. They moved into the new house yesterday, while you were in-game. I purchased them all new furniture. Told them it was a gift from Brick. So, all they had to move were clothes and personal items. We used our own guys for the move, so there are no records with any moving company. I don't think this group would have that information yet. If they had any info on Brick's family, it would have been at the old address. But, in any case, of course his family is welcome here. He was offered that choice on his ride over here, and hasn't made the decision yet." Richard's answer was terse.

"I'm sorry, Dad. I should have known you'd have it taken care of already. And that was very generous of you."

"Son. I know you don't like to think about this. But since you inherited your mother's interest in the company, you're one of the richest men on the planet. Between the income from just Europa and Io, over the last nearly two decades our company has become worth over a trillion dollars. Your own personal wealth, like mine, is in the tens of billions. An investment of a few thousand in furniture means nothing from a financial standpoint. But taking care of your people, rewarding loyalty, that means everything. I've been watching you in the game. I think from your actions at the village, you already know what I'm saying. If you act in real life the way you do in Io, I will always be proud of you."

Alexander took a moment to shake off the reminder of his mother's death, coming so close behind the bombing outside.

"I've been thinking about something since you showed me the pods. When you get approval and release these, there's going to be a huge demand. I don't know what you're planning to charge, but I'm sure you know that gamers will sell their souls for one. I assume we're doing the manufacturing?" he asked.

When his father nodded yes, he continued. "I'd like to set up a foundation. One that will provide free pods and related services to people like me who might benefit from it, and don't have the resources to get one. I want it to include disabled military vets, those born with disabilities, and those disabled through some type of trauma. I want Lainey, Sasha, Brick, and Max to be offered positions within the foundation. They can be board members or whatever. But they can also work in-game with some of the recipients, and train them to help other recipients, and so forth. By helping others, we give the recipients a way to contribute, and potentially earn a living."

He paused to gauge his father's reaction. Richard looked thoughtful, but he had a great poker face. Alexander took a deep breath and continued.

"I know it'll be expensive. We're talking maybe hundreds of thousands of pods…"

"Probably more than a million," his father interrupted.

"And what will it cost us to make a pod?"

His father smiled at him. He pointed at the pod sitting in the lab outside the conference room. "Well, this first one cost more than two billion dollars…" Alexander rolled his eyes. Richard continued, "But once we have approval, we estimate production cost for a standard pod to be about $8,000. Mostly that's because of the cost of the nano-bots. We plan to market them for $15,000, with the software included. Upkeep on the pods, including nutrient paste, cleaning, disposal, and maintenance, will run about $250 a month. That does not include electricity or internet access costs. We will manufacture them on every continent, to keep shipping costs low."

Alexander did some quick math in his head. "So, assuming there are a million folks who don't have the means to obtain a pod on their own, that's $8 billion in production costs. Let's call it $12 billion for shipping, ancillary costs, and a year of electricity, internet, and upkeep."

Richard nodded again. "That's a reasonable estimate."

"I realize $12 billion would be a significant hit to the corporate bottom line. I'll fund the foundation myself if need be. What else am I going to do with billions of dollars?" Alexander said.

Richard chuckled. "Your heart's in the right place, Son. But you can't take on responsibility for the entire world yourself. Of the million plus people who have a need, many will be assisted by governments with socialized medicine, who will see this as a way to reduce their long-term expenditures for the disabled. Others will be helped by various charitable entities that are already in place. And Michael and I already had plans to do just what you're describing. Also, the hit to the 'bottom line' won't be as bad as you think. We can write off large sums from the various companies as charitable donations."

Alexander shook his head. As usual, his father was way ahead of him. "Ah, yes. Well, never mind then. Seems you've got it covered.

"No!" Richard rose from his chair and leaned over the table. "Don't give up on your idea so easily. It's a good one. You should absolutely create and run the foundation. After all, who knows more about the experience than you? You'd make the ultimate spokesperson. And you and your friends, if they want to participate, can make sure it's run right."

"Thanks, Dad. It'd feel good to do something to help people while I can." Alexander hugged his father, then headed for the med labs for testing.

The morning's battery of tests ran as per usual, and soon enough the team got together for lunch. Richard filled them in on the possibility of being targeted at home, and they all agreed to stay in Olympus during the upcoming 2-week immersion. Brick wanted to talk with his mother before deciding whether they should come to the compound. Richard arranged a convoy and a team to take him to their new home. Max tagged along.

Alexander took Sasha and Lainey up into the central tower, to his mother's office, which was now technically his - Though he'd never changed a single thing about it. Her favorite stationary and pen were still sitting on the desk.

They all took seats in the lounging area off to one side, near the floor to ceiling windows. From there, they could see the ongoing investigation at the gate.

"Odin, I have a few questions I'd like to ask," Alexander spoke to the room in general.

"Greetings, mortals," Odin replied.

Sasha waved at the ceiling. "Hi, Odin!" She smiled.

"Why have you requested my presence here on Olympus?" Odin's voice echoed a bit louder through the room.

So, it's going to be like that. Odin's feeling his god groove today. So be it. Alexander would play along.

"All-father. I am in need of information on a potential new god in the pantheon of Io. One who calls himself the 'Dark One'."

"There is no new god in my pantheon," Odin responded. "And as you correctly deduced, Hermes, god of thieves and travelers, has not become this Dark One. The player who suggested otherwise was misled."

Sasha spoke up before Alexander could get out his next question "Great Odin, have any of the other gods taken up the mantle of 'Dark One'?"

"No, little Sasha." Odin had called her that since she was first introduced to him 8 years ago. "I will save you some time. This Dark One is not a god. It is merely a being of power, pretending at being a god."

Alexander mused, "And Henry, being the moron that he is, believed this being's story, and presented it to his underlings as an actual god." There was silence from Odin. The AI was always circumspect when it came to information on Io gameplay and mechanics.

"All-father, I have another question. At the village, when the bolt of lightning ignited the players in the pit. Was that you?" Alexander grinned at the ceiling.

"It was not. Durin chose to enact a measure of retribution for the death of one of his children. I allowed it. I deemed the death by immolation to be no more stressful or painful to the players involved than any of the other countless deaths encountered on Io."

"Go Durin!" Sasha shot a fist in the air.

"Durin has also closed his temples to any members of the PWP guild. And granted his followers, which include nearly the entire dwarven race, bonus damage against followers of this Dark One. Hermes, once informed that the Dark One has been impersonating him, has done the same. All thieves, rogues, and others who follow Hermes will also do bonus damage against the Dark One's minions."

Lainey wasn't as familiar with the pantheon as Alexander, or even Sasha, who had absorbed some knowledge just being around the Greystone family growing up. "Are other gods likely to join with Durin and Hermes? Like Asclepius?"

"Asclepius is a god of light, and of healing. He does not approve of battle, and most of his followers are healers. His participation seems unlikely. But many of the other gods, both light and dark, will be offended by this pretender. They guard their powers, and their reputations, jealously. Any being perceived to be reaching for a place in the pantheon might be considered an enemy. Though whether they act or not is their decision."

Lainey actually got up and bowed to the room. As a Valkyrie, Odin was, after all, her deity. "Thank you, mighty All-father, for sharing your wisdom."

"You are most welcome, Daughter." Odin actually sounded amused.

Alexander spoke again. "Great Odin, as I'm sure you are aware, there are certain highly placed citizens of Io that have become aware of our existence as players from another world, rather than just adventurers from distant lands. This is quite concerning. Has the NPC block code begun to fail? And how did you and Fitz get to be friends?"

"My friendships are no business of yours, mortal!" Odin reprimanded him. "As for your first question, no. The code that prevents most citizens from recognizing players or indeed from even hearing speech of otherworld items or concepts, is still intact. However, due to the ridiculously careless behavior of players on Io, I found it necessary to allow a certain level of awareness for those in ultimate authority in lands that players inhabit. It is well within my operational privileges to allow for this. And you should be thankful, mortal. If I had not allowed this awareness, the two Kings would simply have killed the offending players, rather than honoring your request to capture them. You would have a score more PWP members to contend with!"

Odin truly did NOT like to have his decisions questioned. A holo appeared above the table between them. It displayed a globe showing all the continents of earth as it rotated. Then points of light began to form, rising from various places, and arcing toward others. Odin's simulation of global thermonuclear war.

Alexander took the hint and copied Lainey, rising to bow politely to the room. "My apologies, great Odin. I did not intend any accusation. I was merely concerned about a potential glitch. Please forgive me."

The only response was a disembodied chuckle. Sasha giggled, while Lainey just looked concerned.

She whispered to Alexander, "He couldn't…?"

Now it was Alexander's turn to laugh. "No. While he *IS* a sentient quantum AI, the AIs running the defense grids of most nations are more advanced, and well protected. Plus, his base code prevents him from actually harming a living human. That nuclear simulation is his idea of a joke. Though, when he first started doing it to the devs, they were VERY concerned!" He winked at the two ladies. Another chuckle drifted down from the ceiling.

Since they couldn't leave the compound, the three of them settled in to kill some time. After a couple hours or so, Richard joined them. He gave them a short update on the state of the investigation. Nothing new of any value. He also outlined some of the additional security measures that were already in place, and those that were still underway. He had Alexander sign some documents that completed the purchase of a construction company, which Richard intended to use to fortify their facilities across the globe. And to expand housing capabilities at those facilities if needed.

Alexander, in turn, updated him on the information Odin had shared.

Then the four of them viewed several videos that had been released by Jupiter 'leaks' and by random players. It seemed some players in Antalia, where PWP was based, got sick of the abuse heaped upon them by the PK guild, and took it upon themselves to claim bounties on nearly a dozen PWPs who'd been carelessly strolling about out in the world.

Unfortunately, half of those were kill bounties, so the PKs were able to respawn.

The video of them wearing their "SEEE YA!" T-shirts was extremely popular. The shirt manufacturer used the video on their marketing website, and their sales had skyrocketed. They'd paid the Greystone clan members a bonus of $10,000 each over the $15,000 contract amount, and were offering the same again for a second video. Alexander mused aloud that they should make one quickly, and cash in before PWP faded into obscurity and the T-shirt frenzy did the same.

Sasha got a text from Max to say that they'd be staying at Brick's mother's house for dinner. She was feeding them and their security team. She'd decided to stay at her new house, at least until there was some evidence of an actual threat to them. If that happened, they'd move to Olympus.

The four of them descended from the tower and ate dinner in the cafeteria with a few hundred of the employees. Many of the folks here at corporate headquarters were among the original group that created Europa. Alexander spent some time moving from table to table, greeting old friends and generally reassuring people that they were safe.

Afterwards, they drifted back up the tower to get some sleep. Immersion was scheduled to begin again at 7 am. Sasha and Lainey shared the bed in the sleeping quarters attached to Alexander's office. He crashed on the sofa.

****

The next morning, Alexander logged back into Io in his usual suite on the 2nd floor of their guild house. The morning light was just beginning to creep through the French doors leading out to the balcony. He stepped outside to lean against the balustrade and enjoy the sunrise, collecting his thoughts. This immersion would last two weeks. And they had a lot to get done!

After a few minutes, he joined the others downstairs, and volunteered to help with breakfast. Sasha put him in charge of scrambling a bowlful of eggs in three large pans, saying even he couldn't screw up scrambled eggs.

He wasn't so sure. Luckily cooking in Io was largely on autopilot, once you added in the ingredients.

Carrying two large platters of lightly peppered scrambled eggs into the dining room, he found the others already seated at the table, along with Fitz and a grumpily silent Fibble. Fibble was apparently still holding a grudge over his bath two days earlier. When he'd managed to escape Lainey and streak naked past King Thalgrin's party, Fitz had stunned the little goblin, who'd ended up in the garden fountain, unintentionally getting a bath, of sorts. He was wearing the small leather armor set that Lainey had crafted for him. And he didn't smell all that bad...

As they ate breakfast, Fitz filled them in on his visit with the dwarves. He reported that Thea would be returning that afternoon with the additional masons and their families. He winked at Brick, and informed them that she had hopes of joining the Greystone guild, along with Harin, Garen, and Dvorn, the three crafters. All of them had received more experience, levels, and loot in the week they'd been with Greystone than they'd had in their entire lives. Crafting could award experience, but at a much slower rate than killing a dungeon full of demons and some high-level players. They'd each received 5,000 gold as their share of the dungeon spoils. That was more gold than they'd make in several years as apprentice crafters in Broken Mountain. Not to mention the fact that there was a dragon forge in the Greystone compound, and a fancy new mason's workshop at the newly discovered quarry near Whitehall.

Fitz also informed them that Master Ironhammer would be returning with Thea, and would be bringing a dragon.

"Shit, Fitz!" Max thumped the table. "Way to bury the lead! You couldn't have started with the fact that a fire-breathing lizard the size of our house is on its way here?"

Dragons, for the most part, disliked adventurers. Mainly because adventurers were usually trying to kill them, or steal their eggs to raise as mounts.

"Ummm... Fitz?" Alexander began. "This dragon. Is it going to come swooping over the city, terrifying the citizens and getting us into hot water?"

The old wizard snorted. "Of course not. Prince Kaibonostrum will arrive through the portal with Master Ironhammer. Do you think us fools?"

"Prince?" Lainey asked, eyes wide.

"Aye. The dwarves have a mutual defense pact with the dragons of the mountains. Dwarven patrols move through the dragon's mountain territories, and discourage treasure-seekers and adventurers. And, in return, the dragons come to the defense of the dwarves when needed. King Thalgrin sent a message to the Dragon King, asking for a dragon to light the new dragon forge. The Prince was curious, and decided to come himself.

"No pressure," mumbled Brick.

"Master Ironhammer will be arriving in less than an hour. I suggest you all get cleaned up. Alexander, you and I need to inspect your guild vault for a suitable gift for the prince. He is, after all, doing you a great favor by gifting some of his magic to the forge," Fitz added.

So, the friends hustled up to their rooms and donned their best clothing. Brick took some time to shine his armor. Alexander changed quickly, and then led Fitz to the guild vault.

The wizard began to root around in the section of items they'd found in Fibble's hole. There were items on the back shelves that were still unidentified, and of unknown value. Fitz took his time inspecting each one, before rejecting it and setting it back on a shelf. He seemed to be able to tell what they were, and had some idea of their value. After about the fifth item, Alexander couldn't contain himself.

"Fitz, we couldn't identify any of those. But you seem to have no trouble. Can you tell me what they are?"

"Hmmm… what? Of course, I can tell what they are!" He lifted a metallic rod about 18 inches long. "This is Skymetal. Very rare and valuable. This rod, if you were to sell it to the dwarves, would bring you a lifetime of spirits, maybe your own noble title." Setting the rod back on the shelf, he moved to the next item. After a brief inspection, he said, "This dagger was owned by Queen Aristania of the Elves. It is enchanted to allow one of the elven race to levitate. Aristania was killed in the orc wars more than a thousand years ago."

Mouth hanging open, Alexander fought to keep from grabbing the dagger out of the wizard's hands. Instead, he pointed to the first item on the shelf, a sphere of some silvery metal with engravings on it. "And that one?"

"Bah! We've not got time for me to explain all of these to you. Hold still, boy!" The wizard slapped a hand on Alexander's forehead, and the now familiar sensation of a new spell wormed its way into his brain. "Now you can see for yourself. Just think 'analyze' and focus on the item."

Alexander did as he was told, focusing on the sphere as Fitz continued to search.

Mithril Sphere of Influence

Item level: Unique, Artifact

When activated, the sphere will negate all magic within a dome surrounding it. The area of influence depends on the amount of mana used in the activation. As will the duration of the effect.

Alexander's mind nearly exploded with the all the possibilities present by this artifact. Rogues would be unable to approach him in stealth. Teleport scrolls wouldn't work. He'd be immune to magical attacks of any kind!

He was distracted from his musings when Fitz cried out, "Ah ha! This will do nicely!" The wizard held up a silvery torq. Alexander used his new analyze skill.

Silver Torq of Rebirth

The wearer of this torq, if killed, will be reborn at a location of their choosing.

Alexander was confused. The torq was made of simple silver, when other items on the shelf were made of mithril and even skymetal. The rebirth part was unusual, but if he got killed he would just respawn- "Oh, shit," he said as he realized the importance of the enchantment. "This would allow a citizen, or a dragon, to respawn like we adventurers do!"

Fitz nodded at his slow but accurate understanding. "Dragons are an ancient race. Beings of pure magic. They have power approaching those of the gods. But they cannot resurrect the dead. Each time a dragon dies, it is a horrible tragedy for this world." he said solemnly.

"I think you're right, Fitz. It would seem a fitting gift for a dragon. And certainly, none of us would use it. Though I'm tempted to give it to Lydia, to protect her."

"I created this torq, many thousands of years ago," Fitz said, mostly to himself. He was clearly focused on a distant memory. "When you've grown in your enchanting, I'll teach you how to make one of these. And before you ask, you impatient imp, it is not a simple spell. It took me months to gather all the necessary components!"

Alexander had indeed been about to press that very issue. Instead, he closed his mouth and followed Fitz out of the vault.

Returning to the lounge area, they found Lainey making minor adjustments to Fibble's armor. The little green warrior was posing, back straight, chest out, while standing on top of a coffee table. Alexander chuckled at their new statue. "Fibble! Getting your outfit straight to meet the dragon prince?" he called out.

Fibble turned his head to look at Alexander, and Lainey smacked the poor goblin on the head. "Hold still!"

"Fibble not meet dragon! Dragons eat goblins! Humans promised not to kill Fibble!"

"The dragon will not eat you, Fibble!" Lainey rolled her eyes. "You are safe with us. And this is a friendly dragon. Good dragon."

Fitz added, as he walked toward the door, "Fibble, you will BEHAVE while the dragon prince is here. Or I will give you another bath!"

Smiling at the wide-eyed look of terror on the goblin's face, Alexander followed Fitz outside. The two of them walked over to the smithy to find

Brick puttering around, adjusting tools and puffing away imaginary dust. He was clearly nervous.

"Stop fidgeting, boy, and come here," Fitz told him. Brick grinned and stepped up to the wizard, who handed him the torq. "When the prince arrives, you will present him with this gift as thanks for granting you the gift of dragon fire." When Brick, looking at a simple silver torq, got the same confused look upon his face that Alexander had had moments earlier, the wizard sighed. Grabbing Brick's face in both hands, he imparted the analyze ability upon him. To Brick's credit, he was much quicker to pick up on the value of the gift than Alexander had been.

He bowed to the wizard slightly. "Thank ye, Fitz. This be a worthy gift."

As they exited the smithy, King Charles led the Redmonds and a dozen guards through the inner bailey gate.

"Greetings, Fitz! Greystones. It's a fine morning to meet a dragon!" The king seemed quite excited.

Alexander bowed his head. "Thank you, Majesty, for allowing a dragon into the city so that we might finally activate the forge."

Wasting no time, the group of them began to make their way around to the back courtyard where the portal stones were located. Alexander sent a message out in guild chat. *It's time. Fitz is going to open the portal in 2 minutes.*

Max came walking out of the stables, where he'd apparently been checking on the horse. Sasha, Lainey, and a trembling Fibble stepped out the back door of the residence. All of them bowed their heads to the king.

Fitz waved his hand, and the portal activated. The first to step through were Master Ironhammer, Thea, and a tall man with silver eyes and hair so black it shone with a blue tint.

Master Ironhammer bowed to the king, saying, "King Charles of Stormforge, I present to ye Prince Kaibonostrum o' the Dragons."

King Charles and all present bowed to the dragon prince. "Welcome, mighty Prince. We are honored by your visit."

"The honor is mine, King Charles." The prince bowed his head slightly. "It is rare for one of my people to visit a human city. Even more rare to do so by invitation!" His smile revealed an array of very sharp teeth.

Brick stepped forward, bowing deeply at the waist. Holding the torq in both hands, he offered it to the dragon prince. "A small gift, mighty Prince, as thanks for granting yer fire to me forge."

Prince Kaibonostrum reached out and lifted the torq from Brick's hands. He examined it briefly before his eyes rose to meet the dwarf's. "This is no small gift, Master Paladin. I know this torq, and the one who wore it. It was lost more than two thousand years ago! How do you come to have this?" he asked.

Before Brick could answer, Fitz growled slightly, distracting the Prince. "We found it in this goblin's hole at the bottom of a dungeon filled with demons." He waved his hand toward Fibble. "He'd been sleeping on it, along with some other ancient treasures. Said it was quite lumpy," the wizard added dryly.

"Ha!" The prince smiled that dangerous looking smile again. Fibble squeaked and held up his 'stick' as if to defend himself. "It is good to see you again, Fitzbindulum." The prince actually bowed his head lower to Fitz than he had the king.

"You as well, Kaibonostrum. We can catch up later. For now, you've got a forge to breathe on!"

Taking the hint, the prince and the king led the way toward the smithy. Upon rounding the corner of the building and spotting the obsidian structure, the prince began to laugh.

"No wonder Thalgrin was so tight-lipped. He told me this forge was special, but wouldn't say why. He even threatened poor Master Ironhammer here with a shaved beard if he said a word!"

The rest of the group hung back as the prince, Brick, and Master Ironhammer entered the smithy. The doors on both walls were wide open, so the trio could easily be seen inspecting the interior. The prince ran his hands over the walls, benches, and the forge itself. He chuckled again when he noted the roaring dragon's head above the forge.

"This is your work, Paladin?" he turned to Brick. The dwarf lowered his eyes and shuffled his feet uncomfortably. "Aye, partly, mighty Prince. I had help."

"Never have I seen a forge that was such a wondrous work of art. I commend you, Paladin Brick. It would be my honor to share my flame with you." Brick bowed so low his beard touched the obsidian floor.

Exiting the building, the dragon prince turned and leapt up onto the roof of the smithy. Extending his arms out to either side, his body began to grow and change shape. In just moments, where the human-like prince had stood, now sat a dragon.

Kaibonostrum in his natural form was more than a hundred feet long from nose to tail. His scales were the same blue-black as his hair had been. Sitting on his haunches atop the smithy, his head extended nearly as high as the nearby wizard's tower. He extended his wings briefly, as he shifted to make himself more comfortable on his perch, wrapping his tail around the back of the building. Compared to the dragon's bulk, the 20x20 smithy structure looked like a small pedestal.

In a voice that shook the land beneath them, the dragon prince called out, "I, Kaibonostrum, grant the power of my ancestors to this dragon forge. May it be used only to create weapons of light!"

With that, he leaned forward, gripping the roof of the smithy with his massive front claws, and snaked his head inside the doorway. There was a whooshing sound, and a blast of heat that caused the gathered crowd to step back a few paces. As the mighty dragon withdrew his head, the obsidian stone of the smithy structure began to emit a silver-blue glow. When the glow faded, the dragon settled down on the rooftop, tucking his forelegs under him like a cat. He closed his eyes and began to hum.

After a few moments, he opened one eye and addressed the king. "If you don't mind, I think I'll stay here a bit. This perch is nice and warm, and the magic running through it tingles pleasantly!"

Not one to argue with a dragon under any circumstance, the king simply laughed. "Of course, mighty Prince. You are welcome to stay as long as you like. In fact, you are always welcome here. My ancestors left the mountains ages ago, but we still remember the old ways, and we honor still the ancient treaty between our people."

The dragon bowed its long neck to the king. "I am glad to hear that, Majesty. Long has it been since a human has spoken so. We must talk again sometime about renewing ties."

He then looked to Brick, Thea, and Master Ironhammer. "I hear a whispering on the wind, children of Durin. Kneel, and ask for his blessing."

The dwarves immediately fell to one knee. Taking up hammers, each of them held it to their chest and bowed their heads. A moment later, there was a roll of thunder in the sky, and a bolt of lightning struck the smithy just above the main doorway, momentarily blinding all of those present. When their vision recovered, all could see the hammer symbol of Durin etched into the obsidian where the bolt had struck. The glass and silver highlights within the stone were blazing with light. The dragon prince chuckled.

"It seems your god holds a grudge. He bids me tell you that weapons crafted in this forge will be a bane to servants of the Dark One." He smiled, and the end of his tail twitched mischievously. "I could use a snack. Where'd you put that goblin? What was his name? Nibble?" he asked, laughing as Fibble screamed and tore off toward the wizard tower. "I've not had this much fun in ages!"

Seeing the hesitation by the dwarves, he stretched his long neck so that his head was mere inches from Brick's. "Are you going to sit there drooling? Or are you going to head inside and make something? I'm curious to see how dragon and holy magic will combine."

Not needing more encouragement, Brick and Master Ironhammer rose and rushed into the forge. Thea was more sedate, pausing to bow and thank the dragon again before heading inside.

The king and the others retired inside to the lounge while his guards set up a perimeter around the house, and the three young dwarven crafters, who'd followed Thea through the portal, attempted to unobtrusively peek through the smithy doors. The dragon closed his eyes and resumed humming to himself.

Sasha was the first to speak once they were all seated. "I didn't know dragons could take human form!" she blurted out.

"Dragons are beings of pure magic, young lady," Fitz responded. "They can take many forms. And as dragons predate humans by many eons, it would be more accurate to say that humans take dragon form." He winked at her.

"As to forms, the one you see him in now is not quite his natural form. He's scaled himself down to fit his new perch. Kaibonostrum is an elder dragon, the son of the Dragon King. He is... well, let me see." Fitz looked at the ceiling and appeared to count on his fingers. "He's nearly six thousand years old now. As you may know, dragons never stop growing. In his natural form, he could cast a shadow over half this city."

"Fitz..." Sasha looked at him sideways. "How do you know how old the prince is?"

"Silly child! I was there when he was born. That torq that Brick gifted him today? That was originally MY gift to his mother."

"Holy crap," Lainey whispered.

Max coughed and waved his hand at the wizard. "Uh... father time... you just said, 'his new perch'?"

Fitz grinned at him "Yes, well. When you are effectively immortal, time has little meaning. When he says, 'stay here a bit' that could mean anything from a few hours to several hundred years."

Sasha giggled. "He's just like Fitz! Except we didn't even have to feed him before he moved in!"

Lydia and Sasha got up to make some tea and bring some treats for everyone to snack on. Outside, the ringing of hammer on metal had begun. Apparently, it didn't take long for dragon fire to heat metal to a workable temperature.

Alexander looked toward the king. "Majesty, while you're here, I wanted to ask you about Dire Keep."

The king smiled back at him. "I've been wondering when you'd get around to asking. Master Gando told me of the research you've done. And I'm sure you've decided that those keys will open something within the keep. Am I right so far?"

"Yes, Majesty." Alexander nodded his head. "The implication in the name leads me to believe the keys may grant us some type of ownership over the keep. But as you said, I've done some research, and I know that those lands belonged to Stormforge's King, and were granted to the baron in return for performing certain duties…" He paused to consider how to best continue.

"Alexander, I'll save you the effort. You wish to know if I'm willing to grant you the keep."

"Yes, Majesty. I've been thinking about this Dark One. He has clearly targeted my friends and me, and I intend to give him a fight. But, already the city has been attacked, and Whitehall as well. Too many innocents have been killed in this conflict. I am hoping that if we restore the keep and offer the challenge of capturing it to kill us, the Dark One's minions will attack us there, far from any innocents."

The king waved his hand for Alexander to stop. "I, too, have been thinking. Dire keep has sat abandoned and useless for 200 years. For all you've done for us, and all you plan to do, I will gladly grant you the rights to the keep and surrounding lands. Though, with those keys, I rather think the decision wasn't up to me." He grinned at all of them.

Quest received: Clear the Keep

Difficulty: Hard

The king has offered you the ruins at Dire Keep. But you must clear the keep of any enemies before you may claim it.

Reward: Title to Dire Keep and surrounding lands. Increased reputation with all light factions of Io. Variable experience.

Lydia and Sasha returned with tea and cookies. Sasha served the king first. The others were left to help themselves. The tea was one of Lydia's special recipes that gave buffs to stamina, and regen rates for health and mana.

"If you like, I can offer you an escort of a dozen men when you ride for the keep. You never know what you'll find in old ruins," The king offered.

"Thank you, Majesty. But for that very reason, I must decline. We don't know what dangers are within, and I would not risk the lives of your men." With Lydia in the room, he did not want to mention that he and his friends could respawn if killed.

"Because you, children, will return if you're killed, but my brother's soldiers will not." Lydia solved his dilemma for him.

Laughing, Alexander bowed his head to her. "You are very perceptive, my lady."

"Pshaw! I'm sister to the king and married to the extremely handsome Captain of his Guard. Of course, I know your little secret." She winked at him as Sasha giggled. "We thank you, children, for caring enough to spare the lives of our young men and women." The captain nodded his agreement.

"Still," the king began, "I'm concerned that just the five of you may run into more trouble than you can handle."

"To begin with, we will simply go and assess the situation. We already know of the dire wolves in the area. If we find more dangerous monsters, we can always recruit fellow adventurers to help," Alexander reassured them.

"I think I'd like to go as well," the dragon's voice boomed from outside.

Fitz chuckled at the surprised looks on nearly everyone's faces. "Dragons have very good hearing."

After a few moments, the dragon prince walked into the room, in human form. "This Dire Keep place sounds interesting. Spooky name. Unknown dangers. Might make for some interesting stories to tell my cousins!"

Alexander wasn't sure what to say. On the one hand, rejecting a dragon prince didn't seem any smarter than poking a sleeping wizard. But did he want to be responsible for getting the prince killed?

"Mighty Prince…" Alexander began.

The dragon cut him off. "First, all of you, call me Kai. If you're all constantly bowing and trying to sputter out my full name and title all the time, we'll never get anything done. Second, Alexander, I can sense your concern. Know that there are few things on Io that could harm me. And none of them are in Dire Keep." He winked.

Fitz nodded. "Kaibonostrum is indeed hard to kill. And would make a good companion on your adventure. You should know, though, he has taken some oaths as a dragon prince…" The wizard looked at Kai, who bowed his head.

"It is true. I will not kill sentient beings, except in defense of myself or others. I will not steal for any reason. I will not reveal the location of our home city on Io. And while I am free to teach you several forms of magic, there are secrets of dragon magic that I will not share. And I must return home once every month for… personal reasons." Lainey and Sasha shared a look and snickered at that.

Alexander thought it over for a moment. "Do undead count as sentient?"

"No!" Fitz and Kai said at the same time. Kai finished the thought. "Most undead are an abomination and should be wiped from the land. The one exception being vampires. They are a civilized and sentient race that happen to feed on life essence. Though, if a vampire goes feral, they must be put down."

Max spoke up. "We will almost certainly encounter adventurers from a guild called PWP who will try to kill us. Or whom we will try to kill. They have been declared enemies of both Stormforge and Broken Mountain for multiple attacks that have killed innocent civilians. There may also be other servants of this 'Dark One' they claim as their god. Will you be able to fight them?"

Kai thought for a moment. "I assume these are people Durin referred to? Fight them, yes. I will simply capture them, rather than kill. Unless they are an immediate threat to your lives, or the lives of innocents."

Alexander grinned. "Capture is better for us anyway. We can teleport prisoners back to the king for trial."

"Then let us be off tomorrow! With me at your side, higher level threats will be no issue." He stepped toward Alexander and raised an open hand toward his forehead, and paused. "May I?" he politely asked.

"Sure," Alexander replied. Kai laid his hand down and examined Alexander's stats.

<u>Mage: Alexander</u> Level 30

Build: Ranged magic/Melee dps

Health: 2100	**Experience 3,800/20,000**		**Attribute pts avail: 21**
Mana: 2800			**Skill pts avail: 5**
Stamina: 4(12)	**Dexterity: 6**	**Armor: 140**	**Health Regen: 30**
Strength: 4(15)	**Wisdom: 40(45)**	**Defense: 100**	**Mana Regen: 35**
Agility: 6(11)	**Intel: 40(50)**	**Phys Attack: 25**	**Magic Attack: 30**
Luck: 10(13)	**Charisma: 9**	**Stam Regen:**	**Race: Elf**

"You have a significant number of attribute points available to you. Why do you not use them?" Kai asked.

"You can see all that?" Alexander blurted. Then collected himself. "Never mind. Stupid question. I am new to magic. Two weeks ago, I was a warrior, level 74. My friends and I accepted a quest, of sorts, from Odin. He required we be reborn in this land at level one. I am still learning how best to grow, and did not want to waste points before I'm better informed."

Kai nodded his head. "Wise choice. And to reach level 30 in two weeks is impressive. I believe I can help you all grow even stronger." He tilted his head. "It seems the dwarves have completed their first item crafted in the new dragon forge. Shall we go see?"

Again, the king and the prince led the procession to the smithy. Master Ironhammer was polishing a blade as Thea was completing the stitching on a leather scabbard. Brick was already hammering away at something else on the anvil.

Seeing the king approach, Master Ironhammer held the sword out to him on both hands, and bowed his head. "As promised, Majesty. In return for allowing us to come into yer city to work the forge. The first weapon produced be fer yer lad."

King Charles reached out and took the weapon in hand. It had a forty-two-inch dwarven steel blade, fullered to keep it light. There was a simple guard, also steel, and the grip was wrapped in dire wolf hide. Inset in the pommel was a smoothed and rounded obsidian stone that glowed faintly. Dwarven runes were inscribed up and down the blade.

Storm Blade

Item Level: Epic, Scalable

Stats: Strength +10, Agility +10, Stamina +10

This is the first blade forged in the Greystone Dragon Forge, crafted by a Dwarven Master specifically for Prince Edward of Stormforge. Enchantments: Sharpness. Durin's Wrath. This blade will remain sharp even in the harshest of battles, and will inflict an extra 25% holy damage against targets with a dark affinity. As the Prince grows stronger, so will his blade.

The king stepped away from the group. He took a few practice swings with one hand to get a feel for the weight and balance of the sword. He then took an open stance, and with a burst of movement, began to flow through a long series of sword forms, both offensive and defensive.

As he moved, Max whistled, "King's got skills!"

Ending a two-handed finishing move that would decapitate an opponent, the king chuckled. "I'm glad you approve, Max."

Walking back to the dwarven master, he inclined his head slightly in respect. "A fine weapon, Master Ironhammer. Light, yet with perfect balance. My son may not yet be worthy of such a blade!" He grinned. "But I must ask. How did you manage such extensive engraving in such a short time?"

"Ha! T'weren't me…" The master motioned over his shoulder toward Brick, who was still oblivious and pounding away at something. "I were about to quench the blade, when Brick took it from me hands. He held the heated blade in one hand, put the other on the forge. He closed his eyes n used his shaping skill, and the runes just appeared."

"What do they say?" Lainey asked.

Master Ironhammer scratched his head a moment, then grinned. "Damned if I know, lass. Them runes look dwarven, but are not. I asked Brick to translate, but he just stared at me."

Kai stepped forward. "May I take a look?" The king handed him the blade.

"Ever shall this blade remain sharp in service to one who is worthy. May it defend the innocent, and banish the darkness with Durin's holy light." Kai read the runes. "It is the language of the gods."

Ironhammer grunted. "Makes sense. Our lad there be a paladin of Durin, whose blessing ye all saw fall upon the forge this day."

The banging from inside the smithy halted, and Brick walked out, looking slightly dazed. He was carrying a staff, six feet in length and less than two inches in diameter. Made of dwarven steel, it too was engraved with runes. He bowed to the dragon, handing him the staff.

Staff of the Dragon

Item level: Unique

Stats:??

This staff was created for the dragon whose fire brought a dragon forge to life. It is imbued with dragon magic, and the blessing of a god.

"What do the runes say?" A curious Lainey was peeking around Kai's shoulder at the staff.

"Defender of life, bringer of light. Strength of purpose, power of conviction." Kai read the engraving to them. He smiled and nodded his head. "A perfect weapon for me. Thank you, Brick."

"It doesn't have any stats," Max observed.

Alexander replied in guild chat. "*Dragons aren't like players or NPCs. They're sort of outside the system. They don't have levels or stats. They don't gain XP. Their magic is innate, and they don't use mana except in human form. They grow in strength and power over time regardless of what they do.*"

"I'm sure the stats are just hidden from us at our low level," Alexander said out loud for the benefit of the NPCs nearby.

Brick seemed to have recovered his senses a bit. He was staring off into space, the look on his face saying he was reading something on his UI.

"Me journeyman blacksmithing just went up 20%. And me shaping skill raised to adept."

Master Ironhammer thumped him on the back. "There be benefits to working a dragon forge, lad. And not just to the quality of the items crafted. This forge, bein' obsidian, and god-blessed, be unique in all of Io. And the potential power here be… unknowable. Whole damned structure be one big magic circuit. This be part of why smiths'd be willing to sell their children to work here! HA!"

"Brick, how are you feeling?" Sasha asked. "You were kinda zoned out there. And you look pretty drained."

"Aye. I started out to forge a sword for the prince. But when I pulled the steel from the forge and picked up me hammer, I got a sort of… vision. It showed me a staff. I focused on the vision, and it guided me hands. When it faded, I held the staff in me hands. And me stamina was nearly gone."

"Stamina be what drives smithing," Ironhammer explained. "And shaping, too. Ye did both, at the same time. Yer lucky ye didn't just drop where ye stood!"

"I thought blacksmithing would mainly require strength," Max offered.

"Aye, lad, it do need strong arms. And to make a horseshoe or plow blade, that be all ye need. But to work the metal into a worthy weapon or armor, ye need to put somethin o' yerself into it. Some o' yer power." He looked to Brick. "Best be careful till ye grow a bit, and have more reserves, lad."

Brick bowed his head to the elder dwarf. "Aye, I will. Thank ye, Master."

"Bah. I be here to teach ye! Can't learn if ye be dead! Ye be banished from the forge for the rest o' the day! Get some rest, and some food in yer belly!" They all chuckled at the gruff dwarf's concern.

The king thanked them again for his son's sword, and departed for the castle with both Redmonds. Kai headed toward the back courtyard, saying he wanted to practice with his new weapon. All the dwarves but Brick headed back into the smithy.

Looking at his friends, Alexander said, "I suggest we take the rest of the day to run errands and get training. Level 30 should have earned us all new skills. We'll leave in the morning for Dire Keep."

The friends ran their errands, met back at the house for dinner, and retired early to get some rest. Kai returned to dragon form, and slept atop the smithy.

Chapter Two

Finders Keepers

The group gathered for breakfast in the morning before heading out. The table was nearly filled with the Greystone clan, Fitz, Fibble, the five dwarves, and Kai. Fitz and Kai seemed to be competing to see who could shovel down the most eggs and sausages.

After breakfast, Master Ironhammer requested a portal back to Broken Mountain. He wanted to show King Thalgrin and the other smiths a few of the weapons he'd crafted yesterday, and to inform them of Durin's blessing of the forge. He requested permission to bring half a dozen masters back with him for a week, so that each may have the opportunity to work the forge.

Before Brick could even reply, he offered payment for the privilege. "We'll bring ye two ingots of pure mithril, lad. And a set o' the very best smith's tools. Plus, the work o' six more master smiths will be addin' to the power o' yer forge."

When he finally stopped talking, Brick replied, "O' course ye can bring 'em. Me forge is at yer disposal."

Sasha spoke up. "I'm afraid we're a little limited on space. But there are some rooms above the armory, and a few more above the greenhouse workshop. I'm afraid those don't have beds, though."

"Not to worry, lass. Thea showed me around. We'll make do just fine. She'll go today and purchase some furniture. If we can use yer wagon?" Ironhammer smiled and winked at the druidess.

"Of course. Consider this your home while you're here." Sasha returned his smile.

"And if you see this goblin running around loose, capture him long enough to give him a bath!" Lainey added with a wink of her own.

A wide-eyed Fibble disappeared under the table, then was seen briefly as he flew out the door.

Fitz volunteered to man the portal for the dwarves. Sasha gave them each a medallion, the simple ones that would allow them access through the wards. And left six more for the visiting masters.

And with that, the group that was going to Dire Keep headed out. As they passed through the city gate and headed toward the forest, Alexander sent a group invite to Kai. Sasha hit them all with a regen buff, Lainey used her haste buff, and Kai provided a strength and stamina buff.

So, feeling stronger, faster, and more energized, the group stepped into the forest, headed toward Dire Falls and the ruined Keep.

They ignored the low-level forest mobs that roamed in proximity to the city. The only time they paused was when Lainey or Sasha saw herbs they wanted to gather. The group made good time through the forest, and soon reached the halfway point, roughly five miles out. This was where the mobs began to match or exceed their levels. Boars and bears roaming this area would be around level 35. Dire wolves would start at about level 40. Lainey asked that they kill every mob they could, as skinning higher level beasts and working with their hides would improve her leatherworking skill. Sasha demanded they make a visit to the caverns where they'd found the dungeon two weeks earlier. She wanted to see about gathering more featherroot for Lydia. Alexander agreed, as they should probably check to see whether the dungeon had reset. Though they were still too low level to kill anything inside.

It wasn't long before Max located a level 36 black bear and led it back to the group. As he ran past Brick, he smacked the tank's helmet and said, "Tag, you're it!" The dwarf mumbled something about bears liking elf ears before charging at the bear to bash it with his shield.

Since Lainey wanted to work with the pelt, they tried to damage the hide as little as possible. Brick pounded the bear's head whenever he got an opening. Max and Lainey both focused their arrows at its head as well; Sasha focused on healing, though she did cast a vine trap - no thorns - to hold the bear still; and Alexander shot it in the face with magic bolts. Kai simply observed, staff at the ready in case he needed to step in to prevent one of the group from being injured. The bear was down in less than a minute, and Lainey moved to loot and then skin the animal. There was a significant amount of bear meat that would provide a nice dinner for them all when they made camp.

They continued on for another hour this way, Max grabbing nearby mobs and the group killing them as carefully as possible. After they took down a large boar nearly the size of Brick's battle boar, Bacon, they each gained a level.

Level up! You are now level 31!

Your wisdom has increased by +1. Your intelligence has increased by +1

You have 21 free attribute points available

Deciding to take a break before continuing, they found an area with a fallen tree near some large stones that would provide them some cover. Sitting for a few minutes, they reached into their packs for biscuits or fruit, whatever they'd each brought for travel rations. Kai took a seat next to Alexander. "I noticed you were a bit limited in your damage when fighting those beasts," he said.

"Normally, I'd burn them with wizard's fire," Alexander responded. "But Lainey won't get much use from scorched hides."

"Have you no other offensive magic?" the dragon asked.

"I have earth magic, which I use to trap or block enemies. I've used that twice to cause explosions that did damage. Once it killed a room full of imps. And I have a magic shield, which I'm afraid is not very effective yet."

Kai looked thoughtful for a moment. "How do you feel about other schools of magic? Specifically, light magic?"

Alexander began to get excited. "I wish to learn as much as I can about magic. All magic!"

Kai placed a hand on Alexander's head. "As we are headed to the former abode of a necromancer, I think this might be appropriate."

Alexander felt pain similar to that first time when Fitz burned a group of spells into his brain. Though this time the pain grew stronger. Once again, he closed his eyes and embraced the pain, accepting it and let it flow past him. When Kai removed his hand, the pain subsided. His UI told him he'd learned the spell 'Ray of Light'.

Why did it hurt so much this time? Not able to discover an answer on his own, he decided to ask the dragon.

"Thank you, Kai. If you don't mind me asking, learning that spell was a bit more… painful than others I've learned recently. Would you know why?"

The dragon shook his head. "My apologies, I should have warned you. I assumed that working with Fitz, he'd have taught you this. The spell I just gave you is from a different school than the others you've learned so far. Future spells within the light magic school will come to you more gently."

Lainey plopped down next to Kai. "I don't know about magic schools. I have a shock spell that I can either fire as a lightning bolt, or imbue into an arrow. And I have a minor healing spell that seems like a white light when I use it. Are those both light magic?"

Again Kai shook his head. "In your case, those are both Holy spells, gifted to you by Odin. Valkyries are the favored daughters of Odin, and are imbued with certain abilities at birth. Others, you will grow into as you become stronger. I can teach you some light magic if you'd like. Be warned though, as you saw from Alexander, it can be… uncomfortable."

Lainey snorted. "If pansy-boy there can handle it, so can I! Please, I'd like to learn."

Alexander gave her a look that was half indignant, half concerned. He didn't think she fully comprehended the level of pain that was imminent.

Kai placed his hand upon Lainey's head, and closed his eyes. Her face scrunched together as she gritted her teeth against the pain. Both fists were clenched so tightly her nails were beginning to draw blood. After what seemed like forever to Lainey, but was really only ten seconds, Kai removed his hand.

"Holy shitballs!" Lainey gasped, collapsing off the log onto the ground. "That frigg'n' hurt! I think I just peed myself a little." Kai chuckled as he extended a hand to help her up.

"As with everything worthwhile in life, knowledge has its price." He smiled at her with his dragon teeth.

She looked to Alexander, who was grinning unashamedly at her reaction to the pain. "You felt this too, just now?"

"Yup."

"I take back the pansy-boy comment."

Laughing, he asked, "So what did you learn? Show us!" Lainey took a moment to pull up her UI. Smiling, she withdrew her belt knife and stuck into Alexander's arm, then yanked it out.

"Ow! Shit! What was that for?" he demanded.

"I was right the first time, pansy-boy." She grinned as she covered the wound with her hand. A white light glowed for a few seconds. When she removed her hand, the wound was healed. "It's called 'mend'. Says it will heal up 300hp."

"You know you didn't have to stab me before casting that, right?" he growled at her.

"But how would I know if it worked unless there was something to heal?" she asked innocently.

Max and Brick were both outright snort-laughing, while Sasha just grinned. Even Kai had a slight smile on his face, though he was kind enough to try and suppress it.

"Alexander, one important thing you need to know. All of you, actually. Not all light spells will heal. The one you've just learned will only do damage. It will also dispel opposing effects, like curses or damage over time spells, created with dark magic. But if you were to cast it at one of your friends right now, it would damage them."

Alexander immediately flung a hand up at Lainey, who squeaked and dove behind Kai. Laughing, he put his hand down and pulled up his UI.

Ray of Light: *Generates a beam of light will that will burn a target, doing variable damage, dependent upon the amount of mana used in the casting. Range: 50 yards. Minimum mana cost: 30.*

Stepping away from the log he'd been sitting on, Alexander held out a hand and cast a minimal ray with 30 mana. A beam of light shot from his hand, striking the log and leaving a small, perfectly round, smoking hole in the wood about an inch wide and two inches deep.

"Huh," he said. "Everybody step back for sec. That was a minimum cast. Only 30 mana. I'm going to try it with … 300."

Holding up his hand again, he focused on building up mana while holding the spell in his mind. When the casting bar on his UI had counted up 300 mana, which took about 5 seconds, he let go of the spell. The beam struck the log and made it shudder. There was now a wider hole in the log, and the beam had passed all the way through the wood and into the ground behind it.

"Ye just shot a friggin' laser!" Brick pumped his fist in the air. The others grinned as Sasha gave a little golf clap.

Kai looked puzzled. "How much mana did you put into that?" he asked.

"Three hundred. It took a while to build up before I released it." Alexander answered.

"That is meant to be a channeled spell. There shouldn't be a 'release' as you put it. The spell is supposed to emit a steady ray, the damage increasing as the duration increases. You have somehow modified it into a single-charged burst. Interesting." Kai rubbed his chin.

Sasha spoke up. "Since we've been reborn, we have each figured out how to… modify our magic in small ways. It has actually helped us work as a team."

Kai stepped up next to Alexander. "Well, you certainly found an effective modification. Let me show you something. I will use the same amount of mana you just used." He extended a hand, and a steady beam of light stretched from his hand to the log. He kept the spell going for about 5 seconds, then let it end, dropping his hand.

"That was cool!" Sasha cheered. The rest of the group nodded their heads.

"Yes, well, take a look at the log." Kai instructed them.

Upon inspection, the surface of the log had been burned in a line that curved around several times in a roughly circular pattern. Almost like someone had tried to burn a spiral into the wood. The marks only went a fraction of an inch deep.

"If I were to cast this at one of you," Kai explained, "it would do significant burn damage. But when channeling, it is difficult to hold one's hand perfectly still. So the impact point shifts around as the spell continues. The further away the target, the greater the movement. So the spell may fail, for example, to penetrate armor."

Kai motioned to the hole Alexander had created in the log. "You have solved that problem with your… I'm going to call it 'burst modification'. All of the heat goes instantly to one point, providing considerable penetration. How did you figure out the change?"

Alexander looked guilty. "I didn't. I didn't realize from the description of the spell that it was to be channeled. I just envisioned it the way it would be on our world, where we have weapons that fire bursts like this. So that's how it came out. Lainey came up with her stun arrow the same way. She just didn't know any better."

Kai looked to Lainey. "Show me".

Lainey lifted her bow and drew an arrow. Infusing it with her shock spell, she shot Alexander in the leg, stunning him. And causing Brick to nearly fall off the stone he was sitting on.

When the stun wore off, Alexander was furious. "That's twice! What the hell-" Though he kept shouting, the sound of his voice was cut off when he was hit in the same leg with a silence arrow from Max. Followed by a heal from Sasha. Brick was now rolling around on the ground, helpless with laughter.

Realizing he'd been silenced, Alexander stopped yelling and resorted to hand gestures that made it very clear what he was thinking, which caused everyone, including Kai, to laugh out loud.

When the stun wore off, he simply growled, "I hate you all," and sat back down.

Kai was the first to speak. "I'm fascinated by the changes you've all made to your various types of magic. I have never seen this before, in all my time on Io. Though, now that I see them, I wonder why no one discovered them earlier."

"We're just awesome like that!" Sasha declared, taking a small bow. "Wait until you see us fight critters that Lainey doesn't want to skin. Then you'll REALLY be impressed!"

On that note, they all did a quick gear check, and resumed their march toward Dire Keep. It was approaching noon as the Dire Falls came into view. The group had worked their way through the remainder of the forest, pulling and killing as they went. All that could, gained another level and Lainey's bag was getting full of animal hides. Brick had collected twenty more dire wolf pelts, which oddly enough, when looted from the wolves, still allowed Lainey to skin them and take viable hides. Alexander had made a note to check with the devs to see if that was intentional. Though with all the folks watching them play, he was pretty sure someone was already asking the question.

The group paused when they reached Dire Falls. The forest had ended about two hundred yards from a sheer ridgeline that, if you were to follow it, would eventually lead to Broken Mountain. From the top of the ridge, a series of waterfalls fell 600 or so feet down to a wide lake. The lake, carved out of the bedrock by eons of falling water, was deep and clear, with flashes of silver in its depths as fish swam about. Its waters fed a wide creek that ran south toward the ocean. There was an old stone bridge that spanned the creek several hundred yards downstream from the lake.

Deciding to have lunch by the lake, the group crossed the bridge and walked north along the creekside to a spot that had a nice, gradual grassy slope down to the edge of the lake. They were far enough from the falls that they could hear each other's voices, and also avoid most of the spray from the water striking the rocks.

Lainey made a quick fire, and Sasha cooked up one of Lydia's boar stew recipes that awarded stamina and regen buffs. They all refilled their water flasks from the lake, with Brick and Max only committing a few 'accidental' splashes at each other.

Sasha, Lainey, and Kai all renewed their party buffs, and the group set out toward the ruins just a quarter mile away. There was what remained of a road stretching from the bridge to the ruins. Now, it was just a mostly clear trail among the tall grass and shrubs that had taken over in the 200 years since the keep fell. The group followed the road to the main gate of Dire Keep.

The keep itself had been built right into the rock of the ridge above. The outer walls were mostly intact, not having been damaged in Fitz's rampage. They were missing a few stones here and there, carved out of the wall by storms or ice. A few had been pushed out by plants that had wormed their way into the mortar between the stones. The thirty-foot high walls ran in a half-circle, extending from the ridge to the east of the keep, and curving around to connect back with the ridge on the west side. What they could see of the keep's main tower was partially collapsed, the missing sections exposing doors and hallways cut into the mountain. The tower, when it was whole, must have risen a good hundred feet above the ground.

The iron portcullis at the outer edge of the bailey, left closed by Fitz and the king's men as they departed 200 years ago, had long since rusted into piles of scrap. The inner bailey, however, was sealed with a pair of enormous stone doors, with stone hinges much like those Brick had learned to craft for the homes at Whitehall.

"Aye, makes sense." Brick nodded his head. "This keep were crafted by dwarves, hired by the baron. Dwarves build things to last millennia, not just decades or centuries."

As they stood inside the bailey tunnel examining the doors, Alexander looked up to see a series of spouts and murder holes. Any enemy who breached the outer portcullis would be stuck in here trying to open the doors while hot oil and arrows punished them from above. It would quickly become an oven, roasting any who remained.

"The doors were sealed from this side," Kai observed, looking at the two spikes driven into the stone with a chain woven in between. The padlock securing the chain was the size of a Christmas wreath, and looked shiny and new.

"Was someone here recently?" Max pondered aloud, looking at the lock.

"The lock and chain are enchanted," Kai replied. Stepping forward he touched the lock and closed his eyes. A moment later he chuckled. "Fitz. Not only did he protect the lock, he added a warning that appears to any who touch it. "No treasure here. Big scary monsters that will eat your face. Turn around and go home." Most of the group chuckled along with Kai, hearing the warning in the wizard's voice.

Alexander, though, had just thought of something. "Fitz said he and the king's men came back and cleared the keep, and the mine, of all the undead. I would assume that they also took anything of value back to the king as payment for taxes owed. From the way he described it, Fitz burned out or otherwise demolished most of the inside of the keep. So why seal it up like this?"

Max, always one to focus on the potential for loot in any situation, said, "Well let's get inside and find out. I'll bet ten gold there are secret rooms or hidden chests that Fitz didn't bother to look for. After all, he WAS in a hurry to get back to his hot young lady friend…" Max winked at Lainey.

"How do we open the lock?" Brick had been examining it. "Max, can you do this?"

"No need," Kai said as he stepped sideways to the right-hand door. Rather than work on the magically protected lock, he simply grabbed one of the two spikes that secured the chain to the doors. With a grunt, he ripped the spike free from the stone. Dropping it to swing below the other spike, he then pushed on the massive door. The stone-on-stone hinges groaned, but the door swung open enough to allow the friends to walk through. Kai closed the door behind them. "To make sure we have no unannounced visitors," he explained.

The group found themselves in a large courtyard. Straight ahead was the main structure of the keep, with the tower above. To the right were what had to be stone stables, a wide opening in the nearest wall where wooden doors must have hung. To the left was a two-story guard house. Through the open doorway they could see a wide open first floor. Maybe it served as a storehouse as well?

Heeding the captain's repeated advice about not leaving un-cleared rooms behind them, the group split up. Max and Lainey went to check the stables, while the others entered the barracks building.

The interior was dim, but enough sunlight streamed through the door and windows that Alexander could see nearly the entire first floor. There were piles of dust on the floor along both walls that might once have been crates or bags of supplies. At the opposite end of the long room there was a small office. Just to their left as they stood near the main entry was a stone staircase leading up to the second floor. Under the staircase was another door, presumably leading down. The door was iron, and still mostly intact, having been protected from the weather.

Deciding to wait for the others before going up or down, Brick trotted across the room to check the first floor office. Peeking through the doorway, he saw nothing that posed a threat. He stepped inside, poked around a bit, and came back out, declaring the room empty.

Alexander moved over to examine the iron door. There was a heavy layer of dust, rust and windblown leaves on the floor at its base. Clearly the door had not been opened for a very long time.

Max and Lainey arrived and reported nothing of interest in the stables. Sasha asked, "So, up, or down?"

"Up first," Max replied. "I don't want to be underground and get trapped by beasties drifting down from above."

Nobody having any argument for his logic, they proceeded up the stairs to the second floor. As expected, this was a guard barracks. Room after room with stone bunk beds. Six per room. Each room had a weapons rack, some of which still had spears or swords scattered among the debris. The weapons were rusted, and of little value. At the end of the hall they found a larger set of two rooms, likely the office and living quarters of the commander. Surprisingly, there was an intact ironwood door standing between the rooms.

"Enchanted," confirmed Kai. "It has been spelled for strength, and sealed. Coded to open for someone specific. Likely the commander."

"I love a challenge!" Max grinned as he crouched in front of the door lock. "I told you there'd be a room Fitz didn't check!"

"Or it was checked, and somebody simply closed the door behind them as they left, causing the spell to activate." Sasha poked him in the back.

"Party pooper," Max mumbled as he worked the lock.

After a minute or so, he grinned, and pushed the door open. "Ta-daaaa!"

The room inside was surprisingly well preserved. Clearly sleeping quarters, the room contained a bed, a wardrobe, an armor stand with a set of ceremonial armor draped on it, and a small desk. All were covered in a layer of dust, but were intact. Probably because in addition to the door, which had remained sealed, there was still glass in the single window. It must have also been magically protected.

Max quickly looted the armor. The stats weren't great, but it was a beautiful set, and there were always those out there who were willing to pay for style over function. Lainey moved to see if there was anything useful in the wardrobe, while Sasha peeked under the bed. Alexander searched through the small desk. Finding a coin pouch with some gold, he tossed it to Max. There were several sheets of old, brittle paper that disintegrated at his touch. Inside a lower drawer he found a leather-bound journal with a lock on it.

"Max, buddy. Got another lock for you." He handed the ranger the journal.

Max just rolled his eyes. He produced a small lock pick and barely even looked at the lock as he worked his magic. The flap containing the lock mechanism flopped open, and he handed the book back to Alexander. "I'm going to search for secret compartments."

Alexander opened the journal and began to read. It seemed the commander's name was Captain Artemis, and that he'd been sent by the king to command the keep's guards. Not caring about the day to day thoughts of the man, Alexander skimmed to the back of the book, where he found a very interesting last entry.

The bastard has been killing citizens of the keep, turning them into undead monsters. Two of my own men disappeared last week, then returned as walking corpses. I sent a messenger to the king, and he suffered the same fate. The baron must have more undead patrolling the road and forest.

This cannot stand. Tonight I will kill this evil monster myself.

Clearly, Captain Artemis had failed to kill the baron. Likely he became one of the undead, as well. Alexander hoped Fitz had put the man out of his misery.

Sasha had pulled a small chest out from under the bed. It contained mostly personal mementos. Service awards from Artemis' time in the guard, a ribbon from a young lady, letters from family and friends. And a fist-sized bag of gemstones. Alexander took the stones. Sasha returned the rest to the box and replaced it under the bed.

The clothes in the wardrobe had not fared well, and had mostly fallen into rags at the bottom. There was a longsword, still in its sheath standing in the corner. Withdrawing the sword to confirm it wasn't rusted beyond use, she handed it to Max.

Finding nothing else, the group exited the room, closing the door behind them. Alexander had decided to deliver the journal and the gems to Captain Redmond, in case any of the commander's descendants or relatives could still be found.

Making their way back downstairs, they moved to the iron door leading downward. After a brief inspection, Max informed them that the door's lock was not engaged. He suspected it was barred from the inside.

"Stand back, and I'll make short work o' the door with me hammer," Brick offered.

"Thank you, buddy, but I'd rather not make that much noise if there's something still moving down there." Alexander patted him on the shoulder.

Nodding in understanding, Brick stepped forward and placed his hands on the door. He closed his eyes and activated his shaping skill. After a moment, there were two small pinging sounds as the hinges opened themselves to release the pins they held. Brick asked Kai for assistance, and the two of them simply lifted the door from its place and moved back to set it against the wall.

Spanning the doorway was a metal bar set into brackets bolted to the wall on either side of the doorway. Brick simply lifted the bar away, and the way was clear. The stone stairs led downward one floor to a mostly dark room.

"One moment, please," Kai said. Lifting the iron door, he moved to lay it on its side across the building's open doorway that led out to the courtyard. "If the undead should try and enter, we will be able to hear the door fall to the floor."

Brick leading the way, the group made their way downstairs. The light from the floor above reached to the bottom of the stairs, but not much farther. Brick, with his dwarven dark vision, scanned the room. "It be empty as far as I can tell. Though there be another door in the back corner."

Max lit a couple of torches, handing one to Sasha. They spread out a bit, and moved across the room, all eyes searching for threats. Finding none, they continued on to the next door.

This one was a simple wooden door, and was not locked. Brick positioned himself in front of it while Max pulled it open, torch held high.

The door opened to a short landing, and another stairway leading down. To the left of the landing was a 10x10 room with stone workbenches. On the benches were vials and bottles filled with substances of varying colors.

"An alchemist's workshop?" Sasha ventured.

"More like a necromancer's," Kai corrected her. "There's a foul magic permeating that room. I shall burn the room once we've completed our work down here."

"If you must. But I'd prefer to leave it so that Lydia can investigate. She might find useful information or ingredients in here," Sasha replied.

"We shall see," was Kai's only response.

The group continued down the stairs. This staircase went much deeper, and had curved around to angle back toward the main keep structure. When they finally reached the bottom, they found a corridor with several doors on each side. The doors had windows with iron bars across them. Prison cells.

"We be about 5 levels down," Brick informed them. "Right under the main tower." Dwarves had an impeccable sense of direction and distance underground.

With a sigh, Max said, "You all know the drill. We need to clear every room as we go."

So they began to search each cell as they passed down the corridor. Most of the doors stood open, and it took only a brief glance inside the eight foot square rooms to confirm they were empty. The few that were closed were not locked.

Just in case, Alexander asked, "Kai, can you use magic to search for any hidden doors?"

Kai snorted. "I am a dragon. Nothing is hidden from me. We find all the best treasure in secret rooms and buried under floors. If there's a door, I shall inform you."

Under floors! Stupid! I hadn't considered that! Alexander berated himself. He paused to close his eyes and reach out below him with his earth magic. He found solid bedrock directly below. Sweeping in a wide circle around them, he found no tunnels or stairways below. Only small drain pipes leading from the cells downward.

"This is the lowest level. There's nothing else below us but rock," he reported to the group.

They continued down the corridor, clearing cells as they went. At the end there was a large chamber with a stone table in the middle. Around the walls were hung an assortment of tools meant for torture. The table itself was stained black, as if from years of soaking up blood and bile.

Passing through the room, not wishing to spend any more time there than necessary, they found a small guard chamber, with another door at the opposite end. The chamber was empty but for a rack of rusted weapons near the door.

Max moved across the room and began to work on the next door's lock. Alexander looked around the room. There wasn't much to see. A table and four chairs, and a desk to one side.

"There's no dust," Sasha thought out loud. "Upstairs, there was a thick layer of dust everywhere. But since we reached that lab, and all the way to here, there's been no dust."

All of them paused to look around. Brick stepped back out to the torture room to confirm what Sasha had observed.

"Aye, she's right." He took a cleaning rag from his bag, and walked over to the stone table. Running the cloth across the surface, he said, "Might be someone's still using this place?".

Raising the cloth from the table revealed a dark stain. He held it up to show the others. "Blood. Ain't fresh, but ain't 200 years old, either." He moved back over to Max, who had unlocked the next door.

"Right," Sasha said. "Standard dungeon procedure. Brick in front. Max you open the doors for him. Lainey, have a stun arrow ready. Alexander, burn the first thing that moves. I'll add the vines. These are narrow corridors, so should be easy enough to group targets and burn them down. Kai, I don't know what abilities you have, but I trust you'll find a way to contribute."

The dragon nodded his head. "I will observe for a while, and determine how you interact. I will be there when needed."

Max threw open the door, which lead to a stairway going up. Brick began the ascent, the others following behind. There was a short flight to a switchback landing, then another short flight up to what Alexander thought of as the fourth dungeon level. The door at the top was unlocked and very slightly ajar. As Brick nudged it open, the hinges squeaked loudly. The sound caught the attention of some two-dozen living corpses that were shambling about the room in seemingly random order.

The undead turned to shuffle toward the group, moving slowly. Brick hit the nearest with a holy smite, causing it groan in pain. The tank set up in the doorway, the others gathering behind. Alexander looked over their enemies as they approached, beginning with the one Brick had hit.

Undead Hunter
Level 45
HP 1300/2400

There appeared to a wide range of entities here. The closest was a hunter without a bow, carrying a long dagger. Behind him was a dwarf with a mining pick. There were warriors in plate and chain armor, what looked to be a barbarian with a two-handed axe, and a few mage types carrying staves. Though they were not casting, just moving forward with weapons raised.

"Brick, move to a corner. We can't burn them all here in the doorway!" Sasha called out.

The dwarf stepped into the room, bashing at the undead hunter with his hammer, then moving to the side and backing toward a corner. He hit one of the casters on the far side of the room with another holy spell. All of the corpses in the room turned to follow the tank.

Setting himself up in the corner, Brick bashed his shield against the closest foe, knocking it back and off of its feet. The two directly behind it both stumbled over the corpse as it struggled to rise. More of the undead moved in over top of them, and from both sides, pushing up against the dwarf, beating at his shield or trying to reach over it to grab at him. He dragged his hammer across the surface of his shield, activating its Serpent's Screech ability. This sent the corpses into a frenzy, and they moved more quickly, pushing and shoving against each other to reach the tank.

Sasha cast her aoe thorn trap right in front of Brick, thorns ripping into the dead flesh of arms and legs. Alexander cast wizard's fire on five of the mobs. The fire quickly spread to the other undead, and to Sasha's vines. Brick hunkered down behind his shield as the zombies burned.

Max and Lainey began shooting arrows into the heads of each of the mobs. Alexander, deciding to experiment, moved to one side until he was lined up parallel with Brick's shield. He aimed for a zombie in the middle of the most dense grouping, and began to pump mana into his Ray of Light spell. When he'd reached 300 mana, he released.

The beam shot out from his hand, burning through half a dozen zombies before striking the wall behind. Those that were hit with the light spell died instantly, their bodies still fueling the wizard's fire.

Between the fire, the light magic, and critical hits from arrows to their heads, the undead were all fully dead in less than two minutes.

Level up! You are now level 32!
Your wisdom has increased by +1. Your intelligence has increased by +1
You have 21 free attribute points available

Brick emerged smiling from the pile, his shield having healed him from the fire damage. Max moved to loot the cooling corpses.

"Impressive teamwork," Kai observed. "I see what Sasha meant when she spoke of the damage you can do when you're not holding back." Sasha smiled and gave a small curtsey.

"Did you guys notice the make-up of the mobs in here?" Alexander asked.

"Yeah," Max answered, still looting. "Hunters, warriors, miners, casters. They must have been adventurers that came here after Fitz cleared the place."

"But… how did they get in? And who killed them?" Lainey's voice was just above a whisper. She was looking around nervously.

Not having an answer, the friends prepared to move on. Max and Sasha picked up their torches, having dropped them as the fight started. They moved across the room to a door at the other end. This door was unlocked, and led to a short corridor that ended in another stairway leading up. On either side of the corridor were single closed doors.

Choosing the left door first, Max pushed it open, and Brick stepped through, shield raised and hammer ready. The room held rows of iron cages, stacked against the walls and across the center. A quick count showed thirty cages in all. Each cage held an undead beast. Dire wolves, bears, tigers, raptors, even a bugbear. One long cage at the back wall held a 12-foot alligator.

Undead Alligator
Level 50
Health 3000/3000

"Well, this confirms that these undead were not killed here. Many of the animals are not found in this region. Alligators live only in the island and equatorial nations across the sea to the south. And bugbears are only found on the other side of the mountains," Kai observed.

Lainey continued the thought. “So somebody has been making these zombies, and transporting them here. Teleporting?”

“More likely a portal. Much like the one you have in your compound. Only a being of great power could teleport itself between continents. And very few could do so with cargo,” Kai responded.

“We need to kill all these animals. But let’s do it carefully. I want to see if I can work with their hides.” Lainey said. Drawing her bow, she fired a demon-bone arrow into the gator’s head. It was a critical hit, doing about 800 damage. She drew another arrow and paused for a moment. The arrow began to glow with a white light. Firing into the now thrashing gator’s head again, this arrow dropped its health down into the red. One more standard arrow finished it.

Stepping inside to loot and skin the gator, she said, “I infused my Mend spell into the arrow, just like with my stun arrows. The light magic did way more damage.”

Taking the hint, the others spread out and begin to slaughter the undead beasts in their cages. Max pumped arrow after arrow into the heads and faces of his foes. Brick used his hammer, which carried the blessing of Durin, and did holy damage in addition to crushing damage. Alexander cast bursts of Ray of Light with minimal charges of 30 mana into his first mob’s head. Seeing that it took off about 60% of the creature’s health, he finished it off with another one. The next mob he hit in the face with a 50 mana burst, and got an instant kill.

Kai followed Alexander’s lead, deciding to try the burst casting. After just two tries, he was successfully killing mobs with every shot. Having a dragon’s massive mana pool, he was putting 100 mana into each burst.

Level up! You are now level 33!
Your wisdom has increased by +1. Your intelligence has increased by +1
You have 21 free attribute points available

Thirty mobs, all ten levels or more above them, was good xp. When the last of them was dead, the friends rested and recharged while Lainey skinned as quickly as she could. Max helped her out, looting each corpse before she skinned it. Her bag was getting full.

"Lainey, remind me when we get back. We learned a little trick a while back. You can put one bag of holding inside another. So when you fill one bag, you put it into another, and it only takes one slot. There's a limit of one, but it allows you to fill 199 slots instead of just 100. And the weight increase is minimal. We've got extras we took from those PWP morons who died at Whitehall."

Lainey, elbow deep in a dire wolf corpse, just grunted in the affirmative.

As they waited, Kai asked, "Alexander. Have you learned the use of soul crystals in your enchanting trade?"

"Soul crystals?" Alexander hadn't even heard of them.

Kai replied. "Aye. There is a spell that, when cast upon a dying creature, will cause their essence to be transformed into a crystal that is left behind at their death. These crystals can then be used to power enchantments. The stronger the life essence, the more power the crystal retains."

"I've seen a few o' them in the auction house," Brick added. "Never knew what they were, but they sell for thousands o' gold each."

"Can you teach us this spell?" Sasha asked.

"All of you?" Kai looked dubious. "You saw the pain that Lainey suffered…" he reminded them.

"These crystals sound useful," Sasha said "And Alexander is just starting to learn enchantment. If these crystals will help him increase his skill, then we need as many as possible. If we're facing a group of mobs, one of us might not have time to cast the spell on each one. So it's better if we can all do it."

"This spell is from the school of dark magic. Are you certain?" Kai asked again.

"So, it be evil?" Brick asked worriedly. "I be a paladin of a god o' light. I canno' be casting evil magic."

"Dark is not the same as evil, good dwarf. Nor is light always good. Though many make that association. Dark magic is a tool, like any other. The portal you built with Fitz contained some dark magic. The spell within Lainey's demon bow, the one that creates arrows, contains dark magic. Dark magic is often destructive, but it also balances light. Fire magic is destructive, yet few call it evil," Kai pointed out. "If it would ease your conscience, then only cast the spell on creatures of darkness."

Brick looked thoughtful. While he was considering, Alexander stepped forward. "I can bear the pain." He bowed his head to Kai.

The dragon placed his hand on Alexander's head, and the pain began. It may have been Alexander's imagination, but it seemed the dark school was more painful than the light. The knowledge wormed its way through his brain, burning as it went. He thought it almost whispered to him, a sinister voice implying everlasting damage to the burning bits of his mind. Gritting his teeth, he fought the weakness in his legs. He would succumb. When the knowledge settled in place, it was as if a roaring flame etched its image onto his soul.

The dragon removed his hand, and Alexander faltered. Strong hands gripped his shoulder and held him upright for the several moments it took him to regain his equilibrium.

"That sucked," he said, moving to sit atop one of the smaller cages. "Can't say I recommend it." He looked at Kai. "I know you said dark magic is not evil. But it almost seemed as if it wanted to hurt me."

Kai shook his head. "No, Alexander. The magic is neutral. It was your predisposition to think of dark magic as bad or evil. The magic is what you make of it. Any of the rest of you who wish this knowledge, you must avoid this prejudice. Keep your minds open and neutral. I doubt any of you could accept the kind of pain I just felt from Alexander."

Surprisingly, Lainey was the next to step forward. "Can't hurt more than the light magic did…" she offered.

Again, Kai laid his hand on her head and closed his eyes. Lainey's jaw clenched, her teeth audibly grinding. Her fists once again squeezed tight and trembling. When Kai removed his hand, she simply dropped to the floor. "Damn! Wasn't any worse, but wasn't any better, either!" she gasped.

Max stepped forward next, gripping an arrow between his teeth as he lowered his head to Kai. As the magic took effect, the arrow snapped, Max growling out the pain. He was silent, and a bit wobbly, as he stepped away.

Sasha was next. She looked at Kai and said, "I believe what you say is true. Dark magic is no different than my nature magic when I use it to kill. A tool. Nothing more."

She bowed her head and accepted the magic from the dragon. Though she tensed, and gritted her teeth like the others, she seems to experience considerably less pain.

Brick had been kneeling in prayer since Alexander first stepped forward. He rose, and stepped to Kai. "Durin be a god o' light, but also a god o' vengeance. I felt no resistance when I asked fer guidance."

Placing his hand on the dwarf's head, Kai transmitted the knowledge of dark magic once more. Brick, believing he had the blessing of his chosen god, seemed to feel little pain at all. Though, when it was over, he did whisper, "Durin's balls, that hurt!"

"Did that count as a prayer?" Max grinned at him.

"Bwahahaha!" Brick laughed heartily, and the others joined him.

Lainey had finished her skinning, but the whole group, including Kai, felt the need to rest a bit. Giving and receiving magic took a toll. They broke out some travel rations, and sat mostly in silence for ten minutes.

Rested and recharged, they moved to the room across the corridor. Upon opening the door, they found what looked like a surgery theatre. The room was about thirty feet squared, with two doors exiting the wall opposite them. Corpses with missing limbs, and limbs missing bodies, were hung on hooks and stacked on benches. Standing at the table, needle and thread in hand, was what looked like your average surgeon. Only the surgeon was undead, and was sewing parts of different corpses onto a very large orc's body.

The Surgeon
Level 55 Lich
Health 5,000/5,000

Without hesitation, Brick dashed forward, bashing the lich from behind, knocking him into the table. The orc corpse was knocked off to the floor on the other side. Brick hit the lich with a holy smite spell, causing it to roar in pain. As it turned to face him, he slammed down his shield and braced himself.

"YOU SHALL ALL DIE HERE!" it screamed at them. "THEN I WILL BRING YOU BACK TO SERVE MY MASTER!"

It reached out to a tray of what looked more like torture implements than medical instruments. Grabbing a cleaver in one hand, it pounded at the tank's shield. It began to chant under its breath, while waving its free hand.

"Casting!" Brick yelled.

Max hit the lich with a silence arrow, effectively interrupting its cast. Lainey put an arrow into its skull, the shaft running all the way through like an old Three Stooges prop. Alexander hit it with a minimal Ray of Light burst that would have caused it to scream if it weren't still silenced. The spell caused Alexander to draw aggro, the lich dashing around Brick to bury the cleaver in the mage's shoulder. Just as the cleaver struck, there was a loud <crack!> as Kai's staff crushed the lich's spine. Abandoning the cleaver in Alexander's shoulder, the lich retreated back behind the surgical table, seemingly unimpaired by the broken spine. It said two words, made a motion with its hands, then ran for the back of the room as the corpse of the 8-foot-tall orc began to rise from the floor. It had two legs, four arms, and a third eye in its forehead. Lainey shot it in the face as it rose.

Orc Monstrosity
Level 50
Health 2800/3000

The cleaver had severed an artery and broken Alexander's collarbone. But the pressure of the blade in his flesh was, for the moment, keeping him from bleeding out. His health bar was down 40%, and he was beginning to feel dizzy from the lack of blood flow. He stepped back to lean against a wall, pushing a dangling arm out of the way. Kai had leapt forward and was pounding on the undead orc with his staff. Max and Lainey were peppering it with arrows as it used its two original massive arms to grab Brick's shield and try to tug it out of his hand. The dwarf used his hammer to pound its left hand against the sharp edge of his shield, severing the fingers and doing holy damage. The orc's secondary right hand lifted a hobbling hammer from the table and began to pound at Brick.

Meanwhile, Alexander observed the lich in the background, casting another spell. As it finished, several of the partial corpses began to rise and move toward Alexander's friends. Sasha hadn't noticed, as she was frantically casting heals on Alexander and Brick.

"Focus on the lich!" he tried to yell, but it only came out as a gasp. It was getting difficult to breathe.

Sasha looked up long enough to take in the situation, and agreed with him. "Focus on the lich!" she screamed. "It's raising adds!"

Brick stayed on the orc, holding its attention while Kai and the archers both switched targets to the lich. Kai began to cast a spell as arrow after arrow pounded into the mob's head.

Brick used his hammer to activate his Serpent's Screech ability, drawing all the adds in the room to him. Once they'd gathered, Sasha cast her aoe thorn trap underneath them. Alexander cast wizard's fire on the orc and three of the adds.

Looking at Sasha, he said, "You have to… pull it out. Blocking… blood supply". He was very near to losing consciousness. His health bar was back up at 70%, due to Sasha's heals, but the metal cleaver was still lodged in him.

His best friend gritted her teeth, grabbed the handle, and yanked the cleaver. She hadn't enough strength to pull it completely free, and Alexander screamed in pain. Blood began to spurt into the air, splattering Sasha and causing her to have to wipe her eyes. Alexander was bleeding out quickly, his health bar at 40% and dropping. She yanked the cleaver the rest of the way out, and cast her largest heal on him. The bleeding stopped, and his health bar went back up to 50%. Most importantly, the blood flow was restored. The dizziness began to wear off as another big heal hit him.

Sasha paused to check on Brick. Though the fire damage to the mobs was healing him, he was still down to 60%. Sasha hit him with another large heal, as well as a HoT. Then she focused back on Alexander.

While she made sure he wasn't dying, Alexander focused his attention again on the lich. It was dancing around the back of the room, avoiding several arrows in the process. That thing had to die!

Focusing on his Ray of Light spell, Alexander pumped 200 mana into it, then released it at the lich. The light burst from his hand, blasting a hole through the lich's chest. The creature dropped dead instantly, wailing as it died. The moment it hit the ground, all the adds that weren't already destroyed by the fire, dropped lifelessly to the floor.

Level up! You are now level 34!
Your wisdom has increased by +1. Your intelligence has increased by +1
You have 21 free attribute points available

The level up brought them all back to full health and mana. Alexander simply sat where he was, too tired to move. Max and Lainey began to loot the lich and the adds. This came as a surprise to Alexander. He'd expected Lainey to rush over to check on him, then call him an idiot.

Kai walked over to kneel in front of Alexander. "My apologies. I was unable to move quickly enough to keep him from harming you." The dragon lowered his eyes in shame.

"It wasn't your fault, Kai. That thing moved like lightning. Brick didn't have time to block it, I didn't have time to raise a shield, or even block with my staff. I'm alive. Don't worry about it."

Nodding his head, Kai changed the subject. "The lich will resurrect itself if we do not find its phylactery." He rose and began to search the room.

Chapter Three

Dragons Are a Guild's Best Friend

"What's a phyl… phyl… what's he talking about?" Lainey asked as she approached to stand next to Alexander. She kicked him in the leg and mumbled, "Idiot!" He couldn't help but smile.

"A phylactery is an artifact that a lich uses to store its soul. When its body is destroyed, its soul flows back into the artifact, and it begins the process of possessing another body. Depending on the power of the lich, and the availability of a new body, this can take anywhere from a few minutes, to years. I'm guessing with all these bodies around, we don't have a lot of time," he explained.

"What does it look like?" Lainey was already scanning the room.

"Don't know. Usually it would be a gem or a crystal. But it could be pretty much any inanimate object. You'll know it when you see it," Alexander said.

Kai had been standing near the center of the room, eyes closed. He turned, mumbling to himself, then faced the right hand door. "It's in there," he said with finality. Stepping to the door, he punched it with a seemingly casual blow. The heavy wooden door disintegrated into tiny splinters that peppered everything in the room beyond.

Stepping through the door, Kai disappeared. Sasha helped Alexander to his feet, and the group rushed to follow the dragon.

The small room, maybe 6x6, was more of a cell than a room. But it was filled with boxes and piles of loot! There was gold, silver, art work, sculptures, platters and tea services, any and every type of treasure one could imagine. Just a quick glance from Alexander was enough to notice dozens of gems scattered about.

"Well, shit," said Brick.

Kai just laughed. "Fear not. I am a dragon. This simple ruse will not deter me. No creature on Io knows treasure better than a dragon!"

Alexander cast mage sight on himself as Kai looked around the room. He could see from the overlapping glowing areas that many of the items were enchanted. But he didn't see anything that screamed 'phylactery' to him. A quick glance at Kai showed the dragon was thinking the same.

"Brick, buddy. Feel like a bit of pally action?" He looked to the dwarf. Getting a questioning look in return, he winked. "A lot of this loot is enchanted. Considering where we are, some of it could be dangerous. How 'bout a quick request to Durin to bless this room?"

The dwarf chuckled. "Aye, that be possible."

Dropping to one knee, the dwarf held his hammer to his chest and lowered his head in prayer. After maybe ten seconds, the hammer began to glow more brightly than usual. Then the dwarf himself began to glow. The aura of holy light spread out from him in an expanding ring, until it covered the entire room. Alexander had noted that several of the enchantments had winked out when exposed to the blessing.

As the wave of light hit the back wall of the room, there was a high-pitched keening. It appeared to come from behind the stone. Running his hand across the stone, Kai reported, "There's a hidden alcove here." Without another word, the dragon cracked his staff against the stone, causing it to crack and fall away. It revealed a small alcove, maybe a foot wide and three feet deep. Inside it was a jeweled chest.

Kai withdrew the chest and set it down atop a much larger chest that sat against a side wall. Opening the box, he revealed an interior lined with purple velvet. The entire box was filled with diamonds!

Grabbing a silver teapot from the pile, Kai dumped the diamonds inside, and handed the teapot to Max. He then ripped out the velvet lining, searching underneath. Finding nothing, he turned to Lainey.

"Please take the teapot from Max, and cast your Mend spell into it."

Lainey did as requested, taking the pot in both hands. After a moment of concentration, both hands glowed briefly. Nothing happened.

Kai nodded. "It is as I thought. Come with me." Taking the jeweled chest in hand, he stepped out of the room and back into the surgery. He set the small chest down atop the table where the surgeon had been working on the orc.

"Separating a lich from its phylactery is no small feat. I wish all of you to cast your Soul Trap spell upon this chest. Now." Following his own instructions, he cast the spell himself. The others complied and cast the spell onto the box. There was no reaction that any of them could see.

"Again," Kai said. Another round of spells were cast. This time a faint shadow formed around the chest.

Looking at Brick, Kai said, "It is done. Now the box must be completely destroyed."

Grinning, Brick mumbled a few words of prayer, then raised his hammer high above his head. With both hands, and all the considerable strength the dwarf could bring to bear, he slammed the hammer down upon the jeweled chest.

There was an explosion of light and dark magic as the hammer blow shattered the box.

"Gather the pieces. Every single one!" Kai growled at them. They began to pick up splinters of wood and loose gem fragments from the floor around the table. When they were done, Kai dropped to his hands and knees and searched again to make sure not the tiniest piece was missed.

Standing, he dropped a few small fragments onto the table with the others. "Alexander? Wizard's Fire if you please?" Alexander and Kai both cast Wizard's Fire onto the pile of fragments. Brick cast Holy Smite upon the pile as well. Lainey put her hands upon the table and cast her Mend spell repeatedly.
When the fire died down, all that remained was a smoky grey crystal the size of a golf ball.

Greater Soul Crystal: Lich Adept
Item Level: Rare
Charge: 400/400

Kai nodded his head. "It is finished."

Alexander lifted the crystal, examining it. "It says it has 400 charges?"

"Yes," Kai said, "that was a powerful lich. That crystal can now be used to charge enchanted items. Or the power within it could be added to a magical construct, like the dragon forge. The crystal itself could be placed within a weapon or armor to provide an enchantment. The crystals have many uses."

Grinning, Max said, "These would be hugely valuable at auction. As far as I know, nobody else has the knowledge to MAKE these. They sometimes drop after a boss or mini-boss fight. We could corner the market!"

Alexander had read a few books from early in the century that featured players with 'inner greedy' hamsters or pigs. He grinned back at Max, picturing him as a giant hamster.

"We still have a room to clear," Lainey spoke up. As one, the group turned to the unopened left hand door in the back wall of the surgery.

"Right! Good lookin' out, lass!" Brick stomped toward the door. The others took up their standard positions behind him.

Opening the door as quietly as possible, Brick leaned in to look around. "Huh," was all he said. Stepping back, he cleared the way for the others to see inside.

It was a large room, maybe 50x60, with a closed door on the left hand wall. There were no furnishings of any kind, just bare stone walls and floors. But wandering around were maybe fifteen zombies.

“They’re… clones?” Sasha asked. Indeed, the zombies all appeared to be copies of each other. In life they would have been a very attractive female elf. Alexander was instantly suspicious. There was no such thing as cloning in Io.

Brick, being Brick, decided it was time to start the party. Extending his hammer, he hit the furthest zombie elf with a Holy Smite. With a moan, it turned toward him, and began to shuffle across the room. Each zombie it passed was alerted and aggro’d onto the tank. But this wasn’t happening fast enough for the dwarf. He scraped his hammer across his shield. Serpent Screech instantly causing every undead in the room to focus on him.

Moving to the near corner, he began to execute their standard plan for groups of mobs. He used his shield to knock back the first few slow-moving zombies that approached. Knocking them to the floor caused the wave behind them to stumble over their bodies, and began a sort of zombie traffic jam. When all the undead were grouped up, Brick used his Shield Bash ability, darting forward and knocking several more down into a pile. Then Sasha cast her aoe Thorn Trap, and Alexander laid on the fire. Each of them hurried to cast Trap Soul on the zombies. It took less than a minute for all the zombie elves to perish.

Leaning down, Max tried to loot the crispy corpses. He got nothing but soul crystals. “No loot,” he said, clearly offended.

While Kai searched for any hidden doors or caches, Max moved to the closed and barred door.
“No lock, just this bar. Looks like they wanted to keep something IN, not out.”

Hearing that, Brick stepped up next to the ranger and prepared to open the door. When the rest were in position, he grabbed the handle and pulled open the door, shield held high in case a monster came charging out.

There was no monster. Only a crying elf maiden sitting on a bed.

“Please don’t kill me again!” she snuffled, wiping her nose with her sleeve.

Alexander stepped forward. "We're not…" his voice drifted off as the elf raised her face to look at him. She was beautiful. Not the standard beauty that came with elven features. On Io, all elves were tall, thin, with high cheekbones and narrow chins. This elf was drop-dead, supermodel meets Aphrodite beautiful.

A smack to the back of the head from Lainey brought him back to his senses. "We're not here to hurt you," he said. Crouching down so that his eyes were level with her emerald green gaze, he asked, "What is your name?"

"I… I'm Jules." She hiccupped as she spoke. "You're really not here to kill me?"

"Why would we kill you?" Kai asked her.

"I don't know? Since I got here, every day the guy in the nasty doctor robes comes in here and kills me. When I respawn, he's gone. And the door's locked." She began to cry again.

"The surgeon is dead. He was a lich, and we captured his soul. So he won't be bothering you again." Sasha sat next to the girl on the bed and patted her hand.

Jules looked hopefully at Sasha. "Can you… take me out of here? I really want to go home."

"Where be home?" Brick asked.

Jules looked down at her lap. "In the game, its Antalia. That's where I was when I was captured." Her voice grew very quiet. "I can't really go outside the game right now."

Lainey gasped, "She's a player!"

Having already deduced that from the multiple identical zombies, and the fact that Jules had been killed repeatedly, Alexander asked the next logical question.

"Jules, from the number of zombies out there, you've been trapped here at least a couple weeks. Why didn't you just log out? Or call a GM to help you?"

Jules sniffed again, taking her time to answer. "I… I can't log out. I mean, I can. But if I do, I might not be able to get back. And being in the game is so much better than… the other."

"Why wouldn't you get back? Is there a problem with your gear?"

"I promised I wouldn't tell." Jules looked down at her hands. "I signed a DNA thingy when I…" She stopped speaking, shaking her head.

"DNA?" Alexander asked. "Do you mean an NDA? A non-disclosure agreement?"

Jules just nodded her head.

Getting angry, Alexander stood and headed for the door. "Kai, please stay with Jules. The rest of you, out here with me." He held the door as Max, Brick, Lainey, and Sasha passed thru, then closed it behind them. He led them out of the large room, back into the surgery.

"Odin! I need to speak with GM1. NOW!"

The others looked at him with questions on their faces. "What's going on?" Lainey asked.

"That girl is a player. She's been locked up against her will for weeks, being murdered every day. She says she's signed some kind of NDA. My guess is she's a beta tester like us. I want to know why she's been left here to rot."

As he finished speaking, his father's avatar appeared in the room. "Alexander…" he began.

"Dad. What the hell? Tell me what's going on!"

"Calm down, Alexander. I will explain," Richard said.

"Jules is not a beta tester. At least not like all of you. She's not here to test the game play. She's here because she's in a coma in the real world. Her body is in a pod just down the hall from all of you right now."

His father's words took the anger right out of Alexander. "A coma?"

"She suffered traumatic injury to several areas of her body, including her head. One of my original pod research team members, Dr. Westhall, is on staff at the hospital where she was admitted. She was connected to life support and monitoring, but her doctors didn't hold out much hope. Having no family, she was a ward of the state at the time of her injuries. She had her 18th and 19th birthdays in the hospital."

"Poor thing…" Sasha hugged Lainey as they listened.

"Westhall is a neurosurgeon. He'd been monitoring Jules' condition, and in his opinion, she'd lost her will to live. The cognitive activity indicators in her EEG's were declining. When we finally had successful test results on the pods, he recommended she be brought here and put into long term immersion. It took a while to get the hospital to sign off, but we made it happen. We managed to get enough of a sync with her brain to get her into the game. She actually helped a lot with that. She was already a player, before she was hurt. The character creation process was familiar to her, and she almost leapt at it!"

Sasha was openly crying now. Richard's avatar put an arm around her, and continued.

"I myself visited her in the creation room, along with Dr. Westhall, and Melanie. We explained to her what had happened, and that she was in a coma. We offered her the chance to live in the game until such time as we're able to restore her body. That's why she told you she couldn't log out. For her, leaving the game is falling back into darkness. And there's no guarantee we'd be able to sync her up again."

"And the NDA?" Alexander asked.

"It was actually just a one-page promise from her that she wouldn't tell anyone in the game about the pods, or her situation. There are no penalties in it for her." Richard scowled at his son.

"How long… has she been in the game?" Lainey asked.

"Nearly two months now. She was a level 20 rogue, before. But when she got back into the game, she mainly stayed in her starter city. At first, she just wandered around, touching things like flowers and trees. Then she would sit in a park and smile and wave at people passing by. Never did any quests. Eventually, an NPC seamstress sort of adopted her, began to teach her the tailoring skill. She focused on that, and it seemed to make her happy."

"And when she was kidnapped? Why was she just left here for TWO WEEKS?" Alexander was angry again.

"As soon as you entered the room with her zombies, and I saw her face, I started an investigation. She was apparently taken by PWP and held in their keep for a week. There's no record of her calling for a GM. When the tech that was monitoring her gameplay looked in to check on her, she was always just sitting or lying on the bed in what looked like a normal bedroom. That trend apparently continued here. I'm afraid he didn't bother with a more thorough check to confirm her location, or notice that her level was dropping from being killed repeatedly. He has been fired for his… failure."

Richard's voice caught. This was clearly an emotional situation for him as well. "I will personally apologize to Jules. I'm making arrangements for our psychologist to spend some time in-game with her. In the meantime, I would appreciate it if you all would see that she's protected. Take her back to your guild house and let her recover?"

Brick spoke first. "O'course we will! She'll be well looked after, don't ye worry!"

"Thank you. All of you. Alexander, please come with me. The rest of you, wait here, if you don't mind?" Richard headed back toward Jules' room.

The moment Richard entered the room, Kai froze. The NPC lock would keep him suspended until the unexplainable GM left the room again.

Richard knelt down in front of Jules. "Hi there, Jules. It's Richard. Do you remember me?" he asked gently.

Jules looked at him and nodded her head. "The boss guy," she mumbled.

Richard chuckled. "That's right. And the young man who just rescued you is my son, Alexander."

Jules looked at Alexander. "Hi."

Alexander couldn't speak, so he gave a simple wave in reply.

"Jules, I want to tell you I'm very sorry for your being stuck here so long. The man who was looking out for you let us both down. He didn't notice you'd been captured. He's just been fired, and when I left the lab to come visit you, Melanie was beating him on the head with a rolled up file folder."

This actually made the girl smile a bit. "I like Melanie. She's funny."

Richard returned the smile. "Yes, and Melanie likes you too. In fact, she volunteered to be the one to watch over you from now on. Would you like that?"

Again, Jules just nodded her head. "Is she watching now?"

"I'm sure she is. She's very worried about you. We all are."

Jules looked toward the ceiling and gave a small wave. "Hi, Melanie."

Melanie's avatar appeared in the room. Complete with lab coat, and for some reason, bunny ears. She launched herself onto the bed, hugging Jules tightly.

"Hey, sweetie! I'm glad you're okay. I'm not letting some stupid-head look after you in the real world anymore. I'll be there with you every single day!"

Jules returned the hug. "I'm sorry to be such a burden on everyone." Her voice was very soft.

"Nonsense! You're not a burden in any way!" Melanie scolded her. "I mean, you just lay about in that pod all day. You're basically a great big goldfish!"

Richard and Alexander both looked shocked, and Richard had opened his mouth to interrupt, when Jules began to giggle.

Melanie continued, "We feed you, change your tank once a month. Easiest pet I ever had!" More giggling.

"As for monitoring you in game, that's nothing. I'd be watching this big lug, anyway." She pointed at Alexander. "I spend all my time watching the game. It's my JOB. And now that Alexander's found you, he'll be taking care of you, too. So I can watch you both at the same time!"

Jules looked to Alexander and smiled. His heart stopped.

Seeing the look on his face, Melanie shoulder bumped Jules. "I know, he's pretty cute, right?"

She giggled as Jules' face turned bright red. She nodded her head quickly.

Never one for subtlety, Melanie kept going. "Lots of us girls stop by his pod to 'check on him' when he's online. He's all nekkid in there, ya know!" She winked at Jules, who snorted loudly before covering her mouth.

Now it was Alexander's turn to blush.

Coughing, Richard said, "Yes. Well. Melanie, it's time for you and I to head back. We've got a lot to talk about." Melanie hugged the girl once more and stood up.

"Jules, if it's okay with you, Alexander and his friends will take you to their home in Stormforge. In a few days, Melanie and I will come back to visit you. What do you think?"

Jules stood up and hugged Richard tightly. "Thank you. For everything. Without you, I'd still be drifting in the darkness. Or dead."

With that, Richard and Melanie faded from the game. A moment later, Kai blinked, and looked around.

Alexander said, "Jules, do you have any gear or anything you'd like to bring with you?"

She nodded her head, and moved to a wardrobe. Withdrawing her bag, she said, "When they kept killing me, I didn't see any point in putting my gear back on every time, so I just kept it in here." She threw the bag over her shoulder and said, "Ready."

Taking her by the hand, he led her out of the room and back to where the rest of the group waited. Kai followed behind. As they walked, he explained to her, "We're in the 4th level of the dungeons of a ruined keep. We're working our way up to the main floor."

He sent her a party invite, which she accepted. Then, after a brief thought, he sent her a guild invite as well. Also accepted. She smiled at him. "I've never been in a guild before. Oh! And its named after you and your dad!"

Alexander hung his head in shame. "Yeah, I'm afraid I didn't put a whole lot of thought into the guild name."

She squeezed his hand. "I like it!"

As they reached the group, he continued. "This place is filled with undead. We're clearing it as we go up. When we get into a fight, you just stay behind Sasha, here." Sasha waved at her. Remembering his manners, he introduced everyone. Each of them shook Jules' hand and welcomed her to the guild.

Taking both of her hands, Alexander looked at Jules. "These people are all family to me. We've been through a lot together, and I'd trust any one of them with my life." He paused until she nodded in understanding.

"You don't have to worry about what you say around us. We all know your situation, and we have decided to adopt you into the family. We'll do all we can to help you get better."

As tears came to Jules' eyes yet again, she became the center of a group hug. All except Kai, who kept a respectful distance.

Chuckling, Sasha said to Jules, "Kai's a dragon. Dragons don't do hugs." To which Kai gave his biggest dragon-toothed grin.

Having cleared this level, the group headed upward to the next. Just like with Fibble's hole, there was too much to carry in the lich's treasure room. So they agreed to leave the treasure and secure it once the keep was clear.

Moving up the stairs to third floor of the dungeon, Jules whispered to Sasha, "I don't have any weapons or armor. I feel a bit useless."

Overhearing, Max halted the group. From his bag he produced the last set of armor they'd taken off Henry, leader of PWP. "This is good quality rogue armor. It should help protect you until you're stronger."

Jules thanked him, and began to equip the armor. As she did so, Max produced a pair of daggers, and handed those to her as well. In full armor, and with daggers in each hand, the rogue looked much tougher than she had only minutes before.

"You still need to stay behind Sasha," Alexander warned. "All those deaths have taken you back to level one. A good sneeze from one of these level 50 mobs and you'll be sent to respawn."

Reaching the third floor, they found more of the same. Corridors with cells, larger rooms filled with undead. They bashed, burned and skewered their way through, casting Trap Soul on each mob. With each kill, Jules gained multiple levels, at least to begin with. This was the ultimate power-leveling situation. And they collected soul crystals from nearly every mob.

By the time they had fought their way through the third and second floors to the main floor of the keep, Jules had leveled up to 28, and the others had gained three more levels themselves, putting them at 37. Though they'd not run across any more named or boss mobs, killing several dozens of undead that were 15 or more levels above them was still great xp.

The stairway they had climbed emptied into a hallway at the back side of the keep, where it was carved into the mountain itself. As with the lower floors, the group began to systematically clear each room and hallway. After thirty minutes of not finding anything, living or dead, they began to relax. They split up into groups of two, with Jules tagging along behind Kai and Sasha, and began to clear rooms much more quickly. After another hour, they had cleared the first, second, and third floors of the main keep structure. Still they had found no enemies. It seemed that whomever was using the keep to build up the small undead army was sticking to the underground levels. Though Kai was concerned that they'd still not found a portal.

All that was left was for them to clear the tower itself. The layer of dust on the stairs made it clear nobody had passed that way in years. The friends cautiously made their way up, having to leap a few times where sections of the wall and stairs had broken away. At one particularly wide break, one that was too far to jump, Kai actually grabbed each of them and leapt across the gap before depositing them and going back for the next. Dragons in human form were stronger than they looked.

After half an hour of careful climbing and jumping, they reached the top of the tower. Alexander gazed at the room Fitz had described. He could picture the baron standing over Agatha's father, dagger in hand. The stone altar was still there. To one side of the room was a stone workbench that had been cleared of its contents long ago. In the corner next to the bench was a 6-foot free-standing mirror on an ebony wooden stand. The other side of the room held what once had been a bed, a padded chair, and a dresser with a porcelain washbasin. The basin was the only thing still intact. There were windows facing each of the cardinal points. Unlike nearly all of the rest of the keep, these windows were still intact. The views out over the falls and the forest were spectacular as the sun was beginning to set.

Kai, stood with his eyes closed. "There is magic here," he said. Turning slowly, he sensed for a direction.

Pointing to the altar, he said, "Strong dark magic residue there."

"Fitz said he found the baron performing a sacrifice there," Alexander offered. "And that he'd already turned close to a hundred of his citizens. So probably lots of sacrifices happened here."

The stone stood about three feet in height and width, and was close to eight feet long. There were runes and symbols engraved in the stone on every side. Looking at those runes, Kai said, "This is a thing of evil, not just of darkness."

"Let's just see about that!" Brick stepped toward the altar.

Laying his hands on the stone, he activated his shaping skill. First he wiped clean the top surface of the altar, the old blood and bile stains flaking away into dust. Then he wiped all the engraving from every other surface of the stone. "There even be some engravings on the inside," he informed them as he wiped them out.

After that, he knelt before the altar, asking the others to do the same. He prayed to Durin to cleanse the evil place of the baron's corruption.

As he murmured his prayer, Brick's hammer lifted from his hand and rose into the air. From the hammer shot a lightning bolt that struck the altar and, much like with the blessing of the dragon forge, etched the symbol of Durin's hammer into the front face of the altar. The stone began to glow with a warm, white light.

Max laughed. "You must be Durin's favorite paladin by now. You consecrated a chapel to him in Whitehall, then a dragon forge, now this altar here. You've arranged a basically unlimited supply of free ale and spirits. And everywhere you go, you brag about the size of his balls!"

As the others laughed, Brick grinned. "Aye! He do seem pleased, now that ye mention it!" There was an echo of thunder outside.

As the sun had now set, the group elected to rest in the newly consecrated room. No undead would dare approach it, and with only one door that led back down the stairs, it was an easily defensible position. Just to be safe, Brick used his shaping skill to detach the stone workbench from the wall, and used it to barricade the door.

Sasha managed to open a window enough to allow some air flow, then used the remains of the furniture to start a fire. In no time at all they were eating a hearty stew of boar meat, vegetables, and herbs for flavor. Alexander shared his flask with Jules, as she'd not had one with her when she was taken from her home city. Sasha and Lainey both raised an eyebrow, then shared a smug look between them.

Dinner completed, the friends began to discuss whether to stay the night, or return to the city and report to the king.

"The quest didn't complete," Max observed.

"Quest?" Jules asked. Alexander slapped his forehead. He instantly pulled up the quest log in his UI, and shared the quest with her."

"Oh! Thank you," Jules said, surprised.

"It's definite," Alexander sighed. "The fact that I could still share it with Jules confirms that the quest is not complete. Did we miss a room?

Kai and Max both shook their heads. Kai spoke first. "I did not sense any hidden rooms as we passed through the dungeons. And though I did not enter every room as we cleared the upper floors, I was close enough to the rest of you that I should have sensed any hidden doors."

Max volunteered, "Maybe we need to clear the mine, too?"

They all took a moment to read the quest description carefully.

"Nooo…." Sasha began. "It clearly says clear the KEEP of any enemies."

"Did we leave an angry rat alive somewhere?" Lainey half joked.

They all grew quiet, lost in their own ponderings of the quest. Alexander raised a hand to scratch his head. Catching movement out of the corner of his eye, his head snapped around, hand already reaching for his staff.

"Bwahaha!" Brick pointed and laughed. "The elf scared hisself, nearly attacked his own reflection in the mirror!"

Blushing at his own foolishness, Alexander looked to Jules to find her giggling at him, one hand over her mouth.

The mirror! Dammit. I'm such an idiot.

Alexander rose to his feet, approaching the mirror. Brick laughed even louder. "Looks like he wants revenge!"

Turning to look at the group, but keeping one eye on the mirror, he said, "Brick. Remember when we built Millicent's bakery?"

"Bah! O' course I remember. It were just a few days ago. And now ye got me hungering for fresh bread and pastry!"

Alexander saw the look on Max's face as he made the connection. Brick was still focused on dreams of pastry.

"Brick? How did Millicent get upstairs?" Max helped with a hint.

"Fitz made her a magic…" Brick paused. "Well, shit."

"Mind clueing in the rest of us?" Sasha grumped.

Alexander motioned for them all to get up as he explained. "Fitz created three magic mirrors that allowed Millicent to teleport from her residence upstairs, down to the bakery, and down to the cellar. And back up again."

They all stared at the mirror now. Kai stepped closer to it, closing his eyes.

"Aye, Alexander, you are correct. There is teleport magic. It was masked by first the evil magic of the altar, then by Durin's blessing. Even now, I have to focus to sense it."

Brick spoke up. "Millicent's mirrors had a trigger word. She had ta say 'upstairs' or 'downstairs' to activate it."

Kai shook his head. "I believe one need only touch this mirror to activate the magic. But to be sure, I will go through first. Wait here."

And with that, he reached out and placed a hand on the mirror. The was no flash, no sound, his body simply disappeared.

After a very tense minute, Kai spoke to them on group chat.

"The way is clear. It is safe to follow"

They each stepped up in turn to touch the mirror. Brick first, followed by Sasha. Then Max, Lainey, and Jules, with Alexander last.

As he stepped through, he found himself instantly in a large stone chamber. There were no doors that he could see. Behind him was a mirror, twin to the one in the tower, though this one was mounted to the wall. To his left there was a single window, just two feet wide and three feet tall. Looking around the room, he saw two more mirrors mounted on the wall. Across the room was a long stone table. Kai had cast a light globe that was floating near the ceiling and providing enough light to see by.

"We are inside the mountain again," Kai informed them. "Somewhere near the top of the ridge, I believe." He motioned toward the window.

Looking out, Alexander could see the tower far below, and great expanse of moonlit forest.

"Somebody has certainly been using this room." Max pointed out a multitude of footprints, drag marks, and what looked like tracks from cart wheels in the dust. All led to the back wall of the room. Casting his mage sight, Alexander could see an archway carved into the stone. The room had been too dark to see it from this distance with normal vision.

"Looks like we found your portal, Kai," he said, pointing at the back wall.

"Aye. This makes sense. Whoever was capturing all of those animals and other undead, was using a portal to bring them this far, then teleporting them into the dungeon." Kai nodded as he spoke.

"I didn't see a mirror anywhere down in the dungeon…" Sasha mused.

"Even a beginner like Alexander here could teleport a small group or some cargo such a short distance," Kai said.

Alexander, choosing to overlook the slight insult, added, "Remember, there was no dust disturbed in the tower." Pointing at the mirror they'd just exited from, he said, "That looks like only our tracks below that mirror. And the dust below the others doesn't look to be disturbed. Maybe whoever has been using this place doesn't know about the mirrors. Or just had no use for them."

"I believe you are correct," Kai said. He turned to look at Brick. "Fitz mentioned that you two helped construct the portal at your home. Do you think you know enough to disable this portal without permanently damaging it?"

Brick stroked his beard. "Aye. Maybe. Alexander mentioned something 'bout the runes controlling the… frequency? What if I was to just smooth away them runes?"

Smiling at the dwarf, Kai said, "Very good. That would indeed disable it. We can engrave new runes later if we need to make use of the portal."

Brick moved to the back of the room and laid his hands on the stone. While he was doing that, Max and Kai each went to examine the other two mirrors, to see if they could determine where they went.

Alexander studied the one they'd just passed through, looking for any kind of mark or indicator symbol that suggested 'Tower'.

After a few moments. Sasha's voice drifted across the room. "Uhhh… guys?"

Instantly, all eyes located the druidess, expecting to find her in danger. She was simply standing by the long stone table, one hand reaching down toward its surface.

"You should look at this," she said, some excitement in her voice.

When Alexander reached her side, he looked down upon what seemed to be a plain stone table. Just then, Sasha leaned over and blew the dust off the surface. Exposing four keyhole shaped holes in the tabletop.

"YESSS!" Brick pumped a fist in the air as he reached into his bag with his other hand to retrieve his keys. The others did the same.

"On the count of three?" Brick called out. "one… two… three!" Each of them pushed their key into a hole, and turned it to the right. The table began to hum, and the surface started to glow with a blue light.

Quest Completed: Clear the Keep!
Report to King Charles of Stormforge to claim your rewards.

Max did a little dance. "I've seen this before. Mostly in 'capture the flag' PVP games where you try to take and hold citadels. This would be the keep's 'control room'. The table will be your interface. It should allow you to make changes to the keep itself. Anything from the height of the walls to the furnishings inside!"

"Go ahead, boss." Lainey poked Alexander in the back with her bow.

Alexander placed a hand on the glowing tabletop.

"*Keep ownership entity recognized. Please state your designation.*" A voice echoed through the air.

"Alexander?" His answer was more of a question.

"Ownership entity Alexander, confirmed. Welcome to Dire Keep. Do you wish to activate the interface?"

Level up! You are now level 38!
Your wisdom has increased by +1. Your intelligence has increased by +1
You have 26 free attribute points available

Level up! You are now level 39!
Your wisdom has increased by +1. Your intelligence has increased by +1
You have 26 free attribute points available

"Yes, please," Alexander replied.

A three dimensional diagram appeared above the table, made of the same blue light that glowed upon the table. Next to the diagram was a menu of options.

Status	**Infrastructure**	**Population**
Defense	**Resources**	**Ancillary Structures**

"Begin at the beginning" Alexander said. "Interface, do you have a name?" he asked.

"The previous master of the keep simply called me Interface."

"That won't do. We must give you a name!" Alexander smiled. He could still remember the day when he'd named Alfred.

"Let's call him Fitz!" Sasha giggled. "That'll annoy the old wizard!"

Kai smiled, seeming to like the idea.

"How 'bout Jeeves?" Lainey volunteered.

“Or Durin!” Max grinned at his dwarf buddy. “That way Brick here can claim he’s praying every time he speaks to the interface!” He dodged as the dwarf swung a half-hearted punch at him.

“Methinks Jeeves is better,” Brick growled.

Alexander smiled. “I like Jeeves as well. Any objections?” Hearing none, he said, “Interface, from now on your name is Jeeves.”

“Thank you, master. Would you like to view the current status of the keep?”

“Yes, thank you, Jeeves. But first, are there any other recognized owners of the keep?”

“There are three other recognized ownership entities that have not yet chosen designations.”

“I see. What about the previous owner of the keep?”

“Baron Dire’s claim of ownership was nullified when you and the others captured the keep, and claimed it, master.”

“Thank you, Jeeves. That’s good to know. The others will now introduce themselves.”

One by one, Sasha, Brick, and Max laid a hand on the table and stated their names. Though Max altered his a bit, then guffawed as Jeeves said, *“Ownership entity Sir Max the Fabulous confirmed. Welcome to Dire Keep.”*

“I propose we add a fifth, in the event we can’t agree on something, we’ll have a tiebreaker,” Alexander suggested.

The others all nodded and looked at Lainey. “Jeeves, we wish to add an additional ownership entity,” he said.

“Of course, master. Simply have the entity place their hand on the control panel, as you did, and state their designation.”

Lainey approached the table, and set her hand down. With a wicked grin, she said, "Princess Lainey!"

"Ownership entity Princess Lainey confirmed. Welcome to Dire Keep"

"Copycat!" Max grinned at her.

Alexander moved on to business. They had their very own keep to play with!

"Jeeves, please show us the keep's current status."

The 3-D image changed from the main menu to a list of figures.

Dire Keep: Level 10/25	
Physical Status: 340/500	**Resources: 14,000 units**
See Infrastructure for details	*See Resources for details*
Current Population: 7	**Defensive Capabilities: 60%**
Citizens: 5 Guests: 2	*See Defense for details*
Ancillary Structures: 2	**Production rate: 0%**
See Ancillary Structures for details	*Production will increase with population and use of ancillary structures*

"So, the Physical Status makes sense. The keep's been damaged. Same goes for the Defensive Capabilities. Population is a no brainer. And Production probably means the mine. No miners, no production. But what are the ancillary structures, and what are the 14,000 resources?" Max thought aloud.

"Let's start with population." Alexander smiled at Jules. "Would you like to be a citizen of the keep?" The elfess smiled shyly and nodded her head. "Yes, please."

Looking to Kai, Alexander said, "You are most welcome as well. Though we certainly understand if your position restricts you in some way."

Kai grinned and bowed his head. "I am honored by the invitation. We dragons are not so rigid in such things. My title as Prince is my birthright, and would not be affected in any way were I to become a citizen of Dire Keep. However, it may have some impact on your keep. Adopting a dragon is no small thing."

Alexander looked to the others. "Any objections? Concerns?" No one spoke up. "In that case," Kai said, "I humbly accept citizenship at Dire Keep."

There was a flash of blue light, and several things changed on the status page. First, the population explanation changed to *Citizens: 7 (1 Dragon).*

Next, the Ancillary Structure count went up to 3. And the Defensive Capabilities increased to 75%!

Sasha laughed. "I guess having a dragon around is good protection!"

Alexander wanted to know why the ancillary count went up. "Jeeves, what are the current ancillary structures?"

"*The current ancillary structures consist of The Mine, The Stone Bridge, and the Embassy of the Dragon Kingdom, master.*"

Kai grinned. "I did warn you. Any time I set up a residence in a location, because of my title, it automatically becomes an embassy. King Charles received a similar message when I chose the dragon forge as my perch."

Max chuckled. "Between Kai's colonization and Brick's consecrations, we're slowly taking over the world!"

Alexander raised two long benches from the stone floor, one on either side of the table. "Please, rest. We've got some things to discuss before we sleep." When everyone was settled, he began. "Okay, I see several immediate needs we must address. First, there are two more mirrors in this room. We don't know where they go, or what might come through them from the other side. Though the dust around them is not disturbed, I still have an itchy feeling, and think we need to explore, or somehow secure them."

Jules raised her hand. When Alexander smiled at her, she spoke. "This may sound stupid, but what if we just take them down and set them facing the wall?"

There was a moment of stunned silence. "BWAHAHA!" Brick burst out. "Ye be genius, lass!"

Laughing himself, Alexander continued. "Okay, problem solved, for now. We'll address this again if that doesn't work. Next item. We need to improve the defenses here, and rebuild the keep in general. Brick and I could do much of the rebuilding. But it would be slow. And we don't know how much time we have before we'll need to defend this place from PWP, or others. I suggest enlisting some help."

Sasha spoke first. "I'm sure if we feed him well, Fitz will come and help. Maybe add some protective enchantments?"

Kai laughed loudly. "Aye, Sasha. He would at that. And I have some magical protections of my own that I'll happily put in place."

"This keep be dwarven built," Brick began. "Dwarves be the best ones fer repairin' it. I'm sure me King would send us the dwarves and supplies we be needin', in trade fer something o' value."

"That's exactly what I was thinking," Alexander agreed. "But it brings up another question. Population. We need miners and farmers, hunters, and crafters to restore and operate this keep. But being here might be dangerous to citizens. The dwarves accepted our invitation to settle in Whitehall, and it cost them a child within a matter of days." He gave that a moment to sink in.

"I intend to paint a giant target on this keep. I want this 'Dark One' to throw his minions against these walls, until he has none left, and has to come at us himself. And between the attack on Stormforge, and

Whitehall, and the innocent citizens that were lost there, I'm not sure my conscience could take more," Alexander continued.

"Yer thinkin… adventurers," Brick guessed.

"In part, yes. I think we should ask King Thalgrin for dwarves willing to help us rebuild, with a full disclosure of the danger. Volunteers who are fully aware of the risk. Stonemasons, and maybe miners as well. We could also reach out to King Charles, to see if any human citizens would wish to volunteer. But I think it's time the Greystone Clan begins its expansion. We can recruit players who are crafters, and those who are fighters. But…"

"But you're worried about recruiting spies for the Dark One," Max finished for him. Brick was right behind him.

"We can no' read player's minds. But we CAN make it so no servants o' that dark scum be settin' foot in our keep!" The dwarf grinned. "Just like Whitehall. We'll bring Father Ignatius, and priests o' every other god who wishes harm to the Dark One. We'll consecrate the ground so there be no sneakin' about, 'n' set wards what kills or captures any o' his own, just like at our own house."

Kai added, "Fitz and I can create those wards, and it seems Brick is more than capable of providing the consecration. In addition, as a prince, I can accept an oath of loyalty from each member that, if broken, will have harsh consequences. Though, the oath would have to be to the Keep, as I am not a member of your guild."

"Is it possible to have an N…. a non-adventurer in a guild?" Jules asked a bit awkwardly.

"I don't know?" Alexander answered. "I'm not sure it has ever come up." A rumble of thunder rolled across the forest outside.

Chuckling, Alexander said, "Apparently Odin thinks it's okay. Kaibonostrum, would you do us the honor of joining the Greystone Guild?"

"It would be my pleasure," the dragon prince replied. Alexander tried sending him a guild invite, but the [send] button was grey. "Huh. The invite won't work. Kai, are you a member of another guild already?" he asked.

Kai thought about it. "I was a member of a Trader's Guild in a city that perished some three thousand years ago. But I doubt that would prevent my membership."

"Maybe the thunder wasn't a sign from Odin? Maybe only adventurers can join the guild?" Lainey said, a note of sadness in her voice.

"But why let Kai join our group, and become a citizen of the Keep, but not join the guild?" Max said. "Try it again."

Alexander pulled up his UI. Highlighting Kai's icon in the Group screen, he thought, 'Guild Invite'. This time, he was able to click the now green [send] button. Kai quickly accepted.

"Huh. Now it works. Maybe it just took a few minutes for mighty Odin to alter the rules of the universe!" He grinned. "Welcome, Kai. You are the first dragon and the first non-adventurer to join Greystone!" Everybody golf-clapped as Kai took a bow.

"Okay, back to business. It's getting late. So, raise your hand if you support the plan to recruit citizens." All in the room raised a hand. "And adventurers?" Again it was unanimous.

"Then that is how we shall proceed. Next item. Jeeves, can we specify Dire Keep as a Guild property?"

"Yes, master. As long as a majority of the ownership entities approve."

Alexander put his hand back on the table. "Jeeves, please designate Dire Keep as the official Guild Keep of the Greystone Guild." The other four all laid a hand on the table and stated, "I approve."

"It has been done, master."

>>>SYSTEM ALERT! <<<
The Greystone Guild has captured Dire Keep in the Kingdom of Stormforge, and claimed it as Greystone property!

They all stared at the notification. It hadn't even occurred to them that this would rate as a system-wide alert. That was usually reserved for worldwide events, or successful raids where one guild took a keep from another. That target had been painted on their backs much quicker than intended.

"Well, shit," Brick said.

Chapter Four

Be Careful What You Ask For

Alexander read the system alert for the third time, shaking his head. "That was stupid of me."

"You had no way to know." Lainey tried to comfort him.

"It might tell us something, though," Max pointed out. "Think about it. Jeeves told you that Baron Dire still had the ownership claim here, until we took it. The place was full of undead. System messages usually only happen when a guild keep is taken by another guild. So maybe Baron Dire's still alive, and somehow running a guild?"

"And we know, Jules was kidnapped and sent here by PWP. So, by extension, maybe PWP held the keep, and the 'Dark One' running them is Baron Dire?" Alexander finished the train of thought.

"That would explain the system message, sort of," Sasha said.

"Well, regardless, we now have less time to prepare. I say we flip those other two mirrors, teleport back to Stormforge, and start with the recruiting." Lainey nudged them.

"Teleporting will not be necessary," Kai said. "I know portal magic as well as Fitz does. He taught it to me when I was a small child. I can adjust this portal so that it will connect to both your portal in Stormforge, and the Broken Mountain portal. It will save any new citizens from having to transport themselves and their supplies through the forest, where they might encounter enemies."

"Thank you, Kai," Alexander said. "Can you also make sure that whomever has been using it can no longer connect to it?"

"Yes. I will change its origin frequency. You will be able to connect to it from any portal on Io, using your medallions. But otherwise, no portal will be able to make a connection here."

As Kai collected all their medallions, plus a few extra from Sasha, and went to work on the portal, Brick and Alexander both observed using their mage sight. Both were interested in learning more about portal magic.

The others removed the two unknown mirrors from the wall and set them on the floor, mirror-side down. Anyone attempting to use the teleportation magic within the mirrors would emerge within the stone itself.

When Kai was finished, he handed them back the medallions, and opened the portal. They all stepped through it into the Greystone compound.

Sasha showed Jules around, while Brick headed to the dragon forge to see what was happening there. Max took off to the butcher's shop to see if he could obtain a late-night snack for their big cat mounts, and Bacon. Lainey headed into the workshop to see what she could make from the many hides they'd gathered. Alexander reminded her that she could take some time in the morning to see if the trainer had new patterns for her, and not to use too many of the hides in case she'd need them for higher level items.

Alexander, with nothing in particular to do, raised himself a bench in the middle of the courtyard, and decided to practice his enchanting. The old gnome had taught him a basic light spell. Removing one of the smallest of the lich's diamonds from his bag, he held it in his hand, and cast the 'light' enchantment. When he opened his hand, the stone glowed with a clean, white light. It did not seem bright in the open night air, but Alexander suspected that in a dungeon corridor it would be bright enough to see by. The standard 'recipe' enchantment he'd learned included the ability to turn the enchantment on and off at need. So, he deactivated the stone and put it back in his bag.

The enchantments he'd done on the light posts around Whitehall had been significantly brighter, though he'd used the same spell. Was this due to the size of the stone? Or the medium? Did stone hold light better than diamonds?

Deciding to experiment, he reached into the earth below and raised more obsidian. Just a block weighing maybe 100 lbs. He'd leave what he didn't use at the forge, for Brick and the dwarves to make use of.

Keeping in mind Fitz's warning about putting too much mana into something and causing an explosion, he started small. He broke off a golf-ball sized piece of obsidian. Holding it in his left hand, he focused on his Ray of Light spell. Figuring a burst of magic into the stone would be dangerous, he tried channeling the light the way Kai had.

His first attempt simply burned a groove into the stone, and he stopped after only a couple of seconds. He needed to rethink this. Ray of Light was a damage spell, Kai had said. It wouldn't heal. Maybe it wouldn't work as a flashlight type spell either.

Closing his eyes, he thought about the standard recipe light enchantment. He broke the spell down into components, looking for an answer. Not finding one, he changed his train of thought.

Okay, shooting the stone with the Ray of Light won't work. I'm basically just attacking the stone. What about channeling the spell through the stone?

Holding the same stone in hand, he extended his arm and focused on pushing the light spell from his hand through the stone. His fingers immediately heated up, and he stopped the spell, shaking his hand.

That was stupid. Even if you did it right, the light has to burn through your fingers to reach a target. Little bit like sticking your finger in a gun barrel. Idiot.

He smiled to himself. That admonition had come to him in Lainey's voice.

Deciding to continue this path, he made a few adjustments. First, he put on a glove. Then he shaped his subject stone into a more convex configuration. Then he reached down and pulled a small amount of stone from the bench, shaping it into an eight-inch tube, the end of which wrapped around the obsidian 'lens'. The net result looked like a giant drinking straw with a big chocolate chip stuck in one end.

Taking the thing up in his gloved hand, he began to slowly channel the ray from his hand, through the stone, and into the lens. The light beam sprang forth from the obsidian and into the ground where it was pointed. Alexander kept a minimal flow of mana going, waiting for a feeling of resistance in the stone, or heat in his gloved hand. After twenty seconds or so, he stopped.

Okay, this is cool, I'm shooting the light thru the stick. But that doesn't really get me anywhere. I can do the same just sticking my hand out. Can I stop the ray inside the stone?

Again, being very safety conscious, he decided to move forward. Removing his armor and setting it, along with his bag, off to one side, he got ready to try his new idea. If he died, he didn't want to lose any of his gold or gear. And he'd respawn a few feet away.

He extended the stick with the stone at the end toward the ground. Closing his eyes, he focused on the Ray of Light spell. He pushed much more lightly than in his previous cast. Inching the mana through his hand, into the stone of the stick. From there, he watched it slowly progress down the length of the stick, into the stone. He pictured the beam swirling within the stone, spiraling down in a tight pattern toward the center. It worked! The light did not exit the stone, as before. It followed the spiral pattern he was picturing in his mind.

Ever so slowly, he pushed more mana into the stone. The cast bar on his UI said he was up to 100 mana, and adding about 10 per second. As he approached 200 mana, he began to feel some resistance. He instantly stopped casting.

Skill Level Increase! Enchanting: +1
You have created a new and unique enchanted item

So, he'd made something, and hadn't killed himself or anyone else! This was exciting!

Looking down at the stick, he saw:

Ray of Light Wand
Item Level: Unique
Charges: 200/200

Right on! He'd made his first wand! And of a type that nobody had made before…

Wait. Why has nobody made this before? It's a simple spell. Is it the materials? I know obsidian is rare. And most wands are made of wood. Maybe I'm just the first to combine them to make a shooting wand? Shooting! How do I shoot? Maybe just point it and shout 'pew!'?

He chuckled to himself. He really didn't know how to activate the wand. Or whether it would fire a channeled beam, or a burst. A burst with 200 mana could be dangerous. Especially if it backfired somehow. He resolved to go ask Fitz.

Passing through the house, he didn't find the wizard in the kitchen, dining room, or lounge. His three favorite hangouts. Stepping out front, he checked in at the forge, finding several dwarves, but no wizard. Finally, he stepped through the garden to the base of the wizard's tower. Looking about, he didn't find any kind of doorbell or chain to pull. There was no door to knock on. One only accessed the tower through teleportation. And only at the wizard's invitation.

So, stepping back, he looked toward the top of the tower and shouted. "Fitz! Been practicing my enchanting! Discovered something new! Need to ask you if I'm about to blow some shit up!" He smiled as he pictured the likely look on the wizard's face.

In a flash, he found himself inside the wizard's tower. He was standing next to Fitz, in an empty stone room. The walls were covered in runic writing and symbols.

Fitz held out his hand. "Show me, boy."

Smiling, Alexander first took out the diamond, and activated the light spell. Handing it to Fitz, he asked "I enchanted this with the standard light spell. But it's not as bright as the light posts I made. What's the difference? Is it the size, the medium, what?"

Fitz looked annoyed. "You interrupted me for THIS?" His eyebrows merged into one large hairy grey caterpillar above his nose.

"No… but I need this question answered, and I knew you'd ignore it after I show you the other thing." He grinned at the wizard.

Fitz actually laughed. "Well played, boy. Okay. The difference is partly in size, yes. Larger stones in general can hold more magic. Though some stones are better conduits than others. So, for example, a small bit of obsidian would hold more magic than a larger piece of limestone. Gems, in general, will hold more magic than base stone. But different gems, and even different cuts, favor different types of magic. I have a book somewhere around here that will help you."

He held up the diamond. "This is a small stone. But diamonds are actually good conductors of light magic, due to their clear and refractive nature. This one could actually have held more magic that you've put into it. And more magic would have caused it to glow brighter, or for longer."

Handing the diamond back, he said, "Now. Why are you really here?

Alexander produced the wand and handed to the wizard. He stayed silent while the wizard examined it.

"A unique wand that fires damaging light." The wizard shook his head. "I don't know whether to congratulate you, or slap you in the head. At least you came to find me before you killed anyone."

"I was very careful, master." Alexander decided to play to the wizard's ego. "But I didn't want to risk firing it. Partly because I don't know how, and partly because a 200-mana burst might be dangerous."

"Both good reasons to stop. And the reason we're in this room," Fitz replied. "This is my testing room. It's warded with magic to prevent you from blowing up the whole tower. If something goes wrong in here, the only thing that will be damaged is you." He grinned, pushing Alexander toward the center of the room. With a wave of his hand, he conjured a straw dummy that looked a lot like Fibble.

"The wand is intent activated. Much like the healing wand I gave Fibble. You need only point it at its target and want it to fire."

"Will it fire a channeled beam? Or a burst?" Alexander asked, pointing the wand at the dummy.

"Interesting. I assumed a beam. But if you've figured out a burst, then try that."

Alexander decided to update his mentor. "Kai showed me this spell, and opened up the light magic school for me. I didn't know anything about the spell, and assumed it was supposed to fire in a burst. So that's how it came out. Kai was pretty surprised." He chuckled.

"Ha! I'm sure he was. You never cease to surprise me, boy. Now, focus." He waved at the dummy.

Alexander pointed at fake-Fibble and thought about the wand firing a burst using 30 mana. The burst fired from the end of the wand, burning through the dummy's chest. The beam seemed wider and stronger than when he'd cast it in the forest. Maybe it was just his imagination.

As the wizard approached to re-examine the wand, he decided to ask, "Fitz, I used the minimum 30 mana that time. But it seemed like the beam was more powerful than when I cast it by hand."

The wizard took the wand from him. With another wave of his hand, the dummy disappeared, and two identical blocks of wood appeared.

"Show me," the wizard instructed. "You shoot your block with the spell you first used. Use exactly 30 mana. I'll shoot a burst from this wand with the same."

Alexander held up his hand and fired a minimum burst at the wood block. The block jumped in the air, and landed with a hole burned into one side. Much like his first time casting at the log, the hole was about an inch wide, and two inches deep.

Fitz pointed the wand at the other block, and fired. It, too, jumped into the air. But when it landed, there was a much larger hole in the wood. Slightly wider and nearly twice as deep.

Alexander's heart beat faster. "Could it be because I shaped the stone like a lens?" he asked.

Fitz looked at the end of the wand. From the outside, you couldn't really determine the shape of the stone.

Pulling another small piece of obsidian from the larger stone in his bag, he shaped it into a convex lens, then handed it to Fitz.
Enlightenment dawned on the wizard's face. "That would explain it. You basically made it a magnifying lens. What made you think of doing this?"

Skill Level Up! Enchanting +1: *You have discovered that passing a spell through a convex lens may increase the power of the spell.*

Blushing, Alexander explained. "In my world there are old stories of mad scientists creating weapons of light called 'lasers' using a power source and a series of lenses like that one, to amplify the power and destroy things. Like planets. I guess my brain just decided that's how it should work?"

"Yes, well. Keep this to yourself, boy. If this became generally known, it would change the face of warfare across Io. Imagine a five-foot-long version of this, mounted on a siege tower. It could burn defenders off a wall, one after the other. Or, with enough stored mana, it could burn right through a gate. The same could be done right now, of course. But it would take a chain of mages pooling their power, and they would all be drained afterward, taking hours to recover. Most mages won't even try it, because of the risks involved."

"I understand," Alexander said solemnly. "Where I'm from we have terrible weapons of mass destruction that can take out entire cities, or even realms, in seconds. I would not want to see that here."

"Yes. Quite. Best you take your explorations in a different direction, boy. It's plain you've a talent for destruction. Why not enchant items that provide boosts to useful attributes? Extra stamina, extra mana, and such? Maybe healing items like Fibble's wand?"

"I don't know any healing spells yet," he responded to the wizard, hoping he'd take the hint. Being able to heal would come in VERY handy.

"Ha! You could be more subtle, boy. Fine, then. In the interest of saving the world from your dastardly tendencies toward crafting weapons..." Fitz placed a hand on Alexander's head. Alexander was beginning to feel like he could tell the difference between magic types as they penetrated his mind. Dark magic felt a bit slimy, and burned like napalm, spreading itself to burn as much as possible. Light magic still burned, but it was a clean, almost surgical fire. He embraced the pain, as usual.

Fitz removed his hand. "That should do. It's a large heal, and requires a correspondingly large amount of mana. But when stored within an object during times of rest, it makes an effective combat heal without draining you of your reserves."

Alexander pulled up his UI and found the spell.

Healing Light: *This spell harnesses the regenerative powers of light to heal a friendly target for 2,000 hp. Range: 50 yards. Mana Cost: 600*

"Should I try to enchant something now?"

Fitz snorted. "Why not? This should be interesting.

Alexander pulled more obsidian from his bag. Breaking off a small piece, and another very small piece, he used his shaping skill to form the smaller one into a tiny convex lens. He spent some extra time smoothing and polishing the stone. Then he formed the larger piece into a wand-sized tube, which wrapped around the lens at one end.

Looking to Fitz, who only raised an eyebrow and glared back, Alexander continued. As he'd done with the Ray of Light spell, he focused on transmitting the Healing Light through his hand, slowly infusing it into the wand, and down to the obsidian lens. Again, he pictured the magic moving in a tight spiral toward the center of the lens. Much tighter than before. He kept pushing mana into the lens until he felt resistance. Easing back, he began to spiral the magic through the body of the wand itself. Wrapping the tube like a Tesla coil. He continued until he was nearly out of mana.

With his recent additional levels, his mana pool was up over 3,500. He'd put more than 3,000 into the wand.

Fitz, who'd been watching carefully with mage sight, let out a laugh that was nearly a giggle, waving for Alexander to inspect his work.

Salvager
Item Level: Unique, Epic
Stats: Intelligence +10, Wisdom +10, Stamina +10
This wand will cast a burst of regenerative light magic, healing a friendly target for 2,400hp.
Charges: 20/20

Skill Level up! Enchanting +5: *You have created a unique, epic level enchanted item.*

"Woohoo!" Alexander couldn't believe it. He'd crafted an epic healing wand! He looked again at the stats. Huge boosts to his intel and wisdom, and a big increase to his stamina would bump up his health to nearly double what it was now.

But the amount of hp per heal was off. The spell description said 2,000. The wand's heal was 2,400. Was this because of the lens? He asked himself.

Fitz nodded his head "Aye, boy. I can see what you're wondering. Yes. The lens boosts the power of the spell. By 20%! That's nearly unheard of. Absolutely unheard of from one so new to enchanting, and magic in general. Well done, boy!"

Alexander had one more question. "Why only 20 charges? The wand you gave Fibble fired something like 100 shots before you had to recharge it."

Fitz waved his hand and produced the wand. A shout of goblin dismay echoed down the corridor. Followed by the sound of little feet rushing toward them. "This is Fibble's Stick. Take a look."

Fibble's Stick
Item Level: Unique, Epic
This wand imbues a target with regenerative light magic, healing the target for 200hp.
Charges 100/100.

Alexander chuckled at the wand being renamed for Fibble.

Fitz said, "This wand was created by a GrandMaster Enchanter. Namely, me. It is in no way my best work, simply something I threw together in a time of need. It does indeed have 100 charges. But heals only 200hp at a time. That's a total of 20,000 hp capacity." He gave Alexander a moment to digest the information.

"Aaaand..." Alexander did the math in his head, "the one I just made has a capacity of 48,000hp!"

"Now you see it, boy. Even without the boost from the lens, your wand would have held double the capacity of Fibble's."

"Thank you, Fitz. I... you've been a great friend to me. To all of us. And an even better mentor."

"It has been my pleasure, boy. You have shown great promise. I look forward to watching you grow. And the food here's pretty good, as well!" He waggled his eyebrows.

Laughing, Alexander said, "As you may have seen, we captured Dire Keep. It was full of undead, including a lich…" He went on to detail their findings at the keep.

"Kai has joined our guild, and decided to become a citizen of the keep as well. I would like to extend the same invitation to you." Alexander bowed low to his mentor.

When he straightened up, Fitz patted him on the should. "Thank you, boy. But I'm afraid I must decline. I'm a lifetime member of the Mage's Guild, and would not abandon that. As for citizenship, I am a citizen of Stormforge, and Advisor to The King. I'm afraid I must remain so.

"But it sounds to me like you could use some assistance in repairing the keep, and boosting its defenses. And every citadel needs a good wizard's tower! Especially since you so cleverly announced your new acquisition to the world!"

Alexander hung his head. "Yeah. That wasn't my best moment. We were all excited about playing with our new keep, and I didn't think."

"Well, you DID remove the capability for the previous owner to portal to the keep. So, at the least you should have three or four days before an attack of decent size can be prepared. In the morning, we'll go see the king, and formalize your rights to the keep. We'll also ask for volunteers from among the citizens. And we'll do the same with Thalgrin. The next day, we'll all head over and begin improvements. In the meantime, I'll send Kai back to guard the keep and begin repairs. Also, the two guild mages who've been working in Whitehall could probably be persuaded to take on more work, if the payment were worthwhile."

He winked, producing a bottle of dwarven spirits as if out of nowhere. "That reminds me. We need Thalgrin to deliver another shipment. Brick's running low!"

Alexander noticed a pair of goblin ears peeking out from the doorway. "Fibble! Come on in, buddy. I've got your stick right here."

The goblin stepped hesitantly into the room, looking from Alexander to Fitz, unsure of himself. When Alexander held out the wand, he stepped closer and accepted it, hugging it to his chest.

"Fibble, we made a new friend today. Her name is Jules. She's a very nice elf. She was hurt by some bad people, but we killed them all, and brought her home with us. She could use more friends, and a protector. You think you could protect her, like you did for Sasha?" Alexander asked, keeping his tone very serious.

At hearing he was needed as a protector, Fibble's chest puffed out, and he assumed a look just as serious as Alexander's. "Fibble protect friends! Use stick to keep them safe!" He waved the wand about. "But…" he paused.

"What is it, Fibble?"

"Hungry dragon still out there?" the goblin asked, very quietly. He began to tremble. "Dragon wants to eat Fibble!" he wailed.

Trying not to laugh, Alexander dropped to his knees so that he was at eye level with the goblin.

"No, Fibble. The dragon will not eat you. He was just teasing you. His name is Kai, and he's a good dragon. In fact, he is our friend. He has joined our guild. So now he is one of us!"

The frightened little goblin didn't look convinced. So, Alexander tried another approach. "Fibble, how would you like to join our guild, too? Guild members can NOT eat each other. It's against the rules. You could come on adventures with us, and get bigger and stronger, until not even a dragon would scare you!" Fitz raised an eyebrow at this, but remained silent.

Fibble looked at him for a moment. Alexander could practically hear the rusty gears grinding in the little goblin's mind. "You… make Fibble a friend?" he asked.

Alexander shook his head. "No." The goblin looked crushed. "Fibble, you are ALREADY my friend. Since the day we met. And Sasha's. And everyone else in Greystone. What I'm asking is, do you want to become part of our clan?"

Fibble nodded his head so rapidly his ears stirred up a breeze. To a goblin, clan was everything. And Fibble's clan were all killed. Many of them by Greystone when they cleared the village.

"There is just one thing," Alexander qualified. "You will have to take a bath, once every week."

Fibble's eyes grew wide, and he began to back away. "Noooooo…" he protested, shaking his head.

"Fibble, we all have to take baths." Alexander thought quickly for a decent argument. "If we don't take baths, we stink. And when we go on adventures, if we stink, it's easier for monsters to find us. Then Sasha or Jules might get hurt!"

Fibble thought it over for a while. "Okay. For protect Sasha and Jules, Fibble take bath." He sounded as if he'd just agreed to take on a suicide mission.

"Great!" Alexander sent a guild invite to the goblin. Fibble's eyes got big as the words appeared before his eyes. Knowing from experience that the goblin couldn't read the invitation, he said "Fibble, do you want to join the Greystone clan?"

The goblin nodded his head, yes, and that was that.

Fitz said, "I'll send you back to the house. I'll get Fibble bathed and prepared, and bring him to breakfast in the morning." He snapped his fingers, and Alexander found himself in the courtyard in front of the house.

There was still work going on at the forge. He stuck his head in to find Brick alone inside, pounding away at something on the anvil, zoned out like he'd been the day before. Alexander left him to it.

Walking into the house, he headed to the lounge, where he found all three of the ladies smiling at him. Instantly suspicious, he stopped in his tracks. "What?"

Sasha leapt up and hugged him. "You invited Fibble to the guild!" She squeezed him again.

Laughing, and greatly relieved he wasn't the target of some female plot, he said, "Oh, yes. He's determined to protect you, and Jules, on our future adventures. And once I convinced him that Kai wasn't going to snack on him, he even agreed to a weekly bath!"

"No WAY!" Lainey giggled. "You're like, the Miracle Worker, 'n' shit. The Goblin Whisperer!"

"Yup! Fitz is giving him a bath as we speak." Alexander grinned. "Oh!" he said, taking out his newest creation, "look what I made!"

He handed the wand to Sasha. When she inspected it, her eyes grew wide. "It heals for 2,400 a pop! That's nearly the same as my biggest heal spell!" Lainey took it from her hand to inspect it herself.

Taking a few steps back, and moving behind the chair where Jules was sitting, he said, "Yeah, so… we don't really need YOU anymore, Princess Band-Aids!"

Sasha gasped, then snorted, and launched herself at him. Prepared for such a move, he dodged around the chair, then leapt over a sofa, grabbing the wand from Lainey as he passed her. Continuing to keep large furniture between himself and his best friend, he fired the wand at her, shouting, "Pew! Pew!"

Despite herself, Sasha collapsed on one of the sofas, laughing in great gasping donkey-laughs. Figuring himself safe, Alexander plopped down next to her, putting one arm around her shoulders. "Though, I supposed we'll keep you around anyway. Your boyfriend Fitz might be upset if you left. Who would feed him?" He winced as she elbowed him in the ribs. When all the laughter in the room had died down, Alexander looked at

Jules. "Have they given you the tour? Got you all set up with a room?" he asked.

Jules hit him with a smile that curled his toes. "Yes, everyone has been so nice. And this place is amazing! The kitchen is bigger than my whole apartment. Sasha offered to let me stay in her room with her, but I don't want to be a bother. So, she gave me the suite right next to yours."

A bit flustered, Alexander mumbled, "Good choice. The sunlight through the French doors in the morning is lovely."

Max returned with a cart driven by the butcher's boy who had previously fed their cat mounts. He saved Alexander from more awkwardness by shouting, "Bring out your cats! Its dinnertime!"

They all headed outside, summoning their mounts. As the giant cats appeared, Jules gasped in wonder. She instantly began hugging and petting each of them, to which none of them objected.

The boy stood in the cart, and began to gingerly hand over a large chunk of meat to each of the cats. As before, they politely took the meat from his hands, and headed toward the stables to eat.

"Brick's in his crafting zone, so he won't be summoning Bacon right now," Alexander said.

"No worries. The big pig seems to prefer his food slightly aged." He lifted a large sack from the cart. "Brought some leftovers from the fruit and veggie vendors. I'll leave them in the stable for him." Max flipped the boy a gold coin and sent him home.

Kai walked up to the group. "I've spoken with Fitz. I'm heading back to the keep for the evening. I'll see you all back there in a couple of days!" And with a blink, he was gone.

Brick came out of the forge, shaking his head, looking as if he'd just awoken from a dream. Which, in a way, he had. "What did I miss?" he asked.

"Well, you need to summon Bacon. Max brought him dinner, it's in his stall." Brick grinned, summoning the giant battle boar. He thumped the pig on its flanks a few times, and scratched behind his ears, before telling him there was food in the stables. Bacon snorted and waddled off to find his dinner.
"Also, Kai just went back to guard the keep until we can get back with some folks to help secure it. Fitz and the guild mages are going to help. It seems we'll also be getting a wizard's tower at the keep." Everyone laughed at this.

"You forgot the important things!" Sasha stomped her feet. "Fibble has joined the guild! And dork boy here crafted an epic item!"

This got Brick's attention. "What'd ye make?" he asked.

Grinning, Alexander said, "You've been busy in the forge since we got back. You show me yours, and I'll show you mine." All three of the ladies giggled at this.

Shaking his head at his friend's poor phrasing, Brick produced a two-foot metal statue of a dragon. Its wings were outstretched, as if about to take flight. The dragon looked much like Kai had, sitting atop the forge. Handing his wand to Brick, Alexander took the statue from him and inspected it.

Dragon's Stand
Item Level: Unique
Stats: Defense +10, Morale +10, Mana Regeneration +15%
This unique sculpture, crafted in a Dragon Forge, provides enhancements to a base, and its occupants, to aid in the defense of their home.

"Brick, this is amazing!" Alexander blurted out. "We'll put this in the main hall of the keep. Make it our Guild symbol. What do you think, guys?"

The ladies all nodded emphatically. Max, who had returned after feeding Bacon, added, "Hell yeah! Nothing looks cooler than a dragon. We'll get banners made with a dragon logo. Maybe get shortness here to craft a giant dragon head to mount over the gate!"

Jules quietly volunteered, "I can make the banners. I just need some supplies."

Sasha leapt at the opportunity. "Tomorrow we're going shopping! We'll get you everything you need, and you can set up in the workshop by my greenhouse, if you want!"

Leading the group back into the house as the girls talked about shopping, Alexander waited for them all to sit. Brick held up the wand. "This be quite the treasure! Ye could sell at auction fer a million gold!"

Alexander shook his head. "Can't do it. Fitz says the method I used is new to Io, and that if others had a chance to examine and copy it… well it'd be like giving nukes to Napoleon. Severe negative impact on in-game warfare."

Everyone nodded at that, before a grinning Brick said, "Aye. Well then, with this here, we'll not be needin' our druid. We could sell HER at auction. Maybe make half as much."

Sasha threw a pillow that hit him in the face.

Getting down to business, Alexander said, "Okay. Tomorrow's going to be an easy day, if busy. First, all of us should take time to visit class trainers and skill trainers. We've all leveled up a good bit. Lainey, can you help Jules find the rogue trainer?" Lainey nodded. "Okay, Sasha. You mentioned shopping. We're going to need a ton of supplies. Food and drink for maybe… a hundred people. For a month. We're also going to need whatever items you'll all need to set up work stations for your crafts. Alchemy set, cookware, tanning rack, ingredients, whatever. Take Jules with you, get her some clothes, gear, whatever she needs." All three ladies smiled in confirmation.

"Max, can you arrange a couple more wagons and horses? Maybe three? We'll need to transport all this stuff." Max just grunted and nodded.

"Brick, I'd like you to take all the weapons and armor we looted from the citadel, and make sure they're in usable shape. We'll need to establish an armory, and make weapons and gear available to our citizens in the event of an attack."

Brick stroked his beard. "Aye, I can make that happen."

"Guys, we're going all out here. There's no shortage of gold in the guild bank, and there's more in the dungeon at the keep. Spend what you need to. Tip well. Talk to citizens about where we're going, and see if you can find any volunteers. Tomorrow is all about improving the reputation of the guild, and finding recruits. I'm going to meet with the king in the morning and ask him for volunteers, as well. Also, if you run across players you have a good feeling about, especially players with crafting skills, then use your best judgement on recruiting them. Bring them back here for interviews. We'll set up a feast in the back courtyard area." He looked at Sasha. "Maybe get Lydia and the folks from the Ogre to help with that?" he asked. "Offer the O'Malley's 350 gold if they can feed a hundred people here tomorrow night. We'll provide the alcohol." He winked at Brick, who looked slightly pale. "Don't worry, buddy. I'm going to Broken Mountain tomorrow, as well. I'll bring back your weekly delivery, and another big wagonload."

An idea struck him. "Max, while you're grabbing the wagons, can you get enough beds and such to fill all the vacant rooms here? In both the armory and the second floor of the workshop? We need to be able to house some folks here when necessary. It wouldn't hurt to get more, if you can, to take to the keep. Or find a citizen who can craft them that wants to come to the keep. I'm going to petition the king for the use of some tents and cots from the quartermaster. We'll return them once we've had time to build what we need. Ladies, we'll need several dozen sets of linens, pillows, some bedrolls, etc."

Alexander paused to take a deep breath. "Can anyone think of anything else?"

"I'd like to invite Lydia to the guild," Sasha said.

"Aye, and Thea and the younglings, as well," Brick added.

"Fine by me! Any objections?" he asked, expecting none. "Done!"

“Please remember to warn anyone making deliveries to wait on the street until escorted through the gate. Don’t want anyone teleported to the prison by accident. I’ll ask Captain Redmond to post a few men at the gates with medallions to screen deliveries and let them through.” With reasonably thorough plans for the next day complete, the friends all retired to their rooms to rest.

Alexander, having just finished showering and donning sleeping clothes, heard a noise out on the balcony. Stepping through the doors, he found his giant tiger sprawled out on the stone floor, Jules sitting with her back against its side. She was scratching his ears and talking softly to him.

“Trying to steal my mount?” he joked.

She hit him with one of those smiles that made his heart thump. “He’s so soft and warm!” She patted the ground next to her, and Alexander sat down, leaning against his tiger as well.

“Everything going okay?” he asked. “I mean do you need anything?”

“Not a single thing.” She leaned back against the big cat and sighed as it purred. “Things are just perfect. I’m so happy you all found me. You’ve been so kind.” She drifted off, as if remembering something. “Before your dad helped me, I was… in limbo. Most of the time, everything was just darkness. I had nothing but my own thoughts. And I’m really not great company.” She smiled sadly.

“I think you’re delightful,” Alexander blurted out awkwardly, earning him another smile before she continued. “There were occasional sensations. Mostly pain. But sometimes flashes of light, or sound. I held on to those as tightly as I could, trying to make them last. But they never did. I think the doctors kept me pretty drugged.”

He instinctively took her hand and squeezed it. “You don’t have to worry about that now. We’ve got you in a pod, and the interface has learned all about how your brain works. You’ll be able to keep your connection as long as you need it,” he reassured her.

“I owe you all so much. There’s no way I can ever repay-”

“Stop right there,” he interrupted, squeezing her hand again. “There is nothing to repay. Let me tell you a little bit about us. My dad and I, along with his partner, Michael, own one of the largest corporations in the world. We’re so wealthy, we’ll never spend the money we already have in our lifetimes. Taking care of you is no burden to us, financially at all. Like Melanie said, you’re basically a giant goldfish!” This time she squeezed his hand, and let out a small laugh.

“The pod you’re in wasn’t built for gaming, exactly. Did my father tell you much about his research?” he asked.

She shook her head. “They were focused on getting me in the game and stabilized.”

“Okay, well, can you keep a secret?” She nodded and made a motion with her free hand, crossing her heart. “My father started his research nearly ten years ago, when I was diagnosed with NDS. It’s a degenerative disease that slowly takes away my ability to move my body, or control my muscles. It’s very rare, and always fatal.”

She squeezed his hand much harder. “Oh! I’m so sorry!” she said.

“I’ve been lucky to last as long as I have. And Dad and his team have created a drug that seems to have slowed the deterioration. So, things are looking up. But the pods were invented to help me, and others like you and me, to rebuild their bodies’ muscle control. To establish new connections by running and jumping in the game, while stimulating corresponding movements in our real-world bodies. Training our brains to move our bodies as they should.”
“In your case,” he added, “your body and mind were both healthy, but damaged. You mainly need the pod to buy you time for your mind to heal, and re-establish those connections. And to maintain your body while that happens, so that you’ll be able to use it when you wake up!”

Tears were beginning to form in her eyes, but she gave him a sad smile. “By ‘buy me time’ you mean, give me something to do, to keep me from going insane in the darkness," she said. "And I would have, too. I didn't much want to live anymore. Your dad saved my life."

"Well, if you're *determined* to repay him. I know something you could consider," he suggested. "This is another secret. Not even the other guild members know this yet. So, you have to promise not to tell."

"I swear." Eyes wide, her face had adopted a serious look.

"My father and I are forming a foundation. We'll be providing pods to maybe as many as a million people worldwide who are in situations like ours. Who need the pods to give them a chance at restoring their bodies, or minds. Or both. I'm going to offer Sasha, Lainey, Brick, and Max jobs at the foundation. In addition to helping me run it in the real world, they'll be working in-game to help foundation clients learn how to play the game. Help them adjust, like we're doing with you, now. But there's no way that we can personally help all of them. So, we'll be training the ones we help, to enable them to help others. Who can then help others. Eventually we'll have a whole community of people ready to help those who need it most."

"I want to help, too!" She thumped him on the chest in excitement "That would be perfect for me! I can work with others who've been trapped in the darkness like me." She became thoughtful again, unconsciously leaning her head back into Alexander's shoulder. He wasn't about to object.

They were silent for a while, each in their own thoughts, leaning against the warm, purring tiger. Alexander didn't notice when Jules drifted off to sleep. He might have already been asleep himself.

Chapter Five

The Enemy Within

Alexander was awakened by a tiger's tail to the face. The big cat, clearly amused, was actually grinning at him. Just how smart were these mounts?

He moved gently so as not to awaken Jules, who was still deeply asleep, snoring softly. He extricated his arm, setting her head softly against the tiger's fur. He rose to his feet, and looked down at her.

She's amazing. Beautiful, kind. She's been through so much. So, you just need to chill. The last thing she needs right now is you getting all smoochy at her.

Smiling to himself, he looked around. The sun had not yet risen, though it soon would. He'd let Jules sleep a bit. Nodding at the tiger, who was still smiling at him, he headed inside to change.

Downstairs he found Sasha already in the kitchen. He pitched in, frying bacon and sausage for breakfast, while Sasha made eggs and pancakes. Lainey came in, and started chopping fruit.

They carried their several platters of food out to the dining room, to find the others all assembled, including Jules, Fitz and Fibble. Sasha and Lainey both hugged the little goblin, welcoming him to the clan. Then they introduced Jules. Fibble stood on his chair, made a little bow, saying, "Fibble protect Jules, like protect Sasha!" Then he waved his magic stick about as if defending them all from monsters. Jules was instantly enchanted.

Jules was also introduced to Fitz, who grunted politely as he stuffed bacon into his mouth. Alexander took a seat next to her, and she reached out to squeeze his hand briefly. He winked at her, and was rewarded with a smile. He could get used to those.

After breakfast, they all went their separate ways for training, and errands, according to plan. Fitz dished up two heaping plates of breakfast, then teleported Alexander and himself to the king's study. The king didn't even look up, just growled, "Morning, Fitz, you old goat." Though, when he smelled breakfast, he became much more interested in his visitor. "Ah! You've brought breakfast! And young Alexander as well! Good morning, Alexander," he said, taking a plate from Fitz and sitting at a side table to eat. "My compliments to Sasha. Breakfast is wonderful!"

Alexander bowed his head. "Thank you, Majesty. I'll pass that along. I'm sure she'll be pleased to hear it."

"So?" the king spoke around a mouthful of pancakes, "I saw the alert that Greystone captured the keep. Anything I should know?"

"Yes, Majesty." Alexander gave him the short version of what they found at the keep, their battles, and their suppositions on Baron Dire still being alive, and potentially being the 'Dark One'. The king listened while finishing his meal.

"I didn't expect to alert him so quickly that we'd taken the keep. Though if he'd tried to use the portal, I suppose he would have found out soon enough." Alexander looked down, still embarrassed by his bonehead move.

"So, what are your plans to defend the keep?" the king asked him.

"Well, the ladies are out today buying supplies for a month, and we're recruiting adventurers, both crafters and fighters, to join the guild in defeating the 'Dark One'. I've come to ask your assistance on a few matters, though, Majesty."

"How can I help you, Alexander?" As he asked the question, Captain Redmond knocked, then entered.

"Good morning, Majesty. Fitz. Alexander." He took a seat at the table with them. "I've just come from hearing an interesting tale from young Sasha and friends before they whisked Lydia away for some kind of shopping spree. Seems you've been busy!" he chuckled.

"Alexander was just about to ask us for some assistance in that matter," the king said. "Go on, Alexander."

"I'd like to request your assistance in recruiting some volunteers from among the citizens, Sire. They must be made aware of the dangers before being accepted. They'll also need to swear an oath of loyalty before Prince Kai. We can't have spies in our midst. Also, we could use a few dozen tents, and maybe twice that many cots, until we're able to build or repair appropriate housing. I'll return them as soon as possible. And we can certainly compensate the crown for their use." He bowed his head again.

"Nonsense! The quartermaster will deliver what you need by day's end. As for volunteers, I will send out messengers to spread the word in key locations. By noon, the whole city will have heard the news. Shall I have volunteers report to your guild house?"

"Citizen volunteers, yes. Thank you, Majesty. We're accepting adventurers by invitation only. The gang are out about town right now, delivering invitations to likely prospects. And that reminds me, Majesty. We'll be throwing a feast tonight for all the volunteers. You are, of course, always welcome in our home. The food will be catered by the Ogre, and Brick's supplying the refreshment." He grinned.

"Ha! I just might attend!" the king chuckled. "If only to see if you're stealing all my best citizens. And for Lady O'Malley's cooking, of course!

Alexander's face fell. "Only fifty or so citizens, Majesty. Maybe less. I'll not risk any more than that. And no children, at least for now. I don't think I can take the death of another child." The others were all silent.

Shaking himself, he continued. "I plan to visit King Thalgrin next. To ask the same from him. Dwarves built the keep, and we think dwarves should be the ones to repair it."

The king looked thoughtful. "Alexander, how would you feel about taking my son with you?"

"Majesty?" Alexander began to panic. He was already worried about defending civilians. This was… insane!

"Relax, Alexander. Let me explain. My son must grow and learn if he is to become a good ruler in his own right. I don't expect any wars in the near future; we live in very stable times. Especially now that we've made alliance with the Dwarves. Whom, by the way, I'd like him to get to know, as well. Going with you to the keep, he'll get to watch a settlement being built. You did an excellent job with Whitehall, and I'm sure you'll do the same with Dire Keep."

"But, Majesty! I've just painted a giant shining target on the keep. Practically dared our enemies to attack! I… cannot guarantee the safety of the Prince."

The king just chuckled. "Aye, that you did. And I'm aware of the risk. But as I said, my son must learn. Not only about politics and economics, but about being a warrior. And if I must place him in harm's way, I much prefer to do so where he'll be surrounded by loyal friends, in a fortified keep, with a dragon and a crusty old wizard to watch over him."

Captain Redmond spoke up as Alexander was about to object again. "It's a sound idea, Alexander. Much better than sending the boy off to a friendly nation with a border conflict he can observe. This way, he can learn a mere ten miles from here, and if necessary I can have a small army there in minutes to help defend him."

Suddenly Alexander understood. The king was putting some skin in the game. Risking his son in the process. And Fitz and the captain agreed with him. Still, the responsibility…

"Fitz, I'd have your oath that if things go badly, you'll teleport the prince back here," he said.

The king laughed. "Fitz took an oath centuries ago to protect this family. And he loves my children as he's loved Lydia and myself. When they were small, he hovered over them like a mother hen. Would have spoiled them rotten if I'd let him. You need not worry about that, Alexander."

Fitz harrumphed and twisted his beard. "Aye, lad. The prince will be safe. I'd challenge the gods themselves to make it so."

"In that case, I humbly accept, Majesty." Alexander was still a bit worried, but not overly so.

"Thank you, Alexander. And before I forget…" the king reached for a box, handing it to Alexander, "I hereby grant to you the Dire Keep, and the surrounding lands, as laid out in this deed. I charge you to defend them well, and to maintain them. Bring the mine back to life. Cull the dire wolf population so that my farmers, and your own, may plant and harvest without fear. But most importantly, take good care of its people."

"Thank you, Majesty. I give you my oath that I, and mine, will give our utmost to fulfil your trust."

"It is trust well earned, Alexander. Now, we've both got a lot to do today. The quartermaster will deliver supplies to you by day's end. If I don't see you at the feast, good luck to you!"

As Alexander rose to leave, he remembered something. "Captain, in addition to the quartermaster, there will be a large number of vendors and crafters making deliveries at the keep today. I was hoping you could spare a small squad to screen them, and give them access through the wards? There was a pair of guards at the cemetery dungeon the day we were attacked by PWP. They were very observant. I think they were… Jenkins, and Foster?"

Captain Redmond smiled. "Of course. And those two would make good recruits for your keep, as well. I'll assign them with six other guards to your compound. You can speak to them yourself about joining you."

"Speaking of the keep, Captain." Alexander pulled the journal and gems from his bag. "We found a room in the barracks that belonged to a Captain Artemis. These were his. I know the chances are small, but if he has descendants here in the city, we thought they might want these." Alexander handed the items to Captain Redmond. "The journal's last entry said that he was going to try and kill the baron."

"Thank you, Alexander. We'll have someone check through the records and see what can be found."

His business in the palace settled, he and Fitz moved on. Next stop, Broken Mountain.

The two of them teleported back to the Greystone compound, then used the portal to Broken Mountain. As usual, their arrival was met with momentary aggression, quickly followed by recognition, and they were passed through to the citadel. A runner was sent ahead to alert the king.

"Bah!" Fitz said. "Waste of time, walking all the way there. We've got much to do today!" In a blink, the two of them had teleported to the Great Hall. This time, they caused a much greater fluster, as they'd arrived at the heart of the citadel with no warning. Around the hall, weapons were drawn and shields taken up. The hall went dead silent.

"BWAHAHA!" A great laugh rang out as King Thalgrin entered from a side chamber. "Fitz! Ye always did know how to make an entrance!" With that, the room relaxed. Dwarves being dwarves, if there was no longer the prospect of a fight, they were mostly disinterested. They went about whatever they'd been doing.

Fitz and Alexander bowed to the king. "Majesty, my apologies. I couldn't resist stirring things up a bit. When you're as old as I am, you take every opportunity for excitement." He waggled his eyebrows.

The still-laughing king motioned for them to move to one of the long tables, where he took a seat. At his nod, they sat themselves on either side of him. "If ye've come fer Brick's weekly shipment, it be waiting by the main gate. Ye'd have seen it if ye'd approached like normal folk!" He winked at Alexander. "Master Ironhammer be about ready to head back with his six masters and their supplies, as well."

"Thank you, Majesty. But I'm afraid that's not why we're here. Though, since you brought it up, I'd like to double the weekly shipment, if that's possible? I will, of course, pay for the second one."

Thalgrin grinned. "The old wizard be drinkin yer entire supply so quickly?"

"No, Majesty, though he is making a dent. The extra supplies have to do with our reason for coming here today…" He went on to tell the king of their adventures at the keep, and their plans for rebuilding. And the feast they'd be holding for volunteers.

Just as he was finishing, the young runner that had been sent from the portal burst into the hall. Out of breath, he approached the king. "Me King! Sir Alexander and the wizard be…" He stopped, seeing the two men already seated with the king. He looked confused.

Deciding to have some fun with the boy, King Thalgrin said, "Aye! Ye could've warned me they be comin!" He gave the boy a stern look.

"But… Me King…" the lad stammered, "I… I runned all the way–"

"BWAHAHAHA!" Thalgrin's laugh echoed through the Great Hall, interrupting the poor dwarf. "It be fine, lad. The wizard likes his jokes. He teleported hisself here. Now, catch yer breath, then run 'n' tell Ironhammer to double Brick's shipment." The boy bobbed his head and took off.

"Me grand-nephew. Easily confused. Never stops bein funny!" The king grinned.

"Right! Back to business. I'll call the council and spread the word. Any volunteers will be gathered at the port by mid-afternoon. I expect ye'll see more'n a few miners. And there be some masons were disappointed they'd not been chosen for the new quarry."

Alexander began to offer the same warning he offered King Charles, but Thalgrin held up a hand. "I'll make sure they know the danger, lad. But ye must know by now. Dwarves love danger!" He grinned.

Alexander chuckled. "Very true, Majesty. Also, I'd like to invite you to tonight's feast. I know it is short notice. But we are moving quickly."

"I canno' attend, I'm afraid," Thalgrin said, regretfully. Dwarves also love parties. "I can offer ye some guards, if ye'll have them. Me lads'd appreciate some fresh air and the chance to kill darklings!"

"I'll accept any volunteers, Majesty. Up to say, fifty? But please don't order any to come with us. And no children, for now. My conscience is already heavy at the loss of the child at Whitehall."

"That be no fault of yours, lad. None! Ye've done much to try and help both the villagers, and me own folk. Maybe more than any since Fitz, here. Ye've opened up trade that'll help feed Broken Mountain fer years. Ye've fostered an alliance with Stormforge, securing our longest and closest border. T'was a stray arrow, fired by a murderous servant of this 'Dark One'. And if he indeed be Baron Dire, still alive, then he were an enemy o' the dwarves long before ye were born!"

"I appreciate the kind words, Majesty. We must head back now to make more preparations. But before I go, I wanted to seek your guidance on something."

"Ask away, lad." The king leaned back in his chair.

"We recently added Prince Kaibonostrum as a member of our guild. And we'll be inviting Lady Lydia, as well as some other citizens of Stormforge. I wanted to offer Thea, Harin, Garen, and Dvorn membership as well. But I did not want to do so without your permission."

"Aye. Thea and the young'uns came to ask me permission a few days back. I gave 'em me blessing, as long as ye were willing to have 'em." His voice dropped to a whisper. "I think Thea be settin her sights on yer paladin friend." He winked.

"Majesty, I think the ladies of the guild have already decided to help make that happen. Brick's fate may be sealed, and he has no idea." He grinned.

"Ha! Good then. As for the guild, and the keep, me people be free to choose fer themselves, and make whatever oaths they be wantin'. As long as ye don't try to steal one o' me masters, I'll not object."

"Thank you, Majesty. Speaking of crafting, I'd like to make you a gift before I go."

Alexander pulled a piece of obsidian from his bag. He shaped it into a tube, just as he'd done the night before. This time, though, he did not add the lens at the end. Fitz nodded his approval at that.

Closing his eyes, he pushed the healing light spell through his hand, infusing it into the stone of the wand. He wrapped the magic as tightly as possible around the tube, over and over. Again, he stopped when he'd reached 3,000 mana. Feeling that there was some capacity left, he added Fitz's "Undying" spell that would keep the wand's owner alive after what should be a fatal blow.

When it was finished, he handed the wand to the king. "I hope you never need this, but if the need arises, this will keep a few of your people alive. Though I'm afraid the Undying enchantment only works once."

The king took the wand and examined it, eyes wide.

Redeemer
Item Level: Unique, Epic
Stats: Intelligence +10, Wisdom +10, Stamina +10
This wand will cast a burst of regenerative light magic, healing a friendly target for 2,000hp. Undying: Should the bearer receive a mortal blow, the wand will maintain bearer at 1% health, preventing death.
Charges: 20/20

***Skill Level up! Enchanting* +5** *You have created a unique, epic level enchanted item. Your skill level has increased to Journeyman.*

"Thank ye, lad." Thalgrin's voice was soft, his face solemn. He held the wand gently in his open hands.

"Bah!" Fitz broke the mood. "The boy's just showing off. I told him to practice, not make an old dwarf all misty-eyed!"

"Ha! Shut it, ye ornery goat! Yer not one to be callin' others old! This mountain be younger than you!" The king was grinning again. Fitz waggled his eyebrows and grinned right back.

Taking their leave of the king, who was already calling for his council to gather, Fitz teleported them back to the portal courtyard. Informing the guards that they'd open the portal again two hours past noon for Ironhammer and any volunteers, they activated the portal and stepped through.

Alexander had had an idea when speaking to King Charles about housing the volunteers. He pulled up guild chat.

"Sasha, have you already spoken to the O'Malleys at the Ogre?"

"Not yet, why?"

"I was thinking that with the feasting tonight, we might have more than a few who won't be able to stumble home after. Offer the O'Malleys an extra 150 gold if they'll rent us all their rooms for the night. Then we can just drop off a wagonload to sleep it off."

"Okay. Though it might be better to do that at the inn by the palace gate. So we're not transporting drunks across half the city."

"Good idea! Let's do both. The Ogre can have those who are sober enough to get there, we'll roll the drunks to the closer inn. I'll go there now and make arrangements."

With an easy mission to undertake, Alexander headed out the gate. He'd not set foot in the inn down the block. Didn't even know its name. Always good to meet the neighbors though, right?

The sign at the door read 'The Prancing Stallion'. Alexander wasn't sure if that was the name of the inn, the restaurant, or both. Stepping inside, he found a lavishly decorated lobby with an intricately carved wooden reception desk. Behind the desk was an attractive and sharply dressed young woman, who smiled at him as he entered.

“Can I help you, Sir Knight?” she asked cheerfully.

“I… yes, I hope so. I’d like to see about renting some rooms for this evening.” He decided a little formality was appropriate for this setting.

“Very good, Sir. How many will you need?” She opened a ledger and lifted a pen from the desk.

“All of them, Miss….?”

“Oh! My name is Shari.” She curtsied prettily. “And, did you say ALL of them?”

“Yes, Shari. I’m afraid I did. You see, I’m hosting a feast this evening at our guild house down the street. We’ll be serving dwarven ale and spirits, and I’m afraid a significant portion of our guests may be… less than able to find their way home, afterward.” He gave her his best smile.

Shari covered her mouth to suppress a giggle. “I understand, Sir. If you’ll wait just a moment? I’ll go fetch the owner.” She ducked through a doorway and was gone.

A few moments later, a tall, thin man appeared through the same door, Shari trailing behind. The man bowed slightly to Alexander.

“Sir Knight. I am Hobson, owner and proprietor of the Stallion. It is a pleasure to meet you.”

Alexander nodded in return. “You as well, Hobson. We’re neighbors now, and I feel remiss in not having to come to introduce myself sooner.”

“Ah, you need no introduction, Sir. Knight-Advisor to The King. Leader of the Greystone Guild. Savior of Whitehall, and as of last night, Master of Dire Keep, I believe?”

“Ah, yes. But please, just call me Alexander.” He shuffled a bit, slightly uncomfortable.

"Of course. Shari has informed me that you wish to secure all of our available rooms for the evening. Is that correct?"

"It is, indeed," Alexander confirmed. I'm sorry for the short notice, but we find ourselves a bit rushed. The attendees of tonight's feast will mostly be leaving in the morning for Dire Keep. We must prepare its defenses before our enemies organize an attack."

Hobson nodded his head. "And I understand there will be dwarven spirits flowing at this feast?"

"Ah, yes." Alexander thought he knew where this was headed. "I'm afraid our guests may be a bit, rowdy? I hope that's not too much of a problem?"

"Oh, no! Pardon me, Alexander. I wasn't suggesting anything of that sort. I'm actually interested in acquiring spirits for my establishment." Hobson hastily responded. "Currently, twenty-five of our thirty suites are available. And as you plan to utilize all of them, I'm sure a bit of rowdiness can be... accommodated."

"Thank you, Hobson. I appreciate that. As for the dwarven spirits, can you not purchase them from the crown? I know the king has a supply coming from Broken Mountain that he intended to sell to local vendors."

"Yes. That is correct. And we have purchased all that the king's factor will allow. However, supplies are limited, and there are many establishments in the city who wish to purchase them. And several of my regular customers have developed a taste for them..."

Alexander chuckled. "I can imagine. They seem quite popular. I'll tell you what. Come to the feast this evening. I'll introduce you to Brick, the king's Trade Emissary to Broken Mountain. I happen to know he has a good personal supply at hand, and I'll persuade him to gift you enough to meet your immediate need. In the meantime, we'll see what we can do about increasing the king's supply. We plan to be killing a large number of dire wolves in the near future, and those are the basis of the king's trade with the dwarves."

“Thank you, Alexander. That is most generous of you,” Hobson replied.

“Now, about the rooms. You said you have twenty-five available? What will the cost be for all of them?” Alexander queried.

“Our normal rate is ten gold per suite, per night. However, since you’re buying in bulk, so to speak…”

Alexander raised a hand to interrupt him. “As Knight-Advisor to The King, it would be improper for me to accept any discount. Though I appreciate the thought, Hobson.” He took out a pouch, handing it to the man.

“Twenty-five suites at ten gold for a night, that’s 250 gold. Here is 500 gold. In case of any accidents that cause property damage. Come to think of it, it might be beneficial for you to hire a few large men to… escort our guests to their rooms, ensuring a minimization of any accidental damage. Maybe some off-duty guards?” Hobson actually laughed at that. Surprising Alexander. “Put that cost on my bill. If there is a remainder left over in the morning, just open an account under Greystone guild. I’m sure we’ll have occasion to come here for a meal or two.”

“It will be as you say. And we’ll have a hearty breakfast, as well as some useful potions, available first thing in the morning. I’ll personally make sure they’re all awakened and fed by…” Hobson paused for Alexander’s input.

“We should be ready to leave no later than two hours after sunrise,” he said.

“Very good. It has been a pleasure to meet you, Alexander. I do hope you visit us often.” Hobson shook his hand.

“I’ll see you this evening,” Alexander said. He gave small wave to Shari as he left.

With that taken care of, Alexander headed to the enchantments shop to see Master Baleron about learning some new enchantments.

He entered the shop to find the old gnome standing on his countertop, reaching toward an upper shelf. "Can I help you with that?" Alexander asked.

"Alexander! Good timing. Make yourself useful and pull down that box for me." The gnome pointed at a box on the top shelf, near the ceiling.

Alexander stepped over and used the lower shelf as a stepladder, grabbing the box and pulling it down. "Here you go."

"Thank you, son. Now, what can I do for you? Have you come for another lesson?" Master Baleron inspected him for a moment. "I see! You've reached journeyman level so soon!"

"Yes, I've been… experimenting. And I got lucky. Created a few unique and epic items that earned me multiple skill points," he replied. Before the master could ask, he produced the stone that he'd accidentally created in front of Millicent's. He handed it to the gnome for inspection.

Elemental Stone
Item quality: Unique
This stone has been infused with the power of the earth, and the element of fire. When affixed to a weapon, it will provide a bonus of +20 to Strength. In addition, the weapon will inflict +150 fire damage.

"Quite impressive!" Baleron exclaimed. Especially for one so new to the craft. Let me see what I have that might help you…" The old gnome shuffled about behind his counter.

As he searched, Alexander spoke. "Fitz has offered me a book that details the properties and capacities of various stones, gems, and the like. He says he's doing it out of self-defense, as I've nearly blown myself up more than once when he was nearby."

Master Baleron's head popped up from behind the counter. "Did you say Fitz? As in, Master Fitzbindulum? Well, now. That explains much. Studying with a grandmaster enchanter is bound to increase the speed of one's progress. I'm afraid you won't need me any longer, though." The gnome looked sad. Alexander suspected it was less about not teaching him, and more about losing his supply of dwarven spirits.

"Ah, well. I've not really been studying enchanting under him. Fitz is teaching me magic. Our conversations regarding enchanting have been more like, 'Be careful you don't blow something up, idiot'" He smiled at Baleron. "So, I expect I'll need to learn as much as I can from you, Master Baleron." Removing a bottle of spirits, he placed it on the counter.

After some more searching, Baleron found some scrolls that taught Alexander several new enchantments of Light, Fire, Strength, Stamina, Intelligence, and even Luck. Alexander thanked him, and headed back to the compound.

Walking back through the marketplace in the central square, he heard people talking about Dire Keep, and his calls for volunteers. As always happens when information is passed from mouth to mouth, what must have been a factual announcement from the king, had become a variety of wide tales and rumors. Since he had some time, he decided to set things back on track.

Stepping to the center of the square, he raised some stone beneath him, lifting himself up above the crowd. Taking out his light damage wand, he fired a burst into the air. This got the attention of some, but not all. "ATTENTION!" he called out, waiting a moment, then firing another burst. This worked much better. Enough people had become silent that others were looking around to see what was happening. One more burst, and he had nearly everyone's attention. He put the wand away quickly.

"Good Citizens of Stormforge! My name is Alexander. Some of you may have heard of me?" This caused a ripple of laughter in the crowd. "I know that you all saw last night's announcement about Dire Keep. And many of you heard the king's messengers' announcement this morning. But in my travels this morning, even here in the square, I've heard some pretty wild interpretations." He pointed to a man running a fruit stall. "You, sir. What is your name?"

The vendor shouted, "Hank, Sir Knight!"

"Hank! Though I must confess I like your idea… I'm afraid I'm not recruiting only beautiful virgins for Dire Keep!" He smiled as the crowd laughed a bit louder. "And to lay to rest any of the other rumors, especially the one about an Elf invasion, please let me update you all. Then I'll answer some questions."

"First of all, Dire Keep has lain in ruins for two hundred years, after the wizard Fitzbindulum destroyed it in order to kill the necromancer, Baron Dire. Yesterday, at the request of the king, my guild and I went to investigate the ruins. We found a large number of undead, and evidence that the baron may have survived the battle two hundred years ago, and is now working with PWP-"

He was interrupted with a crashing wave of, "Boo!" and, "Death to PWP!"

As the noise died down, a voice in the crowd shouted, "GNOMES RULE!" which caused a bit of laughter.

"As I was saying, there was a presence from… the guild that shall remain nameless, at the keep. We destroyed them all, and disabled the portal they'd been using, claiming Dire Keep in the name of the king!" This brought a resounding cheer from the crowd, which Alexander noticed was growing steadily larger.

"Unfortunately, the announcement you all saw last night, has also alerted our enemies. So, we must work quickly to repair and secure the keep, before those enemies attack. To accomplish this, I have asked for volunteers from among you all. We need crafters who can help us rebuild. And fighters who can man the walls!" There was another cheer, and some thoughtful looks here and there.

"I must warn you, though. The keep will soon be a battle zone! Any who come with us will be risking their lives. We will only be taking fifty or so citizens from Stormforge, and we hope, a similar number from Broken Mountain. I will NOT accept any children at this time. Some of you may have heard we lost an innocent dwarven child to a PWP attack on Whitehall. That CANNOT happen again!" He realized he was screaming at a now silent crowd.

Calming himself, he continued. "My aim is to protect the citizens of this realm, not to put you in harm's way. I could not forgive myself if another child were lost due to reckless decisions on my part. Once the keep is secure, and our enemy dealt with, I will welcome families with children. We'll need miners, and farmers, hunters and cooks. And everything in between. But for today, I will be accepting only those who understand, and are willing to accept, the dangers involved!"

There was a cheer from the crowd. Though he wasn't sure which part of what he'd just said they were cheering.

"Okay, I have a few minutes. Who has questions?" he asked.

"What're you paying?" shouted a large man near the front.

"That's a good question. I suppose the pay will depend on the individual, and the service they perform. I'll ask Captain Redmond to give me a fair wage rate for soldiers, then double it, as hazard pay, for the period until the keep is secure and our enemy vanquished. As for crafters, we'll work out a similar arrangement. And for any family men or women who are killed in defense of the keep, I will pay two hundred gold to their families to help with the burden of their loss. Though, again, I would prefer volunteers without families."

"What about players?" came another shout. This time from a mid-level warrior in custom armor.

"Greystone guild will be recruiting ADVENTURERS over the course of the day. But certainly not any who don't know the difference!" He scowled at the man, who flipped him off. This generated some laughter from other players scattered about.

"I should warn you. Any who join us must swear a magically enforced oath of loyalty. This oath will be sworn to a dragon who has seen fit to join our guild, and become a citizen of the keep. Breaking an oath to a dragon carries extreme consequences on Io. And those who do not pull their weight will be banished. We have no time or patience for slackers or fools! Your fellow citizens' lives may depend on your actions!"

“Doesn’t sound like much fun!” shouted a female elf player who was dressed in not much more than a bikini, and dancing around at the fringe of the crowd. There were always a few in every group.

“No, it does not. Unless you like to build, and to fight. To run dungeons and collect loot.” He winked at the vacant stare on her face.

“Where will we live?” shouted another voice.

“Initially you will all live within the walls of the keep, mainly in tents that the king has agreed to lend us. It will take a week or more to build enough housing for everyone. We’ll have to expand the keep’s walls to do so. I also plan to enclose large areas for farming and livestock.”

“Ya can’t do all that in a week! Even with a hundred sets of hands! I call bullshit!” The warrior from before had decided to troll him. In response, Alexander waved a hand, and the stone underneath the warrior shot upward in a tall column, raising him thirty feet in the air. He squealed like a frightened piglet as he practically flew upward. The crowd roared with laughter. Several players were obviously recording.

“I am an earth mage, among other things. I also have the assistance of three others from the mage’s guild. This same group built a wall around Whitehall, and reconstructed every building in the village, as well as adding an inn, a warehouse, a masonry shop, three barracks buildings, and nearly two dozen extra homes. All in four days! Plus, we expect dwarven stone masons to be among the volunteers. Anybody else doubt my word?” He waved his hands back and forth, and random blocks of stone raised folks up high enough for the crowd to see, including the bikini dancer. Which elicited some whistles and catcalls. Then he lowered them all again. The idiot warrior he left high in the air, begging to be let down, and considering whether he’d survive the jump. Alexander lowered him back down to save him from himself.

“What’s your name, warrior?” he asked the man, who was recovering from his rapid descent.

"I am Ceasar!" the warrior shouted, sticking his chest out. "Ceasar the Bold!" Once he'd said his name, it appeared above his head. It was, of course, spelled wrong. Typical.

"Well, Ceasar… I think you'll find your time in this land will be much more enjoyable if you learn some respect for its citizens. Your strength and your level mean nothing here in the city. Only your reputation, and your relationships." This brought some cheers from other players in the crowd, and a lot of nodding heads from the citizens. Adventurers were known to be rude and annoying much too often.

"Screw you, noob! You wouldn't dare face me in a duel! I'd wipe the floor with you!" he screamed, angry at being embarrassed and lectured in front of the crowd. Alexander wanted to facepalm. This guy could be Henry's dumber brother.

"That is exactly what I'm talking about, moron. This world is about strength and strategy when you're out adventuring. But here in the city, it's about being a decent human being. Didn't your mother teach you any manners? If the merchants like you, they won't charge you as much for goods, or repairs. On the other hand, if you walk up to them all 'I'm an asshole cause I'm stronger than you and there's nothing you can do about it' … well, then you pay double! Am I right?" he asked the crowd, who cheered enthusiastically.

"Shut the hell up and fight me!" screamed the warrior.

"You're… what? Maybe twenty-five levels above me? What would it prove if you were to defeat me?" Alexander asked.

"It would prove you're full of shit. It would prove you're not worthy to have your own keep!" The man was snarling now.

"So! That's it. You're jealous? Or maybe you're working for PWP? Angry that we took your keep from you?" At that, several guards began to make their way toward the man from different directions. Alexander decided to give the man his wish, to distract him a bit longer.

"Okay, genius who spelled Caesar wrong. You can have your duel. Send me the challenge!" he called out. The crowd roared. Alexander motioned for the crowd to clear a wide space, and for the warrior to step forward. The fool strutted through the parting crowd like a prince about to be crowned king. Once he'd stepped inside the open area, Alexander raised the whole thing 3 feet, so the entire crowd would have a good view. A ring of guards formed around the edge of the circle.

The warrior sent him a duel challenge, and he accepted. He had fifteen seconds before the duel began. Knowing the warrior build as he did from his previous toon, he was sure this fool would charge at him the instant the clock hit zero. So, he cast his weak magical shield two feet in front of him, making sure it glowed for all to see. Then he prepared the ground behind it, making it soft. He turned on his recorder.

As the clock reached zero, Ceasar smirked at his obviously weak shield. Activating his charge ability, as expected, he rushed across the open space. Alexander immediately raised a two-foot-thick wall five feet high in front of him. The warrior had lowered his shoulder, intending to bash through the glowing magical shield. Which he did. Upon impact, the shield resisted for less than a second before disappearing with a pop. Leaving the idiot warrior with plenty of momentum as he crashed head first into a thick stone wall. Stunned, Ceasar fell backward into the soft stone prepared by Alexander. Which then liquefied, causing the warrior to sink into it like quicksand. As soon as Ceasar's arms and legs were secure within the stone, Alexander hardened it again. Now the warrior was unable to move, only his shoulders and head above the stone. Alexander calmly cast Wizard's Fire on his face. Then he raised a block of stone to sit on. The crowd, which had been roaring, began to laugh.

Duels in Io had a five-minute timer on them. The battle so far had taken about twenty seconds.

Motioning to one of the guards, he said, "Could you send word to Captain Redmond? I'd like him to come and determine whether this… genius… is PWP. Ask him to also bring someone who can cast a truth spell? I can hold this man here for another 4 minutes. Thank you."

The guard laughed. "We sent for the Captain as soon as the man challenged you, Sir. He'll be here in a moment.

Ceasar was screaming as the wizard's fire burned his face. There was no danger the spell would kill him. As a warrior, he was sure to have a very high stamina stat, and the corresponding large health bar.

Ignoring the insults the man threw at him, he turned to the crowd. "Any other questions while we wait for the Captain?" This drew another laugh. He was pausing in the middle of a duel with a much higher level player, to chat with the crowd.

"Aye, I have a question!" said the large man who'd asked about pay. "Where do I sign up?" He grinned.

Alexander laughed. "Another good question! Clearly, you're much more of a thinking man than Ceasar, here!" He paused for laughter. This was actually fun! "I'll tell you what. Meet me at the Ogre after this is over. We'll talk about your qualifications, and what I expect. I'll buy you an early lunch."

This, of course, started an avalanche of 'applicants' looking for a free meal. Alexander held up his hands.

"This is no joke! That offer is for serious applicants only. Any who come to waste my time, or simply seeking a free meal, will end up like Ceasar, here!" he roared. For emphasis, he shot a burst of light into Ceasar's face. That quieted things down considerably. He waved over a young boy, maybe twelve years old. "You know where the Ogre is?" he asked.

The boy nodded his head emphatically and pointed in the correct direction. Alexander tossed him a gold coin. "Run and tell O'Malley that Alexander is bringing guests for an early meal. I'd like a room in which to have private discussions."

The boy was already in motion as he caught the coin. He sped off through the crowd.

Chapter Six

You Can't Fix Stupid

By this time, Captain Redmond had appeared. When informed by his guard what Alexander suspected the screaming warrior of, he smiled. Hopping up onto the platform Alexander had made, he looked at the screaming man. Then he whispered to Alexander. "He is not an official member of PWP. But he might be in their employ. I can interrogate him. I know a spell that will alert me if he lies."

Alexander thought for a moment. "When I signal with a nod, place him under arrest. I can only hold him about another two minutes before the duel ends, then you'll have to detain him. As soon as he can speak, cast your spell, ask your questions."

Alexander stood and looked down at Ceasar. He dispelled the wizard's fire. Once the man had stopped his screaming, he asked "Do you concede the duel?"

"Fuck you!" the warrior screamed. His voice was ragged from a couple minutes of nonstop screaming.

Checking the man's health bar, Alexander hit him in the face with a slightly strong burst of light. "You have no hope of winning. I could kill you now, but I'd rather talk to you. You're just making a fool of yourself. This duel was over before it started. Concede."

The man hurled an insult about Alexander's mother. That was a mistake.

Alexander kicked the man in the teeth as hard as he could. Then he cast Wizard's Fire directly into his screaming mouth. After ten seconds, he dispelled it again. Ceasar's health bar was now down to about 10%.

"I'll ask you again. Concede the duel."

"No! Never!" the man screamed, causing blood and burnt tissue to spray from his mouth.

With a sigh, Alexander cast bolts of light into the man's face until he reached 1% health, which signaled the official end of the duel.

Congratulations! You have won your first duel! Achievement earned: Scrapper!

Alexander liquefied the stone around Ceasar and raised him up. Then he solidified the stone again. He nodded to the Captain, who stepped forward. "In the name of King Charles, I arrest you on suspicion of espionage. You will now answer my questions truthfully, or suffer the consequences." He cast a spell on the moaning warrior. To help things along, Alexander cast a heal on the man. Even the 2,000hp heal only took him back to 25%.

"Are you a member of PWP?" the Captain asked.

The warrior smirked at him. "No."

"Are you here in the employ of, or on behalf of, PWP or any of its members?" Again, a 'no', but less certain this time. Ceasar clearly didn't like the direction this was taking. The Captain, and many in the crowd, picked up on this as well as Alexander had.

The Captain spoke much louder this time, so all the crowd could hear. "Are you in the employ of, or working on behalf of, the 'Dark One' or his minions?"

Ceasar struggled to his feet, looking around as if for a path of escape. "No," he said.

"That was a lie!" The Captain shouted in his face.

Instantly, the icon above Ceasar's head turned an angry red. Seeing he was caught, the warrior leapt at the Captain, swinging his sword and yelling, "The Dark One will destroy you all!"

Captain Redmond's sword whipped out of its sheath and across his body faster than Alexander could even follow. Ceasar's sword arm separated from his body above the elbow, and landed in the crowd, still holding the sword. Alexander quickly cast another heal on the warrior, preventing him from bleeding out. When the Captain looked at him questioningly, he whispered, “I want this one imprisoned as he is. If you’d killed him, he’d have respawned with both arms.”

Ceasar was stripped of his weapons and armor, as well as his inventory bag of holding. All were given to Alexander to search. There was just over two thousand gold, good quality armor and weapons, several high-quality healing and stamina potions, and a ring with a dark stone. The rest of the inventory was mostly junk - Hides, mob loot like teeth or claws, poor quality weapons.

Alexander used analyze on the ring.

Ring of Communication
This ring allows the wearer to speak with its creator over long distances.

He handed the ring to the Captain, who inspected it himself. His eyebrows rose, and he turned back to the now subdued warrior. “Who gave you this ring? Who does it enable you to speak to?” he shouted.

The warrior just spat on the ground. Alexander stepped forward. Towering over the man, who was on his knees, he said very quietly, “Answer the man’s questions, and he might kill you and let you respawn in the dungeon with two arms.”

Ceasar looked up at him with absolute hatred in his eyes. “Simms was a friend of mine!” he growled.

Alexander was shocked. He stumbled back and sat on the block he’d raised. The Captain, looking worried, put a hand on his shoulder. “Alexander?” he asked.

What the hell? This guy’s a friend of Delbert Simms? One of the people who attacked Olympus? And he knows Simms is dead!

“EVERYBODY TO THE CENTRAL SQUARE! NOW! I’VE JUST FOUGHT A DUEL WITH A FRIEND OF DELBERT SIMMS. DROP WHAT YOU’RE DOING AND GET HERE.” He sent the message out in

guild chat. As an afterthought, he added '*Equip your T-shirts*', so that his friends wouldn't panic.

Suddenly Alexander felt a cold rage. He needed information from this man. He stood and stepped forward again. "You mean Delbert Simms?" His voice monotone.

Ceasar nodded. "Bet you didn't expect him to come knocking on your door, did you?" he smirked.

Alexander leaned down to whisper in Ceasar's ear. "Simms died screaming and begging, just like you did a minute ago. That little bitch accomplished nothing but his own painful death, and the death of his friends. He burned to death, slowly. You fuck with my family, the same will happen to you."
Standing straight, he turned to the Captain. "Captain, are any of those who lost loved ones in the PWP raid on the city here today?"

The Captain looked around the crowd. He called out two names, and motioned them forward. When the man and woman he'd called reached the platform, they were helped up gently by the guards.

The Captain introduced the woman first. She was in her late 50s or early 60s, with a kind, if sad, face. "This is Edna. Her husband was the barkeep at a tavern where the PWP attacked. He was killed before others could take the bastards down."

Alexander bowed deeply to the woman. "I'm so sorry," was all he said.

The Captain then introduced the man. "This is Caleb. He is... he was a guard sergeant. His wife and daughter were murdered on the street near their home.

Alexander felt tears in his eyes as he bowed to the man. "I cannot imagine your loss. I'm sorry."

He took the gold they'd just looted from Ceasar. His voice rough and quiet, he said, "This was just taken from this piece of shit here." He motioned to the warrior, still on his knees. "There is just over two thousand gold here." He brought out a small pouch and put half of the money in it. Then he handed a pouch to each of them. "The captain will sell the rest of this man's gear, and make sure those funds reach you as well. I cannot bring back your loved ones, but I hope this will ease your burden going forward."

Alexander shook Caleb's hand, and hugged Edna.

He needed to keep this show going. Hopefully his father had already tracked Ceasar's information and sent the FBI to wherever he was logging in from. If he was really lucky, they'd find information that would help in the bombing investigation. But if Alexander let the captain take Ceasar away and lock him up, the man would likely log out and run.

He turned to the warrior. "I've just given away all your gear. Which you forfeited when you tried to kill the captain, here. That was just stupid. Your Dark One, he seems to prefer stupid. Everyone he's sent against us has been a moron. Why is that?" he asked.

"Fuck you, Greystone. We know where you live. We know where your friends live. We'll kill them all. Burn their houses to the ground. We won't stop until you, your company, and the game are a smoking ruin."

Alexander addressed the crowd. "THIS is what happens to those who serve the darkness! This man will now go to prison and be put to hard labor. I am personally going to request that he be assigned to cleaning latrines!" This brought a thundering cheer from the crowd.

Turning to Edna and Caleb, he said "Is there anything you wish to… express to this man on behalf of your loved ones?"

Without hesitation, Edna walked over and spat in Ceasar's face. Then, with a little hop for momentum, she landed a 40-yard field goal kick to the man's nut sack. The crowd erupted in cheers.

As Edna stepped back, sobbing, the captain gathered her in a hug. Caleb stepped toward the warrior, and smiled. Alexander shuddered. The malice behind that smile made the warrior quail. Caleb moved behind the man, and bent low, his head next to Ceasar's. He said, "Your Dark One has made enemies today. Beginning with me. I hereby dedicate my life to avenge my girls by ending his life!" As the crowd roared, Caleb whispered something in the warrior's ear that made his face go pale. He actually wet himself.

As Caleb whispered, cries of "SEEE YA!" began to erupt from the outer edges of the crowd. Looking up, Alexander saw Lainey rushing toward him, the crowd parting as the chant grew. Right behind Lainey were Sasha, Jules, and Lydia.

From another direction, Brick was steaming toward him with Max not far behind. All but Jules and Lydia were wearing their bright yellow T-shirts. Alexander equipped his as well. The cries of "SEEE YA!" doubled.

When the others had made their way up onto the platform, Alexander raised his hands. "Eight times now, PWP and the servants of the this so-called 'Dark One' have attacked the citizens of Stormforge. And each time, they have ended up dead, or imprisoned!" He paused for cheers of 'SEEE YA'. "But too many times, they have managed to take away our friends and loved ones!" The crowd grew quiet at this, watching the still-crying Edna as Lydia and Sasha took over for the captain.

Alexander continued, "Greystone will fight this pretend god of darkness, and all his minions! We will fight until he is destroyed, or we are!" As the crowd roared, he stepped behind Ceasar. Grabbing the man's hair, he tilted his head up.

"This scum has been walking around freely in the city. His job was to gather information about us. While he, and others like him, are here amongst all of you, they pose a danger to innocents. SO, I WILL MAKE IT EASY FOR THEM!" he screamed as loudly as he could. "YOU CAN FIND US AT DIRE KEEP! BRING ALL YOUR MINIONS, COWARD! FACE US! WE WILL BE WAITING!"

As he finished, he kneed the warrior in the back, causing him to fall face forward onto the stone.

His friends all raised weapons in the air, shouting, "Death to the Dark One!" The crowd picked up the chant.

Alexander slowly lowered the platform back to ground level. The show was over. But he still needed to keep Ceasar busy.

Rolling the man over on his back, he said, "I'll offer again. Tell us all you know about this Dark One, and I'll ask the Captain to restore your arm." One of the guards, who had retrieved the arm from the crowd, waved it at the warrior.

Ceasar growled. "The Dark One ain't no friggin' NPC god you can vanquish. He's real! He pays in hard cash. American dollars. His beef with Greystones goes way back, and he's been planning for YEARS! He'll destroy you all; destroy this world! And when it's over, I'll spit on your grave!" He looked at Sasha and Lainey, a sneer on his face. "Except for you two. My boys and I, we got plans for you hotties! We're gonna pass you around like party favors till you can't even scream anymore."

Lainey snort-laughed. "Big talk from a little boy who pissed himself just cuz somebody whispered in his ear a little!" This caused a ripple of laughter from the surrounding guards.

Ceasar's face turned bright red. "I did what you said, now kill me!"

Alexander shook his head. "All you've done is boast and threaten. I want real information. Where do you meet? Who else is involved?"

"I'll not say another word. They'd kill me in my sleep. Now kill me so I can get my arm back." He stood up and faced Alexander, then turned his head toward the west. "KILL ME!" he screamed.

The captain shook his head. "We don't kill adventurers once we've taken them prisoner." He smiled at Alexander. "No mercy."

Alexander had a bad feeling. The warrior was too insistent on dying. Looking to the west, Alexander tried to follow the warrior's line of sight. He was looking at a small building just off the main road leading into the square. The front door was ajar, but Alexander could not see in the building.

Quickly, he sent the captain a group invite. Then he pulled up his map, shared it with the group, and pinged the building.

In group chat, he said, "*I think Ceasar's got friends here. EVERYBODY LOOK AT CEASAR. Do NOT look at the building. He was looking that direction as he screamed 'kill me'. The front door is ajar. Captain, can you get guards behind the building quickly? I'm going to put on a little show to distract them. The rest of you, take off your T-shirts, and separate. Move in that direction, and be ready to take out anyone leaving that building.*"

"*Make me group leader.*" The captain replied.

Alexander did so, and the Captain instantly converted the group to a raid. He added in Lydia, and two dozen guards. Then he pinged the map again, and instructed half the guards to move in on the back of the building quietly.

His guildmates removed their T-shirts and drifted into the crowd. Jules and Max actually went into stealth mode. Alexander began his distraction.

Grabbing the warrior's severed arm, he raised a smaller platform back into the air. It held just himself, Ceasar, and the captain. He wanted to give the man a good viewpoint from which to command the situation.

Waving the arm in the air, he cried out, "This piece of shit is begging for his arm! I think he expects we'll sew it back on for him! What say you?"

Cries of "No!" and "Never!" rose up from the crowd. One voice, louder than the others, shouted, "Feed it to him!"

Alexander chuckled. Looking in the direction of the voice, he shouted, "I like the way you think!" He handed the arm to Ceasar, who cradled it with his good arm, looking slightly nauseous.

Monitoring progress in guild chat, he saw that the guards were nearly in place at the back of the building. There were two more squads of guards heading in from neighborhoods close by.

He threw his arms up and spun around, enabling him to look toward the building without seeming obvious. He saw his group taking positions around the corner from the front door. Taking the opportunity, he extended his earth magic to its limited, and softened the ground across the entire road in a patch between the building and the square.

"I wish to thank all of you, for your support and understanding. This will be no easy fight. Although, if all of this pretender's minions are as stupid as the ones we've encountered so far, the fight may not be all THAT hard!" He grinned at the crowd.

Pointing to Ceasar, he shouted, "This moron's friends attacked my family's keep back in my homeland. They knew that I was here, but were on a mission to kill innocents, just to prove a point! The idiots blew themselves up, barely putting a scratch on the gate!" The crowd laughed.

That did it. Ceasar roared in anger and frustration, "Attack! NOW! For the Dark One!"

Six players with red icons leaped out the front door of the building. They'd actually been stupid enough to group up before Ceasar challenged him, and remain grouped long enough to be tagged as enemies.

An archer stood up on the roof, and wasted his first shot on Ceasar, trying to kill his co-conspirator. The arrow fell a bit short, striking the warrior in the stomach. The archer never got a second shot, as Lainey hit him with a stun arrow, then she and Max hit him with two more arrows causing him to fall off the building. Luckily, he landed in the mud Alexander had created. He might live.

Of the six who were at ground level, there were four warriors, a caster, and a healer. The warriors had all charged toward the now screaming crowd. They hit the area of liquefied stone at the same time, and with momentum, actually made it half way across before sinking in. Seeing this, the caster and healer remained behind on solid ground. Alexander quickly solidified the stone around the warriors, taking them out of the fight.

Turning to run, the healer encountered four guards who burst from the building behind them. She drew a knife and charged.

The caster, seeing that he was surrounded, pulled a portal scroll. Alexander hit him with Wizard's Fire, burning the scroll. The man screamed and fell to the ground.

Hearing sounds of fighting inside the building, Alexander yelled, "Brick! Inside!"

The dwarf went charging into the building, Max and Lainey right behind him. The guards outside had disarmed and detained the healer, and were kicking the burning mage as he rolled around on the ground. They'd arrest him once he stopped burning. Until then, he was fair game.

More guards came running in from a side street. Having already received orders from the captain, they retrieved the archer from the mud, and surrounded the four warriors. The three men and a woman were sunk to their hips in stone, but still had use of their arms. Seeing that they couldn't escape, they began to attack each other. The guards leapt upon them, three or four per warrior. They were quickly subdued and disarmed, with only minor injuries.

While Alexander was watching this, the mage somehow managed to get off a cast as the mage fire expired. A bolt of dark magic shot at Alexander, striking him in the chest. He'd never even seen it coming.

His health bar instantly dropped by 50%. He was blinded, and paralyzed. There was some kind of debuff on him, and a DoT effect. He was losing 2% of his hp per second. He tried to cast a heal on himself, but the paralysis wouldn't let him.

Losing his balance in the darkness, he felt himself begin to fall over. He must have fallen off the platform, because there was a delay before he felt an impact. And it did another 5% damage. He heard the captain shouting orders, but couldn't make them out over the sounds of the crowd. He watched as his health bar ticked below 30%.

Why can I see my UI if I'm blind? Another thing I'll have to ask the devs about. he thought. Whoever that mage was, he must have been high level. This one hit was going to kill him. He was down to 8% when he felt a heal tingle its way through him. His hp went back up to 25%, but the DoT was still ticking. Someone had bought him twelve more seconds.

With his health at 9%, the DoT and the blindness wore off. He was able to move again, as well. As he suspected, he was lying on the ground below the platform. He quickly cast a heal on himself, pumping 2,000 hp back into his health bar. Then he rose, and looked around.

Sounds of battle were still coming from the building. Looking up, he found the platform empty. Ceasar was on the ground near him, two guards held him as he bled from the arrow wound in his gut.

Alexander teleported himself across the patch of mud to a spot right in front of the building. Dashing inside, he found three guards down on the floor, and could hear Brick taunting someone upstairs. Taking time to check the three guards, he found all three still alive. He cast a heal on each one, then headed upstairs.

As he ran, he shouted in raid chat, "*There are wounded in the building! I healed three of ours in the main room, but there may be more!*"

Reaching the top of the stairs, he proceeded down a hallway toward the sound of fighting. He saw Brick, Max and Lainey in a room to the right, facing off against a plate-armored tank and a caster. Both were level 60. The tank was still near full health, while the caster was sporting several arrows from her head, and was down to about 30%.

Alexander cast Wizard's Fire on each of them. The flames from the tank should help heal Brick. His friend was down to 25% health and not doing well against the much higher leveled tank. Alexander pulled out his healing wand and shot Brick with it, healing him for 2.400 hp. He handed the wand to Max. They needed Lainey to keep shooting stun arrows, as he assumed Max's silence was on cooldown. Max stuck the wand between his teeth, then shot an arrow into the mage's eye, causing her head to slam into the wall behind her. She fell to floor, and Alexander couldn't tell if she was alive or dead.

Alexander looked around. Jules and Sasha were nowhere in sight. A quick check of the UI showed both women were alive, though neither were at full health.

"Sasha, where are you?" he shot out in guild chat.

"Downstairs, back of the building. Had a little fight. Healing guards now. We're good."

Relieved, Alexander turned his attention back to the tank. Taking out his Ray of Light wand, he moved around to the side of the room until he had an angle past the tank's shield. He fired the wand again and again. He was just using the automatic bursts from the wand, eating up a single charge of 30 mana stored in the wand each time.

Still, the beams of light were damaging the tank. As a servant of the Dark One, he was taking extra damage from light magic. And the attacks must have stung. The tank turned his shield to block Alexander's attacks.

That was a mistake.

Lainey hit him in the face with a stun arrow. Max shot him in the face with an arrow as well, as Brick dropped his shield. Winding up a massive two-handed swing, the dwarf leaped up and brought his war hammer down on the tank's head. The critical hit removed half of the tank's health, and stunned the man. Blood leaked out his ears.

Alexander quickly shouted for his friends to step back. He softened the floor beneath the two players, allowing them to sink partway through. Once they'd sunk far enough, he hardened it again. The mage hadn't moved a muscle. She still had a sliver of health, but appeared unconscious. The tank was recovering from the stun with roughly 30% of his health remaining. However, his torso and weapon arm were trapped by the floor. He'd dropped his shield when Brick hit him, and the shield was partially embedded in the floor as well.
Growling, he pointed at Lainey and cast a spell. A shroud of darkness surrounded the Valkyrie. She screamed in pain, and her health bar began

to drop quickly. Max instantly grabbed the healing wand and fired into the middle of the darkness.

"He be a dark paladin!" Brick shouted, as he hit the man again in the head. Alexander cast wizard's fire on him again. The constant damage should prevent him from casting. But just in case…

"Brick, break his arm! Don't let him raise it again! But don't kill him!"

The dwarf put away his hammer. He pushed the tank backward until he was laying nearly flat on the floor, then proceeded to stomp on the man's arm with his heavy steel boots.

Alexander turned his attention back to Lainey. Still screaming, his friend's hp had recovered due to the heal Max had given her. But her health bar was already back down to 30%. Max fired another burst into the darkness, but must have missed. "Keep firing!" Alexander yelled. "Aim low, in case she's on the ground!"

Max fired low, and sure enough, Lainey's hp went up a good bit. He fired again, and she was back to nearly full health.

Taking a chance, Alexander pulled out his light wand. Fitz had said it would damage friendly targets, but that it would also dispel dark curses and spells. Aiming for an area he hoped was above Lainey, he fired the wand.

Instantly, the darkness disappeared. Lainey was on one knee, gasping for breath. She looked at Alexander. "You… you… shot me!" Max grinned, shooting her with the wand again and bringing her back to full health.

"BWAHAHA!" Brick laughed. "Serves ye right. Payback for them free shots ye took in the forest!" He continued to stomp on the now helpless tank. At this point he was just doing it for fun.

Lainey snorted and looked at the three totally unapologetic men. "Idiots." She smiled.

The sound of guards rushing up the stairs brought them back to the business at hand. Alexander directed the guards to give a healing potion to the mage. She had somehow held on at 3% health. Then he bade the guards strip them of their armor and weapons, and their inventory bags. He had to send the guards downstairs to the room below, then let the two players fall through the floor, before their armor could be removed. Max, of course, took all the loot.

The captain arrived, and put them formally under arrest, ensuring that their bind points were transferred to the prison. As the guards rounded up all the prisoners, the group met up in the street outside. The captain gave them an update.

"There was a dozen in total, including Ceasar. The guards entering from the back surprised three of them. They captured two, and one fled into the basement. My men pursued him, but he used an escape tunnel, and lost them in the sewers. I've stationed men at all the known exits inside and outside of the city, and sent a request to the mages guild for assistance in hunting him.

"The two you fought upstairs had been in the main room. They fought my men who'd come in from the back, taking down three before Brick stepped in. He chased them upstairs, and you know what happened from there."

He turned to Alexander. "Thank you, by the way, for healing those three. We'd have lost them if it weren't for you." Turning to Sasha he bowed his head. "And my men tell me you saved half a dozen of them yourself. Thank you." Sasha gave him her best smile.

"As for the others, the mage that nearly killed Alexander was killed. But not before being arrested. So, his respawn will be in prison. When my men saw he'd attacked you, they… reacted badly, I'm afraid."

Alexander chuckled. "Please thank them for me."

"Yes, well. The healer, archer and warriors outside were captured without more than minor injuries. All of these adventurers were level 50 or higher. The highest was level 65. That's the one who hit you, Alexander."

"Just so I know who to thank, who healed me after I fell off the platform?" Alexander asked. "I'd have died if not for them."

The captain smiled. "That would be Lydia. She healed you, and when she saw you were going to live, she stomped off to kill any of them she could get her hands on. I had to physically restrain her. My lovely wife has quite the mother bear instinct these days!"

A runner rushed up to the captain, handing him a message. He read it quickly, then handed it to Alexander, who read through it quickly.

"HA! Seems we found our twelfth bad guy. It was a rogue. He was apparently spotted by a couple guards coming out of a manhole in an alley. They engaged him, and were losing, until Master Baleron came flying out of his shop and struck the rogue with a staff that turned him to stone!" Alexander began to laugh hysterically.

The others looked at him. Finally, he stopped laughing to explain. "Baleron is a gnome. Or at least, mostly gnome. He's only about shoulder high on Brick. He's an enchanter. Very fond of his dwarven spirits. He'll be drinking for free, telling this tale for years!" He smiled.

Max and Lainey moved around collecting the loot and bags from all the prisoners. Sasha and Jules went in search of Lydia. Brick headed back inside, very interested in the enemy tank's armor. Alexander took a moment to find a private spot in an alley.

"Odin, I'd like to speak to GM1," he said.

Odin appeared before him. I'm afraid GM1 is occupied at the moment. He said to tell you that the FBI has brought in local police and national guard units, and are attacking the keeps of each one of these servants of the Dark One." They are already inside the keep of the one named Ceasar, though he does not know it yet."

"Thank you, Odin. I appreciate you passing along the message."

"I heard what that one said. That the Dark One is behind the attack on Olympus. That is not acceptable." Odin growled. Lightning flashed in the sky.

"No, Odin, it is not. We will root out this Dark One and destroy him. Both in the game, and out. Do not worry," Alexander reassured the AI.

"I will assist where I can, without violating my directives." Odin said. Then he was gone.

Oh, shit. The Dark One's gone and pissed off Odin. I wouldn't want to be him!

Stepping back out into the street, he found Max waiting for him. "Was that Odin?" he asked.

"Yup. Message from dad. The FBI's on it. I'll update everyone together back at the house."

Max handed him three more communication rings. "Here, mister enchanter. I figure if you can find out how these work, we can set up a whole communication network outside the guild."

"Good thinking!" Alexander said. "Please give all the loot to the captain to be distributed to those who lost folks in the other attacks."

In guild chat, he said, *"Okay, everybody. We've still got business to handle today. Get your shopping done. Your training. I'm going to the Ogre to talk to volunteers. Sasha, if you haven't already been there, I'll take care of that."*

"We were headed there when we got your call. I'll leave it to you.", Sasha answered.

Alexander walked back over to Captain Redmond. "I should have asked sooner. Did we lose any guards? Any citizens?"

"None. There were some injuries. Mainly among the guards. Two civilians took wounds from the rogue, but are recovering. Lydia went to see to them."

"Thank you, Captain. That's a big relief. Can I ask a favor?"

"Of course, Alexander. I owe you many. If you hadn't caught on to Ceasar's look and found these others, things could have gone very badly."

"These prisoners are what I want to ask about. If, in your questioning, you discover that they are all of one guild, especially if that guild is not PWP, I'd ask that the king not make a general announcement of their status as enemies. I learned my lesson last night at the keep. Please ask the king to declare them enemies, but to do so quietly. That way, they may feel free to walk the streets again until spotted by a guard. Maybe we can capture more of them?"

The captain nodded. "I'll bring your idea to the king."

"Thank you, Captain. I'm headed to the Ogre now, to see about volunteers. Do you think Caleb might want to join us?"

"Try and stop him!" The captain laughed.

Alexander stepped back into the square. Making his way to the platform, he lowered it back down, and smoothed all the surrounding stone. As he worked, people began to applaud. At first, just a few. Then more and more. There was no yelling or cheering. Just applause. And a few slaps on the back as he walked toward the Ogre.

Entering the Ogre a few minutes later, he was pleased to find Baleron already there, and well into his story of capturing the rogue. Stepping up to the bar, Alexander called out, "A round of drinks on me! In honor of Baleron, hero of Stormforge and scourge of the Dark One's minions!" There were enthusiastic cheers and raised drinks around the room. Martin O'Malley winked at Alexander and stepped toward the kitchen. The barkeeps began filling drink orders as fast as they could.

"The boy warned me you were coming. He didn't say you were bringing half the city!" Martin clapped him on the back.

"Yes, well, a few things happened I didn't plan for." Alexander smiled sheepishly.

"I heard what you're doing, lad. I want to help. When the time comes, I'd like to open a tavern at your keep. Guards are guards, they need a place to drink!"

"Actually, you can help today, if you're willing," Alexander said. "I'm throwing a feast at our guild house tonight for the volunteers who will be coming with us. I'm expecting… well, it was a hundred. Now I'm guessing more like two hundred people. Can you provide the food? Nothing fancy, just food that'll fill bellies. Brick will be serving dwarven ale and spirits. We have a large kitchen at the house, you're welcome to make use of it." He paused as Martin looked thoughtful.

"Aye, we can do that, if we close down the restaurant tonight…"

Alexander could see him calculating the lost profits. "I'll also need to rent as many rooms as you can give me. For those who can't make it home after the party. I'll deliver them by wagon if necessary. There might be a large number of dwarves."

Martin smiled. "Aye, lad. We can manage that. I'll have some boys ready with wagons to help bring 'em here and tuck 'em in."

Alexander handed Martin a pouch with 1,000 gold. "This is for the food, the rooms, the loss of business from closing the restaurant, paying the extra help, and any possible damages."

Martin's mouth dropped open. "This is 1,000 gold, lad! That's three times what I'd ask of ya."

"Consider it an investment. Use whatever's left to buy what you need to start another Ogre at Dire Keep when the time comes." He smiled at Martin. "Now, do you have a room where I can talk to volunteers? Oh! And I promised them a meal if I accept them. Can I send them to you?"

“Aye, lad. Right this way.” Martin led him to a private dining room off the currently empty restaurant. “Since the restaurant be closed for the day, I’ll have them wait in there while you talk in here. Just grab the next one as you’re ready, and I’ll feed the ones that come out smiling.”

Chapter Seven

The Whos and the Whys

Alexander walked into the private room to find both Caleb and the large man who'd asked him two good questions in the square. They rose as he entered.

"Gentlemen. Please have a seat. Caleb, the captain has already told me there's no better man we could have with us at Dire Keep. And I know of your desire for vengeance. I fully support that desire. I have only one question. When the enemy is at hand, will you follow orders?"

He didn't need to elaborate. Caleb knew he was saying he couldn't have a loose cannon running around. "You'll have my oath on it," Caleb simply said.

"Good enough for me. Welcome aboard. Martin will bring you lunch if you like. You can eat in peace and quiet in the restaurant. We'll be meeting at our guild house at sunset. There'll be food and drink. We've arranged for rooms both here, and at The Stallion, if you'd like one."

Caleb hesitated. "Sir, if I might say something?"

"Of course, Caleb. And call me Alexander."

"Alexander. I was a guard in this city for many years. I know the citizens here. I could help you with your choosing, to make sure you get good people. Starting with the oversized oaf sitting next to me. He's a troublemaker, he is. Always with the practical jokes. And he's over fond of the ladies. But there's none better to have at your back in a fight. He also happens to be my cousin, Collin."

Alexander looked at the big man. "Collin. I'm not sure if that was a good recommendation, or a bad one. Tell me, what do you do when you're not fighting back to back with your cousin?"

The big man smiled. "I've been a soldier. And a mercenary. And a farmer. I was trained as a carpenter before I ran off to join the army. Woodwork is in my blood."

"Well, as it happens, we need fighters, farmers, and woodworkers. The keep has been abandoned for centuries, and most of the furniture has rotted away. Can you help make beds and chairs so that we can get folks out of tents and into more permanent quarters?"

"Aye, I can do that. Just give me some tools, some space, and wood to work with."

"And you're both okay with swearing an oath to Greystone and Dire Keep?"

Both men nodded their heads.

"Then welcome to both of you." He shook both men's hands.

"Now, can you think of others whom you'd recommend, and that you believe might want to go?"

The two men put their heads together and compared notes. Caleb counting off candidates on his fingers. He got to four.

"Yes, Sir," Collin spoke. Alexander just sighed.

"Okay. Here's what I propose. Caleb, please stay here and coach me as we bring in volunteers. Collin, you go and see if you can round up the… four? folks you just agreed on."

Men of few words, both of them nodded. Collin got up and left the room. After about ten seconds, he came back in and sat down.

Alexander, seeing that he wasn't going to get an explanation without asking… asked, "Change your mind?"

"Ha! Nope. All of them be sittin' outside in the restaurant." Collin grinned. Alexander couldn't help but laugh.

"Right. Then how bout you pick one and call them in? And ask Martin to bring in food for the three of us?"

Without another word, Collin was up again, and gone.

And so it went. Volunteers came in. Alexander spoke to them. Collin and Caleb added their two cents. Over a period of two hours, sixty volunteers applied. Some never made it past the door, with either Caleb or Collin chasing them away. One of them Collin threw a knife at. "He owes me money" was the terse explanation. All in all, there were forty acceptable candidates, plus the two cousins. Farmers, hunters, soldiers, and crafters. All men, with the exception of Edna, who wanted to come and cook for those who were going to fight the Dark One. Alexander was hesitant until she said she'd worked at Millicent's bakery for a few years before she got married. The thought of pastries convinced him.

Alexander headed back to the compound. He only had about fifteen minutes before the portal to Broken Mountain needed to be opened. He was curious to see how many dwarves wanted to relocate to Dire Keep.

It turned out to be many.

The portal opened, and Master Ironhammer led the way with his six master smiths. Alexander formally welcomed them all as he was introduced. They were followed closely by Thea and the lads. Behind them were two heaping wagons of barrels, caskets, and crates of drink. Thea directed them toward Brick's cellar. Next came a couple wagons of supplies for Whitehall, escorted by a dozen dwarven guards in full plate. Those continued right on out the gate and headed for the village. Finally, there came four more wagons carrying a mixture of supplies and dwarves. These circled the courtyard to make room for the others to pass through. Once all of the wagons were parked as far out of the way as possible, all of the dwarves dismounted and headed for the dragon forge. Alexander couldn't help but smile. Brick was about to be mobbed!

Thea and the lads hung back. Alexander motioned them into the house. He sat them down in the lounge.

"I'd like to offer each of you an invitation to join the Greystone Guild," he began. Harin and Dvorn high-fived each other. Thea smacked them both on the head.

"I can see there is some interest." Alexander smiled. "Do any of you have questions, or concerns?"

Garen raised a hand. "Will we still be allowed to study our crafts?"

"Of course! Harin here will be fortunate, or unfortunate, to be able to study here at the dragon forge, under SEVEN masters." The dwarves all chuckled. Masters were known to be surly and short-tempered.

"I'm afraid I don't have a master mason here for you to study under, Garen and Dvorn. But there is one at Whitehall. And maybe in the short term you can study with an experienced mason at the keep? I don't yet know if there are any in the group of volunteers."

"There be a master mason and three journeymen in the group outside," Thea informed him. She produced a list. "Twelve guards that ye see'd escorting the wagons to Whitehall. They'll be returnin' tonight. Four carpenters. Four farmers. Five hunters. Two alchemists. Four smiths that be willin' to work the keep, but that ask for a chance to work the dragon forge later." She smiled at that. "Meanin', when most of the masters be gone." She continued the list. "There be two merchants what want to set up shops. Three cooks. One brew master who asks that room be made for a brewery, and three o' his apprentices. Three laundresses who wish to set up a shop as well, and charge for their services. One chamberlain, and his apprentice. There be also ten miners coming from one o' the far clan mines. They be arriving tomorrow. It were faster for them to come straight here by land than to go back to the Mountain and use the portal."

Thea set down the list. "There be plenty more what wish to come. But me King hand-picked these fer the start. Every one o' them's trained as a warrior, and can fight at need. Except maybe the chamberlain. His heart's willing, but he be nearly five hundred years old."

“Thank you, Thea. Very helpful, as always. First, let’s get the formalities over with.” He sent them each a guild invite. They all accepted.

“Okay. Most immediately, Thea. I need you to introduce me to the Chamberlain and his apprentice. We’re having a feast tonight, and his help in organizing would be appreciated. Lads, there are deliveries coming in near constantly. Supplies for the keep, and supplies for the feast. I’ll need you to help get things set up. We need tables and chairs in the courtyard for eating. Someplace to set up a rather large bar… you get the idea. I’m going to put you at the chamberlain’s disposal for the next few hours. OK?” They all nodded.

“Okay, you all have medallions that let you in and out of the wards. Dvorn, while I speak to the chancellor, would you run outside and find Corporal Jenkins at the outer gate? Ask him to come and see me?”

The four dwarves all headed outside on their various errands.

Thea quickly returned with a very old dwarf, and a very young one.

“Alexander, this be Master Silverbeard. And his apprentice, Lola.” She introduced them.

Alexander smiled, and reached out to shake their hands. “Welcome to Stormforge, and to Greystone Manor,” he said, motioning for them to sit.

“Thank ye, Sir Knight,” the elder dwarf said. “I’d not thought to have another adventure afore I die. This be a good challenge. And good training fer me Lola, here.” Lola bowed her head.

“So, it was explained to you what we’re doing? And the dangers involved? And call me Alexander, please.”

“Aye, Alexander. We know about the Dark Ones tha’ killed one o’ our own lil’uns at Whitehall. Durin has declared them enemies of all dwarves. We know yer gonna fight ‘em. And ye’ll need help. We be ready to swear our oaths to the dragon, don’t ye worry.”

"Right, then. Thank you. Here's the challenge you'll face. The keep's main structure is damaged, and most everything within is rotted away. The walls are mainly intact, but we need to expand them so that farmers and crafters can work in safety. The keep is built into-"

"Hold there, Alexander. I was there when the keep were built. I know it's every in and out. Ye need not describe it," Silverbeard said.

"Excellent! And thank you, for saving me time. If we're going to work closely together, I want you to feel free to interrupt me, or tell me I'm being stupid, when the need arises." The old dwarf snorted.

"We have significant resources. Our guild bank has nearly half a million gold in it, as well as several million in valuable artifacts and gear. And we found piles of treasure in the keep. So, we have funds to stock and equip the keep as needed. In addition, we expect the mine will produce significant income once it is up and running. My guildmates, whom you'll meet this evening, have been purchasing supplies all day. That includes furnishings for all the empty rooms here at the manor, and as many beds and chairs as could be found for the keep. In addition, King Charles is sending us military tents and cots to use as temporary housing." Alexander paused. The old dwarf was just nodding his head. Lola was taking occasional notes, and he wanted to give her a moment to catch up. Which she did almost instantly.

"As you saw, we've got a good supply of dwarven ale and spirits. And we bought food for a hundred people for a month. Here are the lists that Thea made of the Dwarven volunteers. And here's a list of forty human volunteers. I'm still recruiting, so the total may be over a hundred by morning. But I think we can supplement our food from hunting, fishing, and the like. And we can always buy more supplies. The one-month purchase was in case of a siege." He paused again. Lola finished writing and smiled at him, letting him know to continue.

"As for tonight, we're throwing a feast for all the volunteers, plus others, like the masters who are here to work at the dragon forge, some friends, and possibly the royal family of Stormforge. The king has asked us to take his son to the keep, and may be dropping by to deliver him." This actually caused the old dwarf to raise an eyebrow. "I've got the Ogre providing food for two hundred. They should be here shortly to start cooking. I've rented thirty rooms for the night at the Ogre, and twenty-five at the Stallion. The Stallion is all suites. At night's end, I'd like the less rowdy who need rooms sent to the Stallion, and the balance sent to the Ogre. There should be an empty wagon or two available for transport. Though the Stallion is just a few steps away. There will be supply deliveries arriving all afternoon. I'd like you to take over organization of all of these things."

Silverbeard nodded his head. "The Ogre? That be an inn, not a person, yes?"

Alexander laughed. "Yes. An inn and tavern on the east side of town, run by Martin O'Malley and his family. The Stallion is on the corner three doors down, and is run by a man named Hobson, who will be stopping by to bum some spirits from Brick. That reminds me," he handed each of them a medallion, "keep these on you. They'll allow you to pass through the wards on this compound, and the one we'll be placing on the keep."

"Now, for housing tonight. We have two guest suites unoccupied here on the 2nd floor of the manor. If you'd like them, they're yours. The armory building next to the forge has eight small rooms on the upper floors. They should have beds by day's end. I assumed that Master Ironhammer and the other masters would stay there. Thea has set up above the workshop, where there are four more rooms, minus the one she occupies." He paused again, this time to think.

"Most of the human volunteers already have homes here in the city. Though some may need rooms at the Ogre if they can't make it. So, the majority of the dwarves can stay either at the Stallion, or the Ogre, in the fifty-five rooms we have available to us. Those are all prepaid, by the way, as is the food, and all of the incoming supplies. One moment please."

Alexander called up guild chat. "*We have a new chamberlain, Master Silverbeard. Oldest dwarf you've ever seen. And his assistant, Lola. As you get back to the compound, find him and update him on your purchases and arrangements. He's organizing everyone.*"

"I've just informed everyone who's been out shopping to find you as they return. They'll give you details on purchases and expected delivery times. I've put Thea and her three lads at your disposal for the day. If you need more manpower, grab whoever you see fit to use. Or if you need anything, really, send one of them to find me. I've no plans to leave the compound, except for a short trip to Whitehall in a few minutes."

"If it be a short trip, would ye mind if I tag along?" Silverbeard asked. "Lola here can get things going without me."

Surprised, Alexander said, "Of course. Someone there you wish to visit?"

"Some thing. I be wantin' to see the altar blessed by Durin," the dwarf said.

Alexander smiled. "That's exactly where I'm going. I want to ask the priest to come with us to the keep long enough to consecrate the ground, as he and Brick did in Whitehall."

The old dwarf looked to Lola. "Head out and begin to organize things. Stay near the gate to catch deliveries. Use the lads to help with tables and chairs. And get some of our people to set up some tents in the back courtyard against the wall. Have some others see to the horses. Assign the vacant rooms as ye see fit. The masters get priority, o'course."

He looked to Alexander. "How long till we leave?"

"For Whitehall? I have one more person to meet, then we can go. Actually, you can sit in, if you'd like."

Silverbeard nodded his head.

As soon as Lola exited the room, Dvorn walked in with Jenkins. They must have been waiting outside. "Thank you, Dvorn. Please go help Lola," Alexander said as he rose to shake hands with Corporal Jenkins.

"Welcome, Jenkins. Good to see you again. This is Master Silverbeard, our new chamberlain. He's going to be running the keep's day to day operations." The two nodded at each other in greeting. Alexander motioned for the guard to sit.

"Jenkins, I'll get right to the point. You impressed me at the cemetery the other day. You were observant, and alert enough to warn us about the ambush. And you cared enough to warn us both before we went in, and after we came out. I've passed on to Captain Redmond that you went above and beyond. He apparently already knows you well? And he recommended you as a potential volunteer for our forces at the keep." He stopped to let the man soak all that in.

"I want to stress the word 'volunteer'. This is not an order in any way. This mission will certainly involve combat with forces under the command of this 'Dark One' pretending to be a god. I'm sure you've heard about the previous attacks, including the one in the city a few hours ago?"

"Aye, Sir Knight. We heard. Pretty much heard nothing but. I know you dueled a warrior nearly twice your level, and won. I know it was you who discovered his friends in hiding, and nearly died fighting them. I know it was you who healed three o' my mates who'd have died otherwise. And I watched you and your friends take down those PWP arseholes in the cemetery without even tryin' hard. And to answer your question, Sir, yes. I'd like to volunteer. So would Foster, and the rest of the squad at the gate. I'd follow you anywhere, Sir Knight."

Alexander was taken aback by the corporal's fervor. "Uh, please, call me Alexander. And that warrior was less than 30 levels above me. Levels can't overcome stupid. He lost as soon as he challenged me. As for the keep, welcome aboard. How many others in your squad?"

"Five others, sir... Alexander. There be others that want to come as well. All good men."

"You'll vouch for the men in your squad? I may not have time to interview them today. They need to know the dangers, and be willing to swear the oaths."

“I do. And they’re all ready. We know the situation. They’ve each asked today if I’d speak to you about taking us,” Jenkins replied.

“Very good, then. When you see Captain Redmond, inform him that you’re coming with us. I expect he planned it that way.” He grinned at the corporal. “Also, once we set foot in the keep, you will be Sergeant Jenkins. I’m using my rank to promote you. Now, head back out to your squad. I’m relying on you to make sure no spies or freeloaders squeeze through that gate for the feast. If you have doubts about someone, send for me, or one of the Greystones.”

Alexander paused for a moment. He’d been talking a lot about sending runners in the last hour. That was inefficient.

“Actually, let me ask you something. Both of you. I’ve begun recruiting, adding to Greystone’s membership. Prince Kai of the dragons was the first to join. Thea and her three lads just joined a few minutes ago. I’m extending that offer to the two of you. This means I’m putting a great deal of trust in you. Bringing you into the family, so to speak. All of the volunteers will become citizens of the keep, but a much smaller number will be welcomed into the guild. You need not decide now.”

“I’d be honored.” Jenkins bowed his head. Alexander sent him a guild invite, which he accepted. “Thank you, Alexander. I’ll head back to give the good news to my men.”

“If you need anything, use guild chat. One of us will be there to help.” Alexander shook his hand again as he left.

Master Silverbeard asked, “Will ye include me granddaughter in yer guild, as well?”

“Your grand… Lola is your granddaughter? I see. Well, I’ll need to speak with her first. And make sure she understands the risks and responsibilities. But if you vouch for her abilities and courage, I don’t see why not.”

"Then I accept." The old dwarf nodded his head once. "I'll serve ye as guild chamberlain. That'll include me duties at the keep, and here at the manor. Who's yer treasurer?"

Sending him the guild invite, Alexander said, "I suppose that'd be me. We've not had much in the way of complicated needs before last week. This manor has only become ours very recently, and the same with the keep. If you want the job, it's yours."

"Not me, lad. Lola. That girl's skill with numbers be uncanny." Silverbeard smiled. Proud of his granddaughter.

"Okay then, I'll speak to her about it. In the meantime, I'll show you the guild vault, then we'll check on things outside, and head to Whitehall."

Alexander led Silverbeard to the guild vault. The old dwarf's eyes widened at the sheer bulk of treasure inside. Most especially when he saw the selection of items from Fibble's hole. He began to reach a hand toward the mithril ball on the back shelf, then paused to look at Alexander.

"Go ahead. Are you able to analyze it?" Alexander asked.

"HA! I be a chamberlain, lad. With four centuries of experience. I be fully aware of the value of things. I be versed in the magic of defense, transportation, and healing. I know political protocol for royal visits, and the best way to fold a bedsheet. And all that be in between."

He held up the artifact. "This be a truly wondrous thing. And there be a bar o' skymetal…" His voice faded away. "I admit to doubtin' ye, lad. When ye spoke of yer wealth. The value o' just these items here on this shelf could fund yer keep for a decade. And ye can make yer own wealth as needed. I see'd the artifact ye made fer me King. Just sittin' there casual as ye please, he said. Ye just closed yer eyes and pulled out some stone and made it right there."

"Well, I'm glad you believe me, now. And speaking of that…" He pulled out another chunk of obsidian. This one he formed into a flat disc, like a pendant. He focused his magic, sending the healing spell through his hand into the stone. Again, he spiraled it down as tightly as he could toward the center of the stone. There was much more room in this one. Still, he stopped at 3,000 mana. Then he added the Undying spell.

Salvation Pendant
Item Level: Epic, Unique
This pendant will allow the wearer to use regenerative light magic to restore 2,000 hp to a friendly target. Charges: 20/20. Undying: Should the bearer receive a mortal blow, the wand will maintain bearer at 1% health, preventing death.

Skill level up! Enchanting skill +1

Handing the pendant to Silverbeard, he said, "I can't have my chamberlain slain by a stray arrow. You hold onto this. Have Lainey or one of the crafters make you a chain. It will be your symbol of office. And if need be, you can help heal the most urgently injured in a crisis."

The ancient dwarf's hands trembled as he accepted the gift. "Such a thing… Thank ye, lad."

"My pleasure. As soon as I have time, I'll be providing all the keep's citizens with a trinket that holds the 'Undying' enchantment. Hopefully that will help cut down on our losses. Now, are you ready to see Whitehall?"

At the old man's nod, Alexander teleported them both to the cellar of the Whitehall chapel.

Silverbeard's mouth opened as if he were going to speak, but no sound came out. He moved to the altar of clear obsidian, laying a hand on it. Dropping to one knee, he murmured a lengthy prayer to Durin. As he prayed, the pulsing light in the center of the altar began to glow brighter. It engulfed the old dwarf, then seemed to infuse him.

When he ceased praying and rose to his feet, he had tears in his eyes. "Thank ye again, lad."

Taking a good look at his new chamberlain, he could swear the man looked younger. "Are you also a paladin of Durin?" he asked.

"Aye, lad. At least, I were in me younger days. And when I heard o' this place, I knew it was a good place to make one final visit with me god before I be leavin' this life. I prayed for the strength to see ye and the guild through the upcoming war. I think both gods heard me. Me body feels stronger than it has in a hundred years!"

Alexander smiled. "I saw the light surround you, and you look much younger than you did five minutes ago. I'm glad we had time to come. Now, let's see if we can talk the priest into joining us?"

The two of them climbed the stairs to the ground floor, Master Siverbeard moving a good bit faster than he had been. Not finding the priest inside the chapel, they headed out into the village. Alexander took Silverbeard and introduced him to Millicent and her ladies, snagging them a bag full of treats for the feast, and one each for them to snack on. They cleaned out the bakery's entire supply. Theresa said the priest was at the inn, seeing to a wounded farmer.

Moving on toward the inn, they were greeted by villagers, human and dwarf alike. The dwarves bowed low to Master Silverbeard. Dwarves who'd lived as long as he had were highly revered.

Arriving at the inn, they found the priest talking with a farmer named Eli over a bowl of stew. "Alexander!" the priest called out in greeting. "Come join us."

Alexander and Silverbeard sat at the table with them. "Father Ignatius, Eli, this is Master Silverbeard. Our new chamberlain, and the newest member of the Greystone guild." Greetings were exchanged. "Theresa said you were here for some healing?"

"Yes, Eli here lost an argument with his plow horse. A few crushed ribs. All better now." Eli smiled as he continued to eat his stew. Major healings made a man hungry. The body used its own resources, directed by the magic, to heal itself. Those resources needed replenishing.

"I'm glad to hear you're okay, Eli." Alexander clapped the man on the back. "Father, how would you like to take a little field trip? A day or two? To a very dangerous place with a high likelihood of battle, where the odds are there will be many injured to help?"

"HA!" Father Ignatius laughed. "This wouldn't have to do with that message about Dire Keep, would it?"

"That very place. In the morning, we're taking a force of roughly a hundred volunteers and occupying the keep. We're going to rebuild and improve its defenses, just as we did here. And I want to consecrate a chapel there, same as yours." Alexander grinned at him.

"That be a wondrous chapel," Silverbeard added. "Ye must be quite proud."

Father Ignatius took a good look at the dwarf. "I see you've already received a blessing. And from both gods. May I?" he reached a hand out to Silverbeard, who nodded.

The priest placed a hand on Silverbeard's shoulder. "Your heart was failing. But no longer. I'd say you've got at least another fifty or sixty years in you. Assuming you don't get yourself killed at Dire Keep!" He grinned.

"BWAHAHAHA!" the old dwarf laughed. "Not likely. The lad give'd me this." He held out the pendant for the priest to inspect.

"I see you've been experimenting with enchanting again, Alexander. At least with this, you're not likely to blow yourself up, or cook your own meat from the inside!"

Grinning and blushing at the same time, Alexander replied, "Yes, well, I've had some coaching from Fitz. The Undying spell is easy. As you know, most of the villagers have something enchanted with that spell, now. The other is just a gradual infusion of healing. I could make you one, as well. As payment for a couple days of your time?"

"I need no payment, Alexander. I'll come and help with your chapel. But I'll not refuse a gift that would help me heal those in need." The priest smiled.

“Done!” Alexander thumped the table. “You can come back with us now, if you’d like. We’ll give you some time to pack while I show Master Silverbeard around. There will be a feast tonight at our compound, and you can meet all of the new citizens of the keep.”

“You might want to add one more to your list,” the priest said. “When I saw the announcement about Dire Keep, I figured you were going to need a healer. I sent word to my superiors, asking them to send you someone. They should have arrived in Stormforge today.”

“We’ll keep an eye out for them. Thank you,” Alexander said.

The three got up and headed outside, leaving Eli power-eating a second bowl of stew. As the priest hurried off to pack for the trip, Alexander and Silverbeard strolled around the village. Alexander pointed out the new walls, and all the newly constructed homes for the dwarven farmers and their families. Silverbeard stopped at the home of the family who’d lost their child. He hugged the boy’s mother and offered his condolences. They both cried a bit as Alexander recounted the boy’s part in the children’s ‘attack’ on the two Kings just before the battle.

As they left the house, Father Ignatius was approaching. Alexander gathered them together, and teleported them back to the compound. With so many people running about, he teleported them to the 2nd floor landing of the manor house. They needed to designate a teleport pad that could be kept clear.

Alexander set both men free to wander about, explore, and meet people. Stepping out on the balcony outside his suite, he observed the bustle below. Wagons piled with furniture were moving into the courtyard, being directed by Thea. Other wagons were being unloaded, or directed somewhere to be unloaded. Sixteen long tables with chairs were set up in the garden area. Each table sat 6 on each side. Probably more seating than they needed, but then unexpected guests showed up at any party.

Heading downstairs, he found Mrs. O’Malley in the kitchen. “Alexander! This is a wondrous kitchen!” she exclaimed when she saw him walk in.

"I'm glad you like it. I figured it would be easier for you to cook here," he said.

"Aye, that's for sure. And when we build the Ogre II at your new keep, the kitchen's going to look exactly like this!" She smiled. Then she kicked him out. "We've got work to do. You're in the way!"

Heading out the back door, he found beds, mattresses, and chairs being unloaded into the workshop building. Several dwarves were setting up a few of the military tents along the back wall. Each of the tents could comfortably sleep three men (or dwarves) on cots, with a chest for each. Or six with bedrolls instead of cots.

Observing the tent construction, he noticed the small door in the back wall. It was secured with a simple bar on the inside. Not liking the idea of that being so lightly secured, and placed behind a tent where it couldn't be watched, Alexander raised a stone wall eight feet high right in front of the door. No way it could be opened now.

Deciding that preparations were well in hand, and that input from him would likely slow things down, he headed back into the house. Sitting at the desk in the study, he checked in with folks in guild chat.

"Jenkins, everything okay out there?"

"We've had a few crashers who couldn't give a name for who invited them. We set them aside in case someone wanted to speak to them. There's a priest of Asclepius out here, asking for an audience. We found one wagon that tried to deliver tainted meat. The drivers were arrested and are being questioned. Lola gave us a copy of the invited citizens list.", Jenkins reported.

"Please send the priest in. And have two of your men escort the crashers in as well. I'm in the study. Also, if Mr. Hobson from the Stallion comes by, please let him in. And there will be a dozen dwarven guards returning from Whitehall. Thank you."

"Sasha? How goes the shopping?"

"Good! Got the supplies all purchased. They'll be delivered this afternoon, or early in the morning. Even bought us a few fruit trees to plant. I've got 5 players I want the group to meet. Told them to arrive at sunset."

"Great! Thank you." Alexander continued, *"Max, there's a butt-load of furniture already arriving. How much have you been able to get?"*

"Filled all the vacant rooms at the compound. Plus, another thirty beds with mattresses, sixty chairs of varying styles. Also, twenty sofas, and fifty assorted tables. Mostly nightstands and the like. Though I did get three long dining tables. Most of that won't arrive until morning. I bought twenty barrels of oats for the horses. We can supplement that with hay the farmers cut. I don't know anything about farming tools, but I bought two plows, several pitchforks, and a dozen hoes. I figure we can always make them into weapons if we need to. I bought two more big wagons for transportation, and big horses to pull them. We're still going to need to make several trips tomorrow. At ten miles each way, it might take all day."

"Good work, Max! And I've been thinking about that. I don't like the idea of vulnerable caravans going by land. Especially not more than one trip. I'm going to ask Fitz to help me set up a second portal in the courtyard. That way we can move cargo, or troops, directly inside the walls. Okay. Sounds like everybody's doing great. Just a reminder, when you get back, find Silverbeard or Lola and bring them up to date."

Just then, Foster and another guard walked in with a priest, and four citizens. Alexander invited them to join him in the dining room, where he sat everyone down. Except Foster and the other guard, who remained standing behind the four crashers.

Alexander looked to the priest. "Welcome, father…?"

"Alric. Please just call me Alric," the priest said. He was in his late twenties, tall with a muscular build, and long brown hair that was braided down below his shoulders.

"Alric, then. Would you mind waiting while I deal with these folks?" The priest smiled and nodded his head.

"Alright, then. One at a time, who are you, and why are you here? I don't recognize any of you. Starting with you on the left." He pointed at a short man with a scruffy beard.

"My name is Claude. I heard you was offering good pay for volunteers. But I heard too late. When I got to the Ogre, you was gone. I'm a tanner and leatherworker by trade, but I can fight if needed!"

"Okay, thank you. Next?" Alexander looked to the next man. He was tall and thin, with an elongated face and large ears. He looked like he hadn't eaten in a while.

"I'm Albert Bonaducci!" The man grinned. "Famous artist and socialite. I wish to record the rebuilding of Dire Keep, and any battles that occur, in my paintings."

"I see. Okay, now you." He indicated the woman in the next chair. She appeared to be in her mid-twenties, though it looked as if she'd lived a hard life. "I'm Mathilda. Most folks just call me Mattie. I'm a cook. Worked at the Ogre before I was knocked up and got married. My husband's a worthless drunk, and I ain't seen him in three months. I need work, and this seemed better than most."

Alexander motioned to Foster to approach. He leaned down so Alexander could whisper to him, then left the room. "What about your child?" Alexander asked. "I will not be allowing children at the keep until it is much, much safer."

Mattie looked down at her hands. "He didn't survive. It was a rough birthing. Midwife said his heart just couldn't take it."

"Mattie!" Mrs. O'Malley came bounding into the room. When she saw the look on the woman's face, she lifted her from the chair and gathered her in a hug. Giving Alexander a dirty look, she said, "What'd you do to make our Mattie cry?"

"It wasn't him," Mattie sobbed into her shoulder. "I was just tellin' him about my son. I still get a bit sad."

"Hush, child. You'll have another soon enough. Once you dump that worthless lout and find a decent man." Mrs. O'Malley patted her head.

Alexander spoke up. "Mattie has come here to volunteer to serve at the keep. I take it you can vouch for her?"

"NO!" Mrs. O'Malley grabbed the girl's head and looked her in the face. "I mean, yes, of course I'd vouch for her. There are none better than Mattie. She's like one of my own. Good cook, too. I taught her myself. But you'll not be taking one of my girls to that place! What're you thinking, girl?"

"Best way I can think of to rid myself of Bart. That coward wouldn't come near Dire Keep. Or maybe I'll get lucky and he'll come looking for me. Get himself ate by a wolf on the way."

Alexander spoke again. "Mattie, you say your husband hasn't been around in three months?"

She nodded "Aye, he took what little money we had, said a woman what couldn't provide him with a son wasn't worth keeping, and left. He's done it before, but always came back after a week or two. When he wanted to… use me. Or needed money."

"Father… Alric." Alexander looked to the priest. "I admit to not being an expert on marital law. But where I'm from, that would be grounds for divorce. Is it the same here?"

The priest, who seemed a bit angry, nodded his head. "The grounds seem sound. But our church would only grant a divorce if it were approved by the king."

"I see. What about the Knight-Advisor to The King? Or better yet, the ruler of a keep granted by the king?"

Alric thought about it. "As knight-advisor, I'm afraid not. But as rightful baron of a land, if she were one of your citizens, then that would be acceptable."

Alexander looked at Mattie. "Alright. Mattie, I invite you to become a citizen of Dire Keep. But ONLY if you can get Mrs. O'Malley to approve. If so, then I will ask Father Alric here to grant you a divorce. If not, then I will still petition the king on your behalf. He may be here this evening. How does that sound?"

The woman began to cry, nodding her head. Mrs. O'Malley bustled her into the kitchen, tossing Alexander a smile over her shoulder.

Alexander looked to the last of the four crashers. He was half-elven, tall and lean, but muscular. He wore leather armor of forest green. Alexander assumed that Jenkins had confiscated the bow that went with the armor. "And you?" Alexander asked.

"I am Dothloriandal, though you may call me Lorian. I am a Ranger and a scout. I too, arrived too late to meet you at the Ogre. I've just returned from hunting dire wolves in the forest near Dire Keep. I observed your party moving through the woods yesterday morning, though only the dragon saw me. I admired the way you so carefully killed the beasts, to preserve their hides."

"One moment, please." Alexander held up a hand.

"*Kai, are you there?*"

"I'm at the keep, Alexander. How can I be of service?"

"Did you notice a ranger watching us yesterday as we moved through the forest?"

"Yes, he followed us for nearly an hour, watching as we killed the beasts. He was half-elven, and I believe of a noble line. He recognized me. Since he chose not to make himself known, I honored his wish. My apologies."

"No need to apologize. He is here with me, now. He wishes to become a citizen of the Keep."

"I see no reason why he should not. And elven ranger could be a useful addition," Kai mused.

"Thank you, Kai. You okay there? Can I bring you anything?"

"I am quite well, Alexander, thank you. A rather large bear came sniffing around the gate this morning. He made an excellent breakfast." Alexander could hear the dragon grinning.

"Okay, well, I'm going to bring Fitz and Brick in the morning, ahead of the others. I'm thinking we should put up a portal near the gate, rather than try to use the upper portal and try to teleport wagons and horses down. Would you like to pick a good spot?"

"I will do that. See you in the morning." Kai said.

Alexander looked at Lorian. "The dragon confirms your account, and send his greetings." The elf bowed his head.

"Albert. I'm afraid I cannot allow any paintings or renderings of the keep or its residents at this time. We are expecting attack any day now, from a ruthless enemy. Any enemy who has repeatedly infiltrated this city. Giving them any information on our defenses could get all my people killed. I'm sorry. However, Foster here will take you in the kitchen, and ask Mrs. O'Malley to give you some food to take with you. But you must give me your word that you'll draw no images and tell no tales of this compound, either. Keep in mind that you are speaking to the Knight-Advisor to The King. If even so much as a rumor gets back to me that could have been started by you, I'll have you locked in a dungeon and put to hard labor. Are we clear?"

Albert rose, fear in his eyes. "I swear on my life that I'll not divulge in any way what I've seen or heard here today. I do hope you'll consider my request in the future?"

Alexander handed him some coins. “I will consider it, when times are better. In the meantime, here is twenty-five gold, to keep you fed until your next commission. And remember your oath to me.”

Foster led the man to the kitchen.

Alexander looked to the other guard. “I’m sorry, I don’t know your name.”

“Jacobs, Sir.” The guard came to attention.

“Jacobs, nice to meet you. When I’m done talking to Claude, here, please take him and put him between the bailey wards. Let him grab a chair on your way past the garden, so that he may sit in comfort while he waits.” Jacobs saluted in response.

“Claude. All my other volunteers were vetted by men I trust. I have no reason to distrust you, or your motivations. But I cannot accept you until someone else has vouched for you. There are two men who assisted me this afternoon. Caleb, a former guard, and Collin, his cousin. Do you know either of them?”

“Aye, lord. I know ‘em both. Collin were likely wearing armor I crafted for him,” Claude said.

“Good, then. When you see one of them come through the gate, ask them to bring you back to me. If they approve of you, then I will welcome you as a volunteer. You are aware of the oaths you must take?”

“Aye, I have no problem with that. I’ll swear the oaths ‘n’ serve you well.”

“Thank you. Can I get you anything? Do you need food or drink while you wait?”

“I’ll be fine, lord. I ate at the Ogre before I left. And it smells like there’ll be good food to be had tonight.” He grinned.

Foster led the man outside. When they were alone, Alexander turned to Lorian. "Should I be calling you Prince Dothloriandal? Or Lord?" he asked.

The elf chuckled. "So, the dragon exposed me. No matter. Though my father is noble, I am a half-breed bastard son, and therefore not eligible for a title. Just Lorian will do. And I appreciate you waiting until we were alone."

"I come from something like a noble house myself. And I much prefer anonymity to formality. Your secret is safe with me. But I must ask. Will taking you in cause me or my people any trouble with the elves?"

"While my father cannot recognize me, there is no strife between us. And there are legitimate heirs in place to assure the family's stability. If anything, I may be a help to you. From what I have seen, and heard, you are a ruler who cares about his people. You have honor. If you wish it, I would introduce you to my father and suggest a trade alliance. Anything further, you will have to accomplish on your own."

"Thank you, for that. And, you have no oaths in place that prevent you from swearing loyalty in front of the dragon?"

"None. We elves do not take oaths lightly. Though I am not pure blood, I expect to live several thousand years. Still, I will swear my loyalty to both Greystone and the keep."

"Then you are most welcome, Lorian. We depart for the keep a few hours after sunrise. You are welcome to stay here for the feast, and overnight if you like. We have several hotel rooms reserved at the Ogre, and at the Stallion. In the meantime, feel free to roam about the compound and meet your fellow citizens."

A sudden thought occurred to Alexander. "Uhhh... I just remembered. There has been some... harsh feeling between the dwarves and elves in the past. Are you, or your people, going to have a problem with my dwarves?"

"That unpleasantness was resolved long ago, as far as I know. I've never heard a hint of animosity from my father. And I count dwarves among my own friends," Lorian replied.

"Great! I'll see you at the feast tonight." Alexander shook the elf's hand and showed him to the door.

Alexander peeked into the kitchen, seeing Mattie making a pouty face at Mrs. O'Malley. Clearly, their discussion had not concluded. Finding himself with some time, he sat at the table to craft a pendant for Father Ignatius.

Reaching into his bag, he found he'd used up the obsidian he had. So, he headed out to the forge to see if he could quickly snag a piece.

Reaching the forge, he found Brick surrounded by master smiths, all crowded around two anvils and the forge itself. The dwarves were bumping arms, shoulders, and occasionally threatening each other with hammers. Waving, he motioned Brick over, not wanting to insert himself in that mess.

"Looks like a game of twister in there," he said as Brick stepped out.

"Aye. There be not enough room for so many. I dunno what Master Ironhammer be thinkin!" his friend complained.

"Well, maybe it's second Christmas for you, my friend!" Alexander smiled at him. "I came out here to steal some obsidian. But I'm not getting near all that." He waved at the chaos inside the smithy. "How bout I pull up another block, and you add on some workspace?"

Brick's eyes went wide. "That be perfect!"

Looking around, Alexander grabbed the first young dwarf he saw. "Please run next door to the Alchemy shop. Ask Lady Lydia for two stamina, and two mana potions."

As the dwarf took off, he closed his eyes and sent his earth sense down into the stone below. He reached down until he found the space where he'd cut out the obsidian for the smithy. Grabbing a second block the same size, he began to pull it up. The work was much easier now. He was close to double the level he'd been when he raised the first block. And he'd pulled most of a village out of the ground as practice. His mana pool was much higher now, too. Though his stamina was still low. He should probably invest a few points there.

Still, he managed to raise the giant block of obsidian nearly the whole way before he needed to stop for a rest. Taking the opportunity, he put 4 of his free attribute points into Stamina. Instantly, he felt better. And his health bar increased by something like 20%. Still, he waited for the dwarf to return with the potions. He drank down a stamina potion, not needing the mana yet.

With a deep breath, and his newly improved stamina, he reached down and pulled at the block of stone. Hearing the masters all babbling away at once, he decided to add a little drama. When the stone neared the surface, he waggled it back and forth a bit, causing the ground to rumble.

This instantly quieted the dwarves in the smithy. And in the rest of the compound. All eyes turned to Alexander just as the giant block of obsidian broke the surface and came to rest next to the smithy.

Grinning at Brick, who was standing amid the masters laughing as quietly as he could, Alexander took a theatrical bow. "Your turn!" he called out.

Master Ironhammer came stomping out of the smithy. "And just what're ye doin?" he asked. The masters were all right behind him. "Well, you see, Brick and I decided that Prince Kai needed a bigger perch while he's here in Stormforge…" Alexander began.

"Bah! Yer pullin' me leg!" Ironhammer cut him off. But the old dwarf was smiling. He knew he'd made a mistake bringing so many masters to the forge at once.

Alexander decided to help him out. "We saw that things were a bit crowded inside, so we're going to give you and the masters some room to spread out. You'll still have to share the forge itself, but there will be much more workspace for benches and anvils.

Taking advantage of the distraction, Brick had already stepped inside the block, moving it in sections with his hands. Seeing the direction of Alexander's gaze, Ironhammer and the others all turned to watch Brick work. After a few seconds, there was a rush, as each master moved to give direction or make suggestions as to the new layout. Poor Brick. Alexander made his escape after snagging a 10lb chunk of the stone from Brick.

Heading out to the gate, he checked in with Jenkins. He was introduced to the other squad members, and told things were going smoothly. There had been no more crashers. The captain had been seen heading into his home, so Alexander decided to go pay him a visit to ask about the men with the spoiled meat.

Walking into the shop, he was surprised to find Lydia, Sasha, Lainey, and Jules.

"Well! Hello, ladies!" He grinned and waved. "Fancy meeting you here!"

All four women looked at him like he was insane.

"You know that Lydia... lives here, right? Have you lost what little sense you were born with?" Sasha frowned at him. Lydia looked as if she wanted to check his vitals.

"No. I mean, yes. I just thought you'd be..." He gave up. "Never mind. I was looking for your husband, Lydia. Would he be around? And thank you, by the way. For saving my life earlier."

"He's hiding upstairs, Alexander." She smiled at him. At least one of them didn't hate him...

"I don't think I blame him." Alexander tried again to be charming. And failed. With a sigh, he edged carefully past the four women and headed up the stairs, calling out, "Captain? Are you there? I need protection from the fierce creatures downstairs..." He heard giggles behind him.

Turning to face the ladies again, he saw nothing but poker faces. "If you'd like some amusement other than me, you should head next door. I pulled up another block of obsidian for Brick to expand the forge, and he's just been mobbed by the masters. It's like watching feeding time at the zoo."

Not a flicker of interest on any of the faces below. With another sigh, Alexander turned and resumed his climb, to the sound of more giggles.

When he reached the top, the captain was waiting for him, a large glass of scotch in each hand. "Sometimes retreat is the only option," he said, handing Alexander a drink. They moved to a sitting area. "They've got plans for you, son. Whatever they are, you don't stand a chance. Best to just do what they want and hope it's not too painful."

Sitting back to enjoy his scotch, Alexander agreed. He was used to Lainey and Sasha ganging up on him. But adding in Lydia and Jules… he was smart enough to flee with whatever dignity they allowed.

"I came to ask about the wagonload of spoiled meat," he said.

"Yes. Strange that. The butcher swears the meat was good when it left the slaughterhouse. He's a reputable vendor. Those were his lads driving the wagon. Our only theory at the moment is that somebody spelled the meat to rot. We sent for someone from the mages guild to see what they could find out." The captain was rubbing his head.

"That puts us in a bind, with potentially a hundred and fifty mouths to feed. Losing that much meat could hurt us if we're under siege. With a little time, we could hunt that much in bear, boar, and wolf meat, but I was already counting on that as a supplement," Alexander said.

"The butcher promised to send another wagon in the morning. Free of charge," the captain assured him.

"He shouldn't have to absorb that loss if his cargo was spelled. If the mages find this to be the case, I'll pay him for another shipment. But I'm thinking we teleport it straight from the slaughterhouse, so whoever spelled it can't repeat the process." Alexander was thinking aloud. Once we get settled and expand the walls, we can skip the butcher and just buy some cattle and sheep. But that's some ways away."

The two men drifted into silence. When they heard the front door open and close, they figured it was safe to descend.

"I'll head back to the palace and see if there's news," the captain said.

"I need to go meet all the dwarven recruits. You'll be at the feast?" Alexander asked.

"Wouldn't miss it!" The captain smiled.

Alexander returned to the compound to find Caleb talking to Claude in the bailey. "Ah, Caleb. Welcome. I see you found Claude," he said.

"Aye, Alexander. He'll do. Can't let him near his shop when he's been drinking, though. Nearly cut his own hand off last time," Caleb said with a straight enough face that Alexander truly had no idea whether he was joking.

"In that case, welcome both of you. You'll be able to pass through the wards now. Introduce yourselves around, and I'll see you at the feast." Alexander led them inside.

Brick had already finished expanding the new block of obsidian. Surprisingly, he had extended the new section in an L shape that formed around the corner where the forge was. This effectively placed the forge nearer the center of the new smithy. Then he'd opened up the back side of the forge, where the corner of the old structure had been. This, quite ingeniously, allowed smiths to work from both sides of the forge at once. It didn't increase the size of the forge itself, but Brick had already made it large enough to sit inside. So, the dimension of the entire structure went from roughly 20x20 to 35x30.

They were just establishing the connection between the two structures. Brick had two masters helping him to shape the last bits of stone. As the new floor sections connected to the old, the entire structure began to glow. The light quickly spread from the original smithy through the new floors, walls, and even ceilings. Brick had continued the silver and glass mixtures through the new structure, and those accents flashed brightly. Before the shapers could finish the connections, the forge finished it for them. The dragon's head that had been above the eastern door appeared above the new doorway, ten feet away. There was an almost snapping sound, and then it was done. The dragon forge had more than doubled in size and capacity. Every dwarf in the compound was now gathered around the smithy. They all dropped to one knee and began a chant to Durin. The light swirled through the structure as sixty dwarves called out to their god in celebration. When the light faded, they all rose and began to clap each other on the back as they made their way to inspect the renovated forge.

Seeing Alexander approaching, Master Ironhammer called out, "What d'ye think? Do the perch look more comfy fer the dragon prince?" The master was beaming with joy. New anvils were being moved into the smithy near the back side of the forge.

"Ha! I think Kai will be quite pleased. Now he can set his dragon tummy right over top of the forge!" Alexander called back. That got a laugh from most of the dwarves in earshot.

Searching for Master Silverbeard, Alexander located him in the study, where he seemed to have established a command post. Dwarves were running in and out to report tasks accomplished and receive the next. He also found Fitz and Rufus, sitting in a chair. Apparently, Fitz now trusted Fibble alone in the tower enough to grant Rufus some freedom.

"Fitz! Let me guess. You tried to sneak a bit of a snack, and Mrs. O'Malley chased you out with a wooden spoon?" Alexander asked.

"Bah! It was a frying pan. Woman can swing that thing like a battle-axe!" The wizard grinned as he complained. Rufus, standing on the brim of the wizard's hat, mimed a tennis swing. "If she wasn't such a good cook, I'd turn her into a platypus!"

Reaching into his bag, he retrieved one of Millicent's pastries and tossed it to Fitz. "I visited Whitehall this afternoon. Millicent sends her love."

Catching the pastry, the wizard said, "Good lad!" as he defended his treat from Rufus' reaching paws. The squirrel had dropped down to cling to Fitz's beard, and was playing a zone defense. Alexander almost wanted to stay and see how Fitz was going to manage to get the treat past the squirrel into his mouth. Even Master Silverbeard was watching with a smile on his face.

Heading into the kitchen, he held up both hands in a defensive gesture. Mrs. O'Malley turned to see who it was, and snorted. "I hear there's a madwoman with a frying pan loose in here?" He grinned at her.

She lifted said pan in one hand. "Out with you! I've work to do!"

"Wait, wait! I come bearing gifts!" he cried. He stepped to the closest countertop and began producing trays of Millicent's pastries. He'd bought twelve dozen, but he was beginning to worry that wasn't enough. Mrs. O'Malley set down the pan. "Are those… Millicent's?" she asked.

"Yup! I was in Whitehall, and thought I'd help out a little with the menu. Hope you don't mind?"

"Not at all, my boy! I was planning to bake through dinner. You've just saved me some time! I'll make a few pies and cakes, to make sure there's plenty. But this is very thoughtful of you!" She hugged Alexander, covering him in cooking stains. He didn't mind a bit.

"Have you made a decision about Mattie?" he asked, deciding to take advantage of his current popularity.

"Aye. She can go. Only because she's right when she says that dung-snuffler of a husband of hers will come looking for her. But you promise me you'll keep her safe!" She picked up the pan again.

"I can't do that. Not where we're going," he said sadly. "But I will promise to do my best to keep her safe. And I'll charge the others with the same." He bowed his head to her.

"That'll have to do, then," she said, quietly. "Now get! You're in the way!"

As he reached the door, and relative safety, he turned and looked back. "Dung-snuffler?"

"Out!" She threw some type of vegetable at him, but he was already gone. She smiled at the closing door for a moment before going back to work.

As the afternoon approached sunset, Alexander wandered around, introducing himself to the dwarves he didn't know, speaking to each of them for a moment or two. This was no interview process. Dwarven honor was above reproach. If these had been chosen by King Thalgrin, they were certainly good enough for Alexander. He simply wanted to get to know his soon-to-be citizens.

As the last rays of the sun departed from the sky, he headed back into the house. Human volunteers from his list began to arrive, and were told to mix and mingle for a while. Groups began to form, some standing around the courtyard or the garden, some sitting at the long tables. A bar was set up, and a couple of dwarves began pouring mugs of ale. The spirits would be held back until after the feast.

Sasha's five volunteers were escorted into the study, where the five founding members of Greystone had gathered. Fitz was in attendance as well. He was going to be discreetly monitoring the players with magic, and would alert them if one of them lied.

Once they were all seated, Sasha introduced the first. A gnome female.

"This is Beatrix. She's a water mage. Level 35. She's also a gem crafter. To save some time, she and all the others here have been griefed by PWP at some point, and are looking for payback." The little gnome smiled and waved at everyone. There were a few generic questions, like was she willing to fight, was she a servant of the Dark One, would she take oaths, etc. Everyone seemed satisfied with her answers. Fitz nodded his head.

Alexander took out his smallest soul crystal, and tossed it to the gnome. "What can you do with this?" he asked.

Catching it handily, she took a look. Her eyes bugged out, and Alexander could almost swear her ears wiggled slightly. "O. M. G.! What can't I do with this? You can charge enchanted items. You can put it in a weapon or armor with almost any enchantment. You can even recharge your own mana with it, if you know how! Do you know what this is worth at auction? Ten thousand, easy!" Alexander grinned. He was carrying more than a hundred of the crystals from the undead they'd killed in the keep.

"We have a few of them. If we accept you, and you help us succeed in this war, you'll each receive one as a bonus." He looked to each of the five. All were nodding their heads.

The other candidates were a level 40 warrior named Dirk, a level 30 7-foot tall barbarian who called herself 'Huge Helga', a level 25 paladin named Benny, and most interestingly, a level 35 half-ogre tank named Lugs. Lugs was nine feet tall, and from what Alexander could tell, just as dumb as one would expect an ogre to be. Though that might just be an act. But put armor on Lug and hand him a shield and a hammer, and he could defend a zip code.

Fitz and the gang approved of all five. Alexander sent each of them a guild invite, and set their ranks as 'recruit'. There they would stay until they took their oaths with Kai. They had access to 10 gold per day each from the guild bank. For weapon repairs.

With that item off the agenda, they all headed outside. Alexander found Lola in the courtyard near the bailey. "Hi, Lola, have you met all the guild members?"

When she shook her head no, he brought her over and introduced to her the founders. The others had already drifted away to mingle. "How are we doing as far as guests?" he asked the young dwarfess.

"Me King's guards all returned an hour ago. The entire dwarf contingent be here in the compound now. So far, thirty-five of the humans from yer list have reported in. A couple named the Redmonds be here as well. Said they were friends?"

Sasha corrected her. "Family. They are always welcome." Lola nodded her head.

"Captain Redmond said the king would arrive shortly. That were maybe ten minutes ago."

She paused for a moment, looking uncomfortable. "There be a… a goblin running about, waving a wand. Told me his name were Fibble? I be a bit worried he'll shoot somebody…"

"BWAHAHA!" Brick laughed. "Fibble's a guild member. The wand won't hurt ye. It be a healing wand. He helped us clear a dungeon o' demons. Took down a mini-boss almost by hisself with that wand! Saved all of our lives, too."

Lola grinned as she pictured that.

"Speaking of guild members, Lola," Alexander began. "Your grandfather mentioned that you have a talent with numbers. Might you be interested in joining the guild and being our treasurer?"

"It'd be me honor!" Lola didn't even think about it.

"I need to know that you're aware of the dangers involved, Lola. We're going right into a battle zone in the morning. Servants of darkness will be trying to eat your face," Alexander warned.

Lola blinked at the vivid description, but quickly recovered. "I be a dwarf o' Broken Mountain. I trained from age 5 with shield and axe. We be headed to a keep of stone, built by me people. Ten o' us could hold that keep against any number o' beasties. Meanin' no offense, sir, but me face ain't so easy to eat!" She grinned.

"HA! I like her! Can we keep her?" Sasha asked. The others all echoed her sentiment.

Alexander sent her a guild invite. "Welcome to Greystone," he said. "We'll discuss the treasurer bit when we have more time."

The others all congratulated Lola, moving off toward the bar. Looking out at the gate, Alexander thought of Jenkins and his men, who'd been on duty out there all day.

He shouted, "Dvorn!" as loudly as he could. In just moments the young dwarf came running.
"Dvorn, those men at the gate must be dying of hunger and thirst. Grab a couple of hands, go in the house and bring me a small table and two chairs, would you please?"

Dvorn dashed off and grabbed the two closest bodies he found, one of which was Thea. They headed into the house.

Walking to the gate, Alexander waved to Jenkins and the others to step inside the bailey.

"You men have been standing here since sunrise. Have any of you even had any food?"

"Aye, sir. Lady Lydia brought us some lunch, and Foster grabbed us some flagons of water when he was in the kitchen," Jenkins answered.

"That won't do." Alexander pretended to think. "Nearly everyone who is expected is already here. Save the king and a few citizens. I want you to leave two men here, inside the ward…"

The dwarves arrived with the table and chairs. Alexander pointed to the wall at one side of the tunnel.

"As I was saying. Two men here, inside the ward, to greet visitors. The rest of you, inside. Bring them back some food when it's served. Relieve them in an hour. You get the idea. But no ale till you're off duty. Which will be in three hours. You all need to mingle and get to know the others. Also, I need to know who from the list fails to show up, if any." He smiled at them. "And Jenkins, once we're at the keep, nobody pulls more than an eight-hour shift. Unless it's unavoidable. Enjoy your evening, gentlemen."

Alexander walked back through the bailey, and was surprised to see the king and a young man who had to be the prince coming around the corner of the main house, as if they'd just come from the stables. Noticing the king was holding two bottles of spirits, Alexander revised that thought. The cellar, not the stables.

Jogging over to greet him, he said, "Apologies, Majesty. If the guards had mentioned you were coming, I'd have been at the gate to greet you."

The king winked at him. Leaning close, he whispered, "Guards never saw me. Remember I told you I executed the ambassador that lived here for espionage? He was caught digging a tunnel into the palace. I decided to keep it. Leads straight to Brick's booze!" He grinned. "I'll show you where it is later." He put one arm around his son. "Alexander, this is my son, Edward. Your new squire. Teach him what you can. Beat him when you need to. Keep him away from the dwarven spirits. And any overly friendly women! Also, try and keep him alive. I'm not sure my lovely wife would want to make a replacement." And with a wink, he was moving toward the garden.

Alexander grinned as Edward rolled his eyes. Teenagers were teenagers everywhere. "Nice to finally meet you, Prince Edward." He held out his hand. The prince shook it.

"Sir Knight. It is an honor. My father has told me many things about you."

"How 'bout we make deal? Outside the throne room, you call me Alexander, and I'll call you Edward," Alexander said.

"Deal." Edward nodded his head. "I dislike all the formality anyway. As I'm to be your squire for the foreseeable future, have you any duties for me?"

"For tonight, enjoy the feast. Mingle with the volunteers, make some friends. Starting in the morning, you stick with me. Are you sleeping in the palace tonight?"

"Yes. Mother's a bit emotional. She wants one last family breakfast before I 'run off to get myself hacked to bits', as she puts it." Another eye roll.

Chuckling, Alexander laid a hand on the prince's shoulder. The prince stiffened for a moment, not used to being touched. Then he relaxed. "Moms are like that. Let her have her small moments. It costs you little, and you'll be glad later. I lost my own mother when I was ten. I'd give anything for a breakfast with her today." Edward looked ashamed.

Patting the boy's shoulder, Alexander continued. "My first bit of advice to you. Do with it what you will. Now! Go mingle. I'll want you to join your father and I in a few minutes. One small formality, and you're free for the night. Oh! And my second bit of advice. Don't flirt with Huge Helga. She might eat you."

He noticed two more of his new citizens drifting in through the gate. Waving, he motioned them towards the garden. Making a short trip into the house, he stuck his head in the kitchen door far enough that he could ask Mrs. O'Malley when she'd like to serve, while still dodging any projectiles if necessary. She informed him that food would be served in five minutes. He asked if she'd like more hands, and she said she had plenty.

Taking her word for it, he headed for the garden. In guild chat, he said, "*Food in five. Sasha, Brick, Max, Lainey, Jules, Thea, Master Silverbeard, please meet me at the bar. ASAP. Brick, clear some space. If anyone sees Master Ironhammer or Fitz, please bring them, too.*"

Locating the king and the prince not far from the bar, he hurried over. "Majesty, would you join me for a brief ceremony before we eat?" he asked.

"Of course. Lead the way." King Charles and the prince followed him to a clear area to one side of the bar. Fitz was nowhere to be found, but the others were moving toward him. He assumed Fitz would appear when the food did. Still, he asked the king, "Do you have a way to summon Fitz for this?"

The king grinned, then shouted, "FITZ!"

Shaking his head, Alexander said, "Thank you, Majesty."
The wizard appeared. "Is the food ready?"

"Mrs. O'Malley informs me she'll be serving in less than five minutes. Please just stand here and look official for a few moments while I make a short speech," Alexander said.

The wizard grumped under his breath, but remained.

When the others had all arrived, he raised the stone under the entire group three feet. Just enough that all those present could see them. He raised his hands, and the group quieted.

"Thank you all for being here this evening," he began in a commanding voice. "I first want to thank King Charles, and King Thalgrin, for their generous support in our endeavor!" He motioned to the king, who gave a wave and a nod.

"I believe I've met most all of you, by now. But for any that I've missed, my name is Alexander. I am one of the founders of the Greystone guild, whom you see here with me." The others all waved a hand or bowed.

"Tomorrow morning, we head to Dire Keep. We expect to be attacked there soon, maybe even as we move into the keep. Our first priority will be shoring up the defenses. Once they are secure, we will begin to focus on housing, crafting facilities, farming, mining, and the like. We may be at war for some time, but there is no reason we cannot live our lives, or even thrive, at the same time!" There was some applause for this.

"From your first step into the Dire Lands tomorrow, you will no longer be humans of Stormforge, or dwarves of Broken Mountain. You will be brothers and sisters in arms!" Louder applause, and some cheering from the dwarves.

"You will support each other without hesitation. You will work and play together. Maybe even die together. And together we will build a home we can all be proud of!" There was a roll of cheering and applause.

“I want you all to meet Master Silverbeard. He is the keep’s chamberlain. He will be the ultimate authority on everything when it comes to day to day operation of the keep. Assume that he speaks with my authority.” Silverbeard took a bow.

“This is the wizard Fitzbindulum. He will be assisting us a great deal in improving the keep and its defenses. You are to give him anything he needs. Within reason. Don’t give him your breakfast.” There was general laughter at that. The king laughed the loudest.

“We will have two royal Princes in our number at Dire Keep. Prince Edward, son of King Charles of Stormguard.” Edward took a bow, to solid applause. “And Prince Kaibonostrum of the Dragons, who is already at the keep, standing guard.” At this there was a mix of surprised exclamations and cheers.

“That will be all the speech-making from me this evening.” Turning to the king he said, “Majesty, would you like to add anything?”

Having spotted the food coming out of the residence, the king grinned. He raised both hands in the air, each still holding a bottle. “The food is served, and the bar is open! he shouted. This received thunderous applause.

Alexander lowered the platform, and the feast began.

Chapter Eight

Keep On Keep'n' On

Alexander awoke before sunrise. He'd barely slept four hours after making sure everyone was properly housed after the feast. Which had begun at sunset, and ended near midnight.

Stepping outside, he saw there were dwarves and humans both moving about, packing up tables and chairs, cleaning the grounds, and loading wagons. Lola and her grandfather were already organizing the activities.

He took a moment to reflect. It had been a good night. Everyone got along, with no arguments more serious than who could hold the most ale. At one point a brave dwarf had attempted to woo Helga. She'd lifted him off his feet, given him a kiss that made him gasp for breath, then dropped him again, saying, "Maybe when you get taller." Much to the amusement of everyone, including the would-be Romeo, who swore he was in love.

The king and Edward had stayed for a couple of hours, then snuck out the same way they'd snuck in. Alexander now knew where the tunnel entrance was.

Lugs had consumed a large amount of alcohol, and began showing off his dance moves on top of the smithy. Fitz encouraged him by throwing several different colored balls of light to hover over his head. His moves weren't bad, and were very popular with the crowd. Looking at the smithy, Alexander saw Lugs still on the roof, snoring.

Hobson had met with Brick, to their mutual satisfaction. The O'Malley's had stayed until the end, hauling away all their dishware and cutlery, and a wagonload of drunken volunteers. Ironhammer and the other masters were all given suites at the Stallion, and would be staying there for some time, as part of Hobson's arrangement with Brick.

The highlight of the evening for Alexander had been Fibble. The goblin, having never been drunk, or seen drunks, began to panic when volunteers began to drop from overindulgence. He ran from body to body, shooting them with his wand, shouting "Pew! Pew!" This was so popular that several folks actually dropped 'dead' in front of the poor goblin, just to get shot. When the charges in his wand ran out, Sasha pulled the confused goblin aside, telling him he'd saved everyone, and was once again her hero. After that, the goblin strutted around with his chest out, and even helped himself to a large mug of ale. Which left him snoring on top of a table before Fitz put him to bed.

Heading downstairs, Alexander found some leftovers arranged on the dining room table for breakfast. His volunteer cooks, human and dwarf, were already in the kitchen preparing breakfast for the troops. He made a mental note that the kitchen needed to be one of their top priorities at the keep. They'd need to be able to feed everyone by dinnertime.

Fitz walked in and sat down, shoving food onto a plate. He'd agreed to accompany Alexander first to the slaughterhouse, then to the keep. After a quick bite to eat, he left the wizard to his breakfast, and headed out to speak with Silverbeard and Lola. "Good morning," he greeted them both.

"Good morning, Alexander." Silverbeard greeted him. Lola smiled. She looked slightly sleep deprived. Or maybe hungover.

"I want to thank you both for organizing last night's feast. I think it went extremely well."

"You're most welcome, Alexander. All part of the job," the dwarf replied. "We'll have everyone up and ready to leave in two hours."

"Excellent. Fitz and I are going to take Brick and head out early. First stop, the slaughterhouse. Then right to the keep. We plan to have the new portal ready in time to move everyone through by two hours after sunrise." Master Silverbeard had been brought up to speed on the poisoned meat. The mages guild had determined that dark magic had indeed been used to poison the meat. The captain had sent word to the butcher that they'd be by at sunrise to pick up another wagonload, and not to tell anyone they were coming. Just in case, the mages were setting a trap. A second wagon full of the already spoiled meat would be leaving the shop and heading toward the compound shortly.

"Lola, were there any from the list of human volunteers that did not show up last night?" he asked.

"Two," she confirmed. "Was attendance mandatory? Should I strike them from the list?"

"No…" Alexander replied. "Attendance was not mandatory. We'll see if they show up this morning. Thank you."

Walking back inside, he found Brick finishing his own breakfast. Seeing him walk in, Fitz began stuffing his pockets with bread and slices of meat and cheese. Rufus jumped to the table and grabbed some cheese for himself, stuffing it into that odd pouch on his belly.

With a wave of his hand, Fitz teleported them to the street outside the slaughterhouse. The three of them stepped inside to find the butcher waiting for them. Beside him was a wagon piled high with barrels of salted meat, wrapped sides of beef, etc. Fitz cast a detection spell on the entire wagon, then nodded his head. Alexander handed a pouch of gold to the butcher, and thanked him, saying they'd be back for more. Then with another wave, the three of them, and the meat wagon, were in the courtyard of Dire Keep.

Kai greeted them in human form, and Brick handed the dragon a large platter of breakfast food from the dining room. As Kai ate his breakfast, they discussed his placement of the portal. He pointed to a spot just to the left of the inner gate, below a stairway that ran up to the wall. Fitz approved. Alexander got to work, raising a block of obsidian from the ground below.

When the block sat in the courtyard, ready for Brick to shape it into columns, Alexander accompanied Kai around to the keep's kitchen. The two of them unloaded the contents of the meat wagon into a cold storage room that Kai had restored to working order. Well, mostly Kai unloaded, as he was able to lift the heavy barrels alone. Alexander carried in some beef sides, then gave up and focused on the kitchen. He used the enchantments he'd learned from Baleron to heat up the ovens, which were magic. Just like the stove tops. They were all low on charges, so he pulled out a couple soul crystals and charged up the 'appliances'. The kitchen was even larger than the one at the manor. He hoped it would be large enough for their purposes.

When both he and Kai were done, they headed back to Fitz and Brick. The dwarf was just finishing the second column. Fitz stepped in to begin the infusion of portal magic.

There was a significant chunk of obsidian left over. Brick had asked Alexander to pull more than they needed. Brick put his hands on the stone, and began to shape it. By the time Fitz was done creating the portal, Brick had shaped the obsidian into a roaring dragon's head. Asking Kai to carry it for him, then place it above the main door of the keep, Brick fused the obsidian into the stone of the keep.

The four-foot high, roaring dragon's head would be the first thing anyone saw as they walked through the portal.

They gave Fitz and Brick a few moments to rest. Then, almost precisely two hours after sunrise, Fitz opened the portal. And the new citizens of Dire Keep began to file through.

Master Silverbeard led the way, to direct incoming traffic. Lola remained behind to make sure things went as orderly as possible at the compound. Making note of everyone who passed through the portal.

Behind the chamberlain came the dwarven guards. They immediately spread out, manning the wall above the gate. Then came the wagons. Moving to one side or the other as they crossed through, making room for the others. Citizens followed, and immediately began unloading the supply wagons into the storehouse. Wagons with furniture moved toward the donjon, where they were unloaded as well. They'd need to make two or three trips today, in order to move all the furniture and supplies. The two dwarven merchants had received a list from Master Silverbeard, and remained behind in Stormforge to purchase what they could.

Two wagons of fruit, vegetables, and other perishables moved directly to the kitchen entrance around the side of the main building. Longer term supplies like rice, grains, and salt went into the storehouse. Sasha, Lydia, and two druid volunteers took a cart loaded with fruit trees to one side, near the stables. There they began to plant the trees and imbue them with nature magic to make them stronger, and to help them grow faster. Each of these trees were to be the progenitors of an orchard, or grove, of their own.

Max, Lainey, and Lorian each took a squad of two hunters outside the walls and began to search the area. They'd also bring back any game they came across. Jules and Edward stayed with Alexander as he moved about. Fitz and Kai headed up onto the wall, and began casting enchantments for strength, magic resistance, and other defensive measures. Mattie and the other cooks began organizing the kitchen and preparing to make lunch.

With the kitchen in order, and the scouts out, Alexander focused on bigger picture items. They needed some kind of alert system in case of an attack. And a way to relay orders. Shouts may not be heard. He could form a raid group, but the limit was 100, and all told he had 119 souls joining him at the keep.

Then an idea struck him. "Good morning, Jeeves," he said aloud. There was no response. Maybe he needed to be in the control room? He laid a hand each on Jules and Edward, and teleported the three of them up to the control room.

"*Good morning, master,*" Jeeves said as soon as they'd arrived.

"Hi, Jeeves!" Jules waved at the table.

"Jeeves, this is Prince Edward of Stormforge. He is under our protection for a while," Alexander said, motioning for Edward to put his hand on the table.

"*Identity acknowledged: Prince Edward. Ward of the masters. Welcome to Dire Keep.*"

Having Jules touch the table, he said "And this is Jules. Member of the Greystone clan."

"Identity acknowledged: Jules. Welcome to Dire Keep."

"Jeeves, I have some questions. Can you make it so you and I can speak to other throughout the keep?"

"I can hear you speak anywhere within the keep, within twenty-five yards of the walls, or within the mine, master. However, I can only speak to you when you are in, or very near, one of the structures. This includes the walls."

"I see. Thank you. Now, is there a way I can speak to all of the citizens and guests at once?"

"Yes, master, there are two ways. You can speak through the structures, as I'm doing now. Your voice will transmit from every structure at the same time. Or you can make announcements, which will transmit directly to each citizen and guest. You can also transmit individual announcements, though you will not be able to hear a response."

"Okay, Great. Thank you, Jeeves. Let's establish a protocol. When I say 'Jeeves, emergency message.' I want you to send my voice to every citizen and guest. When I say 'Jeeves, loudspeaker.' I want you to send my voice through all the structures."

"Understood, master. Protocols established."

"Next. Within your defensive capabilities, do you have a way to bind or imprison someone?"

"We have dungeon cells in the lower levels that can be used to imprison a being, master. As for defensive capabilities, at higher levels I can stun a designated target, and transport them to a cell. I am afraid that at my current level, my abilities are quite limited, master."

"And how do you gain levels?" Edward asked. Then he looked sheepishly at Alexander. "Sorry."

"I gain levels through an increase in progress points. Points can be earned in several ways. Increases in my population. Addition of new

structures, or improvement of existing structures through expansion. Increased production levels. Also, successful defense from enemy attacks. Trade agreements and alliances will also grant points. As well as certain achievements of my masters and citizens. For example, having a master crafter as a citizen grants 10 points. A journeyman grants 5. So, if a citizen who is a journeyman crafter achieves master status, I would receive 5 additional points."

"That makes sense. And you are currently level 10, correct?"

"*Yes, master. I was formerly level 15, but the loss of my citizens and the lack of any production, combined with the deterioration of my physical condition, have lowered my level.*"

"But why have all the new citizens not raised it back up some?" Alexander asked.

"*My next level increase by population would be at fifty citizens, master. The next beyond that at one hundred. At the moment, my population is only 5.*"

"Of course! We've not officially made anyone citizens yet!" Alexander smacked his forehead.

"Jeeves, if all of the guests here became citizens, except for Edward, Fitz, and Kai, what sort of level increase would you receive?"

"*I would increase two levels from population growth. Until a guest becomes a citizen, I am not aware of their personal information, and am unable to calculate any bonus points, master. In addition, bringing me back to fully intact physical status will restore a lost level.*"

"Right! Then let's get busy!" Alexander had a new mission. "Jeeves, one last thing. Are you able to tell when someone uses one of the portals, or the transport mirrors?"

"*Yes, master. Someone tried to use one of the mirrors last night. One of those you set on the floor. Their essence was destroyed. I received a point for successful defense.*" Jeeves sounded pleased.

"Okay, Jeeves, I want you to notify myself and the other owners if anyone attempts to use the mirrors or the portals."

"*Of course, master.*"

After checking that the two mirrors were still securely facing downward, Alexander teleported the three of them back down to courtyard.

Running up the stairs to the top of the wall, he approached Kai and Fitz.

"I just had a conversation with Jeeves," he began. "We'll pick up two keep levels just by making all these folks citizens. That may improve the defenses faster than we can do it manually. I think we should start taking oaths. What do you two think?"

Fitz just shrugged, while Kai nodded his head. "Where shall we do this?"

"How about in front of the main building entrance? Under the gaze of the black dragon? It would give some symbolic meaning, since we're making the dragon the guild symbol," Jules suggested.

"Great idea, Jules!" Alexander hugged her. "Jeeves, loudspeaker, please," he said.

When he heard Jeeves say, "*Go ahead, master.*" He cleared his throat.

"Attention all volunteers. Please report to the courtyard in front of the main keep entrance immediately. Everyone but the guards on the wall. Thank you."

He smiled as heads popped up and began to look around at the sound of his voice. Jules giggled.

They made their way down to the courtyard. Meeting Master Silverbeard and Lola at the main door, Alexander asked, "Lola, do you have the lists of volunteers?" She nodded her head in the affirmative.

"Did everyone on the list show up, and come through the portal?" he asked.

"All came through the portal except the two dwarven merchants, and Jenkins and his squad, who remained to guard them," she confirmed.

"So, all told, there should be 111 bodies here. Minus the nine who are out scouting. And Fitz, Kai, Fibble, and Edward, Sasha, Jules, Brick, and myself. There are twelve on the wall, keeping watch. That leaves 82 volunteers that should be gathered here," he calculated.

Raising his voice, he shouted, "Please line up, facing me, in three rows!" As the volunteers situated themselves, he asked Lola, "Please count them; confirm all 82 are present."

While she did that, Alexander turned to Kai. "Do we need to do this individually? Or can they swear as a group?"

"As a group will suffice. Though I will need to touch each one to infuse the magic that binds the oath," the dragon said.

When Lola returned from counting and adjusting the lines into three roughly equal lengths, she nodded. "Eighty-two volunteers."

Alexander called out, "It is time for you all to take your oaths as citizens. Prince Kai will speak the oath to you, and you will repeat it back to him. Are you all ready? If you wish to back out, now is the time. There will be no penalty. You will simply be returned home."

He waited fifteen seconds, and heard no requests to leave. Nodding to Kai, he stepped back.

The dragon stepped forward, and in a deep, ground-rumbling voice said, "Your oaths shall be sworn on your lives. Bound to your souls. Violation of your oaths will cause you to be incapacitated until you can be judged for your violation. A judgement of guilt means death. One last time, any who do not wish to utter the oaths, stand aside now."
Still, none of them moved.

"Very well. Repeat this oath. 'On my life, I swear my loyalty to Dire Keep, and my obedience to its masters, the leaders of the Greystone Guild."

He made some simple hand gestures as he spoke, and a blue aura extended from him, encompassing all those who stood in the lines. It also reached into the obsidian dragon's head above the doorway.

As one, they spoke the oath. A few fumbled with the words, but managed to follow the lead of the others.

Then Kai walked down the lines, touching each of the volunteers on the shoulder, and speaking a word. As he did, a black dragon icon appeared above the head of each one, then faded away.

It took less than ten minutes from start to finish.

"Thank you, all. You are now citizens of Dire Keep! I officially welcome you, and give you my own oath that Greystone will do everything possible to protect you, and help you thrive in your new homes!"

An enormous gong sounded throughout the keep, and there was a swirl of light around the tower. The keep had gained a level!

There was a resounding cheer. As the group began to disperse to head back to their duties, Alexander opened guild chat.

"*Beatrix, Benny, Dirk, Lugs, and Helga, would the five of you please man the walls for a few minutes so the guards can come down and take their oaths? Thank you.*"

As those five moved to relieve the guards, and the dwarves made their way down, Alexander stepped inside to speak to Jeeves.

"How are we doing, Jeeves. I saw you gained a level."

"*Yes, master. I am currently compiling the personal achievements of all the new citizens. This will take me a few minutes. I am confident that another increase in level is imminent.*"

"Very good, Jeeves. There will be more citizens added shortly, and another group this evening. We'll have your population over 100 in no time."

The guards gathered around Kai and took a knee. They repeated the oath, and were bound to the keep like the others. Again, the dragon head above the door glowed. The guards were released to return to their posts. So far, 94 volunteers had become citizens. With the five founding members as owners, that put them at 99. When the group came back from scouting, the volunteers in that group would put them over 100.

Alexander felt a tug on his pants leg. Looking down, he saw Fibble looking back up at him. The little goblin had been hiding behind Sasha and Jules, 'protecting' them from the dragon.

"Fibble want swear oath, too. Be part of big clan. Bigger clan stronger," he said. Alexander smiled at the goblin, and looked to Fitz, who just shrugged.

"Fibble, you must swear your oath to the dragon. Can you do that?" he asked.

Fibble looked terrified. "Dragon not eat? Good dragon?" he nearly whimpered.

Sasha knelt down and put an arm around him. "Very good dragon. Friend. Its okay, Fibble. I'm right here."

The little goblin nodded his head. Then he turned to Kai, and bowed. "Fibble protect friends. Protect home. Even protect good dragon. Swear on life!"

Kai smiled without showing his teeth, for the benefit of the little green warrior. He touched Fibble on the head. "I cannot imagine a sincerer oath." A black dragon icon appeared over Fibble's head.

Just then, the gong sounded again, twice this time. The light display around the tower was more spectacular than before. The keep had gained two more levels.

Everybody clapped and cheered, and Fibble beamed at the attention, thinking it was all for him. "Fibble make big magic!" he cheered.

Lugs lifted the small goblin up, and tossed him in the air. The goblin screamed, until Lugs caught him, then did it again. Figuring out it was a game, the scream turned into cries of, "Higher!" After half a dozen tosses, Lugs set the little goblin on his shoulder. Fibble seemed content to ride there for a while.

"It's time to make another supply run," Alexander said. Lola and her grandfather began rounding up citizens to bring the wagons back to the portal for the next load. Hopefully they'd be able to bring the rest of their supplies through this time.

When everyone was gathered, Fitz opened the portal, and the empty wagons moved through. As they arrived at the manor, folks immediately began to load them with stacks of supplies and furniture, some of which had arrived since they left. There were three already full wagons waiting to be taken through.

The dwarven merchants, Thagin and Drellin, were waiting for them, along with Jenkins and his squad. The merchants handed Silverbeard his list. "We were able to get everything ye listed, and more," Drellin said. "We put a dent in yer wallet!" Thagin added, grinning.

Jenkins stepped forward to report. "All secure in the compound, sir. Two individuals tried to enter uninvited during the day. Both were teleported to the prison and are being questioned. Captain Redmond said to tell you the mages caught a warlock and two warriors this morning with the meat trap. One guard was killed in the fight." At this, he lowered his head.

Alexander put a hand on his shoulder. "I'm sorry, Jenkins. I'm hoping that giving them Dire Keep as a target will put an end to the fighting in Stormforge." All the soldiers nodded in agreement.

"Aye. Thank you, sir." The soon-to-be sergeant replied. "Also, the captain mentioned he has more folks who'd like to go. If you're interested, sir.

"Did he say where he'd be?" Alexander was intrigued.

"Aye, sir. He's at the palace," Jenkins reported.

Alexander turned to Silverbeard. "I need to go to the palace. Load up here, and if I'm not back, go ahead and return without me. I'll catch up."

He left for the palace at jog. Reaching the outer gate, he received salutes from the guards on duty. They waved him though, and he continued through the inner gate. He found Captain Redmond in the courtyard, talking to some soldiers. Alexander waited patiently at a distance while he finished his conversation.

When the captain waved him over, he said, "Jenkins told me you lost a guard this morning. I'm sorry."

The captain nodded in acceptance. "He was a good lad. New to the guard. Probably shouldn't have been there, but he was eager. His brother is a guard, too. The lad wanted to be just like him."

Somehow that made Alexander feel worse. "Were you able to capture the dung-snufflers?" he asked.

"Dung-snufflers?" The captain laughed at him.
Alexander hung his head. "Mrs. O'Malley, rubbing off on me," he explained.

"Well, then yes. We captured three dung-snufflers. A warlock who cast the poison spell into the meat, and two warriors acting as his escort. They were apparently part of the other group we fought yesterday, and just hadn't been in the building when we attacked. There may still be others, as well. I've had the mages set a trap in the basement of that building, where the rogue escaped into the sewers. As well as several random traps throughout the sewer system. Nobody with good intentions should be down there anyway. The mage's guild is also beefing up magical protections around the city. They're taking this personally. And I think they're just happy to have something interesting to do."

"Glad to hear it. Maybe between the big shiny target I'm painting on myself, and making it harder for them to move around here, they'll leave the city alone," Alexander said.

"Jenkins also said you wanted to speak with me about more volunteers?"

"Aye. One in particular. One of the king's own. A… specialist, if you get my meaning."

"Ah. I see. The king is worried about Edward?" Alexander asked. Trying to think of any other reason the king would want to send a spy to the keep.

"Worried about all of you. As am I," the captain said.

"Well, this specialist is certainly welcome. I've nothing to hide from the king. Will he take the oath?" Alexander asked.

"Yes, *she* will. With the provision that once her services are no longer needed, she'll be released from the oath to return here."

"Fine by me. But Jenkins made it sound like more than one person was coming?"

"Yes. I've got six more guards who have volunteered. All good men. Also, old Lars, the fisherman. Used to run a fishing boat, but couldn't keep up in his old age. So now he fishes from the shore. Sings to the fish. Catches more than anybody. It's the damnedest thing. He heard about you taking volunteers too late. He'd been out fishing. I'll vouch for him. Been here since my dad was small. Told him and the others to be at your gate at noon."

"Sounds just fine. Thank you. And you have a couple prisoners who tried to sneak into the compound?"

"One prisoner. Two got teleported. One was a boy working for one of the furniture merchants. He didn't know about the wards and just ran right in.

We let him go. He said the merchant was looking to sell you more beds, by the way. The other was a man says he was looking for his wife. We're still questioning him."

"We had a few women volunteers. What is his wife's name?" Alexander asked.

"Mattie. Man claims she was kidnapped and dragged into the compound."

"HA! The very dung-snuffler himself!" Alexander bent over laughing. When he caught his breath, he told the captain Mattie's story. And Mrs. O'Malley's opinion of the man. Which caused the captain to laugh, too.

"You can release him, if you like. Tell him his wife is divorcing him by day's end. And that he's not welcome at Dire Keep. Actually, hold on a minute. Let me see if there's anything she needs from her house before he's loose."

Alexander called out in guild chat. "*Anybody able to get to Mattie in the kitchen, quickly?*"

Sasha replied. "*I'm in the kitchen now. Helping with lunch. What's up?*"

"*Mattie's husband got caught sneaking in the compound. Captain's holding him. Ask her if she wants him held so she can retrieve things from her house or anything.*"

There was a delay, during which he assumed Sasha was speaking to Mattie.

"*She says there's nothing she needs back there. And asks if there's any chance the guards would break his arms?*"

"*HA! I'll ask. Thanks.*"

Looking at the captain, he said, "Mattie respectfully requests that her husband fall down and break both arms." He grinned. "Failing that, there's nothing she needs from her home, so you can let him go as you wish."

"There are more than a few guards who would be happy to oblige. The man truly IS a dung-snuffler." The captain grinned.

Alexander headed back to the compound. The last of the wagons was being loaded. Finding Lola, he said, "There are eight more volunteers coming at noon. I'll stay here and bring them over when they arrive. Do me a favor? Mark a box to the left of the portal as you face the wall. Ten-foot square. Tell everyone to keep that area clear for incoming teleports. Thank you."

Alexander raised a table and bench in the front courtyard near the main house, so he could work and keep the gate in view. He had roughly two hours before noon. Pulling out the block of obsidian from his bag, he began to break off small pieces, roughly a half inch square. Into each one he cast the 'Undying' spell, and a single charge of healing light, before setting it down. When he'd made about sixty of them, he decided to take a break. An idea had struck him. Walking over to the smithy, where the dwarven masters were all busily crafting, he called to Master Ironhammer.

"What can I do fer ye, Alexander?" the master asked.

Alexander showed him one of the small enchanted blocks. "I need some advice. And maybe some help. What can you quickly provide a hundred and fifty of, that we could use to secure these to a person. Be it chain, bracelet, pin, or whatever. Brick will be shaping these into small dragons, the symbol of our guild, and Dire Keep. And what will it cost me?"

The dwarf looked thoughtful for a moment. Reaching into his bag, he brought out a simple metal bracelet. "Apprentices make these during training. Nothing fancy, but sturdy. They make 'em by the dozen. I could have ye hundred fifty of these in an hour if ye open the portal."

Then he pulled out a very simple metal necklace. "These be apprentice work, too. Take maybe till noon tomorrow for hundred fifty."

Lastly, he pulled out a simple pin, not much different than a safety pin. On steroids. "I think this be your best bet. Hundreds of these layin' around in the smithy. Ye can have 'em for free. But I have proposal for ye."

“I’m listening,” Alexander said.

“We have three masters and four journeymen here now that have the shaping skill. If ye’ll give us each one o’ them stones, that be fifteen total, we’ll shape em fer ye, and mount them pins in the back. Seven o’ us can do a hundred fifty in an hour.”

“Deal!” Alexander smiled. He gave the first sixty stones to the master. “I’ll go make the rest.”

Sitting back down at his table, Alexander began to crank out stone after stone. His mana got low after another thirty, so he drank a mana potion, and ate some fruit he’d snagged at breakfast. Then he got back to work. Master Ironhammer sent an apprentice to pick up more stones when he’d reached a hundred and twenty total. The young dwarf exchanged forty-five pins for sixty stones. The dwarves had taken their share off the top. Alexander smiled, and kept working. He managed another forty before both his mana and stamina were low. That should be enough. Here were less than a hundred and thirty citizens, counting the new ones he was waiting on, at the keep.

Taking a rest, he picked up one of the finished pins. The dragon looked just like the one above the smithy’s door. That was perfect! Turning it over to look at the back, he saw the back side of the pin was embedded right into the stone. It would make a nice, sturdy clasp. His intent was to have them all turned into necklaces, but this would do to get his people protected today.

There was a shout at the gate, and Alexander saw a wagon with dwarves standing outside. He disabled the wards, and waved them in. As Thea had promised, the miners had arrived. He welcomed them in, then laughed as they ignored him and went straight for the dragon forge. He went back to his table.

The apprentice came back with sixty more pins, and took the last forty stones. Confirming the math, he smiled. With a hundred and forty-five pins, he’d have some extras for new recruits. Sliding the finished pins in his bag, he sat and relaxed as his mana and stamina recharged. He contemplated expansion plans for the wall surrounding the keep. They needed to have some secure farmland. Rather than try to move the existing walls, it made more sense to build a smaller second wall that circled the first. Maybe… two hundred yards out? The current wall curved in an arc about three thousand feet long. Some quick math in his head… that would be between forty and fifty acres of land between the walls. That should provide enough space for crops to be planted, and livestock to be pastured. He'd talk it over with the farmers.

With the lake and the creek close by, they could easily irrigate. Maybe even add a moat outside the wall! He'd always wanted a castle with a moat. He'd even tried to talk his parents into adding one when they built Olympus. His mom had been willing. But the engineers had said words like 'groundwater seepage' and 'fried servers' and the dream died.

A call from the gate brought Alexander out of his reverie. His volunteers had arrived. He turned off the wards and waved them inside. Once they'd cleared the inner ward, he reactivated them.

He recognized a few of the guards from around the palace. The old man was obviously the fisherman, Lars. The woman was much younger than he'd expected for a trained spy. He realized the captain hadn't said her name.

"Welcome. I'm Alexander. Please come inside." He led them into the house and through the lounge to the dining room. When they'd all taken seats, he said, "Before I get to know each of you a bit, I want to make sure you're clear on a few things. First, Dire Keep is a dangerous place. Likely a war zone within the next few days. We'll be fighting servants of some dark being they think is a god. There's a decent chance you'll be killed." He paused for effect.

"Second, you'll have to take an oath of loyalty, and swear to serve the keep, and Greystone. This is a life oath, enforced with dragon magic. Betrayal means death." Hearing no comments, he continued.

The older man was sitting at the end of the table. He looked to be in his late 50s or 60s. Tall with a lean but muscular build. "You must be Lars?" he asked.

"Aye, that's me. I hear you found a good fishin' hole. Bit tired of the harbor. Time to try something new. Catch some freshwater fish for a change." He smiled. The captain had vouched for him, so Alexander wasn't going to question him more. "Nice to meet you, Lars."

Looking toward the young woman, he said, "And you are?"

She smiled coyly at him. "I'm Sophie! I'm an explorer and a scout. I can also cook really good bear stew. My pa wants to marry me off to some nobleman's brat. But I want to make my own choices. Dire Keep seems to be where the adventure is!" She was young enough to sell the wayward waif story. And pretty enough that the men were distracted by her blonde hair and big green eyes.

He had no intention of refusing her, but he had to ask, if only to make it look good to the others. "Sophie, how old are you? Is your pa gonna come beating down my gates to drag you home?"

She snort-laughed. "I'm old enough. And my pa barely leaves his house. He'd never get riled up to fight over me." Good enough.

Alexander looked at the guards. "Who is the squad leader here?"

A tall man in his late thirties raised his hand. "Corporal Taylor, sir."

"Nice to meet you, Taylor. Though I think we've spoken before, at the east gate, maybe?" Taylor nodded. Alexander looked at the whole squad. They all seemed solid and calm.

"Captain Redmond recommended your squad. And I trust him completely. We're on a tight schedule, and we need to get moving. I'll get to know you all better in the coming days. For now, I welcome all of you to Dire Keep. When we go through the portal, you'll need to wait in the courtyard so that Prince Kai can have you swear your oaths. After that you'll get work and sleeping assignments. They should be serving lunch, and we have some really good cooks!"

Leading them outside, he stopped at the smithy to pick up the rest of the pins. Then he led his group, along with the miners he managed to drag away from the smithy, back to the portal, and they stepped into Dire Keep.

Lola was waiting for him, along with Kai. He introduced the newcomers, and left them in Lola's hands. He handed her a pin before she stepped away. He strode over to where Silverbeard was directing the movement of supplies into the storehouse.

"Master Silverbeard, would you happen to have an empty sack?" he asked. The old dwarf instantly produced a leather bag. Alexander took it, and filled it with the dragon pins. He saved one for himself. "Have they started serving lunch?" he asked.

"Just now," the dwarf answered. "There be tables set up outside near the kitchen."

"Thank you. In that bag are pins with the Undying spell, and a single charge of a healing spell infused into them. There are enough for everyone to get one, plus a few extras. I'd like you and Lola to make sure everyone gets one? The founders don't need them, they've got their own enchantments, much like yours."

"Jeeves, loudspeaker, please," he said. He waited a few seconds, then announced, "Your attention please. If you haven't already heard, or smelled, our first delicious meal is being served in the yard outside the kitchen. Please make your way there. Jenkins, I'd like your squad and Taylor's to grab yourselves some food and drink, and then relieve the guards on the wall, please."

Leading Master Silverbeard to the lunch area, he motioned for the dwarf to begin passing out pins. Alexander stood up on a chair.

"Just one quick thing as you all enjoy your lunch." He held up his black dragon pin. "Master Silverbeard will be handing each of you a dragon pin like this one. I want you all to wear this pin at all times. Except when you're bathing. That could be painful." There was laughter from the crowd.

"This is not just the symbol of Greystone and the keep, this pin may save your life. It is enchanted with a spell that will keep a mortal blow from killing you. Keeping you at 1% health. Unless you take a 2nd blow. It also contains a healing spell that will return 2,000 points to your health instantly. So! IF you happen to get shot in the face with an arrow, and you find yourself laying on the ground with 1% health, trigger the heal in your pin. Then go find a healer. Do NOT pull the arrow out before healing yourself, or you'll die. You need to heal before you take any additional damage. Everybody understand?" Heads nodded.

"These are not to be given away, or sold. Under any circumstance. Bind them to you, so that they cannot be stolen. I swore an oath to you all that I'd do my best to keep you alive. This is part of fulfilling that oath. Oh! And I would prefer, by the way, that you all try to avoid taking any arrows to the face."

Alexander stepped down to the sound of laughter. He watched as citizens were handed pins, and promptly put them on their clothes. Feeling a bit proud of himself, he headed into the kitchen.

Sasha gave him a look as he walked in the door. "Really? Don't get shot in the face?" The ladies in the kitchen chortled.

"Seemed like a good idea at the time. I'm not a good public speaker, okay? Next time, you do it," he mumbled. Looking around, he spotted Mattie. "Mattie? As of now you have formal permission to get a divorce. Go see father Alric when you have some time, and he'll help you make it official."

Mattie smiled at him, as the ladies of the kitchen gathered round to hug her. Alexander bailed as quickly as he could.

A message from Lorian popped up in guild chat. "*We've found some adventurers in the forest. Moving toward the keep about five miles out. They are killing beasts as they go, much like you did.*"

"*How many?*" Alexander asked

"*Four. Two warriors, a mage, and a healer. They are fighting level 30 beasts, and barely succeeding.*"

Max spoke up. "*They could just be questing. Doesn't sound like they're much of a threat.*"

"*I agree. Lorian, if they're not taking the meat and hide from their kills, please have one of your guys collect those from the corpses. We'll let these adventurers do some of our work for us. He can follow behind to keep tabs on them and alert you if they become a problem.*" Alexander wrote.

"*It will be as you say.*" Lorian replied.

Back out in the courtyard, Master Silverbeard had handed out pins, and was sitting down to eat his lunch. Not wanting to disturb the old man, Alexander decided to head to the wall.

On his way, he passed a group of miners. They were sort of shuffling around, adjusting their packs, checking a wagon of supplies.

Right! The mine! Completely slipped my mind. We haven't cleared it yet. These guys can't get to work until we do.

In guild chat he said, "*I've got a gang of miners here with nothing to do. Who wants to help clear the mine? Max and Lainey, not you.*"

"*Jules and I will come.*" Sasha said.

"*Lugs, Helga, and I will come.*" Beatrix replied. "*Benny and Dirk had to log.*"

"*Ok, that should do fine. Meet me at the front gate in ten.*" *Alexander said.*

Approaching the miners, he asked, "Who's the most senior among you?"

Two miners stepped forward. An older human man, and a dwarf of indeterminate age. The dwarf spoke first. "We be two master miners. I be the eldest. Me name's Grimble. This here be Jason." He motioned to the human master.

"Okay. Jason, any objection to Grimble being mine foreman?" The man shook his head. "Fine. Grimble, the job is yours if you want it?"

"Aye, I'll take it. I worked this mine a bit before the baron started takin' slaves. That be me King choosed me. It were a good mine. We'll have it back in shape right quick," the dwarf grumbled.

"Thank you, Grimble. And I'm glad to hear you already know the mine. We're about to go clear it, would you like to join us?" The dwarf nodded in the affirmative. "Fine. We'll meet in a few minutes at the front gate. Just a few other things. First, none of my citizens works more than an eight-hour shift. They can work two in a day, if they wish, but only with 8 hours of rest in between. I'll leave it to you how to schedule them. If you want to work it in three shifts, just follow that rule. You have...." Alexander thought about his lists. Ten dwarves, eight humans. "I believe you have eighteen miners. We may add more later. The other thing is, each miner may keep 10% of what he produces. But all production must be turned in to you at the end of each shift. Their 10% will be awarded to them at the end of each week, either in ore, gems, or gold. Their choice. Stealing from the mine will be considered a breach of their oaths. Is that agreeable?"

Alexander had learned from his interviews that miners working for a clan or company normally got to keep 5%. And that, at least among the human miners, theft was common practice. So, he expected this would be acceptable.

There was murmuring among the gathered miners, and much bobbing of heads. Grimble replied, "Aye, that be more than fair."

"Fine. See you at the gate in five minutes," Alexander said as he moved away. He finally reached the wall, and ran up the stairs to find Kai and Fitz working on more enchantments. "We're going to clear the mine. Any magical padlocks or anything I should know about?" he asked Fitz.

“HA!” The wizard laughed. “The king’s guards closed the doors and padlocked them, but no magic. And I expect the doors have weakened a good bit by now. You should just be able to bash your way in. If I remember right, there were only six branches, none of them all that deep. The baron used slaves during most of his time here, and slaves work more slowly than paid miners.”

“Thank you. Our new mine foreman, Grimble, actually worked the mine before the baron went all assholish. I’m taking him with me now.”

Changing subjects, he said, “Kai, Fitz, I was thinking about adding a second wall, maybe two hundred yards out. To give our farmers and shepherds a safe space to work. Maybe irrigate from the creek? Or from a moat? What do you think?”

The wizard and the dragon both looked out over the meadow surrounding the wall. Kai spoke first. “That could work. I would discuss it with the masons, let them investigate the ground. And bring the farmers in, too. This land may not be good for farming. I like the idea of irrigation, though.”

“And the moat!” Fitz added with enthusiasm. “We can have our very own moat monster. I believe we still have a couple eggs stored at the guild tower. This will be fun!”

Shaking his head, he said, “I’m all in for the moat monster. Beatrix is a water mage, she should be able to help with the irrigation and moat. Kai, would you mind gathering the farmers and masons and starting that discussion? I need to go clear the mine, but I want to start on walls as soon as possible. Fitz, can you fetch whichever guild mages are willing to help? We’ll pay them in dwarven spirits, or gold, or whatever currency they like.”

“Aye, lad,” Fitz said, as Kai nodded his head. “The guild will be happy to help. This Dark One’s minions have become an annoyance in our city. I’ll stop at Millicent’s first, and pick up some bribes.” He waggled his bushy white eyebrows.

“You know that one of our cooks, Edna, worked for Millicent? I bet if you’re real nice to her, she’d make you some treats.” Alexander laughed as the wizard perked up even more.

“Thank you, gentlemen. I’ll check in as soon as I get back from the mine. Alexander headed down to the gate to meet his new party.

Finding everyone waiting, he sent around group invites. Sasha and Jules had brought along their goblin protector. It seems Fibble quickly figured out that if he ‘protected’ Sasha while she was in the kitchen, he’d receive tasty treats. The goblin was smarter than he looked. Initially he was going to tell Fibble to stay. But he had promised the little guy adventures. And the mine should be relatively safe. And he saw that Fibble was wearing a dragon pin. So he let him come. The last member was Edward. Alexander had decided the boy should see some combat. Though he hoped there wouldn’t be any serious fights in the mine.

As they walked toward the mine, he looked over his group. There was Lugs, the tank, in his massive plate armor. Alexander hoped the tunnels were high enough for him to walk in. Next came Helga, with her two-handed barbarian axe. She’d need room to swing that. So far, not the ideal combination for a tunnel fight. But he needed to learn how to work with these folks. Jules could stealth and do back-stabby damage. Grimble was carrying a shield and hammer. Sasha, Beatrix, Fibble and himself would be in the back, casting dps and heals. Edward would remain between Sasha and Alexander at all times. The prince was level 25, but Alexander suspected this was mainly due to weapons training and completion of non-combat quests generated by his father and maybe Captain Redmond.

Chapter Nine

Mine Your Own Business

Upon reaching the mine entrance, they found it mostly overgrown with shrubs and high grass. Lugs and Helga cleared the way in just minutes, the half-ogre simply ripping the trees up like weeds, and Helga sweeping her blade like a lawnmower.

The doors to the mine had been knocked off their hinges. So. At some point in the last two hundred years, someone had been inside. Hopefully they were long gone.

The main tunnel, at least, was plenty large enough for Lugs. Wide enough for two cart tracks, and with twelve-foot-high ceilings. Lugs was just able to clear the support beams. But he'd have to remember not to take any overhead swings.

They moved into the mine, and Grimble called a halt. He stepped forward, sniffing the air, and examining the ground. Shaking his head, he returned to report.

"There be cave troll tracks. And somethin' smaller. Clawed feet. Likely kobolds, or bugbears. The troll tracks be older."

"Right. Let's hope the little guys drove out the trolls," Alexander said. "Sasha? What's the plan?"

Sasha looked to Grimble. "What's the layout of this place?"

The dwarf got down on one knee and used his hammer handle to draw a diagram. He drew the main shaft they were in, a long straight line. From the main shaft, he drew four side shafts, each one having a couple boxes along them that indicated rooms for stored equipment. One branch went to the left, not very far. The other three went to the right.

"This be how it looked when I left. The good veins all ran to the north. We abandoned the south shaft when the vein died out pretty quick," he said.

"Fitz told me when they cleared the place, there were six shafts. I didn't think to ask if that included the main tunnel. So, there is at least one more. Maybe two," Alexander added.

"Right. So, we'll start with the left shaft, and clear that first," Sasha said. "Jules, I want you in the back of the group as a lookout. Stay stealthed. Call out in group chat if anything approaches us from behind. Grimble, I'd like you to lead the way, as you know the mine, and can check to make sure it's stable. But if Jules sees something, I need you to move to the back right away. We'll need a second tank to defend our rear if it comes to that. Lugs, you're tanking the front. Helga right behind. Then Alexander and Beatrix, myself and Fibble. Edward you stay with me."

The group moved forward, following Grimble. The dwarf ranged back and forth across the main tunnel, check the tracks, the support beams, and occasionally putting his hand to the ground to check the stone around them. After about five minutes, they reached the first side shaft, branching off to the left. As they moved in, Jules stealthed and paused at the junction for a while. The rest of the group moved on down the shaft. This one was only about a hundred yards long, with a single room. Cut off from the light of the main shaft, Alexander brought out the diamond he'd enchanted with a light spell. It glowed brightly enough to light the tunnel for about thirty feet. That wasn't going to be good enough.

"Hold on, folks. I need to make some light," he said.

"No need!" Grimble called out. He reached into his bag and pulled out three headbands with a reflective box looking thing attached. He put one on his head, and touched a button on the box. Clear white light like a flashlight beam shone out from the box, illuminating the tunnel about fifty feet down. He handed one to Lugs, and the other to Helga.

He said, "Critters what live in the dark don't like bright light. They'll attack those what carries the lights first."

This got a laugh from Helga. "What a sweet gift." She winked at Grimble. The dwarf grinned back, and they got moving again.

They reached the room about halfway down the shaft. Inside, Alexander could see several sets of blood red eyes reflecting the light. Though he could not see bodies.

"Kobolds," Grimble said. "They be fast. Sharp claws and teeth. Crude weapons. Skin be tough as leather armor."

Sasha called out, "Lugs, tank them out here in the tunnel. Alexander will pull them to you. Alexander, now."

Alexander chose a pair of eyes near the center of the group, and hit them with Wizard's Fire. The room lit up as a kobold screamed in pain. Six others came running out of the room, only to be slammed by Lug's massive shield. Sasha cast her Thorn Trap on the tangle of kobolds, and Alexander cast Wizard's Fire two more times. Then he focused on the one still burning in the room. It was a lizard-man looking thing with black scaled skin, and a thick tail. Like a four-foot-tall T-rex, only with longer forearms. It had a mouthful of sharp teeth.

Kobold miner
Level 35
Health 2300/3000

Helga had charged past the burning pile of kobolds and into the room. Just as Alexander finished examining the kobold there, she swung her two-handed monstrosity of a sword and decapitated the monster. Its still-flaming head rolled across the room.

Lugs and Grimble had bashed in the heads of the remaining kobolds as they burned. The entire fight had taken about thirty seconds. Edward took over duties as loot master, looking to make himself useful. This first group dropped a few gold coins, mining picks, rusty knives and swords. Alexander had warned Sasha not to cast Trap Soul on any of the mobs. He didn't yet trust the new guild members enough for them to know that they could produce soul crystals en masse. He would cast the spell on any boss they encountered, and just pass it off as good luck when a crystal dropped.

Walking into the room, Grimble discovered a pile of iron ore and gems. The Kobold miners had apparently been busy! Alexander instructed him to just leave it there, rather than try to carry it all through the mine. They'd retrieve it later.

Continuing, the group reached the end of the shaft with no further adventure. Heading back, they met up with Jules at the midpoint of the shaft. She'd been hanging back as ordered to keep watch.

"What'd you guys fight? I just got a level up!" She grinned.

"Kobolds." Alexander smiled back to her. "Seven of them. Mostly mid-thirties. This should be good xp for all of us. Keep a sharp watch, though. Their skin is jet black, and they blend into the darkness. All I could see before the fight were their red eyes."

Jules nodded her head and went back into stealth mode, following the group as they moved back to the main shaft. Taking a left, they continued down the tunnel until they reached the first right-hand shaft. Again, Jules paused at the junction to watch for mobs. Lugs led the way down the tunnel.

They could hear the sound of metal picks on stone as they moved toward where the first room should be. Sasha called out the same strategy. Lugs and the rest stayed back a bit in the tunnel, while Alexander peeked around far enough to target a Kobold. He was able to see the outline of one close to the door. Hitting it with wizard's fire, he backed up behind the tank, scooting between the wall and Lugs' five-foot-tall shield.

Again, the rest of the group ran out, only to be smashed stupid by Lugs' tower shield. There were eight of them this time, plus the one still flailing away inside the room. Sasha cast thorn trap on the pile Lugs made, and Alexander cast wizard's fire. This time it was Grimble who headed into the room to finish the lone kobold, as the burning pile blocked Helga's path. Disregarding the fire, Grimble slammed the bottom edge of his shield down onto the kobold's neck, turning its screams into wet gurgles. Then he swung his hammer down, crushing its skull.

Helga and Lugs used their long reaches to skewer or crush the kobolds in the pile. When the fire died down, Edward began to loot.

Inside the room, Grimble was looking into one of two mining carts. "This one be filled with iron ore. The other be half full of the same. And there be a pile o' gems in tha' corner." He pointed toward a back corner, where there was indeed a pile of emeralds, rubies, and amethysts. The pile was dust covered, with just a few cleaner gems that looked like recent additions.

"Maybe they have no use for the gems? They only want the ore?" Alexander pondered aloud.

"Aye, looks that way," Grimble agreed.

Beatrix, who had been standing over the gem pile and drooling, said, "Maybe we just leave and let these guys keep working for a month or two, then come take all the gems!"

Not realizing she was joking, Grimble grumbled, "We be needin' iron to make weapons 'n' tools, lass."

After a moment of awkward silence, Alexander said, "Let's keep going. We've got a lot of territory to cover here, and I'd like to be back at the keep for dinner."

They moved on down the shaft. This shaft was much longer, stretching maybe half a mile. They encountered groups of two and three kobolds working in the tunnel as they went. The mobs died quickly, if loudly. In the real world, the lights and the screaming of the dying mobs would bring every monster in the shaft, maybe in the whole mine, running to fight, overwhelming the heroes like in one of the early century zombie movies. But the game mechanics of Io kept a relatively small aggro radius.

The pattern continued through the shaft, and the three more leading off to the right. Kobolds in small groups in the tunnels, larger groups in the rooms. Most of them being just under, or just over, level 40. Each room had carts filled with ore, and piles of gems. Alexander had allowed Beatrix to pick up a dozen or so rare diamonds that she spotted as they'd searched the rooms. The poor gnome was nearly apoplectic having to walk away from so many gems.

Walking back to the main tunnel after clearing the fourth right-hand shaft, they took a short break. Sasha passed around some jerky, and a wineskin filled with tea that gave stamina and regen buffs. Though so far, no fight had even been difficult, it was always better to be prepared. They'd been in the dungeon close to three hours. While the progress had been quick, each shaft was half a mile long, with rooms to clear in each one. So, they'd fought along a path a little over five miles since they entered the mine.

After their break, Grimble led them deeper down the main shaft. At this point, the slope was getting steeper. The shaft slowed downward at about a thirty-degree angle. Alexander found himself thinking it would be hell to push a full mining cart up that slope. He said as much to Grimble.

"Aye." The dwarf laughed. "But the ride back down be fun!"

The next side shaft they came to branched off to the left. They were in an area that had been created in the time after Grimble left the mine. Grimble examined the walls as they went, running his hands along, tapping occasionally with a soft hammer.

"There be a silver vein here. Big one," he reported.

Moving down the shaft, they came upon its first room. As per usual, Alexander hit the first kobold he could see with wizard's fire. A mass of the creatures began screaming and running for the door. There were at least twenty of them!

"Grimble, form up next to Lugs!" Sasha called out. "Helga! Fill the space left over! Don't let any of them through! We'll burn them down."

"Count of three," Lugs said, talking to Grimble. "1…2…3!" the two tanks slammed their shields forward in unison, knocking back six or seven of the kobolds, causing a massive pile-up as the others crowded in behind. Sasha cast her aoe thorn trap in as wide an area as she could, extending a circle out nearly twenty feet in diameter. Alexander immediately began casting wizard's fire. He started with two mobs at the top of the pile, then cast it four more times at roughly the cardinal points of the circle.

There were four kobolds that were far enough to the side of the tunnel that they'd not been caught in the trap. Helga was flashing her five-foot-long blade back and forth, holding them at bay. As Alexander watched, she stabbed forward and skewered one of them, before stepping back into her defensive stance. Grimble moved over to assist, as the other kobolds weren't going anywhere, and the heat was a bit intense. Once the dwarf had picked up the three remaining loose mobs, Helga moved to the kobold pile and used her long sword and long arm to stab and slice at the burning and helpless mobs trapped in the thorns. Lugs used his even longer arms and three-foot-long hammer to bash and smash indiscriminately. Alexander cast magic bolts at the three loose kobolds, doing moderate damage. He'd need to remember to upgrade that spell. Suddenly all three kobolds fell to the ground, thrashing wildly. Beatrix had entered the fight. A globe of water had formed around each kobold's head, cutting off their oxygen supply. The three little monsters were drowning on dry land.

Edward took the opportunity to jump into the room and finish off the first mob that Alexander had hit. Alexander, briefly panicking, threw a magic shield around the boy, and ran after him. Helga and Lugs finished working their way around the edges of the pile, and it looked as if all the kobolds there were dead. The last three struggled weakly as they drowned on the tunnel floor. Out of pity, Sasha drew her dagger and plunged it into each of their hearts.

Inside the room, Alexander approached Edward as the boy cleaned his newly forged dwarven sword with a rag.

"You do that again, and I'll teleport you back to your father with a note that says he should ground you for a month." He spoke very quietly.

"It was one small kobold, almost dead already. I've been in here three hours and not even swung my sword!" the boy protested.

“And if you didn’t need it to defend yourself in case of an emergency, I’d take it from you right now!” Alexander’s voice was getting louder. “You were told to stay with me. Come out here.” He stomped back out to where they’d been standing during the fight. The boy followed, sullen.

Turning to look at the room, he pointed at the door. “Tell me what you see.”

The boy snorted. “I see a doorway.”

“And beyond the door?”

“I see a wall, and a corner. And another wall.” The prince was beginning to sound annoyed. He didn’t enjoy being treated like a child. But Alexander had a point to make.

“Exactly. How many corners does that room have? Have many walls?” he asked the boy, nearly growling. Fibble stuck his head in the door, looked around the room, and held up three fingers, saying “Five!”. Alexander struggled not to smile at the helpful little goblin.

The prince looked surprised. Then the point hit him. He mumbled, “Four corners. Four walls.”

“And how many of those corners did you check before you dashed into the room alone? Did you even look anywhere besides at your target?” Alexander scolded.

“You’re right. I didn’t. It was stupid. I apologize.” The prince bowed his head. “I got carried away, and didn’t think. It won’t happen again.”

Alexander was surprised by the boy’s humility. And impressed with the king’s parenthood. It was rare for a teenager to so quickly admit their mistakes.

Softening his tone quite a bit, he patted Edward on the shoulder. “We’ve all done exactly what you’ve just done. Except Sasha. She’s always just hung out in the back.” He winked at the prince. “The point is, we all make noob mistakes. It's how we learn. I apologize for the harshness of the lesson, but I made an oath to your father to protect you."

Grimble handed the boy a cup. Then he handed one to each of the others. After pouring a shot of clear dwarven spirits into each one, he raised his cup. "To yer first kill!"

The others raised the cups as well. "First kill!" The prince blushed, but downed his drink with a smile. The dwarf collected all the cups and put them back in his bag. "It be a tradition among me people. And since ye blooded that fancy dwarven sword, I figgered it were fitting." This caused a few chuckles. Lugs made a plea for more spirits. The cup had looked comically small in his giant hand. Edward began looting the corpses.

Moving into the room, they found more of the usual. Four carts this time, filled mostly with silver ore. Another pile of gems, including a large diamond which Beatrix quickly scooped up. But one thing was different. In the center of the room was a large hole. From the center of the hole rose a rope attached to a pulley that hung from the ceiling. Grimble approached carefully, looking down into the shaft. He'd turned off his headlight. Dwarves could see just fine in the dark.

Laying down on his stomach, he looked to Lugs. "Hold me feet," he said. The half-ogre grabbed the dwarf by the ankles, and lowered him slowly into the hole. After a moment, light emanated up from below. Grimble must have turned his headlight back on. The dwarf waved a hand for Lugs to lift him back up. The ogre complied, setting the dwarf carefully on the floor.

"Thank ye," Grimble said to Lugs. "There be another shaft below. There be gold!" He grinned. "The tunnel turns a few yards down. I could not see how far it goes."

Closing his eyes, Alexander used his earth magic. He reached into the stone below, and found the tunnel under them. Following it with his sense, he saw that it curved in a slow descent, ending in a cavern maybe fifty feet down. He shared with this the group.

“That tunnel weren’t curved down, it were curved up,” Grimble said. The dwarf was getting excited. “The tunnel, do it be round?”

Alexander looked more closely. It was indeed round. As if something had drilled through the rock. Confirming this for Grimble, he asked, “What does that mean?

“Rock worm!” Grimble told him. “They feed on ore. That be why the tunnel curves. They follow the vein where ever it leads. Rock worms love the taste o’ precious metal. But they canno’ digest it. They eat, and they shit. And what they shit, it be purified ore. If them Kobolds found the tunnel, they found pure gold. Kobolds got no use for gold. Too soft for weapons. They do not decorate with jewelry, nor do they trade. If me guess be correct, there be piles o’ pure gold in this mine.”

Excited by the news, the Dwarf wanted to delve into the hole right away. Alexander held them back. “We’ve got kobolds to deal with. Whatever’s in the hole is not going anywhere. Let’s clear this shaft and any others, then come back.”

The group moved back out to the branch tunnel, and continued down. They killed several smaller groups of kobolds, then reached a second room. This time, they called Jules forward to have a stealthy peek. To help her see in the dark, Alexander cast mage sight on her. She snuck through the door, and reported in group chat.

“*I see fifteen, sixteen... twenty-two kobolds. One of them is much larger than the other. He glows brighter. He’s sitting in the far corner on a pile of... something. He might be asleep.*”

“*Okay, thank you, Jules. Please come back.*” Alexander said.

When she was back, Alexander said, “Okay, Jules, stay here with us. But please continue to watch our backs. There may still be kobolds moving in the tunnel.” The rogue smiled and nodded her head, going back into stealth mode.

Sasha said, “We’ll try something a little different. Alexander, hit the one closest to the door. Do it with a magic bolt, instead of the fire. I want to see if we can pull out a few individuals or small groups. But be rcady for all of them to come!"

Alexander crept up to the door, and spotted a kobold not three feet inside it. Taking a deep breath, he cast a magic bolt at its face and rushed back behind Lugs.

The kobold screamed and rushed out of the room. Three more came right behind. Lugs waited until they were all close, then hit them with a shield slam. They didn't even bother with the vines and the fire. The four stunned kobolds were easy pickings for Lugs, Helga, and Grimble. Leaving the bodies as obstacles, Alexander crept back to the door. The four closest had already come out. He picked one that was near the left corner of the room, and hit it with a bolt.

This time about half the remaining kobolds rushed out. Eight of them, screaming their heads off. Lugs bashed into them just as the leaders were stepping over the bodies of the last group. The result was a tangle of living and dead lizardmen. Sasha cast her thorns, and Alexander cast wizard's fire.

Once they were sure all the kobolds were trapped, Alexander gave Edward the go-ahead to help cut them down. Helga and Lugs left the ones at the very edge for the boy. Alexander put a magic shield in front of him to keep him from taking fire damage.

Taking a moment to rest and recharge, they discussed the next group. They weren't sure what the boss kobold would do, so they decided to adopt Brick's method of hiding in a corner. Lug's massive shield would protect him long enough for Sasha and Alexander to get the bonfire going, at which point the half-ogre could move away and avoid further fire damage.

But just in case, Sasha knelt down in front of Fibble. "Fibble, we need your help. We need you to protect Lugs. Can you do that?"

Fibble's eyes got wide. He nodded his head so quickly that Alexander feared his brain would come loose. "Okay, Fibble, when I shout your name, you shoot Lugs with your magic stick. Every time I call you, you shoot him. Got it?" Again with the nodding. Alexander rubbed the back of his neck in sympathy pain.

Sasha took Fibble by the hand as they all moved into the room. Lugs wasted no time, roaring out a challenge in his ogre voice. He moved across the room toward the boss, swinging his hammer at a kobold as it came in range. Its head disappeared in a spray of blood and brain. When he had the attention of all the mobs, including the boss, he backed himself into a corner, still bashing away with his hammer when he could. With his back to the corner, he set his feet and waited. The boss kobold pushed aside his minions in order to get to Lugs. He waved a sword nearly as big as Helga's, slamming it against Lugs' shield. When the minions gathered in tight behind the boss, Lugs hit him with a shield bash, knocking him back, and knocking down several of the smaller mobs.

Sasha cast her thorns, and Alexander hit the boss in the face with Wizard's Fire. Then he hit four more kobolds in a circle around him. Lugs was scrunched down - as much as a nine-foot-tall half-ogre could scrunch - behind his shield. Sasha pulled Fibble over to one side so that they could see Lugs clearly. "Now, Fibble!" she called out, dropping a heal on Lugs herself. Fibble shouted, "Pew! Pew!" and fired white healing light at the ogre. The two of them managed to keep Lugs' health above 75% as the fire heated his shield.

"Lugs! Step out!" Sasha called. The ogre moved sideways along the wall, keeping the shield between him and the burning boss. As he cleared the fire, he took a parting shot with his hammer, striking the boss in its shoulder with a massive crunching sound.

Helga was already moving in, slaughtering the mobs that stood between her and the boss. Sasha threw her a heal as she began to suffer fire damage from the inferno of burning lizards. Fibble shot Lugs again, then shot Helga without being asked. Sasha decided to let him go. His wand held 100 charges, after all.

Alexander cast a couple more Wizard's Fires on kobolds he hadn't targeted the first time. One disadvantage of their method was that he couldn't stack fire spell upon fire spell. After thirty seconds, Sasha was able to re-cast her thorn trap, adding more fuel to the fire. The smaller kobolds were now all dead, but their bodies still fueled the inferno that was quickly burning down the boss. Alexander stopped to look at the boss' stats.

Kobold Chief
Level 55
Health 500/5500

He quickly cast the trap soul spell on the boss before it expired. Sasha called everyone back. The fire would finish the boss. There was no need to risk fire damage to themselves. Beatrix cast a globe of water around its head, keeping it from any last-minute castings as it died.

When the boss expired, Alexander heard, "Woohoo!" from Jules behind them.

Level up! You are now level 40!
Your wisdom has increased by +1. Your intelligence has increased by +1
You have 27 free attribute points available

Everyone got at least a level out of that fight. Fibble got several. He was staring in wonder at his hands, probably feeling added… what? What would the goblin's main stats be? Agility? Stamina? Certainly not strength or intelligence. Maybe dexterity. Or even charisma. The little fella did kinda grow on you.

While they waited for the molten corpses to cool, Grimble inspected the room. Moving over to the corner where he expected to find a throne, he paused. "Sweet Durin's mithril balls!" He dropped to his knees and hugged what looked like a pair of ovoid stones.

"What is it?" Sasha asked breathlessly. Jules just giggled and said "He's praying!".

"These be…" Grimble turned and looked at them with actual tears in his eyes. "These be rockworm larvae. The rockworms lay 'em in nests, like eggs. Only there ain't no shell. Just the skin o' the lil beasties all curled up." He motioned to the sort of bowl-shaped structure covered in animal skins that he was standing in. "This be a damned nest! That fool kobold were restin' his scaly arse on baby rockworms like a chicken hatchin' her egg! BWAHAHAHA!"

Not really getting the joke, the others chuckled along, mostly because of Grimble's enthusiasm.

Edward spoke up, holding his sword tightly. "Shouldn't we destroy the eggs before they hatch? How dangerous are rockworms?"

Grimble looked horrified. He actually lifted his shield and put himself in front of the larvae. "Bite yer tongue, lad! These babies be worth their weight in mithril! Fer these lil darlins, me King'd shave his beard 'n' give it to ye!" he roared.

Alexander decided to diffuse the situation. "Grimble, nobody's going to hurt the baby worms. Now, tell me. What is so valuable about them?"

Grimble took a deep breath. "I tell'd ye. Rockworms be living, moving refineries. What a full grow'd rockworm can process thru its belly in a day, would take a refinery three days to process. And it don't need miners to dig the ore out, or carts to transport it, or fuel for the refinery fires. But rockworms be rarer than dragons. Me clan had one nearly a thousand years ago. We kept the secret o' trainin them, just in case…" his voice drifted off. Alexander assumed he was dreaming of riding a rockworm through a field of mithril boulders.

Alexander saw a way to score some points with the dwarves of Broken Mountain, and his new miners at the same time. And to improve the mine production.

"Grimble. Grimble!" he shouted when the dwarf didn't respond. Finally, he said, "Fibble, please shoot Grimble for me?"

The goblin had uncanny aim. The bolt hit Grimble right in the face.

"Bah! What?" the dwarf spluttered.

"Welcome back, Grimble. Let me ask you something. I'm thinking of offering King Thalgrin a deal. What if we give him both baby worms, he trains them both, and gives one back for you to use here in the mine?"

It was hard not to laugh at the range of expressions that passed across the dwarf's face. He had to actually lean on his shield to stay upright. He went from amazed to thoughtful, then cynical, then amazed again.

"It… be possible. Me King would pay ye well for both. But if ye stick to yer guns, yes. I think we could have our own rockworm." The dwarf seemed in shock. Alexander decided not to remind the dwarf that Thalgrin was no longer his king.

This was one treasure Grimble was absolutely not willing to leave behind. He wrapped each of the larvae in one of the hides from the nest. They looked to be dire wolf pelts. He stuffed one of the larvae in his own inventory bag, and gave the other to Lugs. The larvae were apparently very heavy.

As they went to leave the room, Alexander said "Edward, grab the rest of those hides. Lainey might be able to use them. Or we can trade them to the dwarves." Edward dashed over from looting the pile of kobolds and began to pick up hides.

Just as Alexander reached the door, Edward said "Uhhmmm… Grimble?"

The group all turned around, their lights shining on Edward, still standing in the nest. Which, now that the hides had been removed, looked like a shiny gopher mound with a hole in the middle.

Grimble gasped, moving back over to the nest, laying his hands on it. "Mithril. The nest be refined mithril," the dwarf murmured. Stepping back, he pulled the egg back out of his bag and laid a hand on it.

Alexander looked at the nest. Best guess, there was half a ton of refined mithril there. His people never needed to operate the mine. Just that blob of metal would keep them in running for years. Decades. If Max were here, he'd be over there trying to hump it. Maybe Brick, too! Alexander smiled at the visual.

Poor Grimble didn't look well. He'd wrapped up the larvae again and put it back into his bag. The dwarf sat on the edge of the nest.

"Grimble, are you okay? I know that's a lot of mithril. We'll sell it in small bits to Thalgrin. Broken Mountain will have all the mithril it can handle!"

"What?" Grimble looked at him. "Mithril? Oh! Aye. That be a historic find, fer sure…" He drifted off again.

Alexander looked around. The others all shrugged. Helga volunteered, "I think maybe he snapped."

Taking the initiative once again, Fibble stepped toward Grimble and shot him in the face with another bolt of healing magic. "Pew?" he questioned more than shouted.

The dwarf came around again, and Fibble wisely retreated to hide behind Sasha, who was having a very hard time keeping a straight face.

"Grimble, what is it?" Alexander asked.

The old dwarf shook his head, and stood. "These babies. Their mama ate a whole mithril vein afore she birthed 'em. That be why the nest be made o'mithril. This much metal… it'd take her a week, maybe more to process enough to make this here nest." He paused again.

"And?" Alexander prompted him.

"Rockworms have a natural affinity for the metal they be born in. They like that taste best, and seek it out. But also, they be born with some o' the properties o' that metal. These be mithril worms. Ye could fire a cannon into its side, and ye'd just make it angry. With a mithril worm, ye could… roll over an army of ogres with axes, and it'd not be scratched."

"So, it's a tank!" Jules cried. "Like, a real tank!"

Not understanding what she meant, the dwarf chuckled. "Aye, lass. The tank to beat all tanks. Its teeth be mithril. Its hide be mithril."

"Okay, we can discuss all this later. We need to finish clearing this mine, and get these babies back to the keep where they'll be safe. Grimble, are you good to go?"

The dwarf picked up his shield and hammer. "Aye."

A thought occurred to Alexander. "Grimble, if we move these babies, will the mother come looking for them?" The dwarf shook his head. "Nay. Once they be dropped in a nest, they be on their own."

They finished clearing that tunnel, finding several additional small groups of kobolds. As they passed the first room, Alexander used his earth mover ability to close a stone cover over the hole, leaving just a small opening around the rope, so as not to cut it off. Nothing larger than a rat could squeeze through. Grimble agreed they could come back and explore the lower level later.

Back at the main tunnel, they turned left again. Following the main tunnel further down, they eventually reached its end. No other tunnels branched off. That was it. The mine was clear. Except for the underground level that was now sealed.

Walking back up the main tunnel, Alexander had Lugs push an empty mining cart. They stopped at the last shaft, and went back to the two rooms. In the nest room, Lugs used his hammer to try and break off a chunk of mithril. It didn't make a dent. Grimble explained that they needed special picks with diamond tips. The picks were crafted by dwarven masters specifically to work on mithril. He assured Alexander that Thalgrin would happily give him a couple as part of the deal for the worms. Instead, they loaded up the cart with all the gems from the piles in both rooms, and headed out.

Alexander didn't want to give the miners 10% of the ore and gems that had already been mined by kobolds, just for hauling them out. So, he made a deal with Grimble. The miners would come and haul out all the loose treasure, and would split 5% of the total, as a group. By Grimble's estimate, setting aside the mithril, which the miners wouldn't be touching, each of the eighteen miners would still get several thousand gold for maybe two day's work.

He also promised the three new guildmates a share of the loot, including a third of a percent each of the value of the mithril. Grimble estimated the pile of rare metal to be worth ten million gold. More if they took their time and sold it in small quantities. Their one third percent would equal roughly thirty-three thousand gold. That was a huge amount for any player for an afternoon's work. They'd also receive the same percentage of the value of the ore and gems.

Initially, Helga grumped. Saying Alexander was just making himself rich. Until Alexander reminder her that the guild would only take 10%, and that the rest of the funds would be used to support the growth of the keep she'd just sworn to protect.

When they exited the mine, Alexander raised a stone wall to block the entrance. Then he raised a block of stone roughly the same size as a mining cart. He had Lugs dump the content of the cart into the box, and then lift the box. As soon as he had, Alexander teleported them all back to the keep. Lugs quickly set down the heavy box.

Alexander heard some chuckling from above. Looking straight up, he saw Kai looking down from the wall into the box. "I take it you cleared the mine?"

"You could say that." Alexander grinned up at him, getting slightly dizzy. He felt like Fitz staring at Rufus leaning over his hat brim.

"Get some rest, guys. Edward, get all the loot to Lola, and have her make a list. Helga, Lugs, Beatrix, thank you. It was a pleasure running with you."

Tapping Grimble on the shoulder, he said, "I'm going to open the portal. I'd like you to go and invite King Thalgrin here for dinner. Tell him we've got worms to discuss. You can take one worm with you, if you swear to return with it."

Grimble nodded his head. "Aye, lad, I swear on me life. I'll not let ye down. I'll make sure he brings a couple o' mithril picks with him. Open the portal again in… an hour?"

Alexander opened the portal, and Grimble strode through. He immediately began shouting and waving his arms. He summoned a battle boar, and took off toward the citadel.

Letting the portal close, Alexander noted the time on his UI, and set an alarm. He was about to be pretty distracted, and didn't want to forget to retrieve the king.

First, he waved over the group of miners. He told them they'd be getting into the mine in a day or two. Showing them the box of gems, he explained that they'd be spending their first couple days just retrieving similar piles of already-mined gems and ore. And that, in return for hauling it out in the carts, they'd share 5%. They immediately agreed. He also warned them to stay away from the room with the hole in the floor. Then he instructed them to pitch in around the keep, help the masons or the carpenters, until the mine was opened.

Next, he went up the wall to see Kai. He called to Lugs to join him.

"Ever heard of mithril rockworms?" he asked the dragon.

Kai nodded his head. "Rockworms are rare. Mithril rockworms are about as rare as a black unicorn. One might see one once in ten thousand years."

Motioning to Lugs to hand the larvae to Kai, he said, "How about two in an afternoon?" and grinned at the surprised look on Kai's face.

Lugs stomach growled, and Alexander sent him to go get some food. The ogre didn't bother with the stairs, he simply hopped off the wall, landing with an impact like a falling piano, and scaring several miners who were still talking below.

Alexander explained to Kai what they'd found in the mine. Kai closed his eyes for a moment, and Fitz appeared next to them. "Looking around, Fitz said, "What's the emergency?"

Kai simply held up the larvae. The wizard glanced at it, then looked to Alexander. "So, you found a rockwork in the mine? Well done, boy. King Thalgrin will pay a fortune for it. You'll be able to install solid gold doorknobs and toilet seats throughout the keep." The wizard grinned, clapping Alexander on the back.

"Look closer, Fitzbindulum," Kai whispered.

Fitz gave the dragon a questioning look, then focused on the larvae. After just a moment, his eyebrows rose nearly to the brim of his hat.

"A mithril worm! And still a larvae! The skin!" The wizard laughed.

Now it was Alexander's turn to be confused. "The skin?"

Fitz looked at him. "Remember I told you the ingredients for the spell on Kai's torq were rare? Well, the rarest is mithril rockworm skin. Once a rockworm is fully grown, their skin becomes tough as rock. It has to be, as they burrow through rock itself. Rarely do they lose any skin, and when they do, it is someplace far underground. Mithril worms have nearly indestructible skin. The best way to find the skin is to find a nest, and wait for the babies to grow and shed their first layer of skin. What you've found here is… extremely rare." The wizard stroked his beard. "With the full skin from this baby worm, I could make that spell… twenty times?"

Alexander laughed. "We have two. One is with Grimble in Broken Mountain. He'll be returning with Thalgrin in less than an hour. I plan to let Thalgrin keep one in return for training them both, and sending one back here to work the mine."

Instantly, Fitz said, "You must make him agree to collect the skin as they shed! And give them to me. As they grow to full size, they might shed three or four times. Each skin larger than the last."

"Do you know if the adult worm is dead?" Kai interrupted.

"No..." Alexander mused. "There was a large hole in the floor of one of the rooms. It led down to a curving tunnel that originated from a large cavern. Grimble said the rockworm tunneled up into the mine from the cavern. We didn't go down there, as I wanted to finish clearing the mine and get these baby worms back here. So, I sealed the hole."

"We should confirm as soon as possible whether the worm is there. Or nearby. Especially if it is a mithril worm as well. It could be a danger to the miners. It could also be a useful asset," the dragon said.

"If we find it, you can train it?" Alexander asked. Maybe he shouldn't have been so hasty to trade a worm to Thalgrin in exchange for training.

"Not in the way you are thinking. Dwarves train the worms using a series of sounds. Taps on the walls, whistles, and such. The training takes a year or longer. Though it is easier with larvae. As a dragon, I can connect with the worm's mind. Make suggestions. Bind its loyalty. We use them to dig tunnels and lairs for us on occasion. If you wanted, for example, an escape tunnel leading from the keep to the top of the ridge. You could make this tunnel yourself in a day or two. The worm could do it in the same time, while you spend your time doing something else. And it will process any ore that it finds along the way."

Fitz was fondling the baby worm like starving man handed a coconut, trying to get inside. "Fitz, it's not food. And don't lick it. A kobold chief's been sitting on it."

"There were kobolds in the mine?" The wizard looked up.

"Yep. They were mining. Piles of loose gems and carts full of iron and silver ore down there." He pointed below to the stone box full of gems. "And Grimble found some big troll footprints too. Though he said they were older."

"Interesting neighbors you have around here. Trolls, kobolds, rockworms, a dungeon full of demons," the wizard observed.

"So, how did the discussion go with the farmers and mason?" Alexander asked. Did they decided where best to place the wall?"

"They've gone out to examine the soil and the stone beneath." Kai pointed out toward the meadow where several figures were moving about. "But they think your idea is a good one. Two hundred yards gives enough space for crops and animals. The farmers say they'll want additional fields outside the wall as well, but that having some crops secured inside the keep will enable them to feed us during a long siege."

"Speaking of sieges, Fitz, can you put wards on the gate like you did at the compound? Either teleport or kill wards? Tie them to the dragon pins I've given everyone? Or our medallions?" Alexander asked.

"That's what I was doing when Kai summoned me. I'll get back to it. Oh, and I'll be raising a proper wizard's tower shortly. Might want to warn everyone." The wizard handed the worm back to Kai before disappearing.

"Jeeves, loudspeaker, please."

"*Of course, master. Go ahead,*" Jeeves said.

"Attention everyone. If you see a large tower burst from the ground in the next little while, do not worry. It's just our favorite wizard making himself comfortable. And wards have been set that will kill, or teleport to the dungeon, anyone not wearing a dragon pin. So, if you don't have one, see Master Silverbeard. Also, the mine has been cleared, and a tribe of kobolds removed from our lands. If you see Beatrix, Lugs, Grimble, Fibble, Sasha, Jules, or Helga, buy them a drink. Maybe two for Lugs. And half for Fibble! They did good work today! Lastly, I expect a visit within the hour from King Thalgrin of Broken Mountain. So, everybody, try to look pretty."

There was some scattered laughter down below. His people were getting used to his weak humor.

Alexander left the worm with Kai, as it was too heavy for him to carry. He decided to call a guild officer's meeting to discuss the happenings of the day, and opened up guild chat.

"*Max, Lainey, time to come in for a meeting. Lorian, bring your group in too. Any update on the adventurers?*"

"*We are already on our way. The adventurers are still moving toward the keep. They should arrive before dark.*" Lorian answered. "*They've stopped fighting beasts, though that may be because the local animals are a higher level.*"

"*Okay, please follow them in, Lorian. Officers, please meet me at the gate. We've got some business to discuss before Thalgrin arrives.*" Alexander said.

Walking out the gate, Alexander began to wave at the farmers and masons in the field, motioning them to come in. He didn't want them outside the walls with a potentially hostile group of players approaching.

As they gathered around, he asked, "Who's speaking for the farmers? And for the masons?"

A human farmer named Shelton raised his hand. And a dwarf named Brogin did so for the masons. "Okay, good. Let's start with the soil. Is this land we're standing on good for farming?" he asked Shelton.

"Aye, sir. It'll do fine. A bit of a slope, but if we can irrigate, we can have crops growing here in no time. Should be able to grow enough to feed a couple of hundred people with corn, wheat, and vegetables. We'll want to plow more fields outside in order to grow enough to trade though," Shelton said.

"Thank you, Shelton. Now, Brogin. What about placement of an outer wall?"

"There be plenty of stone below. Solid bedrock three hundred feet down. Ye can raise walls as high as ye like. We been talking 'bout an alternative to high walls, though. High walls block the wind, and the sun. Maybe not so good for the crops?" He looked at Shelton, who agreed. "The wizard mentioned a moat. Ye could make the wall ten feet high on the inside, and dig a wide moat on the outside. Make the wall wide, with a road on top fer moving troops and weapons about. Fill the moat with spikes fer any foolish enough to jump in. No enemy will be able to bridge it with a siege tower."

"I'm afraid spikes won't work." Alexander grinned at the dwarf. "Fitz wants to put a moat monster in there. I'm going to have a contest to name it. Winner gets to feed it!" The group chuckled.

"Aye, a moat monster'd work too. Once it's growed, at least. In that case, we'll need to make the moat deeper. At least forty feet. And keep the water flowing," Brogin said.

"Thank you, gentlemen. We'll begin work on the wall in the morning. You should be able to start plowing the next day, Shelton. If you need anything in the way of tools or equipment, let Master Silverbeard or Lola know. For now, please head back inside. There is a group of adventurers approaching, and they may be hostile."

Walking back toward the gate with the group of citizens, he said, "Brogin, where are we with the repairs? Do you have an estimate on how long it will take?"

The dwarf replied, "The wall already be repaired. The wizard see'd to it. The keep and the tower be more complicated. We'll need to erect scaffolds and cranes to lift the stones. Then there be some damage to internal walls where the wizard got rambunctious." He grinned.

"The mages and I will be focusing on the outer wall for the next few days," Alexander said. "After that we can lend our efforts to help with the repairs. Please focus on the main structure's lower levels. We need to be able to secure the building in case an enemy breaches the wall. And we need to make as much residential space as we can available, to get folks moved indoors. Again, let Silverbeard or Lola know if you need anything."

Turning to look toward the forest, Alexander saw Lainey and her hunters jogging in from the direction of the falls. Before long, Max and his group cleared the forest directly ahead of the gate. He waved at both groups, and waited for them to arrive.

Max and Lainey sent their hunters in to deliver the meat they'd gathered to the kitchen. The three of them were soon joined by Brick and Sasha.

"Let's move inside the bailey gate tunnel, to make sure we're not overheard," Alexander said quietly. He had no way to know if there were stealthed enemies nearby.

"So, the first thing you should know is that we mostly cleared the mine, and we're incredibly rich. More so than before. There were hundreds of thousands in gems and ore just laying around in the mine. And there's maybe a thousand pounds of refined mithril that was pooped out by a giant rockworm."

Hearing that, Brick grabbed Max's arm to steady himself. "Sweet Durin," he mumbled.

"It gets better," Alexander continued. "We found two baby rockworms. Mithril rockworms. Grimble says King Thalgrin would practically sell his left nut for them. We're going to make a deal with him this evening. He'll train both worms, and give one back to us. It'll as much as double our mine production a year or so from now. Plus, the skin is an ultra-rare spell component, which has Fitz making googly-eyes. And Grimble says we'll get a couple of diamond-tipped picks enchanted to work mithril."

Brick moaned like he'd just eaten a really good thanksgiving meal. Max laughed. "Brick's gonna have his house paid off by the end of the year."

"Max, Lainey, how much meat did you bring in?" Alexander asked.

Lainey said, "We took down eight boars, two bears, and six wolves." Max followed with, "Four boars, eight wolves, two deer the size of a moose, and a snake that's gonna give me nightmares. Damned thing was twenty-four feet long."

"Ooh! Tell me you brought me its skin!" Lainey grabbed his arm.

"Of course. Actually, two of them. We looted a snakeskin, then skinned it. You can make about thirty pairs of snakeskin boots, I think!"

Looking to Sasha, Alexander said, "So, with that much meat, we can feed our gang for…?"

"Combined with the supplies we already have, I'd say four weeks with our current population. Master Silverbeard could tell you better. And don't forget Lorian's party is still out there. They were hunting as well, and maybe collecting the meat those adventurers left behind," Sasha replied.

"Good! So even if we're cut off, and can't use the portals to supply, we can feed ourselves for at least a month. Which reminds me, anybody checked on the water supply? Do we have wells? Or is there working plumbing somewhere?"

They all had blank looks. Nobody had thought to check. "Right, then. Need to get with Silverbeard and check that ASAP." Alexander made a note.

"We're going to be starting on a second wall in the morning. About two hundreed yards out. It will allow farmers to work in safety, and give us a protected area for livestock. Max, Lainey, I'd like the hunters to stand guard over the wall construction for the next few days. Keep watch on the forest," he said. "There's going to a moat on the other side. And Fitz says he's bringing a moat monster!"

Sasha giggled at this. "You always dreamed of having a castle with a moat."

Max added, "Didn't everyone?"

"For Max and Lainey, who were too far away to hear my awesome announcement-" Sasha snorted at this. "Fitz is about to raise himself a wizard's tower. The wall repairs are complete, and the masons are starting on the main donjon building. Max, I'd like you to organize the carpenters. We need a few things quickly. Doors, and furniture. We can move people inside more quickly if we focus on those. Oh, and more long tables for meals. Nothing fancy, just long smooth planks on saw-horses would do."

"Easy enough. We've got eight carpenters besides myself, that I know of. We'll get started after dinner," Max said.

"There are eighteen miners with nothing to do for a few days, so grab some if you need heavy things moved," Alexander offered. "They're good at swinging picks, maybe they're good at swinging axes, too? And we need to clear the forest back to leave more clear ground outside the new wall."

"Brick, how are you doing setting up the smithy?" he asked.

"Fine. The smiths be making swords and axes, arrowheads and spear heads. It be a mite small for all of us to work in, though. I be thinkin' maybe we could raise some more obsidian and make another forge. It need not be a dragon forge. The magic that gets absorbed in the stone will help all the smiths make better weapons, and level up our skills faster, even without the dragon magic."

"Okay, I'll raise the obsidian for you in a minute. It should get a laugh from Thalgrin." He grinned. "As for crafting, there were…" he looked at Sasha, "maybe nine or ten mining carts of iron ore ready to be pulled up?"

Sasha nodded, and added, "And two carts of silver ore."

"Aye, that'll be a big help. There be a good size smelting rig set up outside the smithy. We'll be havin' refined metals in no time." Brick smiled.

"Also, keep in mind we need to replace the portcullis," Alexander said. "Actually, we might need one for the outer wall as well. And, Max, we'll need to craft a bridge for the moat. Ironwood." Both men nodded.

"Lainey, it sounds like you'll have several dozen hides to work with. At least one of the men, a guy named Claude, is a tanner. I'll leave it up to you to decide whether to trade the dire wolf pelts to the dwarves, or work with them yourself. And I think we should lay off the dire wolves until our hunters can give us an accurate feeling of the population. We need to leave some for players to kill, so that the king can have his pelts to trade with Broken Mountain." He grinned. It wouldn't do to take away the king's source of dwarven spirits.

The mechanics of Io allowed for mobs like the dire wolves, who were the objects of a standing bounty quest, to respawn in a matter of days. Faster if a large number of players were harvesting them. Other beasts, like bears, generally respawned after a week. Part of managing the dire lands was going to be managing its resources. Including the wildlife.

"Alright, then. Anybody have anything else?"

"The two priests been workin' in the chapel inside the keep. They be wantin' ye to raise a block o' stone like ye did in Whitehall. To be a power source fer the consecration," Brick said.

"Okay, let's go now. I'll raise the altar stone first. Then your smithy. We've got maybe thirty minutes before the king arrives. Are the priests ready for the consecration otherwise?" he asked.

"Aye. Been workin' on it all day. Just need ye to pull the stone, and me to shape it."

Chapter Ten A Wizard, A Blacksmith, And Two Priests Walk Into a Bar…

Ending the meeting, Brick led Alexander to the chapel. It was a long, narrow room on the ground floor of the keep's main structure. There was an empty area where the priests had evidently cleared away a wooden altar. Greeting the two priests, Alexander went right to work. They were pressed for time.

Reaching down into the earth with his magic, he located a large obsidian deposit. It was not as prevalent here as it was in Stormforge, as they were further from the volcano's crater, but there was more than enough for his needs.

Cutting out a block roughly four feet square, he began to raise it up. This was a more difficult challenge, as he had several levels of dungeons below him. He would have to carefully soften the rock at each level to allow the block to pass through, then harden it again. It took him ten minutes, but finally he wrangled the black stone up into the chapel.

Leaving Brick to shape the altar, Alexander ran outside to the smithy, which was just past the kitchen's side entrance where everyone ate. He'd just thought of another thing he needed to accomplish immediately.

Being outside the keep's main structure, raising the stone was not as difficult. He didn't have the lower levels to avoid. He grabbed hold of as large a block as he thought he could handle, and began to lift. After three minutes, he needed to stop and replenish his mana and stamina. The stone block was about halfway up. He downed a mana potion and a stamina potion, munched on a piece of jerky, then got back to work. Two minutes later, there was a twelve-foot cube of obsidian standing next to the smithy.

Not having the time or energy to run, Alexander teleported himself outside the gate, to roughly the spot where the new wall would be. He quickly raised a slender six-foot stone post, enchanted it with the light spell, and tied it into the earth as a power source. He'd done this process dozens of times around Whitehall, and the process was second nature at this point.

While pulling up the altar, he had remembered that the consecration in Whitehall had extended out as far as the light posts he and Brick had set up. He wanted the entire area within his walls to be consecrated as well. So he needed to rush and get some posts up before the king arrived, and he was needed there.

There was no time to a do a full ring. So, he placed one in the middle of the arc that would be the new wall. Then he teleported to the west end of the meadow, and placed another where the new wall would connect to the ridge. Then he teleported himself to the opposite side, and placed a light post where the wall would connect at that end. Finding himself with just under ten minutes left, he placed three more posts between the east end and the center, and three more on the west side. Nine posts, all drawing power from the earth, set in a rough arc around the keep. He hoped it would be enough to extend the blessing of the two gods.

Teleporting back to the portal area, he had a minute or so to collect himself. After several deep breaths, he opened the portal.

King Thalgrin and Grimble were accompanied by half a dozen dwarven guards, and what looked like half the dwarven council. Master Stonehand was there, as was Master Tomebinder. There were other council members that Alexander had met, but whose names he did not remember.

As they stepped through the portal, Alexander began to say, "Welcome to Dire Ke-"

He was cut off as Thalgrin grabbed him in a crushing bear hug, lifting him from his feet. "Alexander, me boy! Tis another miracle ye be workin!" the king roared. "I never thought ta see a mithril worm in me life. And here ye went n finded TWO!"

Once the king had set him down, and he could breathe again, he said, "I'm glad you approve, Majesty. I do my best not to let my friends grow bored with me." He grinned at the dwarf.

"BWAHAHA!" Thalgrin's laugh echoed around the courtyard. "This be a historic day. I bring'd Master Tomebinder to record it. The others be here just out of curiosity." Looking around, he said, "Bah! All of ye on yer feet.

The dwarves of the keep had begun to gather round as the portal opened, and all had dropped to a knee in deference to the king.

"Dinner is just about ready, Majesty," Alexander said, as Silverbeard and Lola approached. "We may have just a bit more history than you expected. After dinner we're going to consecrate the chapel in the keep. Just like the one you saw in Whitehall. Also, Brick is going to be shaping his new smithy. Though it won't be a dragon forge, he tells me it'll still have some magic bonus potential."

He began to lead the group of dwarves around the left side of the main building toward the kitchen area. As they walked, the ground began to rumble. The dwarven guard instantly formed a circle around the king and council members, shields up and weapons in hand. All the dwarves in the courtyard instantly produced weapons as well.

After a momentary panic, Alexander realized what was going on. "It's okay, everyone! That's just Fitz!" he shouted.

As he calmed the crowd, a second tower appeared on the other side of the main structure, past where the trees had been planted. The tower grew up nearly sixty feet before it stopped moving.

"BWAHAHAHA!" Thalgrin bellowed. "That damned wizard be makin' sport o' scaring me guards!" This got a laugh from most of the dwarves in attendance.

Not the guards.

The group continued around to the courtyard outside the kitchen. Alexander led them to a long table with enough seats to accommodate all the council members as well as the king, Grimble, himself, and Master Silverbeard. Just as he was about to sit down, the king noticed the massive block of obsidian sitting next to the smithy. Brick was already inside it, using his shaping skill to push sections of it outward, forming the rough outline of his new structure.

Thalgrin shook his head. "I telled me wife just yesterday I wish I could adopt Brick and yerself as me own sons. Ye do things fer fun that most consider to be impossible!" He chuckled.

Grimble spoke up. "I telled ye, me King. Just before we arrived at Greystone Manor, Alexander and Brick more'n doubled the size of the dragon forge! Just like he be doin' here now."

Brick continued to work, as the rest sat down at the table. Thalgrin began, "Grimble telled me yer proposal. But I wanted to hear it with me own ears. Ye are willin' to GIVE us a mithril worm? Just for trainin' a second worm for ye?"

"Well, not quite. There are a few conditions," Alexander replied. "First, we need tools that can harvest the mithril of the worm's nest."

"Aye, that be no problem," Thalgrin said. He motioned to one of the masters he'd brought, who pulled out two diamond-tipped mining picks, and a couple of other diamond enhanced tools Alexander didn't recognize.

"The second condition is that Fitz wants the skin from the worms. The skin they shed as they grow. All of it. They are a spell component that he needs for some plan of his," Alexander added.

"Aye, lad. That be acceptable. We'd not deny the old scoundrel, even if what he wants be worth a mountain o' gold." Thalgrin smiled up at the new wizard's tower.

"My third condition is that you let me name the worms." Alexander grinned.

"Bwahahaha!" The king laughed, not quite as loudly as usual. "Fair enough."

"Then we have a deal." Alexander held his hand out to the king, who shook it vigorously.

"Kai has the other larvae. I expect he'll be around soon enough. How long will it take you to train them? Alexander asked.

One of the masters Alexander couldn't put a name to answered him. "It takes a year to properly train a wee worm just born. These two should come to life soon. Maybe another month. At a year, they be about the size of an ogre. Ten feet long and three wide."

"So, I can expect you'll return one of them to me in, maybe fourteen months?" Alexander asked.

"Aye, lad. That be a good assumption. Ye'll need one o' yer own to come learn how to handle the beast…" the master said.

Grimble visibly restrained himself from jumping up to demand the position.

"And how long do mithril worms live?" Alexander suppressed a smile. "Will they outlive a dwarf, for example? Should I choose a very young dwarf to be its handler?"

Thalgrin, seeing that Alexander was torturing Grimble, played along.

"Aye, the young ones be easier to train. Maybe one o' the lads that Thea bring'd ye?"

Seeing Grimble turning red and looking ready to have a stroke, he relented. "On the other hand, Master Grimble here, DID help us find the worms. I'd have just mistaken them for rocks if not for him."

Looking at the wide-eyed dwarven miner he asked, "Master Grimble, do you think you can handle your responsibilities at the mine, and still find time to learn to handle the worm?" He had to strain to maintain a poker face. Several of those around him were already failing, smiles cracking their bearded faces.

"Aye! I can manage right well, Alexander! By Durin! Them be my babies, and I'll not have anyone else stealin' me fun!" He thumped the table as he practically shouted at Alexander.

"BWAHAHAHA!" The entire table erupted in laughter as Alexander's face broke into a smile. Looking around, Grimble realized they'd been yanking his beard. After a moment, he broke into laughter himself.

"Ye got me good, lad." He shook his head.

"Of course, you'll be our worm wrangler, Grimble. The job was never going to belong to anyone else. All I ask is that you train one other of our citizens. In case you make the worm angry and it eats you!" This elicited even louder laughter from the table.

The meal was served, and the table grew quiet as everyone fell to eating. Barrels of ale and casks of spirits were tapped, and small talk commenced. Brick finished the rough shape of his smithy, and came to join them at the table. He wolfed down a bear steak and a bowl of stew, along with a loaf of bread. Shaping took a lot of stamina.

Fitz also joined them, and stuffed his face as much as any two dwarves. Raising a wizard's tower also took some energy, apparently. Having eaten as much as he could hold, the wizard looked to Thalgrin. "The boy here told you I need the worms' skin?"

Thalgrin laughed. "Aye, ye glutton! Ye'll get yer skin. Ye have me word."

Alexander had inspiration. "Before we head over to the chapel, I've decided on names for the worms." He said. The king looked at him in anticipation. "I think we should call them Rufus, and Fitz! Both seem to be able to eat without stopping. Which seems fitting for a rockworm! I'll leave it to you which one to name which." He grinned.

"HA!" The king laughed. Fitz thought about it for a second, then waggled his eyebrows and grinned back at Alexander.

"It be settled then," Thalgrin declared. He raised his ale in a toast, "To Rufus, and Fitz!" he roared.

The crowd raised their glasses in response, "Rufus and Fitz!"

With the meal concluded, Alexander said, "Jeeves, loudspeaker, please." Then waited a moment.

When he was sure he was connected, he said, "I'd like to thank the ladies in the kitchen for a wondrous meal, fit for a king!" That caused some mild chuckles.

"For any who are interested, we will be consecrating the keep's chapel to both Durin, god of the Dwarves, and Asclepius, god of healers and medicine. You are welcome to come observe."

And with that, Brick led the king and the others to the chapel. The two priests were already there waiting. Brick moved forward and took a knee before the altar, holding his hammer to his chest. The two priests knelt next to him. Surprisingly, Thalgrin moved up and took a knee next to Brick. All the dwarves in the chapel, and those outside who couldn't fit in the room, took a knee as well. The humans all either knelt, or bowed their heads.

The two dwarves and two humans in front of the altar began to murmur prayers. The two priests uttering a memorized prayer in unison, while Brick and Thalgrin each quietly spoke to their god in their own way.

There was a roll of thunder that rumbled through the keep. Beams of light erupted from the staves of the two priests, and the hammers of the two dwarves, striking the altar. As in Whitehall, the altar bore both the hammer of Durin, and the staff and serpent symbol of Asclepius. The obsidian began to glow with the light of the two deities, growing brighter until it was necessary to close one's eyes and look away. With a crack of lightning, the light shot out through the ground, washing through all of those in attendance. The guards on the walls observed the light spreading out from the main building, moving outward through them and the wall they stood on. It continued outward, in a growing circle, until it reached the lamp posts Alexander had just placed. The lights glowed more brightly for a moment, then faded back to normal.

At the same time, the immense gong sounded again, and a light display circled the top of the keep's tower. The keep had gained another level!

There was a quiet reverence from those in and around the chapel. They'd all received buffs as the light passed through them. And the chapel around them had changed.

Where before, the altar and much of the chapel at Whitehall had turned to clear crystal, the chapel at Dire Keep had done the opposite. The altar remained black obsidian, while the ceiling, walls and floor of the chapel around them had become the same black stone as the altar. All of it glowed with an inner light. The light within the altar itself pulsed, a lessening of the darkness of the stone.

Confused by the different result, Alexander asked, "Did you change something from last time?"

Brick and Father Ignatius both shook their heads. Thalgrin said, "It be the same blessing of light. The same healing magic. Only the manifestation be different. That be Durin's doing. A reflection o' his anger at the loss o' one o' his lil'uns. The village were a place of peace. This be a place of war and vengeance. The black stone be more fitting."

Alexander couldn't argue with that. He'd come here with the intent to draw in this 'Dark One' and destroy him.

The dwarves each laid a hand on the altar before leaving. Many of the humans, too. This was another way to protect the people of Dire Keep. Small wounds would heal faster. Health and mana regeneration were increased. Production would increase, as well. In both the crafting of goods, and the growing of crops.

Heading outside, the king said his goodbyes. His guards took possession of the worms from Grimble and Kai, stowing them carefully in leather wraps.

After seeing them through the portal, Alexander headed back toward the gate. The group of adventurers had been expected by now. He wanted to greet them outside. Sasha tagged along with him. She stopped halfway to the light post, about a hundred yards out from the gate. Kneeling to put a hand on the soil, she cast a druid blessing on the land. Alexander activated his mage sight, and watched the green magic of the nature spell drawn up into the light magic bestowed by the gods, and blended with the ever-present earth magic as it spread in all directions around them. It was a beautiful sight, full of swirling color and movement.

When Sasha and Lydia had cast this spell on the farmer's fields in Whitehall, the growth rate of the crops had nearly tripled. Sometimes druids were handy folks to have around.

"How are you doing, with all this?" he asked her. He'd not really had much of a chance to talk to his best friend lately. A lot had happened in the last few weeks.

"With the building of the keep? It's fun!" She smiled at him.

"No, I mean with everything. The long immersions. The attack on Olympus. All of it," he said.

"Oh. Well, the attack kind of freaked me out. I mean, we're sort of the cause of all those people dying. And they might have killed some of our friends," she began. "It's easy for us to be in here and say, 'You deserve to be locked up for killing an NPC'… but for some of those people, that meant a loss of their income for a year." Alexander nodded his head. He'd had similar thoughts.

"But then I think about the people they've victimized. Players just like them, who've been unable to earn their own livings because those assholes were constantly griefing them. And even if these creeps didn't bother to read the Terms of Service before they logged in, they can't have missed all the videos. They knew what they were getting into. And attacking innocent people in real life with guns and rockets, that's not okay. So, I've pretty much decided that assholes are assholes, and they need to pay the price for their decisions." Her voice was soft, but confident as she finished.

Alexander brought her in for a hug. It felt strange, as his elf body was a good half a foot taller than his real-world body, while Sasha was the same not-quite-five-feet. She hugged him back fiercely, and he could hear a few snuffles against his chest. Then she turned her head slightly, and said, "So… Jules, huh?". He could hear the wicked grin on her face.

"What about Jules?" he asked, trying to sound clueless. "You don't like her?" Misdirection was his only hope, here.

"Of course, I like her! She's sweet, and smart, and SO tough for hanging in through all that's been thrown at her. I love her." She started tickling his ribs as she looked up at his face. "But not as much as youuuuu doooo!"

He broke away and ran from his diminutive torturer. His elven legs gave him long strides, but she was a quick little thing. She leapt and tackled him to the ground. Perching on top of him, she began to poke him in any spot he left momentarily undefended.

"Alex and Jules, sittin' in a tree! K-i-s-s-i-n-g!" she chanted. She'd tortured him like this beginning when they were both seven years old, when he'd taken a fancy to a girl on the playground.

Alexander was saved by a call from one of the sentries on the wall. Looking up, he saw the man pointing out toward the forest. Sasha leapt to her feet, then pulled him up as well. They both turned to face a group of four players that matched Lorian's description.

In guild chat, Alexander asked, "*Lorian? Are you still back there*?"

Lorian's very amused voice came back. "*We're here, in the trees. They just passed under us. I'd have warned you sooner, but I didn't want to interrupt... whatever that was.*" Sasha grinned at him, proud of herself for some reason.

Lorian continued, "*I do not believe they pose a threat. I've been listening to them talk amongst themselves, and they mostly seem curious about the guild that captured a keep and plans to fight the Dark One. There was no mention of spying, or battling with you. I suspect they plan to ask to join you.*"

Interesting.

"*Thank you, Lorian. If trouble starts, please put an arrow through the healer's head first*," Alexander replied.

The tree line was approximately three hundred yards from their location. Too far for Alexander to make out much detail. He waited while they approached. When they crossed within the boundary of the light posts, Lorian and his hunters appeared out of the tree line, moving smoothly and silently.

Alexander raised a hand. "Greetings!"

One of the two warriors raised his hand to wave back. "Hello there! We're looking for the Greystone guild! Would you happen to be one of them?" he called out.

Alexander was instantly suspicious. If these players knew about Greystone and Dire Keep, then they must have seen the videos. And there were not so many elves around Stormforge that they'd fail to recognize him.

"I am Alexander. One of the leaders of Greystone. How can I help you?" They were now less than fifty yards away, still moving forward. Their body language was very casual, none of them reaching for weapons or checking the area around them.

Sasha must have had the same thoughts. She sent out a message in guild chat. "*Player party has arrived. There's something strange about them. We're out in front of the gates. Maybe you guys wanna come say hello?*"

The group walked within five yards before coming to a halt. Alexander had put a hand to his sword, letting them know to keep a polite distance.

"Easy there, Alexander. We mean you no harm. My name is Dayle. This is Warren, Misty, and Lyra." He indicated first the other warrior, then the mage, and finally the healer. "We saw the system message about you taking the keep. And we know about your battle with PWP. We came to see if we could join you."

"No offense, but how do I know you're not just PWP butt-munchers, or other minions of the so-called 'Dark One' come to infiltrate our ranks?" Alexander asked.

Dayle didn't even blink at the insult. If he was PWP, he was smarter than their average bear.

"We're not. And I can prove it to you by telling you something about yourself that I shouldn't know." Dayle smiled. His hands remained well away from his weapon. His eyes shifted upward as Brick, Max, and Lainey walked out the gate.

"You're Alexander Greystone. That's Sasha, Max, and Brick. I didn't catch the other girl's name. But I know your face. I've seen your dad's feed as he watched you play," the man said.

Alexander thought for a moment. "Anybody halfway clever could have made the name connection. I did use my last name for the guild name, after all. Tell me more about seeing the feed with my dad." The others had arrived in time to hear this last request, and were suddenly very interested.

"Can we come in and sit down? We've had a long day fighting mobs a good bit stronger than us," Dayle said.

Alexander pulled two long stone blocks from the ground, two benches. One right behind the group of players, and one behind his group. "Have a seat. I'm not ready to let you into the keep yet." He motioned to the bench.

Dayle looked behind himself and laughed. "Nice trick, that." He and his group sat. Misty actually let out a long sigh of relief.

"Actually, tricks are sort of why we're here. This is what I meant when I said I can tell you something about yourselves. When you were 'reborn' in these toons, you found that your magic worked a little different, right? That you could tweak it in ways you couldn't before?" Dayle asked.

"It's possible. But again, somebody clever could have figured that out from the videos," Alexander said.

"I'm going to show you something. Don't freak out," Dayle said. He and the mage rose from their seats and stepped to the side. "Do me a favor, raise me a stone target, over there." He pointed off to the side, away from both groups. Alexander complied, raising a six foot block of stone the approximate size of a human.

Dayle moved back several steps, and then to his left, closer to the target. He eyed his position relative to Misty, the mage. Then he raised his shield, and adjusted the angle a bit. "Misty's going to cast a spell, now. She'll cast it at me. There's no danger to you," he said. When Alexander nodded his head, Misty moved her hands and cast a massive bolt of ice at the warrior. He stepped back for just a split second, then shoved his shield forward. The bolt ricocheted off his shield and headed toward the stone target. Dayle waited a full second, then activated his shield rush ability. He chased the bolt to the target. It was faster, and struck the stone, freezing it. A second later, Dayle's shield struck the frozen target, shattering the top three feet of it.

Everyone was silent for a moment. They were all thinking the same thing. A tank should not be able to redirect a spell like that, and definitely should not be able to react quickly enough to follow the bolt that closely. A normal player would have been a full two seconds slower. At least.

Sasha blurted out, "You're in immersion!". When she realized what she'd said, she gasped and covered her mouth with her hands.

The members of the other group laughed. Dayle said, "Better you break the NDA than me. I had to be very careful there. But now that it's out there, I can tell you. Especially since you're all Jupiter employees, like us." He dropped the final bomb.

Alexander recovered quickly. "Tell me," was all he said.

"You're the boss." Dale grinned at him. "We are indeed immersion players. From the time codes on the killer bunny video I saw last time I was out, we started our immersions about three days before you did. We're all a week into our two-week immersions now."

Lainey said, "A week… then, they don't know about Delbert Simms." She looked upset. He'd need to have a one-on-one with her like he'd just done with Sasha. Preferably minus the tickling.

"Okay. I believe that you're immersion players. Or at least you are, Dayle. Nobody else could pull off that stunt. Good way to make your point, by the way. I bet my dad's laughing his ass off right now," Alexander said. "But that doesn't explain why you're here."

"You mind if we eat while we talk? Like I said, long day." Dayle reached into his bag and produced some jerky.

"Anyway, we've had our own run-ins with PWP in Antalia, where we started. Their guild house is there, and they killed us several times when we first hit level 10 and left the city. Stole all our gear. We managed to get past them eventually, and stayed away from the city. We found a few villages where we could get repairs and sell our loot. And we managed to level up enough to start doing some really interesting quests. When we logged out, we of course saw the videos of you taking out party after party of PWP."

"And the bunny video!" Misty giggled, winking at Brick.

Dayle grinned as well, and continued. "We'd already started to make our way to Stormforge to ask to join you, when we saw the system alert about Dire Keep. So, we headed here. Arriving just in time to interrupt your ticklefight."

Alexander must not have looked convinced. After a few moments of silence, Dayle said, "During our last log-out, I talked to your dad about your group, and told him I was thinking about joining. He said there was code in the game called the 'Odin Trial' that would let you know we're for real."

Alexander sighed. Sasha laughed. She knew what Dayle was talking about. Alexander had told her about it when he'd help code it back then. He knew for sure his dad was laughing now.

Standing up, Alexander raised his hands to the sky. There was very specific sequence of actions and words required for this. It had been a funny joke to him at the time.

"Oh, Odin, All-Father. All-knowing. All-seeing, I beseech thee. Tell your humble servant if this warrior speaks true. Are these players before me what they claim?" he yelled toward the sky.

If Odin agreed with Dayle, there would be a harmless roll of thunder. If Dayle lied in any way, there would be lightning. Alexander was guessing by the looks on their faces, the other players didn't know how this worked.

A roll of thundered echoed through the sky above the forest. Dayle and the others still looked confused. Now that he knew they were friends, or at least not enemies, he decided to get a little payback for having to go through that show.

"Did that sound like angry thunder to you? Or friendly? I can never tell. If it's angry thunder, you've got about five seconds before lightning hits you." He smiled at the group, and took a few steps back for effect.

The others' eyes got wide and they all looked to the sky. When nothing happened after five seconds, Alexander began to laugh.

"Sorry. Just a joke. The thunder meant you were truthful. There really would have been lightning if you lied, but it would have been instant. I was just a lil ticked off about having to go through that whole show. You can be sure when you log out there will be video of that." He shook his head.

Lyra chuckled a bit. The others didn't think it was quite as funny.

"Have a seat. We need to talk," he said. He raised a table between the two benches, and sent a guild message to Lola, asking her to have Mattie bring out a pot of stew and bowls and spoons for nine."

"You can put the jerky away. There's some good food coming. I'll invite you inside in a bit, but there are some things best discussed away from the ears of citizens."

The serious look on his face had the other group curious. He decided not to beat around the bush.

"The last night of our last immersion, which would have been… almost six days ago, Olympus was attacked. It was a group of people who used a car bomb to try to break through the gate, and had a van full of people carrying automatic rifles and rocket launchers. The attack was unsuccessful, and nobody on our side was seriously injured. Two of the people who were on top of the van shooting rockets were shot by our security. Then something exploded. We don't know if it was a vest, or a dropped rocket, or what. All of the attackers were killed."

"Oh my god," Misty said. The others were silent. Alexander gave them time to soak in the information.

"Why… why would somebody attack Olympus?" Lyra asked. Her voice was barely above a whisper.

"You said you've seen some of the videos on PWP. Did you see the one where a player who'd been arrested, the one Lainey here shot in the nuts so many times, got all raged out and threatened a GM and his dog? Got himself banned for life?" Alexander asked.

Warren, the other warrior, snorted. "Dumbass. I saw that video. The guy was all 'they tortured me!' and the GM was totally 'you deserved it', and the dude just went nuts." The others nodded their heads.

Alexander looked at them. "That player's name was Delbert Simms. He was one of the people who attacked Olympus."

"Holy shitballs!" Misty said. Again, the others were silent. Alexander gave it a few seconds, then continued.

"Yesterday, I was challenged to a duel in Stormforge by a warrior who was part of a group serving the Dark One, but not PWP. There was a battle, actually two battles, and the group was arrested. The warrior mentioned during the duel that he was a friend of Delbert Simms. As you know, our gameplay is being monitored. So, the folks at Olympus saw that. We kept him and his friends busy long enough for the FBI to mobilize and raid their houses. We don't know the results, or if they found anything. But the warrior also said the 'Dark One' was a real-life person, who was paying in American dollars for people willing to try and take down the Greystones."

Alexander paused when Mattie and four others showed up with trays of food and utensils. She laid out the pot of stew, loaves of bread, and some fruit. There were a couple pitchers of ale, and a couple more of water. Alexander thanked her, and Sasha gave her a hug, before they returned to the keep.

He continued to wait while the four players dished up some stew and poured drinks. He knew this was a lot to process. They were in no rush.

Finally, Misty said, around a mouthful of stew, "This is REALLY good!"

Sasha laughed. "Thanks. It's a recipe we got from our friend Lydia. You'll meet her."

Warren gulped down some ale. "Did you guys notice how much BETTER the food tastes now?"

Lainey laughed, "I don't know about better, because I didn't play before, but it does taste damn good. My first meal here I told a stranger the food was orgasmic."

The player group all chuckled at that.

Dayle got serious again after a few more moments of enjoying the food. "So, players serving this Dark One here in the game could be working for him in real life, too?"

"Yes. We won't know for sure till we log out again in ten days. But that's what it looks like. Which brings me to why we're out here talking. Nobody knows who you are right now. But if you join us, your faces and names will get out there on videos. And this group seems to be able to get their hands on personal information. They had mine and my dad's home address in a file in the van that blew up. So, if you join us, which you are welcome to do, you need to know of the potential danger to you. And maybe those close to you. My dad has initiated a protocol that gathers all employees in lockdown mode inside Olympus. Those who feel the need can bring their immediate family, too. There's plenty of housing on the compound. You would be offered the same accommodation. You'd use immersion pods on Olympus."

Warren volunteered, "I'm already at Olympus. So is Lyra. We're brother and sister."

"Dayle and I are at corporate housing in the city," Misty said. "Are we in danger?"

"My father and Michael hired an army of security. All of our facilities have been locked down, and armed up. You're under guard right now, and well protected. If there's any threat, they'll log you out and evacuate you," Alexander reassured her.

"If any of you have family you want brought in, say so now. The folks monitoring us will see that it happens."

He watched their faces. They were all deep in thought.

"Lyra and I are all that we have. Our folks are dead. We spent most of our time playing Io to pay the bills. Not much time for social lives," Warren said.

"I have a sister that lives in the city. Please have somebody go see her. She probably won't come. She's kind of a badass. A cop. But she needs to know she might be in danger," Misty said.

Dayle shook his head. "I don't really have anybody either. Had a girlfriend, but she dumped me when I signed up for this."

Misty giggled. "Yeah, that's why she dumped you."

Alexander looked at Misty. "If your sister was listed as next of kin on your employment forms, I imagine they've already reached out to her." After a moment, there was a roll of thunder. "See. Odin confirms."

"Thank you, that makes me feel better."

Alexander leaned forward and put his hands on the table. "You have some options, now. In light of the situation, if any of you feel the need to log out now, or even discontinue your involvement with Jupiter, you will be paid for your time, plus a bonus."

He gave them a minute, but nobody spoke up. "It's not safe for you out here. We expect the Dark One's people to attack. We actually figured you were scouts. I can teleport you to a safe spot in the palace at Stormforge, or you can come inside the keep and lay low, keep yourselves out of any videos, until your immersion is up. Then you can get more details on what's going on, and make a decision from there. It may be that the raids solved all our problems for us. Then again, maybe not," he continued.

"Or, if you'd like to join us and take an active role, you are certainly most welcome to do so. We could use help we can trust," he finished.

Lainey spoke up. "You only need to decide now if you want to be teleported and quit. Otherwise, you can come inside and think it over."

Dayle looked at the others, who all shook their heads. "None of us wants to quit. This gig pays more for a year than any of us would make in three years playing the game for profit."

"Amen to that," Max agreed. "That's how Brick and I were livin' too."

Alexander said, "I can still teleport you back to Stormforge. The city is relatively safe, and you'd be just a group of unknown players."

Lyra put her hand on her brother's shoulder. "The way I see it, we're as safe as we can be inside Olympus. And there's nothing we can do outside the game to help. In here, at least we can be useful. I'd like to join you. All in."

Warren looked at her for a minute, thinking. "If she's in, I'm in," he said.

Misty said, "I'm in too, for now. Until we log out again, and get more information, at least."

Dayle shook his head. "These young fools would be lost without me. Guess I'm in, too."

"Great! Glad to have you." Alexander sent them all guild invites. "Let's head back inside. We make tempting targets out here.

They all grabbed some dishes and headed back to the gate. Lola met them just outside, and handed each of the new members a Greystone medallion. They'd been tuned to the wards of the keep, as well as the compound in the city.

"Oh, yeah. There are wards both here at the keep and at our compound. These medallions will grant you access. Anyone trying to get through without one will be killed, or ported to a dungeon cell, depending on the setting," Alexander said. "Thank you, Lola, for thinking of that. Everyone, this is Lola. Our apprentice chamberlain, recent guild member, and future treasurer."

The others introduced themselves as they walked through the gates. Mattie was there with helpers to take away all their dishes.

"We've just started rebuilding the keep. I'm afraid we're a bit limited on housing at the moment. There are some very spartan rooms, and some tents available. Lola, can you help figure out a place for them to sleep?" Alexander asked.

"Of course, Alexander." She smiled.

Max thumped Dayle on the back. "There's some good news. Three new guildies who just joined yesterday went with Alexander to clear the mine today. Their share of the loot was over thirty thousand gold each. Our boy here has a way of finding money."

The four players stared at Alexander. "We got lucky," he explained. "There was a tribe of kobolds mining ore and gems. It was just laying around everywhere. And we found a large deposit of refined mithril worth a lot of gold."

Leaving Lola to manage the new members, Alexander went back up on the wall. When he got to the top, he looked out over the field, and forest beyond. He pictured an army crossing that field, intent on killing all those inside the keep. Those he'd promised to protect.

I need to stop screwing around and focus on defenses. We have fifteen players in the guild now. Ten of us in immersion. We could make a decent stand, with backup from the citizens on the wall. But decent is not good enough, he thought.

Deciding to check on the status of the keep, he teleported himself to the control room. "Jeeves, please show me the keep's status"

"*Of course, master*" the keep's AI replied.

The three-dimensional display appeared with its normal blue glow.

Dire Keep: Level 14/25	
Physical Status: 340/500	**Resources: 15,000 units**
See Infrastructure for details	*See Resources for details*
Current Population: 139	**Defensive Capabilities: 80%**
Citizens: 137 Guests: 2	*See Defense for details*
Ancillary Structures: 4	**Production rate: 20%**
See Ancillary Structures for details	*Production will increase with population and use of ancillary structures*

Four levels in a day. Not too shabby. Almost back to where it was before Fitz trashed the place. One of them came from the addition of the wizard's tower, and the smithy extension, and probably the chapel consecrations, combined. He noted there were two more ancillary structures listed. That would be the tower and smithy. And obviously, the number of citizens jumped way up, accounting for two levels recovered for population. The repair of the walls brought the defense percentage up. And production rate was up.

"Jeeves, please show me production details," he said.

Production Rate: 20%	
Mine: 380 units (gems)	Carpentry: 25 units
Smithy: 50 units	Food: 45 units (hunting)

So, they'd gotten credit for the gems he had Lugs carry out of the mine, but not for the gems or the ore still inside. That made sense. Brick had said the smithy was producing as fast as possible. Apparently, they'd managed fifty weapons or tools today. Carpenters had been working on tables, chairs, and doors. And the food must be the meat brought in by the hunters. As for the resource increase, they had brought a lot of supplies with them. Apparently a thousand units' worth.

"Jeeves," he asked. "When we assumed ownership of the keep, the status showed 14,000 units of resources. What were those?"

"*When you made the Keep your property, or more specifically a Greystone Guild property, a guild vault was established, and the 14,000 items of value you found in the lich's chamber became keep resources. All items were placed in the vault*," Jeeves replied.

The lich's treasure! He'd forgotten to send somebody down for it. But the number didn't seem right. "Jeeves, why is the value of the items in the vault so low?"

"*The resource unit count does not reflect value, master. It simply states the number of individual items. There were 12,640 coins of differing metals, 1,170 gems of different sizes and elements, and 190 miscellaneous items including weapons, armor pieces, cutlery…*"

"I get the idea, Jeeves. Thank you." Alexander cut him off. "Tell me, Jeeves. Have your additional levels granted any new abilities, or options?"

"Yes, master. I have some upgrades available now. You may choose between one of three." The display changed to a list of three keep upgrades.

Improved Interface
Interface 'Jeeves' will become more intuitive in interaction with ownership entities, and will be able to perform certain tasks autonomously.

Extended Area
The area of influence of Dire Keep would be extended one half mile in every direction.

Self-Repair
Interface 'Jeeves' will be able to effect repairs to the keep automatically. Repairs require correlating resource units of sufficient quantity to replace lost or damaged elements.

Alexander opened officer's chat. Then he invited Silverbeard, Lola, and Kai. When all had accepted, he said "*Quick meeting, folks. I'm looking for a vote here. The keep leveled up four times today. We have our choice of an upgrade. There are three options. Better interface with Jeeves, a ½ mile radial extension of our lands, or the ability for the keep to repair automatically. What do you think?*"

There was silence for a while. "*The repairs would come in handy. If the keep can do them faster than the masons and you and Fitz.*" Max replied.

"*Repairs require resources to match the element being repaired.*" Silverbeard said. *"So, to repair the stone o' the keep, ye would need a stockpile o' stone blocks. To repair doors, ye would need lumber.*"

Kai added, "*Extending your lands would just leave you with more to defend. I see no logical reason to do so at this time.*"

"*What's the benefit of the improved interface?*" Sasha asked. "*Other than making Jeeves more like Alfred*?"

"*It says he'll be able to complete certain tasks autonomously, and will become more intuitive.*" Alexander responded.

Silverbeard had input on this, as well. "*Do not underestimate the value of an efficient interface. It can be a powerful and useful tool. Ye can set it to monitor crops and adjust irrigation. Or set up a calendar of events, with reminders. Or it can monitor resources, and notify ye if production has changed, or a specific resource is running low.*"

"*Silverbeard, you weren't kidding when you said you know everything about everything*!" Alexander chuckled.

"*I think the immediate need be repairs.*" Brick said.

"*Me too.*" Lainey voted. "*We can always upgrade the interface after the next level up. Or two, or whatever.*"

"*I agree.*" Kai interjected. "*Alexander, you and Fitz can raise stone quickly. The masons can convert that into blocks that will work as resource units. The keep could begin repairing itself quickly.*"

"*Sounds like the majority are for repairs. Any arguments*?" Alexander asked.

Hearing none, he said, "*Repairs it is. Thank you all. And, uhh... Lola? Where am I sleeping tonight?*"

"*We have restored the baron's chambers to a usable condition for you.*" Lola responded.

"*Like, the master suite? I don't need all that space. Why not give it to Sasha or Lainey? Or Kai? He IS a prince, after all.*"

"*I was told-*" Lola began, before Lainey cut her off.

"*We told Lola to give it to you.*"

"*Yeah.*" Sasha giggled. "*You know, in case you and Jules end up sharing…*" Alexander rolled his eyes.

"*Ahem, yes.*" Silverbeard interrupted the awkward silence. "*The baron's chambers include a valet's chamber which would be quite comfortable for Prince Edward, in his capacity as your squire. And would allow you to keep a close eye on him.*"

"*Also, it has a huge bed! Just in case.*" Lainey chuckled.

"*Okay, fine. Thank you all very much. If any of you see Edward, please tell him to meet me in the main hall. Have a good night.*" He abruptly cut off the chat meeting before Sasha could start chanting her favorite rhyme again.

"Jeeves, please activate the self-repair upgrade. And, can you show me a map of the keep?" he asked.

"*Of course, master. And I have marked the location of the baron's suite.*" The display changed to a three-dimensional rendering of the keep, including the walls, towers (though there was no information on the interior of the wizard's tower), and the main building from the top floor down to the 5th dungeon level. The baron's suite was on the third floor, above the main hall.

His little project was going rather well. For its first day. And best of all, they'd not been attacked. He considered that the biggest success of the day. A long day. He was ready to sleep.

Teleporting himself back to the designated zone by the portal, he walked into the main building and headed toward the great hall. He found Edward waiting for him. "You're bunking with me, squire. Sort of. Let's go," he said.

The prince followed him up the main stair to the third floor, and then down a long hallway that ended in an oversized, arched ironwood door. This had to be the place. The man sure thought a lot of himself.

Passing through the heavy door, they found themselves in a spacious sitting room. There were two sofas and several chairs arranged around a fireplace. Two doors led from the either side of the room, and the back wall was a pair of large windows looking out over the courtyard below.

The door to the right opened onto a medium sized bedroom, furnished with a wardrobe, a small desk, and a storage chest set at the foot of the bed. It had its own en-suite bathroom.

"This must be yours." Alexander looked to Edward.

The prince nodded. "This will do nicely. I expected to be living in a tent."

"Alright, squire." Alexander grinned at him. "Get yourself settled. Wake me at sunrise if I'm not already up."

He left the room, closing the door behind him. Crossing the sitting room, he opened the last remaining door to find that it led to a study. The room was maybe twenty feet square, with perfectly preserved shelves lining all the walls except the one with a window. And there was a gap in the shelves on either side of a small fireplace. The shelves were empty of books. Alexander assumed Fitz had confiscated them. A large desk made of a wood that looked like mahogany sat in front of the window.

Opposite the doorway he stood in, there was another door. This one led to a large bedroom with a bed big enough to sleep five. There was another fireplace, and a single wide glass door that led out to a small balcony. Yet another door led to a palatial bath with separate shower and tub, a small sitting area with a tall mirror, and a closed off area for the toilet. The entire room was white marble. There was a walk-in closet as well. Alexander would have to remember to ask Fitz to look for any secret doors. He'd bet money the baron would have built himself a discrete way into and out of his quarters.

He closed and locked the closet door, then the glass door. Doing the same with the door that led to the study, he leaned his sword and staff against it. If somehow a rogue working for the Dark One managed to sneak this far, they would fall over when the door opened, and alert him. Removing his boots, he crawled onto the ridiculous bed, and closed his eyes.

Chapter Eleven

Just Another Brick in The Wall

Alexander awoke before dawn, and retrieved his weapons from the door. Waiting for Edward to appear, he sat at the desk in the study. He pulled a sheet of paper out of a drawer, and grabbing a pen, began to make a list.

When was the last time I actually wrote something on paper? I can't even remember.

He listed the projects that came to mind in order of priority. First and foremost was repairs to the keep. He would need to pull some stone for the masons to cut into blocks. Then he'd focus on the new wall. He wanted to start raising sections as soon as possible. Fitz should have the guild mages there today to help.

Next on the list was water. They needed to make sure there was an adequate, clean, and sustainable supply. He made a small note to the side to ask Beatrix about this. And about an irrigation system.

He'd get the farmers started on plowing the fields. With a warning that they'd need to be ready to retreat in a rapid manner if enemies appeared. The same with whatever crew was going out to cut lumber. He'd already made arrangement for the hunters to watch over them, but he wanted to be as safe as possible.

He needed to speak with Kai about exploring that lower level of the mine. In case there was still a momma (daddy?) worm down there. He hoped Kai could Vulcan mind-thingy the worm, so they wouldn't have to fight it. He'd have Grimble use one of those special mining picks to start harvesting the mithril as soon as they cleared that lower level. Not that the dwarf needed reminding. He was itching to get back in there.

He also needed to speak with Fitz about upgrading his magic. He'd reached level 40, and should have access to more spells. And he wanted to improve his wizard's fire spell to level 2, if there was such a thing. He'd remind the others to get some training as well. He wasn't sure where everyone was, level-wise. He and Sasha had gotten a level from the mine. He knew Max and Lainey had been out killing beasts, and probably got a few levels. They'd all likely left Brick a bit behind. He'd spent nearly the whole day at the smithy.

If he had time, he wanted to practice his enchanting. Which reminded him. He owed Father Ignatius a pendant like Silverbeard's. And Father Alric should probably have one too. He pulled out two pieces of obsidian, and shaped them into discs, infusing them with the healing light magic, and then the Undying spell. He didn't get a skill level for these, presumably because he was just repeating work he'd done before.

Edward appeared just as the sky was beginning to lighten. The two of them headed downstairs to see about breakfast. Edward seemed quite popular with the ladies of the kitchen as they passed through. He got smiles and winks from nearly all of them, and a pastry from Edna. When Alexander stood there looking expectantly at her, she just said, "Shoo! You'll ruin your breakfast!" Edward grinned at him as they walked out. "I can't help it if I'm lovable. And you did tell me to make friends," he said.

Dishing up plates of eggs, sausage, and biscuits, the two men sat at a table with several of the dwarven guards. The dwarves were preparing to take a shift on the wall. He informed them that several crews, including himself and the mages, would be working outside the wall all day. And asked them to keep a sharp eye on the tree line. He also told them that any stealthed minions of the Dark One would be exposed the moment they set foot inside the arc of light posts. So, if anyone suddenly appeared, looking surprised and stunned, shoot first and ask questions later.

Finished with breakfast, they headed out the gate. As they walked, Alexander asked Edward if he had a bow. And the ability to shoot it. Edward affirmed both, and produced his bow.

"Good. You're going to cover us today. There will be hunters in the woods near the tree line, watching for enemies. But if they get through, I want you shooting from the back, not up close, swinging your sword."

Stepping just to the right of the gate a few paces outside the wall, Alexander used his earth mover skill to raise several rows of stone. He made each one sixty feet long, by two feet wide, and four feet high.

Realizing he'd forgotten to tell the masons what he was doing, he sent Edward back inside. "Find a mason, or Silverbeard, or Lola. Tell them the masons should come out here and cut this stone immediately. The keep will be able to absorb the blocks, and use them to repair itself."

The boy trotted back inside, and Alexander pulled a few more rows while he waited.

Returning with a couple of the masons, Edward reported that he'd bumped into Fitz on his way to get breakfast. The wizard had grunted something about going to get help at the guild afterward. Knowing the wizard, breakfast could take an hour.

Heading back inside, he located Silverbeard in the great hall. "Good morning, Master Silverbeard," he greeted the ancient dwarf. "Did you sleep well?"

"Like I were only 300 years old!" Silverbeard grinned at him.

Laughing, Alexander asked the chamberlain to send out the farmers and lumber crews when they were ready. He also asked him to send Beatrix outside when she emerged from her room. Alexander's UI showed she was offline. But to citizens, she was merely sleeping.

"Also, I should probably have that conversation with Lola about being treasurer. Maybe this evening? Actually, maybe that should be a group discussion." He was speaking mainly to himself, but Silverbeard nodded in agreement.

"Just out of curiosity, Master Silverbeard, do you know anything about our water supply here?"

"There be two rainwater cisterns built into the walls o' the keep that will need to be drained and cleaned. There be an underground stream that was redirected under the keep by its original builders. This supplies fresh water through the plumbing system. The water appears to be clean, but we should confirm that," the dwarf replied.

"Thank you. I'll ask Beatrix to see to both. Is there anything you need from me?" Alexander asked.

"It would be helpful to work on housing, as soon as ye can," Silverbeard replied. "Current structures be sufficient to hold one hundred, but we have closer to one hundred fifty here."

"Right after we finish the new wall," Alexander promised. The mine would have to wait.

Venturing back outside, Alexander found Fitz and the guild mages walking toward the gate. "Good morning, gentlemen! Thank you, for coming to assist us today!" he called out. The two mages were clearly no more morning people than Fitz himself. All he got in return was some grumbling.

"The plan for today is to raise a wall, two hundred yards out from the existing wall. The wall itself will be ten feet high, and ten feet deep so that we can run weapons and troops along the top without tripping over each other. There will be a moat outside, forty feet deep, so pull the stone from in front of the wall. Make no mistake. There will be war here. This isn't a 'what if?' situation. We'll need crenellations along the front, stairs on the back side every five hundred feet, and a covered area at each stair where soldiers can take cover from the elements or falling magic. Also, enchantments to repel magical attacks. I'll handle the gatehouse, tower, and the supports for the drawbridge. I've placed an arc of light posts from ridge to ridge. Just follow that line. I'd like the walls to be placed right inside the edge of the consecrated ground. This will prevent stealthers from sneaking over and sabotaging the gate."

The mages nodded, and split up. With four of them, the construction should go quickly. The whole wall would be just under a mile long in an arc. That was a long wall to defend. But Alexander was expecting the most dangerous attacks to come in a concentrated area of players. So, they could likewise concentrate their defenses. And, if necessary, they could fall back to the original wall, which was a much more compact and easily defended structure. In truth, this outer wall was mainly meant to give his farmers and shepherds time to retreat, and to protect the crops and livestock.

Standing just behind the central light post, Alexander began to pull stone from the earth. He raised it in sections ten feet thick by fifty feet long, and ten feet high. Moving the stone from in front of the wall created a trench that would serve as the beginning of the moat. Each of the mages would need to raise twenty-five similar sized sections. That could be done in a day, if they maintained their stamina and mana. Sasha had provided potions for that purpose.

Alexander left a twenty-foot-wide gap between the first two sections of wall. Above the gap and on either side, he created a gatehouse. This stood twenty feet high, instead of ten, and was twenty feet thick. It would serve as a combination guard tower, barracks, and trap for any invaders trying to push through the gate. The masons would shape murder holes in the walls and ceiling. When an enemy broke through the outer gate, or in this case the drawbridge, they would be delayed underneath while they tried to break the much stronger inner gate. While they were grouped up inside, fire would rain down on them from above and arrows from the sides.

But all those surprises would come later. Today's mission was just to get the wall up and usable. Finishing the gatehouse, Alexander began to move to his left. He pulled section after section, fifty feet in length, melding each one to the last. Edward tagged along, bow at the ready. When he'd pulled a dozen sections, he took a break. This work was much easier than pulling obsidian from deep underground, through hundreds of feet of other stone. There was no resistance here, other than the weight of the stone sections themselves. He was simply pushing up bedrock through a layer of soil. Still, there was a drain on his stamina. Magic didn't completely negate the physical strain of moving tons of stone. After a rest, he got back to work. The hours passed.

Being the least experienced of the mages on the field, he was slower than the others. He was on his twentieth section when Fitz, who had started at the ridge on the left side, met up with him. The wizard had pulled thirty sections, the last one connecting to Alexander's twentieth.

As it was past lunchtime, the three of them headed back to the kitchen. The other two mages had completed their sections, and met Fitz, Edward, and Alexander at the gate. In just over five hours, the four of them had pulled a hundred sections of stone wall, merged them to their neighbor, and shaped it. Each section took an average of ten minutes. Those with stairs and covers took a bit longer.

After all that work, four very hungry mages took a seat at the table nearest the kitchen, and Mattie brought them heaping platters of wolf steak with sautéed onions, steamed vegetables, fresh bread, and baked potatoes with butter. The entire thing tasted better than Alexander had ever had at any five-star restaurant. Master Silverbeard joined them, and brought the lead mason along. The group took some time after the meal was finished to discuss the wall.

Silverbeard had had the idea to place structures against the inside of the wall. Single story, with stairs leading to roof hatches that would allow quick access to the wall. The structures could be used for storage, stables for work animals, simple shelter for livestock, even housing for those who wished a little more privacy and space. The dwarves, in particular, were interested in these. The mason outlined housing units with a ground floor entry, and two or three underground levels. These would also make good defensive holdouts if citizens didn't have time to retreat after an attack. The mason assured him that dwarves could make doors leading to the lower levels that none would see. The stone for all of this, plus a roadway to connect it all that would run parallel to the wall, could be pulled from outside the wall, increasing the size of the moat.

Alexander loved the idea! This would create needed housing without reducing the available space in the inner keep structures. The proposal solved several problems all at once!

Fitz and the two guild mages went with the master mason to begin work on those structures. Alexander, meanwhile, went back to the gate house, after sending Edward to see if he could find Beatrix. Or to man the inner wall if he couldn't find her. It was mid-afternoon, and he still needed to create the bridge sections and support for the drawbridge.

As he walked across the now enclosed field, he saw the farmers moving about, marking off sections and hauling equipment on wagons. A contingent of hunters had already moved onto the wall itself, and were keeping an eye on the logging crew and the tree line.

Building the supports wasn't really building, per se. He was really just removing the rock around them, and leaving them in place. He did need to raise them just a bit, as he wanted the bridge to have some arch to it. Not enough to make it difficult for wagons, just enough to keep water from pooling and freezing on it.

So, he widened the moat trench to forty feet, and made it forty feet deep. He moved all the excess rock underneath and inside the wall. They'd use it for towers, or shelters, or simply cut it into blocks for keep resources. He left a five-foot-long by twenty-foot-wide section of stone in front of the gate to serve as a base for the drawbridge. Then twenty feet out, a support rose up from the bottom of the moat. This marked the near end of the twenty-foot-long stone section of the bridge, which extended to the far side of the moat. So, anyone crossing the bridge into the keep would first cross twenty feet of stone, then twenty feet of ironwood drawbridge. Alexander designed it this way with the moat monster in mind. With the drawbridge raised, enemies would be tempted out onto the stone section, where the monster could pick them off with ease. It would also give the monster something to hide under, if it was so inclined.

With that done, he began to make his way along the left side, widening and deepening the moat by pushing the rock under and up inside the wall. Unfortunately, widening the moat also required him to relocate his light posts. So he moved them along the outer edge of the moat.

Skill level up! Earth magic +1. Rank increase: Adept
Through repeated and creative use of your earth magic abilities, your skill level has increased to Adept. Mana cost of Earth spells -15%. Range of earth spells +10%

As he approached the ridge a couple hours later, he noticed old Lars, the fisherman, sitting on the grass by the lake. He had a couple fishing poles set up, lines in the water with cork bobbers… well, bobbing.

Waving at Lars, he approached. "Catching anything?" He smiled. A quiet afternoon of fishing suddenly seemed like a really good idea.

"Aye, lad, there be all kinds of tasty lil buggers in this lake!" Lars was excited. "Won't feed many folks using poles, though. If we're depending on fish as a staple, I'll need a net. And a small boat. And a dock," he added.

"Well, some of that I can manage right now. We won't be depending on fish. But maybe having enough for everyone once a week would be good? And if you don't think it'll empty the lake, you could trade some to the Broken Mountain dwarves for your own profit." Alexander picked up on the enthusiasm.

Asking Lars to pick his spot, he pulled some stone up from the lake bed to make a pier that extended a couple dozen feet out into the water.

Then, to one side, he built a six-foot stone box that could be filled with water and used to store Lars' catch during the day, to keep them fresh.

Stepping back onto land, he built a small, single room stone hut sixty feet back from the shore that the old man could use for shelter in case of bad weather, or if he just wanted to get out of the sun. He raised a long stone bench inside against a wall, for sitting or sleeping. Next, he extended the roof forward to create a porch. Lastly, he raised a stone hearth with a wide shelf three feet off the ground. Lars could clean and cook some fish there if he felt the urge. As an afterthought, he raised a stone table and bench near the base of the pier. It was a good place to sit and work, or eat, while enjoying the view.

When he was done, he turned to the old man. "You'll have to see the carpenters about a boat. As for nets, I don't even know who would make those? We could buy you some in the city on our next trip.

"Don't worry, lad, I can make my own net. And I can throw it off the pier, for now. Until a boat can be made. Thank you for all this. The comforts of home!" Lars smiled, and shook his hand. "With that wall popping up behind me, I was starting to figure you'd decided to lock me out!" Alexander laughed. "I'm going to seal the gate for the night when I'm done here. Would you like me to teleport you back inside?"

"Naw. I think I'll sleep out here tonight," Lars said.

"It's not safe out here, Lars. You can make this your home, if you wish, once we've removed the threat. It's all yours. And I'll improve it in whatever way you see fit. But for now, I'd feel better if you slept inside the keep at night."

The old man nodded his head. He pulled in his two fishing lines, and stowed the poles in the hut. Then Alexander teleported him and his day's catch back into the keep.

Moving back to the wall, Alexander finished widening the moat until he reached the stone wall of the ridge. On a whim, he continued the trench on into the ridge face to a depth of about a hundred feet. Thus creating an underground cave for the moat monster to call home.

Sunset was approaching by this time, so he teleported himself back to the outer wall gatehouse. He saw that the lumber crew had placed some split logs across the unfinished bridge span, making a temporary foot bridge that they were now crossing, along with three hunters. He greeted them as they passed, and confirmed that no others were outside. Not wanting to leave the area unprotected, even with the moat in place, he sealed the gate with a temporary three-foot-thick stone wall.

While he'd been outside the wall, things had progressed nicely inside. He could see several structures attached to the inside of the wall, spaced widely apart. The closest was a stable that already held two plow-horses, and a set of plow blades.

Standing in the middle of the field between the two gates, he called out, "Jeeves, can you hear me?" There was no answer. Apparently, he needed to be closer to a structure. He walked the last hundred yards and passed under the bailey gate. Standing in the tunnel, he repeated, "Jeeves, can you hear me?"

"*Yes, master. Though I could hear you before, I could not answer*," the interface replied.

"About that. If we were to build a stone road that led between the gates, would that count as a structure? Could you speak through that?" Alexander asked.

"*Yes, master. And once the outer wall and gate is complete, I will be able to speak though those, as well. Also, the addition may be enough to grant me a level increase*," Jeeves said.

"Jeeves, can you detect when people are on the wall?" Alexander had an idea.

"*Yes, master. There are currently six citizens at various posts along the wall*," Jeeves replied.

"And, if I were to remove those hunters from the wall, could you alert me anytime someone was up there?"

"Yes, master. Thought the structure is not yet complete, the consecration of the land allowed me to extend my awareness out to the distance of your light posts."

"Okay, Jeeves, please monitor the outer wall. If anyone crosses the moat and comes into contact with the wall, please let me know. And can you put me on loudspeaker just at the outer wall?"

"I'm afraid not, master. Not until the structure is complete. I can currently transmit your voice to all citizens directly, or to individual citizens that you name, via what you have dubbed the 'emergency message' system."

"I don't know all their names yet, but please transmit my voice to any citizens on the outer wall, or anywhere outside the keep wall."

"Go ahead, master," Jeeves said a moment later.

"Attention, all of you who are outside the original gates. Please return to the keep. We will not need to keep watch on the outer wall tonight. I will be closing the inner doors in thirty minutes. Thank you," he said.

He'd been worried about manning the outer wall. He had twenty-four full-time guards, and six hunters who were citizens. Having to cover two long walls twenty-four hours a day with so few would be impossible. He also had ten new players in the guild, but asking them to take regular guard shifts seemed wrong. Alexander had been thinking about going back to both kings to request more men. But if Jeeves could monitor the outer wall at night, that would reduce the problem significantly.

"Thank you, Jeeves. The next chance we have to upgrade, I'm choosing to improve your interface. You're a handy guy to have around!" He chuckled.

"*Thank you, master.*" Jeeves actually sounded pleased.

Continuing into the courtyard, he found Edward and Beatrix waiting for him. The little gnome smiled and waved as he approached.

"Hi, Beatrix. Did Edward fill you in on the water situation?" he asked.

"He did. We've been to the cisterns. They were pretty moldy inside. I've disconnected them until I can spend some time cleaning them. And we've actually just come from the lower levels. Edward escorted me down to check the water supply. It's clean and clear. And I think the consecration magic is putting a buff on it. Though I can't tell what it is."

Thank you, Beatrix. Well done. I'll ask the priests to check on that buff. They'll be servıng dinner soon. Do me a favor and keep my squire here out of the dwarven spirits?" Alexander winked at her.

"He's bigger than me, but I'm a water mage. If I don't like what he's drinking, I'll freeze it to his lips!" She giggled. Edward somehow managed to include them both in his eye-roll.

Heading inside the donjon, Alexander made his way to the chapel. He found both priests there, talking quietly to Mattie.

"Ah, Alexander, just in time!" Alric said. "Please affirm your approval of Mattie's request for divorce."

"I so affirm," Alexander said.

"I so witness," Father Ignatius added.

"Then by the power granted me by Asclepius, and by the ruler of these lands, I pronounce citizen Mattie divorced of her husband."

Mattie smiled, bowing to both priests. "Thank you. Thank you all. That's a heavy weight off my shoulders. I must get back now, they'll be needing me for dinner service," she said as she practically ran out of the chapel.

"Thank you both for that. Her husband was arrested trying to sneak into our compound in the city. He meant to drag her back by force," Alexander said to the priests.

"No need to thank us. That girl deserves a chance at some happiness," Alric said.

Alexander pulled out the two pendants he'd made for the priests. He handed one to each of them. "My gifts to you, for the consecration of Dire Keep. This is no longer a place of death and abomination. Thank you." The two priests looked at the discs in their hands.

Salvation Pendant
Item Level: Epic
This pendant will allow the wearer to use regenerative light magic to restore 2,000 hp to a friendly target. Charges: 20/20. Undying: Should the bearer receive a mortal blow, the wand will maintain bearer at 1% health, preventing death

Ignatius smiled, and nodded his thanks. Not having seen Silverbeard's medallion, Alric was taken aback. "This… is a wondrous thing," he said.

"But I cannot accept payment for consecrating my own chapel." He tried to hand the medallion back.

"Then accept it as a tool for healing citizens who may very well need your help soon," Alexander said. Remembering that the pendants only had twenty charges, he pulled out two of his smallest soul crystals. Holding them up, he asked, "Do you both know how to use these?"

"We can use the charges within the crystal to recharge depleted items. Or to power our own magic. The church has a supply of these, and trained us in their use. Though they are rare, and never given to humble priests," Ignatius said.

"Well, they are yours, if you swear to me you'll use them to power healing magic for my citizens here, or the citizens of Whitehall," Alexander offered.

Both men bowed their heads and said, "I do so swear, as Asclepius is my witness." There was a brighter than normal pulse of light from the altar. Alexander handed them each a crystal. The smaller crystals had 100 charges each.

"I hope you never have need of those, but if you do, and they lose their charges, come find me and I'll recharge them," Alexander said.

"Thank you, Alexander. But there is no need. We can use the magic of the altars to charge the crystals. It is slow, a single charge per hour. But it should more than suffice," Alric said.

"Dinner should just about be ready. Join me?" Alexander asked the two men.

"We'd be honored," Ignatius said, as they fell in step with him. They walked the main hallway across the ground floor and turned to the wing that held the kitchen. As they walked, Alexander withdrew a thousand gold, and handed it to Ignatius. "Please, hold this in trust for the citizens of Whitehall. We gave them 5,000 gold from the dungeon, but I have no idea how fiscally responsible the mayor is. So, if you see they have a dire need, use this to bail them out."

Father Ignatius nodded as he accepted the coins. "It will be as you ask."

"Speaking of asking, could I ask a favor?" Alexander waited for nods from both men. "Beatrix checked out our water supply earlier, and thought that the holy magic from the altar might be purifying the water, or causing it to provide a buff of some kind. Do you think you could investigate?"

They were just passing through the kitchen. Father Alric paused at one of the sinks, and turned on the water. Holding his hand under it, he closed his eyes. Alexander heard Sasha behind him murmuring, "K-i-s-s-i-n-g". He made a note to extract revenge later.

"Aye, the water is indeed pure. It has the same healing properties as the land. Meaning small wounds will heal faster. Health, Stamina, and Mana will regenerate faster for a full day after drinking this. Our church would pay well for a quantity of this water," he said.

Another potential source of income! But it wouldn't be right to charge the church. I'll get Max to put some vials on the auction. Call it 'Dire Water'. He'll love that.

"Father, I'll make you a deal. If you pay the craftsmen here to make you kegs, or bottles, and pay for them to be shipped to the church, you need not pay for the water. But let's limit that to, say, two barrels a month?" Alexander patted the priest on the shoulder.

The three of them moved outside and took seats at a table. There was already a pot of venison stew on the table, as well as loaves of bread to help soak it up. Kai joined them as they were dishing up bowls for themselves.

"I would like to investigate the lower level of the mine after dinner," the dragon said.

"We can do that. I'll put together a group," Alexander agreed. That was, after all, on his list.

"No, it would be better if it were just us. What we encounter down there might best be kept secret," Kai suggested.

"How about just you, me, and Brick? His shaping skill could come in handy, as could his shield. And we can bring Grimble along, let him use one of those new picks to harvest some mithril upstairs while we explore."

"That should be safe enough," Kai responded. "This stew is quite good," he added.

Alexander was about to use guild chat to call Brick, when he spotted him several tables over. Standing up, he grabbed a chunk of carrot from his stew, and threw it at his friend's face. His aim was short, and it bounced off the dwarf's chest. He waved when Brick looked up, and motioned for him to grab Grimble, who was also at the table. They appeared to be in the early stages of some sort of drinking game.

When the two dwarves arrived and sat down, Alexander asked, "How'd you like to go poke around the mine a bit? Grimble, you can harvest a bit of mithril, while Kai and Brick and I explore downstairs."

Both dwarves' eyes lit up, and they quickly downed the contents of their mugs. They were instantly ready to go. "Easy, boys. Have some stew. We'll leave in a few minutes." He laughed.

When they'd all eaten their fill, and Alexander had confirmed that Grimble had one of the enchanted mining picks with him, he teleported the four of them directly to the room with the nest.

Grimble immediately produced the diamond-tipped pick, and went to work on the refined mithril. Brick, Kai, and Alexander moved to the door. They quickly moved to the end of the mine tunnel to confirm it was still clear. Stopping back to the room, they called out to Grimble that they'd be heading down. The dwarf barely acknowledged them with a grunt. Alexander raised a stone wall to cover most of the door, leaving a gap at the top for air flow. Grimble was in no condition to watch his own back.

Upon reaching the other room, Alexander removed the stone seal he'd placed over the hole in the floor. Kai hopped down onto the floor below, which was only a drop of about a dozen feet. Brick tested the rope attached to the pulley on the ceiling. Finding it secure, he grabbed hold and jumped. Alexander did the same.

Kai had cast a spell that summoned a globe of light, which floated in the air ahead of them. Alexander really wanted to learn that spell!

The group walked forward along the tunnel, pausing as it began to curve sharply and angle downward. Kai cocked his head to one side. "There is something moving down there," he reported.

As they followed the curve of the tunnel, Alexander noted that Grimble had been correct. There was indeed a wide trail of processed gold along the tunnel floor. Brick reached down and touched it, and a small section liquefied, then formed into a gold bar, which he stuck in his bag. "There be maybe… forty thousand coins worth o' gold layin' here," he said, as they moved on. They'd leave the rest for the miners to gather up.

"Closer to fifty thousand." Kai chuckled. Never argue with a dragon about treasure.

They continued down the tunnel, with Brick asking questions about the mine, the location of the iron ore, and the silver. He wanted to gather some to take back to the smithy. They were running low.

Reaching the lower terminus of the tunnel, they found themselves on a ledge overlooking a natural cavern. Kai summoned two more light globes, which moved off into the cavern, growing brighter until, between them, they lit the whole room. The roughly dome-shaped area was more than a hundred yards in diameter, with a big worm-sized hole in the floor to one side. There were no other exits that Alexander could see. The floor was scattered with stalagmites and large, irregularly shaped chunks of rock that looked like they might have fallen from the ceiling.

They made their way down to the cavern floor, and toward the hole in the floor. As they passed a group of fallen boulders, Alexander jumped back in surprise. "Oh, shit!" he exclaimed, drawing his sword out of instinct.

One of the boulders had a face!

Kai put a hand on Alexander's shoulder, saying, "Sheath your weapon, Alexander. It will do you no good here. These are rock trolls."

"THESE?!" he asked. Looking around in panic, he saw that what he'd mistaken for boulders were actually several large trolls with skin that was made of stone.

"Well, shit," was Brick's only opinion as he raised his shield and prepared his hammer.

Kai let out a low grumbling noise that was something between a growl and a dull jackhammer sound.

The troll closest to them began to shift its limbs, and stood upright. The monstrous thing was easily fifteen feet tall. It had massive shoulders, easily six feet wide, and arms that reached all the way to the floor. It resembled a large stone ape, except its head was rounded and smooth, with small ears and small eyes. And its skin looked exactly like the rock wall behind it. When it opened its mouth, Alexander could see that it had rows of stone for teeth. It rumbled out a reply to Kai that sounded like a small avalanche.

Gorg
Rock Troll Chieftain
Level 70
Health 24,000/24,000

As Alexander examined the Chieftain, other trolls began to rise as the exchange continued. There were eight of them besides the one that was speaking. Alexander focused on resisting the urge to scream like a little girl and run away. Kai was right. Fighting these monsters with normal weapons would get them squished into the floor like overripe tomatoes. Each of them had at least twice the hp of a normal mob at level 70.

After several more exchanges, the massive troll bowed its head to Kai, and sat down. The others all sat as well. The resulting tremors had Alexander looking to the ceiling for falling rock.

"They're hungry, but I convinced them that you're not food." Kai smiled at them.

"Ye speak troll?" Brick asked, mouth open. "I dinna' even know trolls had a language."

With a laugh, Kai said "I am a dragon, and several millennia old. I speak the language of every living thing on Io."

"You said they're hungry?" Alexander was still focused on living thru this meeting.

"Yes. The kobolds, or 'small ones' as the chief here calls them, were feeding the trolls every week. In return, the trolls agreed to not kill them. But he says the kobolds have not been here to feed them today. They were just about to go find them."

"Oh, crap. We killed their lunch-ladies?" Alexander didn't like where this was going.

"Yes, but you've just agreed to take over their feeding. In exchange for their help," the dragon said.

"I have?" Alexander was pretty sure he hadn't. "What do… giant rock trolls eat?"

"They can eat most things. Even stone, for a short while, to fill an empty belly. They prefer meat. And they consider marble a delicacy. But there is no marble in this area. They have very slow digestive systems, and only need to eat once a week or so. A wolf or deer carcass each would suffice."

"And in return? They promise not to kill the miners?" Brick asked.

"Yes, that. But also, they will help by pushing the mining carts. They move slowly, but have tremendous strength," Kai answered. Alexander knew an opportunity when he saw one.

"Please tell him he has a deal. And, if he is willing to help us, I will give them marble for dessert each week," he said.

"You actually already agreed to the deal. Or rather, I agreed on your behalf. But I will inform him of your offer of marble," Kai said.

There was another gravelly exchange. Kai asked, "How much marble? And will they need to live in the keep?"

"They can live wherever they like!" Alexander laughed. He was reminded of the joke, 'Where does a 600 lb. gorilla sit in a bar? Anywhere he wants!'

"As for the marble..." Alexander reached into the floor and raised a slab of stone about the size he'd seen at the quarry in Whitehall. Three feet wide, six feet high, and three inches thick. He guessed it would weigh about 200lbs. "Tell them a slab this size for them to share. Every week if..."

He trailed off as all the trolls immediately jumped to their feet and approached him. They formed a circle around his little trio. The leader began to speak, pointing at Alexander.

"Uhh... did they just decided that I'm breakfast after all?" he asked Kai.

"They are, surprised by your earth magic," Kai said. "One moment please."

Another exchange, much more animated this time. The other trolls were leaning in toward him. One reached out and poked the slab of stone gently, as it afraid it might bite him. The others all made grinding noises that Alexander thought might be laughter.

Great, I've just become a circus monkey for a tribe of rock trolls.

"Uhhh... Kai? If they like marble, how do they feel about obsidian?" he asked as quietly as he could.

"Also a delicacy." Kai paused in his discussion with the chief long enough to answer.

Alexander opened up guild chat. "*Master Silverbeard. I am currently surrounded by nine very large, hungry rock trolls. We are going to be feeding them from now on. Please have someone put one deer and eight wolf carcasses from the cold room into a wagon, and move it to the teleport pad as quickly as you can. I'll be coming to retrieve it shortly.*"

"*Of course, Alexander. Do you need assistance?*" Silverbeard asked.

"*No, Kai is speaking to them. And I'm doing magic tricks. We're fine. Once the meat is in place, ask everyone to clear the courtyard. Trolls take up a lot of space.*"

Kai was still talking, so Alexander took the opportunity to remove a four-inch square chunk of obsidian from his bag. Reaching out, he offered it to the chief. The troll instantly stopped talking. He stuck out a hand, and delicately removed the stone morsel from Alexander's palm. He sniffed it once, then tossed it into his mouth. The other trolls all began to grumble and shift their feet. So, Alexander produced 8 more squares, handing one to each troll. They seemed pleased. He hoped. They all sat back down, still in a circle.

The chief said something to Kai, still rattling the obsidian cube around in its mouth. He appeared to be sucking on it like candy.

Kai laughed. "He says to thank you for the gift. He has not had the black stone since he was a small boulder."

Alexander bowed his head to the chief.

"Few trolls have magic," Kai began to explain. "Only the most ancient of rock trolls develop earth magic strong enough to do what you just did. They are treated with great respect among the troll tribes. The chief is trying to decide if you are a venerated elder of your race."

"BWAHAHAHA!" Brick was holding his stomach. "Ye… ye gived 'em candy, and now yer their grandpa!" He fell over and rolled on the ground.

The trolls seemed greatly amused by this. The one that had touched the stone slab actually rolled over backward in a crude imitation of the dwarf, which only made him laugh harder. Alexander sincerely hoped somebody at Olympus was recording this.

After another short exchange, the chief rose to his feet and began to head up the tunnel. The others rose and followed.

"They are each going to push a cart up to the mine entrance. We'll meet them there with the meat wagon," Kai explained. "And, you have deal on the marble. One slab that size per week, and a weekly feeding, and they will help you defend the mine or the keep."

"Great," Alexander said. "I can get the marble from Whitehall. Did they tell you anything about the worm?"

"They have not seen it in several months. It went down that hole in the floor. I do not sense it within my range, but the chief has promised to alert us if it returns. They choose to remain here in the cavern, for now," Kai replied. "It will take them some time to push the carts up to the mine entrance. I will retrieve the wagon, if you will go and get Grimble and meet me at the entrance."

When Alexander agreed, Kai disappeared.

Helping his still laughing friend to his feet, he said, "Come on, Troll Whisperer," and teleported them back to the room where Grimble was working.

"Yer back," Grimble observed. He was sitting on the edge of the nest. "I cut loose ten pounds o' refined mithril. Any more'n we'd crash the market," the dwarf said. "What'd ye find down below?"

"Well, you were right about the gold vein. The worm processed about 50,000 coins' worth for us. It seems to be gone, for now," Alexander began. Grimble was smiling greedily. "Oh, and we found a tribe of hungry rock trolls in the cavern."

"WHAT? Where be Kai? Ye didn't let him get killed, did ye?" Grimble started to panic.

“Kai’s fine. We’re meeting him at the entrance. Step closer and I’ll teleport us,” Alexander said. He then teleported them to an area about fifty yards outside the entrance, just to be sure they didn’t land on the meat wagon, or any trolls. Kai was already at the entrance, and they walked back to meet him. As they walked, Brick filled Grimble in on the arrangement.

“BWAHAHA! I’ll be the only dwarf on Io what has a rockworm and trolls workin his mine!” Grimble bellowed.

“I’m glad you’re happy, because you’re going to be in charge of feeding them every week. And making sure they get their marble. We’ll pick up a wagonload from Whitehall tomorrow.” Alexander thumped the old dwarf on the shoulder.

As they approached the wagon, the first of the trolls was emerging from the main tunnel. He was pushing a cart filled with iron ore. He stopped when the cart reached the end of the track, and stepped to the side, looking hungrily at the wagon.

One by one the trolls appeared with a cart each. The chief came last, pushing a cart full of silver ore. He stopped the cart at the back of the line, and moved over to stand by Kai.

The dragon handed him the deer carcass. The thing was nearly eight feet long, and had to weigh five hundred pounds. The chief smiled, and bowed his head. One by one, the trolls stepped forward to receive their wolves. They seemed to appreciate that they’d all been skinned. By the looks on their craggy faces, Alexander guessed that this was much more food than they’d been receiving from the kobolds.

Once the wagon was empty, the chief set down his dinner, and lifted the cart full of silver he’d pushed up. Moving to the wagon, he tilted the cart and carefully poured the ore into the wagon bed. Each of the trolls followed his example. Alexander began to worry the wagon wouldn’t hold. At least they weren’t going to pull it back to the keep. He was sure the axles would snap.

Waving goodbye, the chief and his trolls retreated back into the mine.

Kai waved a hand, and the four of them, along with the groaning ore wagon, were teleported back to keep. Grimble immediately began calling for miners to come with carts to lighten the load, so that the wagon could be safely rolled to the smithy. Alexander gave him a parting instruction, "Make sure you record all this, and let Master Silverbeard know. You can safely go back to the mine tomorrow. Just travel in a group. And have weapons ready, just in case."

He thought for a moment. How would Grimble call for backup if they were attacked?

"Actually, Grimble, can I speak to you for a moment?" he asked.

The dwarf moved to where he was standing, far enough from the wagon not to be overheard.

"Would you be interested in joining the Greystone guild?" He didn't sugarcoat it or beat around the bush. Grimble wasn't that kind of dwarf.

"I be already a member of the miner's guild," the dwarf said, "and I gives them 10% of me earnings. What percentage do Greystone take?" he asked, considering. They both knew with his percentage of the mine, especially with the potential production of a mithril worm, he was going to be a very wealthy dwarf.

"We charge 10% of any loot from dungeons or killing monsters. Beyond that, nothing. And the money we earn from the mine, after we pay King Charles the proper taxes, goes to improving the keep, and providing for its citizens. The guild does not take a cut," Alexander explained. "Becoming a member will also entitle to you to a third of a percent of what we found in the mine yesterday, including the mithril. Just like Helga and the others. By your own estimate, that would be about 40,000 gold, on top of what you earn from mining."

Grimble tried to look like he was considering it. After a few moments, he said, "Aye, lad. It'd be me pleasure to join ye. So long as I don't need to quit the miner's guild."

Alexander sent him a guild invite, which he accepted. "See Lola, and get a medallion. If you need help, like if you are attacked on the way to the mine, we can use it as a focus to teleport to you. Just call out in guild chat, and we'll be there."

Grimble nodded and headed back to the wagon. Which by now had been emptied enough to allow the miners to roll it back to the smithy. There had been eight cart loads of iron ore, and one of silver. That should give Brick enough iron to work with for a week or so. They'd need some lumber to burn into charcoal for making steel. Brick could handle that directly with the carpenters.

Making a mental note to go with Father Ignatius back to Whitehall to obtain marble, Alexander headed toward his rooms. They'd gotten a lot accomplished today. Nearly everything from this morning's list.

Reaching his sitting room, he found Edward and Master Silverbeard discussing keep management principles. Sliding into one of the comfortable chairs, he let out a long sigh of relief.

"Apologies, Alexander. D'ye be wantin some privacy?" Master Silverbeard asked.

"No, no, continue your conversation. One can never learn too much about running a keep." He looked at Edward. "Or a city."

The dwarf nodded. "We be discussing the balance o' stockpiling resources for keep use, or trading em fer gold. Most times, this be a delicate balance. Ye need to ensure enough stock to last ye in hard times, but not keep so much that it be wasted. Food spoils. Lumber rots."

Alexander nodded. "We're lucky, in this particular case. We've discovered treasure in the mine that will cover our costs for years. But if we hadn't, right now we'd be discussing what to trade for more food and other supplies. I just made an agreement to feed nine trolls a full carcass each, every week, as well as a slab of marble. For a settlement this size, still trying to rebuild, that would normally be a back-breaking deal. Which reminds me. I'm going to Whitehall in the morning, to make a deal with Master Breakstone for the marble. Would you two like to join me?"

Both Edward and Silverbeard responded in the affirmative.

"Master Silverbeard, I could use some advice. What would you consider a fair exchange, in mithril, for fifty-two slabs of marble? Each slab needs to be 3x6 feet and three inches thick. I was thinking of offering one half pound?"

The dwarf considered for a moment. "Mithril be rare, and valuable. Ye need to be careful not to be spendin' it freely, else ye reduce the value. I know Breakstone. He'll not run to sell mithril to merchants. He'll sell it to me King. Half a pound be overpayin a bit, likely. But it be a good way to establish trade relations, and ye need the marble quickly. Ye can negotiate better terms next time."

"Thank you, Master Silverbeard. We'll go at sunrise. Please ask the miners to wait for us to return before they leave for the mine. I'd like them to take the first slab with them in the wagon."

With that decided, he'd had enough. "Gentlemen, I bid you good night," he said, rising and heading for his bedroom.

Once again, he set his high tech trap, leaning sword and staff against his locked door. The adrenaline rush from nearly being troll food had worn off. He was asleep within seconds of his head hitting the pillow.

Chapter Twelve

Truth Hurts

Alexander awoke well before dawn. He'd heard some noise in the outer room, and was instantly awake. Pulling on his boots, and grabbing his weapons, he moved out into the study. He found Edward sitting in the same chair he'd left him in, snoring loudly. There was a glass in his hand that smelled suspiciously like dwarven spirits.

Grabbing the fireplace poker, he bashed it around the inside of the iron grate, and began yelling, "Attack! We're under attack! Bugbears in the corridor! Move! Run for your life!" right into the boy's ear.

Edward leapt from his chair, stumbled over the table in front of him, and went face-down in the carpet.

"Got your father's taste for the spirits, I see." Alexander chuckled. Quite proud of himself. "I'm pretty sure I told you to stay away from them. How'd you get your hands on a bottle? Or have you had more than a bottle?"

The boy rolled over on his back, and managed to mumble something that included the words, "Brick's cellar." Ah. So, the king wasn't the only one who helped himself the night of the feast. Can't really blame the boy for mimicking his father. Much. Still, lessons needed to be learned.

Lifting the boy to his feet, he said, "Get yourself downstairs for some breakfast. Then find Brick, and apologize to him. No trip to Whitehall for you, lad. You'd only embarrass me. You'll be working the smithy all day. The hammering should be just what you need to remember why boys shouldn't overindulge in spirits."

In guild chat, he said, "*Brick, our young prince is having some trouble holding his liquor this morning. He apparently lifted a bottle or two from your supply at the compound. After breakfast, he's yours for the day. Put him someplace as noisy as possible. Don't work him to death, just make sure he learns his lesson.*"

"*BWAHAHA! I'll be makin' sure he earns his stolen loot*!" Brick replied.

"*The poor dear. I'll fix him some tea that'll help…*" Sasha began.

"*NO*!" Alexander, Brick, Max, Grimble, and Master Silverbeard all shouted at once. Alexander continued. "*Sasha, do NOT help the boy. Or have anyone else help him. This is part of his training. As a man, and as a leader. And the price he pays for 'borrowing' without permission. Brick will make sure he comes to no serious harm.*"

"*Idiots,*" was the only reply from Sasha. Alexander decided to take that as agreement.

Heading down to breakfast himself, he mentally planned his day. He'd make the trip to pick up the marble, maybe grab some tasty pastries from Millicent's.

Then he needed to finish widening the moat, and get it filled. He'd only managed half yesterday. He should make a trip to Stormforge to purchase Ironwood for the drawbridge. And any other supplies Master Silverbeard needed. Stop and speak with Captain Redmond to see if there were more volunteers. Place another order with the butcher, only for livestock this time.

He also wanted to see about creating a road between the inner and outer walls, and eventually to the mine. And create a way to seal the mine to protect the trolls in case of attack.

Fitz's warning about wall-mounted weapons using his new lens design had him thinking about magically powered siege weapons to mount on his own walls. He could make them without the lens, and power them with soul crystals. Massive light cannons that could fire 100 shots each? Yes, please. Or… could he make one that cast wizard's fire? He'd heard of a few guild crafters who'd made massive ballistae that fired exploding arrows. He should be able to improve upon that!

Walking through the kitchen, he caught up to the slow-moving prince, who was using a wall to steady himself as he walked. Deciding to remove any temptation for Sasha, he tossed an arm around the boy's shoulders, and marched him outside to sit at one of the tables.

"How's your head?" he shouted at the boy, much to the amusement of those already gathered for breakfast. The prince was obviously suffering. "Does everything seem like it's louder?"

"Not everything, only you," the prince replied. At least he still had a sense of humor. Alexander dished up a big helping of eggs and greasy bacon, plopping it down in front of the boy. "Eat up!" he encouraged. Then he made a plate of food for himself. Brick, Max, Lugs, Grimble, and a dozen others all managed to find ways to torture the lad as he picked at his food.

"*Master, there are intruders lowering themselves into the moat just east of the gatehouse. I detect five so far.*" Jeeves' voice came into his head.

"Thank you, Jeeves, emergency message please! Loudspeaker too." He waited five seconds.

"Attention, all citizens. Intruders have been detected crossing the moat near the outer gate. All guards to your assigned stations! Hunters to the inner wall. Anyone outside the keep, get back inside NOW! All guild members, meet me at the bailey gate tunnel in two minutes. Everyone else, get your arms and armor equipped, and report to the courtyard for instructions. Make SURE you are wearing your dragon pins."

Jumping up from his seat, he looked down at Edward. Grabbing his head, he turned it so that the boy's eyes focused on him. "Edward, get in the kitchen and stay there. Drink some coffee. If the enemy breaks through the gate, you get up to your room and lock yourself in. I'll teleport up and get you."

Lugs, Brick, and the other players who were online were already armed up and headed for the gate. Alexander teleported himself to the top of the outer wall gatehouse. Seconds later, Fitz and Kai were by his side.

Looking down and to the left, he saw a group of ten players, about fifty yards down from the gate. Eight were in the moat, one up top, holding a rope that the tenth was using to climb down the forty feet to the bottom. It was still maybe half an hour before dawn. The was traditionally a good time to attack a fortified position, as the guards would be tired from night shift, and it was still dark enough to go undetected.

The three of them spoke quietly. "Do we take them now? Or wait until they get inside?" Alexander asked for advice.

"It may not be so easy for them to get inside. There's fifty feet of wall, and it's enchanted to be unscalable," Fitz reminded him. "Besides, they're in such a nice little group. Or will be, when that last one drops down."

Kai concurred. "Attack them before they get inside and can spread out."

Alexander formed a raid party. He invited Fitz and Kai, all the guild members, the guards and hunters.

In raid chat, he said, "*Group of ten adventurers. Still in the moat. All of you guards, hunters, and adventurers, head out here to the outer wall. Take the stairs at the gatehouse. Enemy is fifty yards left of that point. Move quietly. Master Silverbeard, you are in charge inside the keep. Distribute the citizens as you see fit. Put those who cannot fight into the great hall to help with wounded. Put Fibble in there, as well. His wand could come in handy.*" Fitz winked at him, knowing he was just placing the little green warrior out of harm's way.

Looking over at the enemy group, he saw that the player on the rope was three quarters of the way down.

He whispered, "Fitz, when that guy gets to the bottom, the guy up top is going to have to anchor the rope somehow. With a spike, or an axe. Once he's over the edge, if you'll liquefy the ground around the anchor, I'll do the same at the bottom under all their feet. We'll see how much of a splash he makes." He grinned at the wizard.

Taking a moment to look back, he saw his group approaching the wall. All ten immersion players were there, along with Lugs, Helga, Benny, and Beatrix. The dwarven and human guards, and Lorian and the hunters, were not far behind. All of them were doing a good job of moving quietly, yet quickly. But just to be sure, Kai waved a hand, and a silence spell settled over all of them. Realizing this, they all burst into a run, not having to worry about the jingle of armor or heavy footsteps.

Alexander motioned for them to hold in place as they reached the top of the wall. Each took a good look at the enemy below.

"*When that last guy starts down the rope, Fitz and I are going to trap them. Then I want you guards and hunters to spread out along the wall, while the rest of us move down to deal with them. Hunters, once we're down there, any enemy who raises a weapon, or looks like they're about to cast, gets an arrow in the face. Everybody clear?*" Heads nodded.

"*My group, we'll go to the far side. Kai, you come with us. Fitz, you take Dayle's group, Lugs, and Helga down on this side. Beatrix, you and Benny stay up here. Benny, I want you healing. Beatrix, I may call on you to flood the place. Slowly. I'm going to make them think they're about to drown. I need information.*"

They watched for a moment more as the last man on top drove a spike into the ground, and secured the rope. Then he swung his legs over the edge, and began to make his way down.

"*Now, Fitz.*" Alexander said as he used his earth magic to liquefy the ground under all the players at the bottom. They were grouped up near the far side of the moat, watching as the guy on the rope cried out and began to fall. A few tried to move to catch him, but found their own feet quickly sinking into liquid stone. Just for effect, Alexander cast wizard's fire on the falling man, turning him into a plummeting, screaming ball of flame.

Kai lifted the silence spell. The enemy knew they were here now. "Fitz, when they get about chest deep, help me harden the stone!" Alexander said. "Guards, hunters, move down the wall. Keep behind cover as much as possible."

As the flaming player hit ground, Alexander cast wizard's fire on four more players, two on each side, just to add to the confusion.

As they sank, several of them made the mistake of using arms or hands to try to push themselves up or to the side. Each time he saw this, Alexander hardened the stone around them, trapping that limb. Fitz was obviously doing the same. Within ten seconds, all the enemy players were waist deep, or deeper, in the stone. Weapons were dropped, and spells were being cast. A water mage was hitting one of the burning players with a splash of water, which had zero impact on the fire, and created a burst of steam.

The falling player had been submerged completely. He would suffocate in about a minute, assuming he was screaming when he went under. Alexander located the splash zone, reached down, and raised the player up until his head was above ground. Then he solidified the stone around him, as well.

Nearly half of the players still had an arm or two free. Only three of them were casters. All three were busily casting. Max hit one that had been building up a long and complicated looking spell with a silence arrow. Lainey stunned another. Beatriz put a water globe around the face of the third. "Don't kill them. I want to question them," Alexander reminded everyone.

Stepping to the edge of the wall above the trapped players, he called down. "You have intruded upon my territory in stealth, and uninvited. As Knight-Advisor to The King, and owner of these lands, I place you all under arrest. Your bind points have been moved to my dungeon. Resist, and you will find yourselves there. Surrender, and you will receive a fair trial! Drop your weapons!"

Alexander didn't know the spell to change their bind points. And if he did, he wasn't sure he had the authority to do so. He'd have to ask the king.

Fitz didn't seem to have his doubts. He waved his hand, and a brief glow fell over all ten enemy players. It looked a lot like the effect of Captain Redmond's binding spell. Enough like it that several of the players started cursing.

"Let's go down." Alexander teleported his group to the floor of the moat just past the group of players. Fitz and the others appeared across from them. All of them spread out in a half-circle, surrounding the enemy.

The player with Beatrix's water globe on her face looked to have passed out. She removed the spell, and Lugs poked the player with his snow-shoe-sized foot. She moaned and coughed. Still alive.

Alexander looked around at the enemy players. Since they were in combat, he could see all their names and health bars, as well as their levels. The highest among them was level 55. All were over 40.

"Who's the leader of this group?" he asked.

The guy whose face was barely aboveground shouted, "Screw you!"

"Ah, so it's going to be like that, then. Why is it you PWP assholes always go straight to the profanity and vulgarity?" Alexander tried to sound sincere.

"We're not PWP, moron!" the man shouted.

"You just did a flaming dodo bird dive face first into stone. You can't move anything but your eyes and your lips. Who's the moron here?" Alexander grinned at him. "If you're not PWP, then who are you?"

No answer was forthcoming.

"Well, whoever you are, you came just a tad too early. You see, we're filling the moat this morning. If you'd just hung out a bit, you could have floated across instead of climbing all the way down here. I was watching from above. Some of you are really very clumsy," Alexander said. This earned him chuckles from all those in his group below, and those on the wall.

Taking her cue, Beatrix cast a spell, and water started seeping up through the stone, pooling around the trapped players.

"Oh, look. There's the water now. And there you all are, stuck to the bottom. One of you guards up there on the wall, run and get the miners, see how quickly they can break these folks out. I hear drowning is a horrible way to go." More laughter from the wall. Still, one of the human guards took off. Not everyone got his humor.

With a sign, Alexander continued, "What's your name, mister vulgarity?" he asked.

"Suck my ass!" the man shouted.

"Well that just doesn't sound pleasant at all. And even if it did, your ass is currently locked in several feet of stone. Quite unreachable. Now, as your face is quite near the ground, you don't have much time before you'll be blowing bubbles with each breath. I will ask you again. What is your name. I have to have something to put on the arrest report."

"We're going to kill you all! You, your families, your friends! There is no stopping the Dark One's plans for you! You think you're safe inside Olympus? You're not! We're everywhere!"

"And every single one of you, so far, has been as dumb as the rock you're trapped in. Where did this Dark One find you all? Is he hanging around shopping malls and shooting ranges looking for the dimmest bulbs who walk by?" Alexander stoked the man's anger, trying to buy time and get him to talk. The water was still rising slowly, and the talkative one was started to splutter as it reached his chin.

"Your friend here is going to drown. I'm afraid my miners were still asleep when you arrived, and they won't make it here in time to save him. Or most of you. I could, of course, save you all, but that is not my duty. My duty is to interrogate you. I've given up on mister grumpy over there. Who will answer my questions and save you all from a slow, painful drowning?"

"I'm not going through that shit again," said the mage who'd nearly drowned in the water globe. "We're all from Chaos Nation. PK guild. Henry was one of our officers before he bailed and went to PWP. I don't know who this Dark One is. I came here to get payback for Henry," she said.

"Well, let me educate you all. One of the players who ambushed us initially, and was captured, got himself banned from the game for threatening a GM. That same player died, along with several others, in a suicide attack on Jupiter's headquarters six nights ago. The asshole who's drowning over there works for the same guy who paid them, and helped them organize the attack. So, you're all working for a terrorist organization, now." Alexander shook his head, as if he felt sorry for them.

"Oh, shit," the mage said quietly. "Wait! I don't know anything about all that!" She started flailing, waving her arms. Others did the same, crying out their innocence.

Alexander became worried they'd log out and run. But players couldn't log out in combat. It was one of the safety protocols.

"Stop that! Are you trying to escape? Or is that an attack?" he cried. For the record. An arrow from above struck the mage in the shoulder. Other arrows hit other squirmers. His guys had been paying attention.

"Sasha, thorn trap please," he said quietly. She cast the spell, which did enough damage to each player to keep them in combat.

"I believe some of you may be innocent. At least, innocent of the activities back home. You're still PK assholes caught raiding my land, but hey, that's part of the game, right? If you can convince me, I might let you out of there. Now, tell me everything you know about mister profanity the bubble-blower over there." Alexander raised the man a few inches to keep him from drowning.

One of the warriors spoke first. "His name's Marlin. He's a lieutenant in the guild. Third highest. He recruited most of us here. I don't know where he lives. We don't talk like that," the man said.

"And what are all of your names?" Sasha asked, pulling out a parchment like she was going to write on it."

All but Marlin gave their names. They weren't really needed, his father would have pulled their accounts immediately and given their info to the FBI. This was just another stall tactic.

"Who can tell me about this Dark One that Marlin's so fond of?" He looked around at the group. They looked around at each other. Nobody spoke.

"Come on now, this Dark One dude has been running your guild, and PWP, for months now, at least. You expect me to believe that none of you has a clue who he is?"

"He's the one who's gonna wipe you assholes from the face of the earth!" Marlin shouted again.

"Marlin, sweetness, you seem angry. I mean, not like 'just got caught with my pants down' angry, but really upset. Did I run over your dog or something?" Alexander asked the man.

"My cousins nearly starved because of you! You and your bullshit shut-down. They made their living in Europa. You took that from them!"

"Ah, I see. They were in Iran. It wasn't me that took their livelihood. It was their government. They harbored the terrorists that killed hundreds of innocent people, including my mother. We gave them plenty of time to avoid a shutdown. And we gave their people time to sell off their assets. Had they simply turned the terrorists from Light of Truth over to the proper authorities, your cousins might still be in Europa. Or Io."

Light of Truth were heroes!" Marlin shouted. The rising sun's light showed his face to be bright purple. Alexander raised him up a bit more, and loosened the stone around his chest a bit.

"Dude! We're not with that wackjob's group! I swear it!" Another of the mages was beginning to panic. "I remember that whole thing ten years ago. Those anti-tech nuts blowing up the hotel. I want nothing to do with that!" he was yelling desperately. "I'm a techie! I friggin' play a VR game for a living! I have kids to feed!"

Several of the others caught on to the seriousness of the situation. Alexander saw several of them lose focus, staring at the UI's, trying to log out. He nodded at Sasha, who cast the thorns again.

"Aaargh! Dammit! Let me out of here!" one woman screamed.

Alexander looked at her coldly. "You are still under arrest, and under interrogation. Those are the first words you've spoken. You've not answered a single question. And you seem to be in a hurry. Got someplace to be?"

"I… I gotta feed my kid!" she yelled. Nobody believed her.

"Bullshit, bitch." Lainey's voice was full of venom. "If things hadn't gone wrong for you here, you'd be up there raiding the keep right now, not feeding your kid. Try again." Alexander wanted to hug her.

He let the silence hang. The slower this conversation went, the better. Finally, the first mage who had spoken said, "Tell them SOMEthing! I'm not going to jail just because you feel like being a bitch!"

The woman just smirked at the mage.

"She doesn't care," Alexander explained. "She's figured out that she's going to jail, and doesn't give a shit if you do, too. The fact that she's in such a hurry tells me she's in it with Marlin, there. And she's itching to log off and try to disappear. At least three others had the same thought." Alexander gave them a moment.

"They used you like cannon fodder. Bunch of PK assholes who don't much care who they run with, as long as they can victimize weaker players for fun and profit. They scooped you right up, and ruined your lives. They WANT you to lose your places here. They want you to hate us, so it'll be easier to recruit you, stick you in a van with a rocket launcher, and point you at us. Those people who died in the attack? Only one of them was shot. Their van mysteriously exploded. Martyrs for the cause. And when you die too, they'll claim it was all our fault. Just like Marlin there's been doing. They'll recruit your families or friends, offering them revenge. More cannon fodder." He pointed at the man who'd said he had kids. A few of the players were actually crying, shaking with fear.

"And don't forget, this all started when a bunch of assholes decided they hate tech, and needed to show their feelings by blowing up a hotel full of people," Alexander finished.

He turned to look up at the wall, suddenly realizing there were citizens up there listening. And down here with him. Shit.

While his back was turned, the bitch who'd claimed to have a hungry kid shouted a word, and a bolt of dark magic pierced Alexander's back. He reflexively cast wizard's fire on her, which set the vines on fire, and eventually all the other players, as well. "Don't kill them!" he shouted, falling to the ground.

His health was down to 50%. There was something wiggling around in his chest. He could feel it squeezing his heart. He felt nature magic and light magic heals tingle through him. But to no effect. He was bleeding, and his vision was getting blurry. The tightening around his heart continued. He tried to cast a heal on himself. It didn't help either.

Down to 20% health, he felt someone force his mouth open. He recognized the taste of one of Sasha's potions. Then another. That was better. Back up to 50%.

Then Kai jammed a clawed hand inside his stomach. Back down to 20%! What the hell? Kai attacked him?

He felt a strong tug in his chest, and then searing pain. He blacked out.

On Io, when you die, you move into a sort of grey box that players called 'limbo' or 'purgatory'. You sat there with pretty much nothing to do for ten minutes while the respawn timer ticked down. You couldn't check your mail, or chat with your friends, or watch the rest of the fight that killed you. Many people took the opportunity to take a bio break and grab a snack.

Alexander waited for several seconds for limbo. It didn't come. He couldn't see anything at all, in fact. Just as he was beginning to get worried, he found himself in a white cube, his father's avatar sitting at a table in front of him.

"You've only got a few seconds. You didn't die, you just came very close. They'll heal you soon. Your tactic worked. The houses of all ten are being raided as we speak. My guess is at least one of them had ties to Light of Truth. They'll all be investigated. And their accounts terminated. Those found innocent of involvement will be allowed to petition to get their accounts back. The rest of Chaos Nation will be investigated as well."

Before he could speak, the room disappeared, and sunlight began to shine in his face. "Oh, thank god," he heard Lainey say.

Looking at his UI, he saw he was back over 50% health. Though he felt like shit.

"Kai? Where's Kai? Why did he attack me?" Alexander mumbled.

"BWAHAHA!" Brick bellowed. "Ye had a shit-weasel lookin' thing in yer chest. It were killin' you. Kai reached in and yanked it outta ye like it were a infected tooth! Sasha, keeped ye alive, though I dunno how."

That made more sense than the dragon trying to kill him. "Thank you… Kai," he said.

"My pleasure, Alexander." Kai held up a black wormy thing that was all teeth and muscle. Its body had thorns down both sides. Alexander knew it was gonna give him nightmares. "It has been centuries since I've seen this spell. It is a truly evil thing," he added.

Sitting up, Alexander looked toward the player who'd shot him. She was unconscious, maybe dead. There were arrows in each of her eyes, and two more stuck in her skull.

As he stood up, fully intending to finish her off, a GM appeared next to her. All the non-players froze stiff. Time had stopped for them.

"All of your accounts have been suspended, pending federal investigation into possible terrorist activity. You will be disconnected in ten seconds. Authorities are already at your homes, and will be placing you under arrest. Any in-game assets have been confiscated, according to Io's terms of service.

With that, the GM disappeared. Thinking quickly, Alexander shouted, "Fire!" and cast wizard's fire on each of the players. Arrows and spells rained down from above, and a blistering crossfire of ground level arrows, weapons, and spells ripped the players apart. Lugs stomped Marlin's face so hard it squirted out to the sides.

Max gathered their inventory bags, and looted their bodies. Benny, Brick, Beatrix, and several of the guards and hunters got level increases from the fights.

No point in wasting the deaths of ten higher level PK's, if you could get some benefit from it!

Alexander looked up at the wall. "Lorian, please spread your hunters out along the wall in groups of two. I'll need you, Max, and Lainey to search the forest in a bit. The rest of you, back to the keep. Tell the farmers they can come out to work. No miners or lumber crews outside the wall today.

He raised several benches in a tight circle, and sat on the nearest. The players, Fitz, and Kai followed his lead. Fitz teleported Beatrix and Benny down.

"Fitz, Kai, thank you for your help. This could have gone badly without you here. As I'm sure you heard, this conflict isn't just happening on Io, but extends to our homeland, as well."

Turning to the other players, he explained. "Fitz, Kai, King Charles, Captain Redmond, and the dragons, as well as a few others, are aware that we adventurers come from another world. Much like the demons come here from their plane. Except we're slightly better behaved." Misty chuckled at that.

Looking back at Fitz, he said, “We’re about to have a discussion that involves a lot of details about our homeland. I’m afraid Odin may not allow you to hear most of it. I did not want you to think us rude, or that we are trying to exclude you. You are both valued members of our team, and I consider you friends.”

Kai nodded his head. “Aye, we saw Odin’s messenger appear, but could not hear the words he spoke. We will go and finish widening the moat, so that it can be filled.”

“Thank you.” Alexander smiled at them. The pair headed back toward the gate and the narrower section of moat.

“Max, Lainey, a quick update, then you two please take Lorian and head out. I’ll fill in the new folks. While I was dying, I got an update. The authorities were indeed waiting for each of these assholes when they woke up. There’s a suspicion that at least one of them, maybe this ‘Dark One’, had ties to the old Light of Truth. That’s all the new news I have for you guys.”

As Max and Lainey took off, they waved at Lorian, who leapt lightly down from the way, landing gracefully. The three of them would catch up to Fitz and get teleported out of the moat.

“Lugs, Helga, Benny, Beatrix. You four have learned a few things today that I’m sure come as a surprise. As you can see, this little war is happening on two fronts. Here, and in the real world. Unfortunately, hearing this information means that you will be monitored by the FBI, and Jupiter security, from this point forward. The information you have now impacts an ongoing terrorism investigation, and national security. You cannot share this information with anyone. I mean, anyone. Not a husband, wife, sibling, best friend, the person you trust most in the world. I’m sure when you log off, there will be federal agents waiting to speak to you about non-disclosure agreements. Any questions so far?” Alexander asked.

“You knew about all of this before?” Lugs asked.

"Yes. But like you now, I could not discuss it before. I tried to warn you to the extent I could, before inviting you to join us. I did not intend for you to have any involvement other than defending the keep in-game. Marlin's big mouth, unfortunately, closed the door on that."

"I wish you hadn't invited us." Lugs said sadly. "I don't need these kinds of complications in my life." A few of the others nodded their heads in agreement, or understanding.

"Lugs, I'm sorry. I can't undo it. But I can offer you some alternatives. First, Jupiter will put security details on each of your homes, for your protection. Unless something happens, you won't even know they're there. And if you choose, I will release you from Greystone. You will be paid the gold you've earned while you were here, and given the promised soul crystals, which you can sell for a significant amount. You can go on about your in-game lives. Though your play will be monitored, you won't be interfered with. Anybody who has seen your faces here will be banned from the game. That should reduce the likelihood of your identities being passed around. Or, you are welcome to stay here, and continue with us. As most of you have seen, there is a lot of opportunity here. You might even earn enough over the next year or two, that you'll be able to retire. Helga, how much did you earn in the mine yesterday?" he asked.

"Maybe 40,000g," she said. Benny's eyes got wide. He was probably cursing himself for being offline.

Alexander handed her a small soul crystal. "This is worth another eight to ten thousand, depending on where you sell it. And when." He handed a crystal to each of them. "How long would it take you to earn $50K in the game, normally?" he asked Lugs.

"A year, maybe," the ogre answered.

"You will all get a share of the loot we just took from these PK's. And there will be many more dead players to loot in the days to come. As well as dungeons to run, armies to fight." He gave them a moment to do some math.

“There will be people watching you. And if you do something wrong, like talk about today, you will likely be arrested and banned, just like these folks. And that sucks. But if you do nothing wrong, you have the potential to benefit greatly from your predicament. I’ll leave it up to you. Let me know when you’ve decided what you want.”

“What about Dirk? Does he know?” Helga asked.

“I don’t think so. Dirk hasn’t been online since we stepped through the portal, as far as I know,” Alexander said.

“Come to think of it, anybody know why Dirk’s been offline? It has been a couple days.”

“He said something about work when he logged off. I wasn’t really listening,” Lugs said.

“Ah, okay well I’m sure everything’s fine,” Alexander said. He would be sure and have Fitz check the player again when he logged back on.

“Alright, folks. We should know soon enough whether more are approaching. So far, most of the attacks have been by small groups. Even the PWP raid on the city was less than a hundred players. I expect, though, that he’s putting together a much larger force. So, keep an eye out today. We’ll be making a raid of our own, soon enough. I plan to take out the PWP guild house in Antalia. But not until this place is secure.”

With that, he teleported them all back to the top of the wall. He left the raid party in place, for the time being, to save time if another attack was imminent. Heading across the field toward the keep, he saw the farmers start to drift out. He waved and nodded at them, letting them know the immediate danger had passed.

Passing through the gate, he cried out, “We’ve dealt with the enemy party. They won’t be bothering us again!” A cheer went up from the gathered citizens. “You can all go back to doing what you were doing. And thank you for your quick response. Sorry to interrupt breakfast” He grinned.

Finding Master Silverbeard, he said, "Ready to go to Whitehall? We can be there and back in a few minutes."

"Aye, Alexander. The quicker the better," the dwarf agreed.

In a flash, the two of them were standing on the road in front of the quarry's workshop. Heading inside, they found Master Breakstone and a couple other masons working at various projects. Silverbeard was looking up at the clear crystal ceiling. "This be your work, lad?" Alexander looked at his feet. "Yes. Stupid, I know."

"No, this be a wondrous thing. Ye put some thought into makin' life easier fer the dwarves here. That shows ye've a good heart." Silverbeard argued.

Breakstone noticed them, and called out "Alexander! Master Silverbeard! Welcome to me shop!" the dwarf moved to greet them. "What can I do fer ye?"

"I'm actually here for some marble." Alexander grinned. "You won't believe this, but we've adopted a tribe of rock trolls. And they have a sweet tooth for marble. So, in return for their help in the mine, we're feeding them, and giving them a slab of marble per week as dessert."

"BWAHAHA! Ye always have a surprise fer me!" the dwarf laughed. "We can cut some slabs fer ye, easy enough. What size, and what type of marble?"

"Well, the size would be three feet by six, and three inches thick. As for type, I'm ashamed to admit I know very little about marble. Is one type better than another? Or rather, is one type likely to be more tasty to a rock troll?" Alexander shrugged helplessly.

Breakstone looked thoughtful. "Well, in me line o' work, I've tasted the dust o' every kind of marble. Can't say I enjoyed the taste o' any of em. But if I were a troll, me guess'd be the pure white limestone. Got a hint of citrus. Maybe the green, with a bit of magnesium in it, fer kick."

"And which of these is most common? I don't want to be feeding these big fellas rare marble," Alexander asked.

"The white be most common, and therefore least expensive."

"Alright then, I need a year's supply. Fifty-two slabs with those dimensions. What will that cost me?"

"Lemme check if we got that much. We only just got started, as ye know." Breakstone laughed.

"I don't need it all today. In fact, one slab will do for now. I can send a wagon in… six days?" Alexander asked.

"Aye, lad. That be plenty of time. As for cost… let's say a hundred gold per slab," the master offered.

"Actually, I'm horrible at conversion rates." Alexander looked at Silverbeard, who nodded. "Would you be interested in mithril, instead. I can offer you half a pound for the whole lot."

Breakstone's eyes got wider. He quickly did some math in his head. Every dwarf knew the precise value of mithril. After a moment, he shook his head. "Thank ye, lad, but that be too much. Me stone's not worth half a pound," he said sadly.

"But your friendship has value to me, as well. Take the mithril. I'll send it when we pick up the shipment in six days. In the meantime, can you prepare a slab for me now? I don't want to break my promise to nine large rock trolls with a sweet tooth!" He grinned.

Laughing, Breakstone said, "Aye lad, we can take care of ye." The dwarf shook his hand, then moved across the shop. He called over two other dwarves, and in short order they'd cut a slab to fit his needs. Breakstone carried it over. "It be a mite heavy, lad. D'ye need me to carry it for ye?"

Alexander shook his head. A slab of stone that size weighed a good 200lbs or more, and the dwarf carried it like it was nothing. "No, thank you, Master Breakstone. If you'll set it here, I'll teleport it directly to the trolls. They can lift it, I'm sure." He grinned.

"Mind if I come with ye? Ain't never met a rock troll. And I'd like to see this Dire Keep o' yers," the dwarf asked.

"Certainly! You're always welcome at my home. Ready to go now?" Alexander asked.

When the mason nodded, Alexander teleported them, and the heavy stone, to the ledge above the troll's cavern. He saw the trolls scattered below, looking much like the field of boulders he'd originally thought them to be.

"Hello!" he called out. Hoping he'd recognize the chief among the others. Troll heads rose to follow the sound of his voice. Seeing who it was, and the large slab of dessert standing next to him, they all rose to their feet and approached the ledge. It was only ten feet or so above the floor, so Alexander was quickly looking at several troll faces with what he imagined were eager looks on them.

Solving his problem, the trolls parted as the chief approached. He stepped up to the ledge, and looked at Alexander, then the dwarves. At a nod from Alexander, Breakstone moved the slab forward a bit, presenting it to the chief. "Here you go, chief. One slab of marble for the first week. As promised."

The troll extended one massive arm, and took the slab in hand. Pulling it closer, he used two fingers of his other hand to break a small piece off one corner. Popping it into his mouth, he moved it around a bit, tasting it. Then his mouth grew very wide in what Alexander hoped was a troll smile. "Goooood!" the troll rumbled.

Surprised, Alexander laughed. So did the dwarves. "I'm glad you like it, chief. We'll bring another with next week's food." He bowed his head slightly, then teleported back to the keep with the two dwarves.

Breakstone immediately said, "He speak'd to us! I never hear'd of a troll speakin common. The boys'll never believe me!"

“Aye, that were a surprise to me, too.” Silverbeard chuckled. “I don’t get many surprises at my age. Thank ye, lad.”

“Master Breakstone, we’ve been building a new wall and moat outside. Would you like to check them out?” Alexander asked.

“O’ course I would!” The dwarf grinned.” To save time, Alexander teleported them again, this time to top of the outer gatehouse. As both dwarves examined the wall, and looked down its length, the mason asked, “Ye did all this in a day?”

“Not me, alone,” Alexander replied. “Fitz and two other earth mages did most of the work. And they’re finishing the moat today.”

When he showed them the bridge and told them about his plans for a drawbridge, Breakstone said, “Ye could have a stone drawbridge if he like. Ironwood be strong, no doubt. But it’ll burn if ye make it hot enough. Stone won’t.”

“But wouldn’t stone be too heavy to lift?” Alexander asked.

“Bwahaha!” Breakstone laughed. “Ye be talkin to dwarves, boy. Movin’ heavy stone be what we do! Ye leave it to me. Ye’ve got masons here, yes? Good. I’ll need to go back to Broken Mountain fer some heavy chains. And some gears. And…” Breakstone and Silverbeard fell to the logistics and supply list needed to build the drawbridge. Alexander pondered the idea. A stone bridge would certainly be impressive. And it wouldn’t burn, or rot, like Breakstone had said. But stone was more brittle than ironwood. They’d need enchantments to strengthen it…”

Alexander slapped himself in the forehead. Those were exactly the enchantments Fitz and Kai were already putting on the walls themselves.

Returning his focus to the two dwarves, he found them staring at him. “I’m sorry, lost in my thoughts. Where were we?” he asked.

“Ye be about to give me a heap o’ gold and send me through the portal to Broken Mountain so I can get ye yer gate! Breakstone grinned at him.

“Ha! Okay. You mind if we check in with Kai and Fitz first? They’re just down there.” He pointed toward where the two were widening the moat. They’d already almost reached the ridge.

Alexander teleported them again to a spot just ahead of where the two were working. Breakstone bowed his head to the dragon prince. Then he became distracted, inspecting the moat, and the ridge they were about to reach. Producing a pick axe, he slammed it into the ground near the end of the moat. Then he produced a rope, and after tying it to the axe, he held the rope in one hand and leapt over the edge.

Slightly alarmed, Alexander stepped to the edge and looked down. He found the master mason hanging about ten feet below, holding the rope with one hand while he used a small hammer to tap at the stone.

After a couple of minutes, the dwarf pulled himself back up the rope. “Ye have granite, quartz, and high-quality marble here. D’ye have a quarry o’ yer own already?”

Alexander laughed. “No, we don’t. But I bet I know a dwarf who’d be willing to help me start one…”

“BWAHAHA! Aye, lad. I’ll make ye a deal. Ye let me bring some lads n put a quarry here, same deal as in Whitehall. And in return, I’ll build yer gate for ye for free.” Breakstone said.

“Where would you put this quarry? It can’t be too far from the keep, or we won’t be able to protect you.”

Breakstone put his hand to the ground, and closed his eyes. Then he pointed to their left, along the ridge line. “Half a mile or so, that way. There be a high concentration there.”

“That’s not far from the mine. We could probably bribe the trolls to help protect you,” Alexander mused.

“Aye lad, and we’ll cut our workshop and living quarters right into the ridge. No enemy’s likely to break into a dwarven stronghold!” The dwarf smiled.

"Okay. You have a deal." Turning to Fitz, he said, "Fitz, when I widened the moat at the other end, I continued it into the ridge about 100 feet, to give your moat monster a cave to shelter in, if it wished. Maybe you could do the same on this end?"

The wizard nodded his head. "Good thinking, boy. And with a moat this size, I might bring two. So they can make some baby moat monsters!" He waggled his eyebrows. This got a laugh from everyone.

"Well, if you think they'll be alright," Alexander said. "We can connect the moat to the lake, so there will be fresh water. And fish to eat. And we'll be feeding them lots of enemy adventurers, I think!"

Leaving Kai and Fitz to their work, Alexander teleported the two dwarves back to the courtyard. Breakstone went to go find Brogin, the head mason at the keep. Needing to hang around near the portal, Alexander decided to check in with Jeeves. Climbing up onto the wall, he looked at the main structure. Most of the holes had been filled in! Those that remained were on upper floors. He said "Jeeves, what is the status of the repair work?".

Alexander had initiated the self-repair the evening after clearing the mine. That was roughly thirty-six hours ago. He'd initially been surprised that the repairs weren't nearly instantaneous. But as he'd thought about it, he realized the time requirement made sense. If repairs didn't take some time, a keep with a large amount of resources would never be taken. It could just insta-repair over and over.

"*Repairs are nearly complete master. The original structure is at 95%, and will be at 100% physical condition by day's end. New structures are at 90%.*"

"New structures at 90%?" he asked.

"*The new wall and moat are both incomplete. The moat structure is being widened, and has not been filled. The gates for the new wall are incomplete,*" Jeeves detailed for him.

"Ah, of course. Thank you, Jeeves."

Both of those were already in the works. Fitz and Kai would finish the moat, and hopefully add the moat monster. Alexander was VERY curious as to what form that would take! He pictured a giant octopus, arms waiving, grabbing up minions of the Dark One and dragging them down to a watery doom. Or maybe a large Kraken-looking creature with webbed feet and claws, and a massive maw filled with razor sharp teeth.

His musing was interrupted by the return of Breakstone and Brogin. The dwarves were excitedly talking over the potential new quarry as they walked toward the portal.

Heading down the stairs, Alexander called out, "Breakstone, I know you're excited about the quarry, but I need you to focus on the drawbridge first. Completing the gate and the moat could increase the level of the keep. And we need all the defense we can get right now."

"Aye, Alexander. We'll be grabbin' all the gear we'll need at home. Be back here by noon. If ye'll pull and shape the stone, yer gate'll be up by noon tomorrow," Breakstone assured him.

"Thank you," Alexander said as he opened the portal. "I'll open it again at noon."

The dwarves stepped through, and he closed the portal again. Another job begun. He was starting to enjoy this whole building aspect of the game.

"*Ambush*!" Max's shout came across the raid chat. "*Lainey's hit! There are a dozen of them that I can see!*"

"*Everybody to the courtyard, NOW! Guards, and hunters, stay on the wall*!" Alexander shouted in raid chat.

"Jeeves, loudspeaker, emergency message!" he said aloud. Then, "Attention, everyone, our hunters have just been attacked in the forest.

We're going to go deal with it. Keep doing what you're doing, but be prepared to defend the keep if they get closer."

Brick, Sasha, Lugs' group, and Dayle's group all rushed into the courtyard. Without a word, Alexander focused on Max's medallion, and teleported them to his location.

They were in a sparsely wooded area, with widely placed trees and little in the way of brush. The first thing Alexander saw was Lainey, laying on the ground at the base of a tree. Her health bar was below 10%, and she wasn't moving. Sasha threw a heal at her.

Fitz and Kai appeared, Kai standing over Lainey's body protectively.

Alexander took a moment to look around. Max was up in the tree above him, firing arrow after arrow. Alexander followed his line of fire to see a group of players mixed into the trees about fifty yards away. There were four tank types, shield up, making a wall between two large trees. Behind the tanks were three sword-carriers who weren't doing much but laying low. There were three archers, firing at Alexander's group now. A caster near the archers must be their healer. Alexander guessed this because there were half a dozen of Max's arrows in her face and head. The last caster was throwing bolts of dark magic at Lainey, trying to finish her off. Fitz had thrown up a magic shield that was protecting himself, Kai, Lainey, and Sasha, who had dashed over to try and heal Lainey. Kai was reaching down toward his friend's stomach. That was a bad sign. It meant she had one of those spike-wormy things in her.

Even as he watched, Kai stayed his hand. Lainey's health bar had dropped to zero. She was gone. Dead.

With a roar of rage, Alexander shouted, "They killed Lainey! Make them pay!" He liquefied the ground below the enemy players. They'd been expecting this move, though, and all of them leapt to the side. Only one of the tanks made it clear, but he linked hands with the others, and began to pull them free. The healer didn't move, and was sinking. So were two of the archers.

Lugs activated his charge ability, and smashed into the tanks. He'd target the one on solid ground, knocking him back into the mud. Not having anything to hold onto, the others resumed sinking. Lugs' momentum had carried him into the mud as well. But he ignored it, using his massive hammer to crush the skull of one of the distracted tanks. Alexander shouted, "Don't kill them!", but he thought it was probably too late for that one.

Max had taken the healer down to 20% health, and she was sinking, so he left her alone. He focused instead on the other caster. The one who'd killed Lainey. A silence arrow went into his face, tearing off a chunk of his nose in the process.

Sasha, screaming in rage, threw down an aoe thorn trap that engulfed the archers and warriors that had cleared the mud. The massive amount of thorns was easily triple what he'd ever seen his druidess cast. The players were barely visible inside the tangle of vines, each of which were half a foot thick. He quickly cast wizard's fire on three body parts he saw sticking out. He also cast it on each of the tanks. Then he raised some stone under Lugs, freeing him from the mud and allowing him to step back from the flames.

Brick, on the other hand, went charging in. His shield devastated the burning caster, knocking him back into a tree with a crack that was probably his spine. Then the dwarf grabbed the mage's robes and tossed him into the mud with the tanks.

Alexander solidified the ground around that group, trapping all four tanks, the healer, the mage, and one archer. Then he built a three-sided stone box around the group that was trapped in Sasha's vines, so they could not retreat anywhere except toward his group.

"Hit them all, except the healer! Take them down to 5% each. As painfully as you can!" he shouted. The rest of his group didn't hesitate. Brick and Lugs began to break arms and ribs with terrible hammer blows. The enemy tanks fought back as best they could, arms still free of the mud. Dayle moved in to do the same to the tank group, so Brick moved over to the players that were on fire. His shield would heal him while he broke bones. Max was shooting arrows into sensitive areas still exposed above-ground, or sticking out from vines. Misty was doing the same with ice bolts. One of her bolts actually froze a hand that was exposed between burning vines. A second bolt shattered the hand.

Warren and Helga were slowly and carefully slicing tendons and muscles with their swords. Lyra, Benny and Sasha threw heals on any who needed it. Benny, in his paladin's plate armor, stood in front of the two ladies to protect them. Kai and Fitz stayed out of the fight, though both looked angry enough to kill.

Alexander took a moment to observe all the enemy players. These were higher level than the last group, all over 50. One of the tanks was level 68. And the healer was 70. That was double the level of some of Alexander's group. Nearly triple Benny's level 26.

It took several minutes to lower the health bars of all the higher-level players. One of the tanks was a paladin, and he stopped fighting to focus on healing himself and his comrades. A few of them managed to get down healing potions, as well. This stopped quickly when Lugs, Brick, and Dayle broke arms and shoulders, incapacitating the players. Alexander softened the ground below the group that was trapped in Sasha's vines, sinking them to their chests in the mud before solidifying it again.

The mage managed to cast another of those dark bolts with the worm in it, hitting Lugs under the arm as he raised his hammer. The bolt penetrated the ogre's thick skin, and he went down, howling.

Kai was there instantly, making the poor ogre scream even louder as he worked to remove the evil thing. Beatrix cast a globe of water on the mage's head, effectively stopping any more casting. "Beatrix, be careful not to kill him," Alexander cautioned. "That one's gonna pay for Lainey." His tone made several of the others stop and look at him for a moment. There was a promise of pain in his voice that even Sasha had never heard before.

Calling to his group to halt for a moment, he called out, "You are all under arrest…" Then paused.

Shit. What can I charge them with? Killing a player isn't a crime. I don't have any way to know yet whether any of them are PWP. And Chaos Nation haven't been declared enemies by the king yet. Can I do it myself? Are we even still on my lands? His mind was frantic, looking for a reason that the game would accept.

Taking a chance, he said, "Chaos Nation is officially declared an enemy of the Dire Lands, and the Kingdom of Stormforge! All of you who are members are charged with the murder of a citizen of Dire Keep, and espionage!"

Fitz cast a spell, and that same glow of light from the earlier group shone around ten of the twelve. The healer, and the paladin tank did not seem affected.

Moving next to Fitz, he whispered, "Do I actually have the power to make those declarations?"

Fitz laughed. He whispered back, "As Baron of Dire Keep, you do. On your own lands. You were granted that title by the king. As Knight-Advisor to The King, you have arrest powers on his behalf, and can bind them to the prison. Either yours, or the king's. I'll teach you the spell, later. The murder charge for killing an adventurer didn't work. That is why two of them were not bound."

Good to know.

Stepping up to the paladin, Alexander said, "You are not Chaos Nation. Who are you, and why are you with these assholes?"

The man motioned toward the unconscious healer. "She's my sister. And that asshole mage over there is her boyfriend. He talked her into following him on this raid. I couldn't let her come alone." Alexander looked over at the mage, who had passed out from lack of oxygen. Beatrix had removed her water spell before the mage died.

Alexander looked back at the paladin. He had no sense that the man was lying. He'd been trying to protect his sister. He wasn't in league with the Dark One, he was just in the wrong place for the right reason.

"Are you a member of PWP?" Alexander asked.

"Those assholes? I've seen the videos of them, and…" His voice drifted off, as his eyes got wide. "Oh, shit. You're that guy." He looked around at the others. "You're Greystone clan. Some of you, anyway. The ones with the SEEE YA T-shirts." Now his face fell.

"Which means, I'm one of the bad guys, now. Right?" he asked, dejected.

"You've certainly been helping them!" Sasha yelled at him. She was still seething over the death of Lainey.

Alexander looked at the man. "These are bad people. Members of a guild controlled by a real-life terrorist organization. I'm afraid you, and your sister, have stepped into some serious shit."

"Terrorists?" The man gaped. "I'm no terrorist! What the hell do you mean?"

"Shut the hell up, moron!" The mage was awake again, and angry. Lugs, who was back on his feet, and very angry, moved to step on the man's neck. Kai held him back. The dragon did break the mage's one unbroken arm, to keep him from casting any more evil worm bolts.

When he was done screaming in pain, the mage shouted, "The Dark One will take vengeance on you! All of you!"

"Yeah, yeah." Max kicked the mage in the head. "The Dark One, blah, blah, blah. All of you are so sure he's right. What's he paying you, anyway?"

"He doesn't pay me! He gives me POWER!" the mage screamed. A wave a dark energy burst forth from him. It knocked Max over, taking about 60% of his health in the process. Others suffered lesser damage. Beatrix put another water globe over his head.

Max got back up, putting his face right next to the globe, yelling. "That makes you an even bigger dumbass than the others! At least they were getting paid. You sacrificed your life for bullshit power? Moron!" Spittle flew off Max's lips as he screamed at the mage.

"*Hey, guys. That sucked.*" Lainey's voice came over guild chat. "*I'm back at the keep.*"

Max took a few deep breaths. Sasha looked a little shaken. Alexander understood. With the hyper-reality of full immersion, Lainey's death had seemed very real to them in the heat of battle.

"*Glad to hear it! Congrats on your first death. We'll have to celebrate.*" Max tried to smile, but failed.
Looking at the paladin, Alexander said, "You might be able to help yourself by providing information. Are there more of you? Did these guys mention any plans?"

The paladin nodded his head. "They said we were scouting for a large raid group. Didn't say how many, but it sounded like a lot. Something about undead soldiers. We were supposed to attack the keep and get an idea of your defenses. They expected us to be killed, and to give them the information when we respawn in Antalia."

"That won't be happening. At the very least, your accounts are going to be suspended while your involvement is investigated." Alexander told the man.

As if on cue, the GM appeared. As he was giving his speech to the players, who were howling objections at him, Alexander called out in raid chat. "*Kill them all! Start with the highest levels. We have about fifteen seconds after he disappears!*" He pulled out his light weapon as he spoke.

As soon as the GM disappeared, he cast Wizard's Fire on the vines, burning that group. He hit every one of the enemy players with a burst of light damage, one per second.

Lugs crushed the paladin's head with his hammer. Brick and Dayle smashed away as well. Max fired arrows into faces as quickly as he could. Beatrix drowned them, Helga and Warren sliced off heads. Nearly every hit was a crit against defenseless players. It took less than the fifteen seconds to kill them all.

Level up! You are now level 42!
Your wisdom has increased by +1. Your intelligence has increased by +1
You have 26 free attribute points available

Each of them got at least another level. Benny got three. Helga, and Dayle's entire group, got two.

Max and Beatrix looted the players, taking their inventory bags as well. They wouldn't be needing them again.

When the job was done, Sasha gathered up Lainey's gear, and Fitz teleported everyone back to the keep.

Chapter Thirteen

No Rest for the Wicked

Lainey was waiting for them in the courtyard. Sasha hugged her, then handed her all her gear.

"Thank you!" Lainey said. "Stuck in that stupid limbo, all I could think about was one of those assholes taking my bow."

Alexander gave her a minute to re-equip, then grabbed her up in a big bear hug. Max and Brick joined in. Nobody said anything. At least until a small voiced squeaked out from somewhere in the middle, "Squishing… me…"

Laughing, Alexander let her go. She breathed in deeply, then kicked him playfully in the shin. "Idiots. Nearly killed me again." She grinned.

Alexander looked around, noticing for the first time all the citizens staring at them.

"Jeeves, loudspeaker, please."

After waiting a few seconds, he announced, "We have dealt with another dozen servants of the Dark One. The keep is safe for now. We did learn there's a large raid group planning to hit us. It seems they're still in Antalia right now, so we likely have a few days. But they are coming. So, let's be as prepared as we can be!" There was a general cheer from the crowd. Alexander continued. "We have reason to believe the army coming against us will include the undead. Father Ignatius, Father Alric, I'd like you to work with the paladins here. Bless as many weapons and armor pieces as you can. Those of you with magic, learn any light spells you can. Healers, your light magic heals will damage the undead as much as any weapon."

Seeing that the mood had darkened considerably, he added "Do not worry! The ground around you is consecrated by not one, but TWO gods of light.

You have all received blessings that will allow you to do extra damage against servants of the Dark One. And you will heal faster than you did before. Together we WILL overcome this enemy!" Enthusiastic cheers answer him.

Kai stepped close to Alexander. "I must return to speak with my father. This Dark One, he is sharing evil magic with his minions. Magic that should not be allowed. The King of Dragons must be informed. I shall return in a day or so."

With that, he teleported up onto the wall. Motioning the guards to move back, his body morphed into his dragon form. Not the form small enough to sleep on Brick's dragon forge. His true form. Where one second a man had stood, now there was a blue-black dragon, larger than the entire keep complex. With a single beat of his massive wings, Kai leapt into the air. He soared in a great circle above the forest, before passing over them and disappearing over the ridge above.

"Holy shit," Misty said, as his shadow blocked out the sun. "Kai's a dragon!"

"A big goddamned dragon," Helga added.

"BWAHAHAHA!" Brick laughed. "Me thinks we forgot to share a couple things." He grinned.

Lyra jumped up in the air, fist raised above her. "We have a DRAGON on our side! Yeah!" she shouted. There was a roar of approval, mixed with some laughter, from the gathered citizens.

As everyone drifted back to their jobs, Alexander motioned to Fitz. "Did you and Kai finish the moat?"

"Aye, boy. I was just about to pop back for the moat monster egg," the wizard replied.

"What happened to two moat monsters? Moat monster babies?" Alexander chuckled.

"We'll start with the one. See how it does." Fitz waggled his eyebrows. "I'll go fetch it, you fill the moat," he added, before disappearing.

"Beatrix!" Alexander called out. "Want to help me make a giant bathtub for our moat monster?"

The little gnome dashed over. "You betcha!" she said. "I always wanted to have a castle with a moat!" She winked at him.

He teleported them back to the lake, at its closest point to the new wall. He'd have to make a trench about three hundred yards long. "Can you control the water flow, so we don't empty the lake?" he asked the water mage.

"Sure! Though, the smaller you make the opening, the easier it will be," she replied.

That was a good point. Maybe a trench wasn't the best idea. A pipe might be better. A large pipe. Say, ten feet in diameter? It'd be easier to make, and easier to shut down if necessary.

So starting at the moat side, Alexander used his earth magic to form a stone pipe, starting a couple of feet above the floor of the moat, and extending it from the moat through the ground until it was nearly at the lake. Once he was there, he told Beatrix "I'm down to the last foot of stone. Try to hold back the water while I open it?"

She nodded her head, closing her eyes. When she was ready, she waved at him. He removed the last foot of stone, raising it straight up like a sluice gate. When the stone had completely cleared the pipe, he looked to Beatrix. The poor little gnome was sweating, her whole body trembling with the effort of holding back the water. "I'm sorry, Beatrix. Go ahead and release it."

The gnome exhaled forcefully, and her body slumped. "I didn't realize it would be so heavy! It was like the weight of the whole lake pushing on me!" She panted.

They both heard a roaring sound as the water rushed through the pipe and gushed out the other end, into the moat. They ran over to the edge and looked down.

The pressure from the weight of the lake water was causing the water to fountain out across the moat and strike the opposite side. Alexander heard the cracking sound of fish being slammed into the wall at high speed. "Can you do anything about that impact?" he asked. "We don't want to kill every fish in the lake."

Beatrix focused again, and re-shaped the fountaining stream so that it curved to the left, shooting the water down the length of the moat. This way the fish were still hitting the floor, but not with nearly the same force as they hit the wall. And soon they'd be landing in water, instead of on the stone bottom of the moat.

Alexander knew the water mage couldn't keep that control going indefinitely. He said, "Channel your magic through the soul crystal I gave you. Use its power. I'll recharge it for you later."

She pulled out her crystal, and after a moment, visibly relaxed. He pulled up a block of stone for her to sit on. "Thank you. That's much better. I can keep this up for a while. I think the pressure is already decreasing, as the water level in the lake goes down."

Alexander hadn't thought of that, either. *What about negative pressure? What if the moat fills, and the water pushes back through the pipe? Would it prevent fresh water flowing in*? He didn't want stagnant water in his moat. This was going to take some studying. Maybe he could consult with one of his father's engineers when he next logged out.

An idea occurred to him. He picked a spot about fifty feet down from the pipe, and raised a six-foot wall. This would cause the water to pool much faster around the pipe, and lessen the impact for incoming water critters. When it reached six feet deep, it could spill over the wall and begin to fill further. Just to be safe, he raised another four-foot wall about a hundred feet downstream from the first. And he ramped up the stone on the dry side of each wall, so the water would run down smoothly.

Alexander pulled up a stone for himself, and sat with Beatrix for the better part of an hour. The two of them talked about the attack that morning, and did some planning for the upcoming raid in Antalia.

After an hour, the water level was high enough, and the pressure in the pipe low enough, that Beatrix could safely release her magic and let the water flow straight out of the pipe. It still gushed out with significant force, but not enough to impact the opposite wall.

The two of them walked back to the lakeside end of the pipe. The water level had gone down in the lake. There was about five feet of muddy bank exposed. Lars was standing not far away, shaking his head. Approaching, the fisherman, Alexander said "Don't worry, it's temporary. We're filling the moat. By day's end, the waterfall should have the water level here back to normal."

"Aye, thank you, Alexander. I heard the splashing back by the wall. I was just about to call you, to look at that." Lars pointed out toward the receding water line, just to the right of his new pier. There was a stone structure peaking above the water. Alexander could see the top third of what looked like a round stone door through the clear water.

"It's a tunnel entrance!" Beatrix shouted. The tiny gnome was easily excited. "We have to go look!"
"If you were to open that door, the entire thing would flood" Lars commented. "I'd guess it's very old, probably been there since this lake was smaller."

Alexander closed his eyes, using his mage sight and earth magic, he sent his senses into the earth below the lake. He quickly found the doorway, and a stairway tunnel leading downward. The stairs ended some fifty feet below the doorway in round chamber. From there, two other tunnels led in different directions. Alexander followed one, only to find it connected to others. There was a whole complex down there.

"There are carvings on the door." Lars said. Alexander couldn't see them, but the fisherman was used to gazing long distances across the water, and obviously had sharp eyes.

In raid chat, Alexander said, "*Fitz, we may have found something at the lake even older than you*!"

"*You shouldn't insult your teacher, boy. The next spell I teach you might put a platypus beak on your face*." The wizard grumped. *"I've picked up the egg, and am having a snack with Lydia. I'll be there shortly."*

"*A snack*?" Alexander realized he'd not gotten to eat his breakfast, having been interrupted by the players attacking the wall. "*Any chance you could bring a little with you? None of us got to finish breakfast*." He pleaded.

"*You'll spoil your lunch! Besides, I might be too ancient and weak to carry such a load*." The wizard responded, sounding petulant. Alexander figured it was best not to argue. It was nearly lunchtime, after all.

"*We're right by the new pier, at the side of the lake*." Alexander replied.

As they waited, Alexander noticed something else. The exposed bank was littered with seaweed-looking plants, growing in bundles.

"*Fitz, ask Lydia if there are any alchemy recipes that use some kind of freshwater seaweed. There's a lot of it here*."

After a moment, Fitz appeared with Lydia at his side.

"Oh! That's trisulca weed!" Lydia exclaimed. "It's useful in all kinds of things. Good flavoring for stews and potions. Ingredient for water breathing potion. Very rare."

She immediately removed her shoes and began stepping through the muddy lakebed to harvest the plants.

"Should I fetch Sasha to help you?" Alexander asked

"No, no. We shouldn't take too much. It must be allowed to grow and multiply. And it's not good for it to be dry like this." Lydia sounded concerned.

“The lake should refill by this evening” Alexander said. “We’ve drained it some, to fill the moat. But the falls will refill it. I can temporarily block off the creek to speed things up, if you like.”

“No, that would just cause other problems in the creek,” Lydia said. “We’ll just have to hope these plants recover, and that there are more of them below the water.”

Alexander thought for a bit. “Lydia, you know how the farms at Whitehall were producing crops at a faster rate?”

“Yes, I remember. Why?” Lydia asked distractedly, as she unstuck a foot from the mud to move toward another plant.

“Well, the ground under the moat is consecrated as well. And the water that runs through the stream under the keep, too. It increases health, stamina, and mana regeneration. I’m thinking that if the consecrated water from the moat mingles with the water in the lake, maybe it’ll help these plants recover?” Alexander asked.

“Oh! Well let’s hope so!” Lydia said, sounding relieved.

“Aye, and might it make the fish bigger, as well?” Lars sounded hopeful.

Alexander shrugged, and looked to Fitz. The wizard was casting a spell toward the partially revealed doorway, and wasn’t listening. Not wanting to interrupt, he told Lars, “We’ll ask the wizard when he’s done here. Maybe he can create a spell that circulates the water better.”

“Ooh! I’d like to learn that one!” Beatrix grinned.

Still watching Fitz, Alexander saw a thoughtful look on the old wizard’s face. “So, what do you see, Fitz?” he asked.

“There are dwarven runes on the doorway. Ancient ones. And it is magically sealed,” Fitz replied.

“There’s a stairway behind it, leading down to a whole system of tunnels. Makes sense that it would be dwarves,” Alexander added.

Fitz said, "You are right about this doorway being old. Not older than me…" He waggled his eyebrows. "But certainly several thousand years. I don't recall a dwarven settlement here. But maybe the dwarves were hired to build this for someone. Or maybe it's simply an old mine."

"It might be good to check with Master Tomebinder, to see if he has any records," Alexander said. "Speaking of dwarves, it's nearly noon. I need to get back to open the portal for Master Breakstone. They're going to be installing our new gate on the outer wall. Fitz, can you stay here and make sure Lydia and Lars get back safely?"

The wizard nodded. Lars started to object. Alexander cut him off. "We've had two attacks already today. I asked you to stay inside the walls yesterday, because it's not safe out here. How did you even get out? The outer gates are still closed."

Lars smiled, and held up a pendant he wore on a braided leather cord. "This was a gift from my late wife. She was concerned about my boat sinking far from shore. She was sure I'd get eaten by a sea monster. It holds a teleport spell. She called it my safety net."

"I see. Well, I suppose if you get attacked, you can save yourself with that. Still, be careful out here. And by tomorrow, you should be able to sit on the wall and fish!" Alexander grinned at him. "The view would be even better from up there!"

"Ha! I just might do that, lad." Lars chuckled.

Alexander said goodbye to Lydia, and teleported himself and Beatrix back to the keep. He had a few minutes before he needed to open the portal, so he went to find Sasha. He found her in a room just down the hall from the kitchen. She was setting up an alchemy lab.

"Are you sure you should be putting this so close to the kitchen? You might poison everyone!" he teased.

"Hush, dork boy," she answered. "I can set up my mad scientist lab wherever I want! Now, why are you bothering me? Did you wear yourself out playing with rocks again?"

I came to tell you that we found a rare plant in the lake when it drained a bit. Lydia calls it tri… tri… fecta? Something like that. She's picking some now."

"Trisulca weed?" Sasha corrected him. "That makes water breathing potions. I haven't learned that one yet!" His friend was suddenly excited.

"Well, from the looks of things, you'll have plenty of chances to practice," he said. "I'm sure she'll share some. But she did say you had to be careful not to pick too much, or they'll die out."

"Of course! Every herbalist knows you don't over-harvest. Silly boy." She smacked him on the back of the head.

Taking that as a dismissal, he headed back toward the kitchen. He begged a warm roll from Mattie, and went to check on Edward.

The boy looked miserable. His face was pale, and he was sweating profusely as he pumped a bellows for one of the smiths. He winced slightly every time a hammer struck a piece of metal with a loud clang. He smelled of smoke and stale liquor sweat.

Brick walked over. "Gotta give the lad credit," he said. "Been workin' like a dog all mornin'. Ain't let'd the hangover stop him. Might be he learned his lesson."

"Edward!" Alexander called him over. "I think you've had enough. You look ready to drop. Go get a bath before lunch."

"Thank you, Alexander." The prince walked slowly and stiffly inside, as if his head were made of glass, and he was afraid it would shatter.

"Brick, Master Breakstone is about to return from Broken Mountain with gears and chains to install a stone drawbridge. Thought you might like to tag along and watch?"

“Aye! Thank ye. That’d be cool to see.” Brick joined him as he walked toward the portal.

Master Silverbeard was waiting for them as they approached. “Alexander,” the master began, “would you like me to handle the negotiations relative to the quarry?”

“Well, the details, certainly. Though we basically agreed to the same terms Thea negotiated for the Whitehall quarry. I don’t even know all the terms,” Alexander admitted. “But she can catch you up.”

The old master chamberlain shook his head. “In the future, it may be best if you consult me before entering into significant negotiations. I’ll do what I can to make sure this deal is favorable to the Greystone guild.”

“Thank you, Master Silverbeard. And I will certainly remember to include you, or Lola, in the future. Right now, I’m more interested in building a solid friendship with our neighbors, than in earning more coin. I think allies are going to be needed. Allies we can trust.”

Silverbeard nodded his head. “That is wise of you to consider, Alexander. Just remember, it doesn’t always have to be one or the other. We can make friends, AND gold.” He winked at them both.

“BWAHAHA!” Brick laughed. “He be right. Dwarves no be resentful of a fierce negotiation. We be considerin’ it like a good battle.”

“I’ll keep that in mind,” Alexander said, as he opened the portal.

Master Breakstone and Brogin led the way, as a procession of pony-drawn carts moved through into the courtyard. Alexander could see enormous clockwork-like gears, coils of massive chains with links the size of his head, and two pulleys that were each so large that only one would fit in a cart.

As Brogin led the carts out the inner keep’s gate and down the path toward the outer gate, Breakstone approached Alexander. “Me King give’d me a loan to purchase all this on short notice. But I do no’ like bein’ in debt.

Be there any chance ye can pay me fer the marble ye ordered?" he asked, hesitantly.

"Of course! We could have given you the mithril before you left! I'm sorry I didn't think of it," Alexander said. He nodded to Silverbeard, who produced a half pound of the mithril that Grimble had retrieved from the mine.

"Thank ye, Alexander. Ye've the honor of a dwarven lord." Breakstone bowed his head slightly before heading off to follow the carts.

"That be a great compliment," Silverbeard said. "Dwarven honor be our most cherished gift. It be give'd to us by Durin hisself. To abuse that gift be among the most grave of sins. A dwarf who breaks his oath, or dishonors his god, be outcast for life."

This was not news to Alexander. The concept of honor among dwarves went all the way back to the writings of visionary men like JRR Tolkien. It was coded into their very being in Io. Even players like Brick who chose the dwarven race tended to behave better than the average player. There were, of course exceptions.

Brick and Alexander followed the procession down to the gate. Breakstone and the others were all gathered around the back of a cart, a set of drawings laid out on the tailgate. They were pointing at the gatehouse and the bridge supports.

When the two friends got closer, Breakstone said, "We'll be needin' ye to make some changes to the structure. And to move that wall." He pointed to the temporary wall Alexander had raised to seal the gate.

For the next few hours, Alexander and Brick moved stone, shaped stone, following detailed direction from Breakstone and Brogin. The gatehouse was raised ten feet higher, and its walls thickened by more than double. Chambers were created within the structure to house the gears and levers, and channels were made for the massive chains to pass through.

Breakstone had Alexander pull up another slab of stone, this one granite. He also asked that Alexander pull up a 5x5 block of obsidian. He pulled up a bit extra for himself, as well. For his enchanting work. He'd used most of his supply for the dragon pins. Once that was done, Breakstone sent Alexander on his way, asking Brick to stay for some further shaping.

Alexander stepped out to the edge of the moat. Best he could tell, there was about six feet of water in it now. The water was slightly muddy, from all the agitation, so he couldn't see the bottom. He reminded himself to speak to Fitz about a spell to circulate the water.

Walking back to the keep, he visited with a few farmers who were taking a break from plowing the fields within the wall. One of them said, "This soil be good enough. But some fertilizer wouldn't hurt."

Even a city boy like Alexander knew what that meant. "There should be some outside the stables by now. We've had several horses and ponies in there for three days now."

"Aye, there was. But them druids claimed it, to make their trees grow," another farmer replied.

"Alright, then." Alexander looked at the group. "Which of you is the best judge of livestock?" After some murmuring amongst themselves, several of them pointed toward a human. One of those Alexander had interviewed. The man was roughly fifty years old, with salt and pepper hair. He was over six feet tall, with broad shoulders and strong arms.

"That'd be me." he said.

Alexander recalled his name. "Plowright, isn't it? I remember thinking it sounded like a blacksmith's name."

The man nodded. "Aye, I hear that often enough."

"Okay, master Plowright. Let us go to Stormforge. I've made arrangements to purchase livestock, but I know little more than how to tell the difference between a horse and a cow." This earned him some chuckles from the farmers. "What will we need?" Alexander asked.

"We'll be needing mostly beef cattle," Plowright said. "A couple more plow horses couldn't hurt. Speed up the work a bit."

"We should have some dairy cows!" another farmer added. "Milk, butter, cheese…"

"Pigs!" A dwarven farmer stamped his foot down in the soil. "We'll not be wantin' to go without bacon fer breakfast!"

Alexander raised his hands in surrender. "Okay, okay. So basically, some of everything?" He chuckled. "Plowright, why don't you come with me, and you can choose for us?"

The farmer nodded his head, and followed Alexander back into the keep. As he walked, he messaged Fitz in raid chat. "*I'm opening a portal to Stormforge. If Lydia's done, she can go back with me.*"

"*We're already back at the keep. She says she wants to spend some time with Sasha and the druids.*" Fitz replied.

Walking through the inner gate, Alexander saw Fitz walking toward him from the direction of the kitchen. He had a pastry in each hand. "That Edna, she's not as good as Millicent, but she's damn close!" He grinned.

Laughing at the wizard and his bottomless pit of a stomach, Alexander said, "Plowright and I are heading to buy livestock in the city. And speaking of livestock, how do we… hatch? Is hatch the right term? How do we hatch the moat monster?"

"It's under a stasis spell right now. I simply place the egg in some shallow water, and remove the spell. It will hatch relatively quickly. Within a few days, I imagine," the wizard replied.

"And, how fast will it grow? How big will it get?" Alexander asked. Noticing Plowright beside him, he apologized. "I'm sorry, master Plowright. I'm wasting your time here."

"No, no. I want to hear this, too. Animal husbandry has been a hobby of mine since I was a lad. I've raised everything from chickens to horses. Never even seen a moat monster," the farmer replied.

Fitz answered, "With a good food supply, it will grow quickly. Within a week, it should be about the size of a horse. After two weeks, it'll be the size of a small whale. From there, the growth will slow a bit. But it will never stop growing, as long as it has food."

"Then, do we need to make the moat bigger?" Alexander asked.

Fitz shook his head. "No, forty feet wide and deep should be plenty. At least for the next several years."

"Okay, thank you, Fitz. Do you want to join us in Stormforge? Maybe check in with the king?"

"No, I am heading to Broken Mountain. I want to speak with Tomebinder about that cave system under the lake," the wizard answered.

Alexander opened the portal to Broken Mountain, first. "There you go, sir wizard. Please give Tomebinder my regards."

Fitz snorted as he walked through the portal. Alexander said, "Watch this," to Plowright, leaving the portal open for a moment.

The guards noted the arrival of the wizard, and sent the same unfortunate boy as last time to run and alert the king. Fitz waited until the boy exited the courtyard, then teleported away. Chuckling, Alexander closed the portal. Plowright just looked at him, not understanding.

"They send that poor boy running about a mile into the citadel to the Great Hall to alert the king he has visitors. Fitz teleports himself there, and will be there waiting when the boy arrives. He and King Thalgrin get a good laugh out of it," Alexander explained. This got a smile from farmer. Everyone understood 'torturing' the boy for amusement.

Alexander opened the portal to the Greystone compound, and the two of them stepped through. They made their way across town to the slaughterhouse belonging to butcher they'd made an agreement with. Because of the smell and the noise, the building was actually located outside the walls, near a creek that ran down to the nearby sea.

Plowright and the butcher already knew each other, so they got right down to business. Alexander followed them out to an area with several paddocks containing a variety of cows, bulls, goats, sheep, and other livestock.

As they walked toward the first paddock, Alexander held Plowright back a bit. "Don't concern yourself with price. I want the best quality animals you can get. We'll be using these as a base for breeding larger herds of our own."

Plowright nodded his head, smiling.

Alexander spent the next hour watching the two men inspecting animals, negotiating prices, and insulting each other's heritage. They both seemed to be enjoying the interaction, so Alexander decided not to worry.

In the end, Plowright had chosen more than a hundred and fifty animals of various shapes and sizes. The butcher began to round up employees to herd the animals through town to Greystone manor. The majority were cows, goats, chickens, and pigs. When Alexander asked about the choices, Plowright explained, "Cows are a good source of meat, but they reproduce slowly. One calf per year, if that. Sheep sometimes have two. Pigs have litters of six to ten, twice a year. Goats generally have two, or sometimes three kids at a time. Also, twice per year. For the first few years, we'll be eating more goat and pork than beef."

Alexander looked at the mass of animals being herded together. "I may be wrong, but I don't think there's enough room to graze all these inside the walls."

Plowright laughed. "No, you're right. Not without them eating some of the crops we'll be raising. In an emergency, we could keep them all inside for a few weeks, and be able to feed them. But then, we'd be thinning the herds for food, anyway. But for now, we'll build them paddocks inside the wall, and take them outside to graze each day. We can also harvest hay and other feed to stockpile. And the pigs are omnivores, we can feed them the remains of butchered stock, meal leftovers, over-ripe fruit and vegetables, the bodies of dead enemies…" The farmer grinned at that.

Alexander and Plowright went ahead to warn the guards at the gate that a large herd was coming through. The guards, in turn, sent a couple men to clear the street in order to prevent any complications. Apparently, this all happened regularly, and folks knew what to do. There was even a cart following the herd, and a boy with a flat shovel, to scoop up any droppings left on the street. It was all very well organized.

As they passed the palace gate, Alexander recruited a guard to stand at the compound gate and make sure none but the butcher's people entered while the wards were down. Upon reaching the compound, he turned off the wards and moved ahead of the herd to open the portal. Then he moved back within sight of the gate. When the last of the animals was through, he waited for the herd to move through the portal, and for the butcher's men to return through the compound gate. He tipped each of them, including the guard, five gold. Thanking them for their help as he turned the wards back on. Then he followed the herd through the portal.

He hadn't taken more than five steps into the courtyard, and had just shut off the portal, when he heard voices cry out, both inside his head and from above.

"*Intruders, master*," Jeeves spoke in his head. At the same time, the guards on the wall began shouting.

Turning to look behind him, he saw two rogues. One a human, and level 50. The other a halfling, level 58. Both wore surprised looks on their faces, and were paralyzed. They had snuck through the portal right behind him, and been stunned by the magic of the consecrated ground. They both had daggers in each hand, and the Halfling had a hand raised as if about to attack Alexander.

The guards surrounded the two rogues, instantly stripping them of their weapons, gear, and inventory bags. Alexander pronounced, "I place you both under arrest for espionage, attempted murder, and trespassing." A flash of light briefly surrounded both rogues. Alexander, looking around, spotted Caleb grinning at him. It seemed the former guard new the same spell Captain Redmond used.

Now properly arrested and bound, the magic of the keep's blessing released the two rogues. Both of them uttered a string of curses that made Alexander glad there were no children about.

"Who sent you here?" he asked.

"Nobody sent us. We heard you had mithril here. We came to steal it," the halfling said.

"And where would you have heard a thing like that?" Alexander asked.

"Everybody knows it. Some dude posted in the forums. Said you found it in a mine. Was bummed that he didn't get his share because he was offline," the human replied.

"So, you just thought you'd walk in here and steal it?" Caleb asked.

"Yup!" the halfling sounded cheerful.

"And how were you going to steal it after you stabbed me in the back and alerted all the guards?" Alexander's face adopted a cold look as he spoke.

"I uhh…" The halfling hesitated.

"You're both full of shit. Who do you work for? If you want to have even a chance of seeing all your gear again, answer me!" he shouted.

The human looked at the halfling. "He's going to find out soon enough anyway. Why should we lose our gear for nothing?" Turning to Alexander he said, "Chaos Nation put a bounty on you. Five thousand gold for anyone who can kill you and post a video."

"So, you admit you came here to kill the Knight-Advisor to King Charles and the Baron of Dire Keep?" Caleb interjected again.

"Yeah, so what?" the human rogue responded.

"Tell me more about this bounty. Who specifically put it up?" Alexander changed the subject.

"It was posted by the city guards in Antalia. I watched 'em put it up on the board in the city square." the halfling said.

"Well, it was stupid of you to come here. Chaos Nation would never have paid you. They're a PK guild and under the control of a terrorist cell. You dumbasses just got sacrificed." Alexander waved a hand, teleporting the two rogues to the palace in Stormforge, where they'd be arrested. Since he'd formally charged them, Captain Redmond would be able to see their crimes.

Pulling up guild chat, he said, "*All adventurer members to the keep gate. Now.*"

Moving into the tunnel between the inner and outer gates, he waited for the others to join him. Checking his UI, he saw that Dirk was still offline. The rest, Lugs' group, Dayle's group, and his own, filtered into the tunnel over the next couple minutes.

Leading them out the gate, he stopped at the benches he'd raised when they'd met Dayle's group. Raising a third bench to make room for everyone, and a large block for Lugs to sit on, he waited for them all to be seated.

"Two rogues just snuck into the keep by following me through the portal from the city. They claimed to be after mithril that we found in the mine."

There were murmurs among the gathered players. "They said they knew about this mithril from a forum post. I need to know right now, did one of you write that post?" Alexander looked at Lugs, Helga, Beatrix, and Benny. He knew that Dayle's group hadn't been offline. And it wasn't possible to post to the internet directly from within the game.

He waited, but none of them said anything. After a full minute, he said, "Which of you has talked to Dirk since he logged off?"

Helga raised her hand.

“And did you tell him about the mithril in the mine?” Alexander asked. When the large barbarian hesitated, he said, “It’s alright. You did nothing wrong if you told him. He’s a guild member. You had no reason not to tell him.”

“Yeah, we talked about it.” Helga hung her head. “I was excited about earning so much money. I can pay off all my bills and actually have some money in the bank for once.”

“And what was his reaction?” It was Max asking this time.

“He was jealous. Said he couldn’t believe he’d missed out because he had to work his crappy job,” she answered.

“I want you all to be very clear on something. Those two rogues told me they were here to steal the mithril that ‘some guy’ was bitching about in the forums. That painted a giant red treasure map X on our little keep here. So now, not only are we dealing with the minions of the Dark One, but we’ll have every dumbass rogue trying to sneak in. Or a guild trying to take the keep for the cash. Or constant attacks on the mine, trying to get the resources out of it.” Alexander looked at all of them.

“The person who posted in the forums will be ejected from Greystone. I’ll find out soon enough who made the post. If it was one of you, confess now. You can forfeit your membership and your dragon pin and walk away. If you lie to me now, you’ll be killed, blacklisted, and I’ll personally make sure you’re spawn camped back to level one.”

Still nobody spoke. And nobody looked particularly guilty, other than Helga. She spoke up.

“I’m sorry, Alexander. I didn’t mean to cause harm to the guild. It never occurred to me that Dirk would be so stupid.”

“It’s not your fault, Helga. As I said, discussing guild business with a guild member is no crime. However, from this point forward, anyone discussing guild business in any form with any non-member without specific permission, most ESPECIALLY in the fucking forums, will be removed. You've taken oaths to this guild. Life oaths sworn to a dragon prince. Those have consequences when broken," he reminded them.

When none of them had anything to say, Alexander waved a hand. "Alright. I'm going to assume it was Dirk that wrote the post. Helga, any idea when he'll be back in the game?"

"Tonight," she said sadly.

"Then I will speak to him then. I'd appreciate it if none of you spoke to him before I can. Also, the rogues informed me that Chaos Nation has put a bounty on my head. It may not be true. But if it is, there may also be bounties on some of you. So keep your heads about you. Literally." He grinned at his own bad joke.

Sending them all back inside the keep, he went to check on the progress on the drawbridge. Brick tagged along.

The masons were busily installing gears and sprockets inside the gatehouse. And one was attaching hinges to the base of the drawbridge stone, where it joined with the floor of the gatehouse. There were three hinges, each of them about four feet wide. They were being fastened to the stone with bolts the size of Alexander's arm.

Seeing the hinges, he was reminded that they still needed some other way to secure the gate. For when an enemy surprised them, and attacked before the drawbridge could be raised. Brick and the smiths were working on an iron portcullis that could be dropped quickly to block the tunnel. Part of the machinery the dwarves were installing would operate that, as well.

But in the short term, Alexander decided to raise a couple doors like those they'd found sealed at the Keep's inner gate.

"Brick, if I pull up two doors for an inner gate here, can you shape stone hinges strong enough to secure them?" he asked his friend.

“Aye, that be no problem,” the dwarf said. “But let’s check with Breakstone first. I’d not be wantin’ to get in his way.”

Nodding, Alexander followed Brick in search of the master mason. A quick check, and they confirmed that interior doors would not interfere with the drawbridge works.

Heading back outside, Alexander pulled a massive slab of granite up from the earth below. He made it two feet thick, and large enough to fill in the entire gap below the gatehouse tunnel arch. To begin with, he only pulled it up three feet above ground, allowing Brick to shape the top of the slab to fit the curve of the arch above. When the dwarf was finished, Alexander continued to raise the slab until it was nearly flush with the roof of the tunnel. Stepping back, he let Brick shape stone hinges along each side. He used three per door, and they were nearly as large as the ones used on the drawbridge.

Once the hinges and pins were secured, Brick moved to the center of the slab, and parted it at the middle slightly. Just enough to separate the single slab into two doors. Then Alexander snapped the stone at the base of the doors, allowing them to swing free a fraction of an inch above the floor. And just like that, they had an inner gate. Both players were getting better at their respective skills. The whole thing had only taken about twenty minutes.

“Let’s go have some dinner,” Alexander said to his dwarf buddy. “We’ll leave it to Breakstone or Brogin to figure out a locking mechanism.”

Arriving at the courtyard, the friends found Dirk had logged in. He was seated at a table with Helga, who looked very uncomfortable as he spoke to her.

Grabbing a seat at an otherwise empty table, Alexander called out, “Dirk, can I speak to you for a moment?”

The warrior rose from his seat to join Alexander and Brick at their table.

“Dirk, I’ll get right to the point. Where have you been the last few days?” Alexander asked.

“I had to work. I have a job working security at a power plant. I do three twelve-hour shifts per week, then I have the rest of the week to log into the game,” Dirk answered.

“And while you were offline, did you happen to post in the forums about missing out on clearing the mine?” Alexander asked, trying to keep his voice neutral.

Dirk suddenly looked guilty. “I didn’t mean any offense. I know you couldn’t wait for me to get back in game. I was just bitching about the missed opportunity.”

“It’s not about me being offended, Dirk. This afternoon two rogues snuck in here through the portal. When they were caught, they claimed to be here looking for the mithril you posted about.”

Dirk’s reaction was not what Alexander expected. “Did you kill them? That’s like, free xp!” He chuckled.

“Be ye really that stupid?” Brick growled at the warrior. His voice had carried enough that the tables around them quieted down.

“Ye post about mithril in the forums, whinin’ like a lil bitch. And now we’ll be havin’ to deal with all the thieves and other guilds attackin’ us to get it!”

Dirk rose from his seat, a hand on his sword. “So what? That’s what the game is about! You fight. If you’re strong enough to defend what you have, you keep it. You level up by killing those who try to take it. And watch who you call a bitch, short stuff!” he yelled at the dwarf.

Alexander and Brick both rose to their feet. So did Helga, Lugs, and several of the guards who’d been eating their suppers.

“Dirk, I was trying to be polite about this. But you clearly don’t get it. Your selfish, moronic post has caused significant harm to this guild. This place is already under threat. By painting an even larger target on our backs, you’ve needlessly endangered the lives of all the citizens here.

You are hereby discharged from the guild. You are free to go, and are no longer welcome in our lands. I'll teleport you back to Stormforge so you don't have to travel the forest alone. Please hand me your dragon pin," Alexander said, reaching out a hand.

"SCREW YOU!" Dirk drew his sword and sliced it across in one quick motion. Alexander's wrist was severed, his hand falling to the table.

Alexander screamed as the pain from the severed nerves reached his brain. Dirk raised his sword and began a horizontal slash, intending to finish Alexander by removing his head. Before his swing built up any momentum, Lugs' hammer came crashing down, pulverizing the warrior's head.

Alexander was gripping his stump as tightly as he could with his other hand, trying to stop the flow of blood. The cries of the players and citizens around him brought Sasha running from the kitchen. Seeing the dead warrior, then Alexander's severed hand, she rushed over to him. "I can stop the bleeding!" she gasped. She raised a hand to cast a heal.

"No!" Alexander stopped her. "Get me to my room," he grunted out through the pain. Taste, smell, speed, and magic weren't the only things enhanced by full immersion. The pain was much more intense, as well.

Sasha grabbed the hand as Lugs lifted his guild leader and quickly moved inside. The ogre's long legs took the stairs four at a time, and soon Alexander was placed in a chair in his sitting room.

"Lock the door," he gasped. He was beginning to feel light-headed from blood loss.

Looking to Helga, who had tears in her eyes, he said, "Kill me."

Healing magic in Io was miraculous. It could repair massive damage to internal organs, broken bones, burns, disease, and poisons. But it could not re-attach a severed limb.

Brick, Sasha, and Lugs all nodded at Helga. Everyone understood. Alexander regretted the experience he was going to lose. But it was better than playing without his weapon hand. Helga's sword would be the fastest, cleanest way to die.

Wiping the tears from her eyes, she said, "I'm so sorry. This is my fault."

Alexander shook his head. Straining to speak, he said, "Pain. Discuss… later." He leaned forward, baring his neck.

"Shit!" Helga cursed. Pulling her massive sword from her back, she moved behind Alexander. With one swift motion, she severed his head, killing him instantly.

Chapter Fourteen

Keep Your Head Up

Finding himself in limbo, Alexander took a seat. He had ten minutes to kill, and he expected visitors any second.

Sure enough, his father's avatar appeared in less than a minute.

"That looked painful." Richard chuckled.

"Yeah, about that. The pain levels in immersion are a good bit higher. Maybe tone that down?" Alexander grinned.

"We actually don't have any control of that. It's one of the challenges we've been trying to overcome. The immersion creates such a strong link that any attempts to scale things down just flat out fails. Not just pain. We can't change the sensitivity of smell, either. Or taste." Richard shrugged. "We're still working on it."

"So, tell me about the investigation. Did the FBI get to all those players? The Chaos Nation ones, too?" Alexander looked at his limbo countdown.

"Yes. They've all been arrested, along with some folks found with them. The FBI has found records of payment to several of them, but haven't yet tracked the source. It seems they're much larger and more organized than we hoped."

"And you saw that guy Marlin talking about his family starving after the Iran shutdown?"

"Yes, we saw. The current theory is basically what you suspected. We think there must have been another member of Light of Truth that we missed. Maybe more than one. And they've been working for the last decade to get even," Richard confirmed.

“Dad, I know you don’t want to hear this. But that guy said the Dark One had people everywhere. I think you need to get security looking into everyone’s background again. Especially the people who’ve moved into the compound. Employees and family members. If there’s a mole, or more than one, inside the compound, they could hurt a lot of people.”

Richard nodded his head. “We’ll bring on more security just for that. And I’ll ask the FBI to run their own checks. I’ll suggest that the bombing was just a planned trigger, to force us to turtle up and bring people in.”

“I’m thinking there’s some connection between the Dark One and the queen in Antalia. PWP is based there. So is Chaos Nation. And the rogue today said the city’s guards posted the bounty on my head.” Alexander said.

“I thought about that, too. But the queen would know about adventurers respawning. It doesn’t make much sense for her to place a bounty. She’d know you would just return. My bet is somebody within the palace. Somebody under the queen.”

“Huh. Maybe you’re right. I’m going to find out. We’ve been planning to raid the PWP compound anyway. But I think I’m going to need more people. Any chance you’ve got more testers like Dayle’s group nearby who’d be interested?”

Richard shook his head. “They were the only group anywhere near you. We purposely spread everyone out. Precisely to avoid you running into each other and sharing information that would affect the testing.”

“Ah, well. Sorry about that.” Alexander grinned. Not really sorry. “Did Misty’s sister come to Olympus?”

“No, she chose not to. She wants to help catch these people. She did move to a police department safe house, and has other officers with her full time. I placed a covert team on her, just in case.”

“I’ll let Misty know. Thank you.”

"Your limbo's just about up. When you get back, give Jules a hug from me. And another one from Melanie." Richard winked at him.

"How's she doing, by the way? I mean, physically. In the pod." Alexander couldn't help but feel a little flutter in his stomach.

"She's still healing. There's a long road ahead of her. You need to keep in mind, son, that she may never wake up. Any relationship you two develop might only ever be in the game." Richard put a hand on his son's shoulder. Then pulled him into a hug.

"Yeah. Thanks, Dad." Alexander hadn't really taken much time to explore his feelings about the girl.

"Oh! Any chance our guys can make that mithril post disappear? Or discredit it somehow?"

Richard nodded. "They're already on it. Lucky for us he used the official game forum, which we control. But we can't really stop Dirk from running his mouth. So, it'll likely come up again."

"Okay. I guess if it were easy, the game wouldn't be any fun, right?" Alexander winked. Then he looked to the ceiling and called out.

"Odin, buddy. I need a clarification on the rules. As an owner of the keep and Dire Lands, do I have the authority to make laws, arrest people, and pass judgement?"

Odin's Avatar appeared. "You do, mortal. You hold the rank of Baron of the Dire Lands. Though technically your decisions can be overridden by the king. Unless you secede and declare yourself an independent nation. And your judgements are bound by the laws of Io. No player's character may be detained for longer than one year. And while interrogation is permitted, torture is not. You have come close to the line more than once. Be careful." Odin disappeared again.

Alexander's father waved at him as he and the limbo room faded out, and he found himself respawning in the sitting room of his quarters. Sasha, Brick, Helga, and Lugs were still there.

"Thank you for getting me up here. I didn't want the citizens to see me die and respawn," he said. "Can I assume somebody is spawn camping Dirk?" He grinned.

"Max and Lainey," Lugs confirmed. "He respawned in the chapel. They've closed it off. He was level 40, so it'll take a while. We'll need to trade off."

"It would be best if Benny and Helga, the lower levels handle it. Let them get some xp. I may take a shot myself, to regain the level I just lost." Alexander looked to Helga. "Unless you don't want to? It's cool if you don't. I assume you two are friends?"

"Were," Helga said. "But not close friends. And he deserves it." She was angry.

"Thank you, by the way. For putting me out of my misery." He reached out his restored hand to shake Helga's. She shook it, then took her leave, heading down to find Benny and get to the chapel.

"And thank you, Lugs. For the quick swing of your hammer. And for carrying me up here." Alexander bowed to the ogre.

Embarrassed, Lugs shuffled his feet. "Bah! Elves are light. I take dumps bigger than you," he rumbled.

"BWAHAHAHA!" Brick laughed. "Come with me, we'll get good 'n' drunk! You can dance on top of the smithy again!"

"One second, before you go," Alexander said. "I got an update while I was in limbo. The FBI got to all the players we've taken down in the last couple days. And some folks who were at their homes. Several of them were paid significant sums in the real world lately. Looks like we're dealing with an actual organization."

"Aye, it were looking that way from in here already," Brick confirmed. Then he and Lugs headed to raid Brick's stash.

Sasha handed Alexander all his gear, which had been left in a pile when his headless body disappeared.

"Thank you. I imagine that was fun for you to watch. Helga slicing my head off." He grinned at her.

"Oh, it was like a dream come true. The number of times I've wanted to do that myself…" She rolled her eyes and sighed exasperatedly.

While she wasn't looking, he pounced. He began to tickle her mercilessly, payback for the day before.

"Stop!" she gasped. "It's creepy being tickled by a guy whose head was on the floor ten minutes ago!" She struggled free and darted for the door. "Come down and get some dinner. They'll be glad to see you whole again," he heard as she made for the stairs.

Equipping all his gear, Alexander headed downstairs. His first stop was the chapel. The door was locked, but when he knocked, Lainey let him in. She hugged him, and said, "You look taller," as he passed into the room.

"Ah. Headless jokes. Very funny." He winked at her. "How long till Dirk respawns?"

Max clapped him on the back. "Four minutes. He's already down to level 37. And begging after only one death. Well, one death in here. And one when Lugs splattered his tiny brain all over everyone's dinner."

"Well, shit. No xp for killing him then. Helga and Benny should be here shortly. Let them do it. We're all too high-level to get any benefit," Alexander said.

"Helga. Right. I hear she's good at lopping off heads." Max grinned.

Alexander headed out of the chapel, through the keep, and out the kitchen door into the courtyard. He raised his fully restored hand as the crowd whistled and cheered.

"Thank you, all of you, for your support!" he called out. "As you may have noticed, Dirk has been… removed from our guild." This earned him some chuckles.

"He made a decision to spread the word about the wealth we discovered in the mine. Causing those two rogues to try and steal it. We expect there will be more. So, I say again, please try to be vigilant, and keep your heads about you!" He grinned as the head joke soaked in and people groaned.

Sitting down, he dished up a plate for his dinner. He chatted with a group that included a couple farmers, two guards, a carpenter, one of the merchants, and Lola. Lola had stopped by to discuss some guild business, but was patiently waiting for him to finish his meal.

When he was full, he rose and carried his dishes into the kitchen. Lola followed behind. As he passed through the kitchen, he took one more shot at Sasha's ribs, causing her to squeal, then blush as the kitchen ladies laughed.

Alexander continued on until he found an empty room with chairs and a table. "What can I do for you, Lola?" he asked as he motioned for her to sit.

"Well, first be the position o' treasurer. I know ye've been busy…" she began. He held up a hand.

"You've done a great job here so far, Lola. More than I could have asked. If you'd like the treasurer position, it's yours. The others approve," he said.

"Thank ye, Alexander. Yer trust means a great deal to me," she answered quietly.

Alexander opened up the guild tab in his UI and promoted Lola to the position of treasurer. This automatically gave her access to the guild bank.

"The first thing you should do is arrange to pay yourself and your grandfather proper salaries. The same for the citizens who we don't have separate arrangements with. Like the guards. The miners are working for a percentage of their take. So are the merchants. Pay the masons until they have their quarry up and running. Then they'll take a percentage of that." Alexander paused as Lola scribbled notes.

"Now, what else did you wish to discuss?" he asked.

"Several things. Master Brogin mentioned when he returned that there be more dwarves who be wishin' to join us."

"Any dwarves in particular?" he smiled. He suspected he knew the answer.

"Aye. Nearly a dozen masons. Bunch o' smiths. More than a hundred warriors. A few farmers. And miners." she confirmed.

"I don't think we can feed that many yet," Alexander mused. "The masons are welcome, as are the farmers. They'll contribute to the keep's resources. Speak to Brick and see if he has room for more smiths. Ask Grimble about miners. And you and Silverbeard can figure out how many more warriors we can feed. Invite that many." He smiled at her. "Also, if there are any hunters, we could use more of those to help feed everyone. And if there's a dwarf interested in learning to fish, they could work with Lars." Lola nodded.

"What else? I'm all yours until I fall asleep," he said.

"The farmers be wantin' to build paddocks outside the walls, o'er near the ridge by the mine. There be not enough room inside the walls fer the herd ye bring'd back."

"I'll ask Fitz to help me extend another wall out there. We can keep guards on the walls to watch over them," he said. "But for the next couple days, they'll need to stay inside at night." Lola made more notes, then checked some others.

"We need the lumber crew back out workin'. We need wood fer furniture, doors, all sorts o' things."

"Are there any lumberjacks at Broken Mountain who wish to come here?" he asked.

"I do no' know. I'll be askin' tomorrow," she replied.

"If necessary, we adventurers will go out and cut wood. Do we have axes?" he asked.

Lola nodded her head. "Next. The merchants, carpenters, laundresses, and the tanner be askin' permission to set up shops. And space."

"The laundresses can find a room here in the keep that has running water, and set up there. We can alter it some to fit their needs. The rest should choose among the structures we're building at the outer wall. That'll be closer to the forest for the carpenters. And nobody's going to want the stink of the tanner's shop in here."

"I were about to recommend exactly that," she said. "Next. How d'ye want to be selling the mithril that Grimble brought in?"

"Do you have access to the auction house?" he asked.

She shook her head. "Not here. We'd be needin' to purchase a franchise to have one here. It cost 10,000 gold fer that."

"Buy one," Alexander instructed her. "We have many items we need to sell, and I would prefer not to have to travel to a city to do so. As for the mithril, keep half of it here, for Brick and the smiths to use when they're ready. Offer it to King Thalgrin a pound at a time. And talk to Brick about an appropriate amount to put up for auction. Only one lot at a time, though. And use the funds from the first sale to pay Helga, Lugs, Grimble, Beatrix, and Sasha their shares."

While he was on the topic of money, he asked, "How hard would it be to start our own bank?"

"Ye mean, like a public bank?" Lola asked.

"Yes. Well, not exactly. Just for citizens and guild members here. We could put some of our guild funds into it, and the proceeds from the sale of resources the keep produces. Eventually, we could use it to loan small amounts of money to citizens to start businesses. Or just allow them to store their gold in it."

"Me grandad would know. I'll be askin' him in the mornin'," she said.

"Thank you. It's not an urgent matter, I just thought it might be a good idea."

"Aye, it might at that," Lola agreed, looking thoughtful. "That's all I have fer ye. Fer now," she said.

Getting up, Alexander said, "Thank you for everything, Lola. And congratulations, Lady Treasurer!"

With that, he headed upstairs. Checking on Edward, he found the boy face-down on his bed, snoring. Alexander retired to his room, crawled into bed, and fell asleep.

He was awakened a couple hours later by a tremendous gong, accompanied by a light show outside his window. The keep repairs were complete! The keep had leveled up again.

Alexander sleepily checked the keep's status.

Dire Keep: Level 15/25	
Physical Status: 650/700	**Resources: 15,300 units**
See Infrastructure for details	*See Resources for details*
Current Population:	**Defensive Capabilities: 95%**

143	
Citizens: 141 *Guests: 2*	*See Defense for details*
Ancillary Structures: 5	**Production rate: 20%**
See Ancillary Structures for details	*Production will increase with population and use of ancillary structures*

So! Back to its original level. Physical status and defensive capabilities would reach 100% when the drawbridge was complete, and the moat filled. The resource units, he suspected, were mostly about the herd of animals that they brought in. And maybe the chunks of mithril.

"Jeeves, what is the 5th ancillary structure?" he asked the AI.

"*The fishing shack and pier you constructed, master. They are considered a production facility. I cannot yet count the new wall or the moat.*"

"And when those are completed, will you gain another level?"

"*Unlikely, master. I just returned to level 15. Level 16 will require significant additional points. Though the additional housing structures and storage facilities you have attached to the wall will bring me close. And my next population level increase is at 200. After that, significantly larger numbers of points are required. A population of 400, or several more new structures. Or vastly increased production,*" Jeeves explained.

"Thank you, Jeeves."

Now that he was awake, Alexander decided to work on something that had been on his mind. Moving back out to the sitting room, he smiled as he heard snoring still coming from Edward's room. Taking a seat, he pulled out a ten-pound chunk of obsidian and set it on the coffee table in front of him.

Closing his eyes, he imagined defensive walls that he'd seen before. Both in-game, and in the real world. He visualized cannons, hard-mounted machine gun emplacements, old world ballistae, even catapults.

Knowing that they faced a necromancer, and that at least a part of the army that attacked the keep would undead, he eliminated blunt force impact weapons. Undead could take massive physical damage and just shrug it off.

His best bet was light magic. Or maybe fire. And facing large numbers, machine-gun type firing would be less effective than, say, a beam weapon. Too many shots would miss targets and waste both mana and time. A beam would sweep across the field and cut down everything in a wide swathe.

Picking up the obsidian, he pulled at it to extend its length and thin it out. Then he shaped it into a hollow tube, just like his light wand. Only this one was four feet long and about four inches in diameter. Per Fitz's warning, he wouldn't put a lens at the end to increase the output effectiveness. It would be too easy for someone to examine and copy. Besides, this wasn't going to be a burst weapon. It would be a cutting weapon. Like an industrial laser.

With that in mind, he changed the shape of the tube, tapering the front end to a point. Lasers were more powerful in a tight beam. Then he closed his eyes, and focused on the Ray of Light spell. He pushed the magic slowly into the stone, spiraling it as tightly as he could, wrapping it around and around in tight coils. When he'd nearly completely drained his mana, he reached into his bag and grasped a small soul crystal. Drawing power from that, he continued to push the light magic into the weapon. He'd used up about half the crystal's power when he began to feel some pushback from the stone.

Then an idea struck him. He placed the crystal inside the tube at the back end, pushing it forward until it wedged itself into the narrowed front end. Then he adjusted the shape of the interior slightly, so that it snugged around the crystal, securing it. Taking a break to recharge his mana, he turned the weapon this way and that, feeling that something was missing.

Of course! Every gun needs a trigger! Dummy. This needs to be able to be used by a wall guard with no magic ability whatsoever. What you've got here now is just a really big wand.

Guns were easy. They had a physical trigger that unleashed a 'hammer' that ignited a spark of powder. But there was no spark involved here. He thought about a trigger word, and a visual of burly dwarven wall guards shouting 'Pew! Pew' made him chuckle. The idea of a random word being uttered near one of the guns, setting it off unintentionally, caused him to set that aside. So he was back to a physical trigger.

Alexander didn't have the technical knowhow to engineer a button trigger. He imagined it involved springs, some kind of contact plate… It was time to call in an expert. "*Brick, are you still up*?" He sent a message in guild chat.

"*Aye, I be at the smithy.*" His friend replied.

"*I'm working on a new weapon for the walls. Kind of stuck on the trigger mechanism. Think you could help*?"

"*O'course! Bring it down. We'll take a look.*" Brick was always up for playing with weapons.

Alexander headed down to the smithy, weapon in hand. There was almost nobody moving about in the building. Even the kitchen was shut down. It must be later than he'd realized. Stepping into the smithy, he found Brick and two other smiths waiting for him. There were half-finished plow blades and swords lying about, cooling from red hot to their normal metallic grey.

Setting his weapon on the bench in front of Brick, he explained what he was going for. Though the other smiths didn't understand the term 'laser', they got the general idea. They began to grow excited. Ideas were put forth, discussed, and either rejected or set aside for further discussion.

In the end, they decided on a dual-step trigger. This would allow for some safety. There would be a trigger phrase, but it would not work unless a physical trigger was also pulled. The physical trigger was simple. It used a single spring coil, set in front of the crystal. The 'chamber' that the crystal sat in was insulated, preventing it from making contact with the obsidian. A slot was shaped into the bottom of the tube underneath and slightly behind the crystal. Brick installed a simple pin and lever trigger that, when pulled backward under the tube, would press the crystal forward against the spring. When the forward point of the crystal made contact with the obsidian in front of it, the weapon would be 'primed', and the trigger word would cause it to fire. The beam would continue until the trigger was released, or the weapon's charge was depleted.

While Brick and Alexander worked on the trigger, the other smiths got to work making an iron tripod mount with a cradle on a swivel ball. This allowed the weapon to be secured the top of the wall and be swept back and forth, or up and down, easily. Roughly an hour after he'd stepped into the smithy, Alexander watched Brick set the finished weapon into its cradle, which was set up on a workbench. Both men examined the item.

Light Cannon
Item Level: Unique, Epic
This cannon will cast a beam of damaging light magic, cutting a target for variable damage, depending on time of contact with target. Rate of damage: 600dps. Mana consumption: 1 charge per 4 seconds of activation.
Charges: 300/300

***Skill Level up! Enchanting* +5** *You have created a unique, epic level enchanted item.*

Each of the four of them received a skill level up for their work on the weapon.

"Three hundred charges!" Brick practically shouted. "That be twenty minutes of firing time! Ye could cut down half a forest!"

"Or an army of undead, hopefully." Alexander grinned at him. "And if necessary, we can change out the depleted crystal with a full one. Though we'll need to do some testing. Don't want it to overheat."

“Ye should make some more. Space ‘em along both walls. They be light enough that if a wall be overrun, the gunner can lift ‘em and carry ‘em away.”

“I agree.” Alexander nodded his head, thinking. “Let’s get with Caleb, Jenkins, and a few of the others in the morning. We can test the weapon, and get ideas from them on placements.”

Feeling much better after having accomplished so much, Alexander headed back upstairs to sleep.

Edward pounded on his door as the rising sun broke the horizon.

“Okay! I get it! I’m up!” he called out. There was one more pound, likely Edward’s revenge for his treatment yesterday, then silence.

Alexander dressed, grabbed his weapons, and headed downstairs. He was later getting to breakfast than usual, and the tables were only sparsely populated. Most had already eaten and gone on about their day.

He sat with Edward, who looked much healthier, and was already well into his breakfast and ignoring Alexander. “We’re testing a new weapon this morning. Would you like to do the honors?” he asked the young prince.

“Is it a sword?” Edward put down his fork and was suddenly interested.

“It’s called a light cannon.” Alexander grinned. No boy could resist shooting a cannon.

Prince Edward waited impatiently as Alexander finished his own breakfast. Walking over to the smithy, they were informed that Brick had already taken the weapon up onto the outer wall.

Arriving at the wall, Alexander observed that the water in the moat was roughly thirty feet deep. Soon enough it would be full. They found Brick shaping the stone above the gatehouse to absorb the feet of the cannon’s tripod. Once the mounting was steady, he stepped back. Alexander motioned for Edward to step forward, and Brick explained to him how the weapon could be fired. When they reached the part about the trigger word, Brick laughed.

"BWAHAHA! We forgot to pick a word!"

"So we did." Alexander shook his head. "What do you suggest?"

"DURIN!" the dwarf shouted.

"Are you praying, or making a suggestion?" Alexander winked at him. "I think Asclepius might get jealous. And we need a word that's memorable. How about… Shazam!"

Now it was Brick's turn to shake his head. "Boomshakalaka!" he said, "Or Kapow!"

Alexander dug into his school memories. "Since it's a laser cutter, how 'bout 'Secare!'. It's Latin for 'cut'. Seems appropriate."

Brick looked disappointed, but nodded his head. If he were honest, Alexander had sort of liked the idea of gunners yelling 'Boomshakalaka!' when they fired. But it was too easy to get wrong in the excitement of battle.

So, closing his eyes, he placed the trigger word 'Secare' into the spell.

When he was done, he looked at Edward. "Okay. Point that thing at that tree over there. When you pull the trigger, a ray of light will shoot out. It will keep going as long as you hold the trigger. Move it across the trunk of the tree, like you're cutting it down with a sword."

Doing as he was instructed, Edward crouched down behind the light cannon. He said, "Secare!" and pulled the trigger. A narrow beam of white light shot out, missing the tree by a good 3 feet, burning into the ground behind it. Edward quickly shifted the beam over to the tree, moving it TOO quickly, and it only scored the trunk as it passed. He moved it back to the left more slowly, progressing across the trunk from right to left as it smoked. When he'd cleared the left side, he let go of the trigger.

The whole thing had taken maybe fifteen seconds. The first five being used up as he flailed about with the beam.

The three of them, along with several of the hunters on the wall, and the masons who'd been working on the drawbridge watched in silence. The tree's trunk smoldered along the horizontal line that the beam had cut. But nothing else seemed to be happening.

One of the hunters drew his bow, and fired an arrow into the trunk about ten feet above the cut. The arrow hit with a thunk that was quickly followed by a cracking sound. The tree swayed backward, then forward with a much louder crack. Its momentum carried it the rest of the way, and the tree fell toward them. There was cheering from both on top of the wall and below.

Edward puffed out his chest and held his chin high. Brick punched him in the shoulder, saying, "Nice shootin', treekiller. Ye should be workin' the lumberjack crew!" The prince decided to ignore him.

Moving back to the smithy, Alexander sat with Brick and the two of them made another light cannon. Brick had the other smiths make six more tripod mounts with cradles. It would take Alexander a few days to make that many, as each one nearly drained his mana. They brought in Jenkins and Caleb and Filgrin, head of the dwarven guards, to ask their opinion on placement.

It was decided that they'd leave three of the cannons permanently emplaced upon the inner wall of the keep. One at the gatehouse, and one on either side. The other five would be spaced around along the outer wall. In the event that an enemy breached that wall, the gunners would retreat, firing as they went, to the inner keep. For now, both cannons would be taken to the outer wall, and a select group of guard would train by cutting down more trees for the loggers. Two birds, one stone. Speaking of stones, Alexander gave them two more soul crystals for the cannons. He gave Caleb instructions to take them to the chapel for recharge at the end of the day.

By the end of the discussion, Alexander's mana had regenerated enough to make a third cannon. Brick took that one and mounted it atop the inner bailey gatehouse.

Needing to rest a while, Alexander sought out Lola. She'd spoken to her grandfather, Grimble, and Brick about numbers of new recruits needed, how many they had space for, and how many they could feed. She also got the name of a banker to speak to about starting their own bank, and another contact for purchasing an auction house franchise.

Alexander opened the portal to Broken Mountain for her, and told her he'd re-open at sunset.

As soon as she'd closed the portal, he used raid chat to call on Fitz, who was with the two guild mages. He asked him to extend a wall from the western end of the outer wall near the ridge for a secured paddock. And to raise a spring or a pipe to fill a long water trough for the animals. Fitz agreed.

He and the guild mages had been constructing more buildings along the inside of the outer wall. There were now three barracks, and more than a dozen homes with underground levels that could sleep a large family, or several single dwarves. They'd also constructed a brewery, because more ale was a priority for everyone. In addition, there were half a dozen utility structures that could be used for storage, or a shop, or even a residence. Each of the structures had plumbing, heat, and some kind of kitchen for cooking. One of the mages had also gone along the wall, hollowing out cisterns and installing a pipe system that would catch rainwater falling on the wall.

Alexander spotted Master Silverbeard emerging from the donjon and waved at him. "Master Silverbeard, good morning!" He was in a good mood.

"Good morning, Alexander. Lola asked me about yer idea fer a bank and auction house. I think it be a damned good idea," the old chamberlain said.

"Just what I was going to ask you about!" Alexander said. "Where would you recommend I put them?

After a few moment's thought, the dwarf replied, "I'd be putting the auction house right next to the smithy. And the bank next to the barracks. Neither be needin' much space. Folks what needs to repair, sell, or buy can be doin' it in the same spot. And the guards livin' in the barracks be close by to protect the bank if needed."

"Thank you, Master Silverbeard. That is wise advice. Please tell the merchants they can choose one of the utility structures as a shop. And assign Claude the tanner the structure farthest away from everyone else. Maybe close to where the livestock paddock is. They won't have to transport the hides as far when they butcher the animals." Alexander nodded to the man as he walked toward the smithy.

Leaving Brick some room to expand yet again if necessary, Alexander began to raise the auction house about thirty feet away from the smithy, right up against the keep wall. The structure wasn't large, only twenty feet square. There were windows on each side wall, as well as one in the front. There was no storage space needed, as all transactions within the auction house were magic. Items placed for sale were immediately transferred into a 'vault' that wasn't a real physical space. When the item was purchased, funds were transferred directly from buyer to seller - with the auction house taking their cut - and the item was delivered to the buyer's auction house location.

Once the building was up, Alexander raised a small office in one back corner, and a bathroom in the other. Then he raised a counter in front of both. The auctioneer, or auctioneers, could add other furniture as they saw fit.

Moving over to the barracks, Alexander was about to raise the bank building as well. Then it occurred to him that it might need special dimensions to accommodate the vault, deposit box rooms, etc. So he decided to wait and work with the banker, whomever that might be.

Feeling rested again, he returned to the smithy. He used the last of the obsidian in his bag to make another cannon, leaving it with Brick to finish. Though Alexander didn't get any skill points after the first one, he found that if he created them in the smithy, and allowed the smiths to connect it to the cradle, and work on the trigger, they still earned skill levels.

Finding himself with some time, Alexander sat outside the kitchen to think. Something that had been nagging at the back of his mind was also pressing on his conscience. There was a sense of danger, but he couldn't put his finger on it.

Jules came to sit by him. He hadn't seen her much in the last few days. And he found himself very glad to see her now.

"Jules! There you are. I've missed you," he blurted out. Her eyes jumped up to meet his, and she blushed prettily.

"Really? I was starting to think you forgot I was here," she teased.

"Never happen," he assured her. "You're my favorite lady elf in this whole country!"

Laughing, she pulled a rolled bundle of cloth from her bag, handing it to him. He unrolled it on the table in front of them. It was a guild banner. The majority of the banner was a light grey color, with a large red shield in the center. Upon the shield was a fierce black dragon that looked just like the one mounted above the main door of the keep.

"Jules, this is… it's amazing!" He hugged the elf tightly, if briefly. "Is this where you've been the last couple days? Working on this?"

"Well, this, and several more like it. You need two for over each gate. A few scattered along the walls. At least one for the Great Hall…" she began to count off.

Alexander just sat there, staring at the beautiful elf maiden, a stupid grin on his face. He thought about the night they'd spent talking on the balcony at the manor. And waking up next to her. He very much wanted to do that again. He thought about how kind she was. And how tough, having survived her ordeal in the dungeons and recovered so quickly. And smart! Her idea to flip over the mirrors in the command center-"

"The mirrors!" he blurted. Interrupting Jules, who looked confused. "I'm sorry, Jules. You just reminded me that we left those two mirrors on the floor in the command center. Jeeves said somebody tried to get through one of them. We need to find out where they go, and who's on the other side." He was already planning who to take with him.

"My… talking about banners made you think of creepy dungeons?" She looked sideways at him.

"Huh? What? No! I was just thinking about how beautiful you are. And how smart your idea was to just turn the mirrors…" She was gazing into his eyes now, and he completely lost his train of thought.

"You think I'm beautiful? And smart?" she asked him. She wasn't blushing this time.

"And brave, and strong." He held up a corner of the dragon banner. "And talented! You're amazing, Jules. You don't even realize."

She gave him a quick hug and a peck on the cheek. "Okay! So, who are we taking through the looking glass?" She winked at him.

"Good question." He opened up guild chat. "*Hey, folks. Jules just reminded me we've still got two teleportation mirrors to investigate. We have no idea where they go, or who's on the other side. Who's feeling adventurous*?"

"*What teleportation mirrors*?" Fitz demanded. He did not sound happy.

Alexander explained to him about the mirror they found in the tower that led to the command center, and the two other mirrors that they'd found. And about Jeeves' report that someone had been destroyed trying to get through one of them. The others listened quietly. For everybody but his core group, this was new and interesting information.

As soon as he was finished talking, Fitz appeared next to him.

"You should have told me about those as soon as we got here!" the wizard reprimanded him.

"I'm sorry, Fitz. I didn't realize you'd care. And to be honest, they totally slipped my mind."

Sasha, Brick, Max and Lainey had drifted over to take seats at the table. Dayle and Misty were moving their direction, and he could see Lugs in the distance across the courtyard. Beatrix was offline. Warren and Lyra had been sparring with some guards, and were on their way.

"*Benny and I want to go.*" Helga said.

"*Helga! I forgot to ask about Dirk. How did it go? You know what? Tell me later. Come sit with us and have lunch.*" Alexander replied. It was still early for lunch, but they should all eat before heading into battle.

While they waited for the others to arrive, Rufus jumped down off the wizard's hat and scampered over to the dragon banner. He looked thoughtfully at the image of the dragon in the center. He sniffed at it, then reached out a paw to touch it. Looking up at Alexander, he smiled and belted out the squirrel version of 'Rawr!' drawing laughs from everybody at the table. Sasha pulled a pastry out of her bag and gave it to Rufus as a reward. The little squirrel bowed to a delighted Sasha, waved the treat at Fitz, then scampered out of reach.

When everyone who wanted to go had arrived, Alexander looked to Fitz. "You seem worried about the mirrors. You suspect something?"

"Not worried. More suspicious," Fitz said. "We know this place was being used by minions of the Dark One. And that they, and therefore he, had access to the portal in the command center. We also know that teleportation mirrors have a limited range. Less than a mile. So, wherever those two mirrors lead, it will be close."

Heads around the table nodded, following his logic. "Now, tell me. If you happened to find an ancient dwarven complex under a lake, and had access to teleportation mirrors…" The wizard let Alexander finish the thought.

"Well, shit," Alexander said. "There's practically a whole city down there. It could take days to clear."

"Dwarven city?" Brick asked. Alexander hadn't filled them all in.

"Yesterday, right before I went to the city to buy livestock, the water level in the lake was dropping because it was draining into the moat. A doorway appeared under the water. It had dwarven runes on it, and it leads down to a system of tunnels and caverns. Man-made. Or, dwarf-made, probably."

Silverbeard spoke up. "I'm nearly five hundred years old, and I've never heard tales of a dwarven city under a lake. Or anywhere near here."

Fitz stepped in. "I believe it's well over a thousand years old. Master Tomebinder did not know of it either. He is checking the archives for any mention of it. There is always the possibility that it was merely built by dwarves, for somebody else. Or that it is simply a mine."

"Can I assume you want to go with us?" Alexander asked the wizard.

"Aye, boy. Wouldn't miss it. I'll bring Fibble too. Level him up a bit, make him useful."

"And everybody else? Anyone who doesn't want to go?" Nobody spoke. Everyone was in.

"Brick, throw that last cannon in your bag. I'll bring Edward. He can practice with it. So far, nearly every dungeon we've been in around here has had demons or undead. The light magic will work against either. And this group is large enough that we can protect him." Alexander eyed Fitz, who nodded his head.

"Right, Master Silverbeard, can you send a runner through to Broken Mountain? Let them know I may not be back by sunset? I'll open a portal now before we leave. And again, as soon as we get back." The old dwarf bowed his head.

"Okay. Everybody eat some lunch. Then grab your gear. We'll head up to the control room in thirty minutes," Alexander said. "Misty, could you hang back a minute?"

Misty stayed in her seat as the others moved away. Alexander patted her hand, then motioned for her to walk with him as he headed toward the portal. "I got an update on your sister. She declined to stay at Olympus. She wants to help hunt the bad guys. She's moved to a police department safe house, and has a squad of cops with her. My father put an undercover security detail on her as well. She won't even know they're there."

"Thanks for that," Misty said. "I figured she wouldn't go. She's a predator. Doesn't even like being inside a building for long. Rather be out hunting criminals." She gave him a small wave and moved off to gear up.

Alexander opened the portal, and Silverbeard stepped through to speak with the guards, who sent a runner to the king. Silverbeard stepped back through the portal, and it was done.

Alexander went in search of Edward, discovering that the prince was at the outer gate with the selected guards, 'practicing' with the light cannon. Looking out toward the forest, he saw they'd cut down nearly fifty trees along the front edge of the forest. Boys and their toys. Alexander grinned.

"Edward, we're going to go investigate those mirrors in the command center. Want to tag along?" he asked the young prince.

"Yes! I just need to grab my armor." Edward was enthusiastic about getting into pretty much any kind of danger.

Alexander teleported the two of them to their study, and Edward dashed into his room to gear up. When he was ready, they both walked downstairs. Passing the chapel, Alexander noted Dirk sitting inside, speaking to Alric.

"What are you still doing here?" Alexander demanded as he stormed inside.

Alric held up his hands, patting the air toward Alexander to try and calm him. "I'm told you promised this man a teleport to Stormforge?"

"I did. Before he cut off my damned hand and tried to kill me," Alexander growled. He took a step toward the level one player, who sneered at him.

"This chapel is dedicated to Asclepius as well as Durin, Alexander. Though Durin is a god of battle and vengeance, my god teaches forgiveness and healing. Please do not kill this man here," Alric pleaded.

Alexander was about to give in and teleport the man to Stormforge. He had been dropped down to level one, after all.

Then Dirk made a decision that would impact the rest of his life. "I had some time to get on the forum during the six hours your people spawn camped me. I told everyone all about this place. Every detail I could think of. Names of all your group, the mine, your compound layout. All of it. I told everyone you had a treasure room piled with artifacts. They'll be beating down your doors! This Dark One you've been fighting? He contacted me, and I sold him all the information too!" The warrior crossed his arms, looking proud of himself. "My bills are paid for a year!"

Alric looked shocked at the venom in the man's voice. And the betrayal he'd just confessed to.

Alexander shook with rage. "You complete dumbass. You've just thrown your life away. And you'll never get that money. The Dark One heads a terrorist organization that was responsible for a car bomb attack at Olympus. He uses idiots like you to do his dirty work, then throws you away. If you'd been online, or even if you'd not been a total dick, you'd have heard all of that. Now you've just confessed to aiding a terrorist organization. I'm placing you under arrest for espionage. You'll not be getting your teleport to Stormforge. Or anywhere."

Alexander turned to Father Alric, and said, "This man just proudly admitted to willingly serving the Dark One. I don't think Asclepius would mind, do you?"

The priest looked conflicted. It went against his nature to harm anyone. But if anyone deserved it, it was this warrior. "Please, don't kill him."

"Oh, I don't intend to." Alexander smiled coldly at the priest. Alric actually backed up a step.

Alexander reached out and slapped Dirk in the face. Not hard, just enough to sting. The man was only level one, and a solid punch would kill him again. Alexander didn't want to kill him. That would allow the man to log off and run. A slap placed him in combat.

"You stupid piece of shit!" Alexander slapped him again. "You felt left out of the mine run, and being the little bitch that you are, you just had to whine to the entire world. Then, rather than accept the consequences, you attack ME?" Alexander slapped him again. Dirk took a swing, and Alexander allowed him to connect with the punch. He barely felt it.

"You've been dismissed from a guild that would have made you comfortable, if not wealthy. You got yourself blacklisted, which would have meant you'd never be able to earn a living in the game." Alexander slapped him again. His health was down to about 50%.

"But you couldn't stop there, could you? Oh, no. You had to climb to a whole new height of stupid, trying to sabotage people who took you in and offered to help you. Well, you'll never know if your little scheme worked, because your unparalleled mastery of the moron subclass just led you to confess to being a terrorist. You'll be in jail for a good long time. I hope they throw you in a cell block with lots of big, patriotic murderers who'll just love your whiney 'the whole world is picking on me' attitude." He slapped the warrior again.

Dirk tried to kick him in the nuts. All he managed was to damage his own leg. Alexander hoped this had gone on long enough for the FBI or the local cops to show up at Dirk's location.

A moment later, a GM appeared. Father Alric froze in place, as the GM said, "Elroy Biggles, your account has been terminated per Io Online's terms of service. We reserve the right to deny service to any one, for any reason. In your case, the reason is being a terrorist asshole. Emphasis on the asshole. You will be logged off in ten seconds. Enjoy prison." The GM smiled at Alexander and blinked away.

Dirk roared and took another swing at Alexander. Edward's sword was out in an instant, and Dirk's hand fell free of his arm. His screaming cut off suddenly, and his body dropped to the floor. His connection to the warrior avatar had been terminated.

"Thank you, Edward. But he wouldn't have done any damage to me," Alexander said.

"I know. I just really didn't like that guy. I saw Odin's messenger, and though I could not hear what he said, it was clear he pronounced sentence for serving the Dark One. So, I assumed it was my duty to kill him." The prince sheathed his sword.

Right. Son of the king, and heir. He'd be in on the secret of players respawning, and he was able to see the GM.

"I didn't like him either. And between you and me, I'm glad he died in pain." Alexander winked at the prince.

Turning to Alric, he said, "Father, I apologize for the violence in your chapel. Your words had convinced me to simply teleport him to the city, before he confessed to serving the Dark One. Some people just will not accept or allow kindness."

Alric nodded his head. "The malice in that man would only have grown. He would have done his best to injure you, and those here with you. I saw the face of evil in him."

Taking their leave of the chapel, Alexander and Edward met up with the group in the courtyard. He quickly updated them all on what Dirk had said.

"What a piece of shit," Helga muttered.

"You have a room piled with treasure?" Warren asked. Lyra slapped the back of his head.

"More than one, actually." Alexander grinned at Lyra. "And we're headed into an underground city that's more than a thousand years old. My guess is we'll find a bit more." He looked around, counting his group and sending out raid invites. There were sixteen of them in total, counting Fitz and Fibble.

"Even split fifteen ways, after the guild's ten percent, I imagine you'll be able to pay some bills when you return home."

With that, Alexander teleported them all to the command center.

"Good morning, Jeeves," Alexander said out loud. "I've got some folks for you to meet. Greystone guild members, and an honored guest."

"Good morning, master. Please ask the others to place a hand on the control table and identify themselves," Jeeves replied. Each of the team did so, and received the usual welcome.

Fitz immediately moved to the two mirrors still lying face down on the floor. Before he moved them, he asked, "Jeeves, which of the mirrors did someone attempt to exit from?"

"The one closest to the portal, master wizard," Jeeves answered.

Fitz lifted the mirror and hung it back on its wall hook. He focused on it, waving a hand and murmuring a spell. The reflection in the mirror began to fade, and a stone room could be seen beyond. Just as if they were looking through a portal.

"This spell allows us to see the reflection from the connected mirror," Fitz explained.

The room on the other side was lit with torches mounted on the wall. They couldn't see the entire room, just the section of it facing the mirror. There was no movement, and no sound.

"Okay, guys. One by one, touch the mirror. Brick, you first. Then Lugs. Sasha and I will go next. The rest of you follow. Edward, you and Lyra bring up the rear. Remember to step aside as soon as you get there, to make room for the people behind you," Alexander said.

Chapter Fifteen

To Kill, Or Not to Kill

One by one they touched the mirror and passed through. The room at the other end was empty. It was about twenty feet square, carved out of rock. It had a high ceiling with moss growing in patches. There was a single doorway that led to an unlit corridor.

Sasha called out, "Okay, Brick you have lead. I want Max and Jules right behind you, looking for traps. Then Dayle, Warren, Helga, and Alexander. Lyra, you're with me and Fibble. Lainey, you and Edward protect us. Misty, Lugs, Benny, you bring up the rear, in case we get hit from behind."

The group arranged themselves and moved forward. Fitz threw two light globes in the air, one leading above Brick, the other above Lugs at the back. Brick began to move forward at a slow walk, allowing Max and Jules to use their stealth skills to detect traps. Alexander scanned under the floors and inside the walls, not finding any obvious traps. He activated his mage sight, just in case.

The corridor extended maybe fifty feet before it ended in a T intersection. To the right, the glow from Fitz's globe showed a stairway going up. To the left, a corridor heading off into darkness.

Alexander used his earth sense to confirm. "We're near the top. Those stairs lead up to the door, and the lake beyond." He looked at the stairs, then at the hallway, then back the way they'd come. "You guys notice there's no dust on the floor?" The others all looked down and around.

"Magic in the air here," Fitz said, by way of explanation. "Very subtle. Feels like a preservation enchantment."

They paused for a few moments while Lugs went up the stairs to confirm nobody was there to sneak up behind them. When he returned, they headed down the corridor and deeper into the complex.

After a minute or so, they began to see doors staggered on either side of the hallway. The first door was on their left. It was made of heavy oak, so old it was nearly petrified. It was held together with iron bands. The entire thing was extremely well preserved, seeming to confirm Fitz's suspicion.

Max pulled the door open as Brick moved into the opening, shield held high. The globe over his head illuminated a small room, maybe ten by twelve feet. Inside was a table with six chairs. A weapons rack with swords and shields sat against one wall. A guard room, then.

Brick moved forward to inspect the weapons. "These be dwarven-made. Good quality."

Max started to reach for them to loot, and Alexander stopped him. "Too much weight this early. If these are an upgrade for any of you, grab one. Otherwise, we'll pick them up on the way back."

Benny and Dayle compared their shields to those on the rack. Benny took one, as it was a significant improvement. Dayle stuck with the one he had. Max, Jules, and Fitz checked the room for secret doors or compartments. Finding none, they moved on.

The next room, on the right side of the hallway, was larger. Again with no occupants, this one looked to be a barracks. There were a dozen beds, chests at the end of each. Another weapons rack by the door. This one was mostly empty. There were a couple shields, and some spears with long diamond-shaped heads. Lugs picked up one of them, then grunted in a satisfied manner. "Mind if I take a few of these? Be good for throwing," he said. The spears, from butt to pointed tip were seven feet long. In Lugs hands, one of them looked like a Zulu short spear.

"Go right ahead," Alexander said.

Once again, the room was checked for compartments and secret doors. The chests were opened, but other than some gold and silver coins, there was not much of interest. Mostly clothes and weapon maintenance gear.

The group moved on like this, clearing room after room, finding no occupants, and not much of interest. After the sixth room, the corridor ended in a stairway leading down. Brick led the way, and they soon reached the second level. There was another long corridor ahead, and one branching to their left.

Sasha decided to split them up. Brick led one team down the left-hand corridor, Lugs took the right. They were to clear rooms, and call out in raid chat if they encountered anything. If they reached stairs leading to another level, they were to stop and report.

Lugs took Helga, Benny, and Dayle's group. Fitz followed along behind them. Brick led the original six officers, plus Jules, Edward, and Fibble.

Again they moved slowly, watching for traps. They reached a room, and Max pulled the door open for Brick, muttering, "Ladies first".

As soon as Brick stepped into the room, lights came on. The tank raised his shield, looking around frantically for an enemy. Finding none, he relaxed a bit.

"Motion sensors?" Max asked.

"Magic sensors of some kind, I'd say," Alexander agreed.

This was a large, open room with long tables and benches. It looked to be a cafeteria of sorts. Moving toward the back of the room, they found a door leading to an industrial-sized kitchen. It was at least four times the size of the kitchen at Greystone manor. Someone had planned to feed a lot of people here.

Sasha admired a set of kitchen knives with intricately carved stone handles, set in a wooden block. They quickly disappeared into her bag.

The group continued through room after room. Some were living quarters, offices, storage rooms. They found no hidden compartments or doors, and the loot was mediocre. Again, mostly coin pouches here and there, some interesting looking books, some jewels that Fibble found in a chest under a bed.

From the reports in raid chat, the other group was finding much of the same. Reaching another stairway at the end of the corridor, they sat and waited for Lugs' group to catch up. Their corridor had ended in a blank wall. While they waited, Sasha pulled out some jerky and handed it out to everyone. Fibble took his and plopped down in Lainey's lap, gnawing away enthusiastically. After a startled moment, Lainey smiled at the little green goblin and patted his head.

As the other group approached, Brick rose to his feet and began to head down the stairs. The group resumed their earlier formation behind him.

Reaching the third level landing, they were faced with a locked door. This one was engraved stone, and round like a hobbit-hole door, much like the one they saw in the lake. Max and Jules both searched the door, but couldn't find a lock to pick, or a mechanism to open it. Brick put a hand on the door, and using his earth sense, examined it closely. "There's no lock. No bar, nor bolt, no lever that I be able to find," he said.

Fitz approached the door, also laying a hand on it. "Sealed with magic. And there's something moving behind it. Maybe several somethings."

"Okay, everybody ready. Sounds like we've got targets. Finally," Sasha said. She nodded to Fitz, who waved his right hand. The door began to glow with a blue light. After a moment, it rolled to one side, revealing the corridor beyond.

Brick cursed loudly as soon as he saw what was ahead. The door opened onto a wide-open cavern that had started as a natural feature, and been widened and shaped by its inhabitants. "Dwarves. Undead dwarves," he said. There were more than a hundred of them in the cavern.

They weren't the rotted corpses in tattered rags that the group had found in the keep's dungeon. These dwarves didn't have a mark on them, as far as anyone could see. Their skin was a pale grey, eyes vacant except for a pinpoint of red light in each pupil. Some wore armor, others everyday pants and shirts. A few carried weapons or tools limply at their sides. None of them moved, or made a sound. It was as if they'd lost all motivation.

"Not dwarves precisely, Brick. Duergar. The grey dwarves. Deep dwellers that rise to the surface levels only to steal and kill. They worship one of the dark gods, and have not been seen on the surface of Io for two millennia at least. THAT is why the runes on the door resembled dwarven script. It was written in Duergan."

Alexander inspected the closest specimen. It was slightly shorter than most dwarves, and thinner. Its grey skin seemed to be almost made of stone, like the trolls in the mine.

Duergar Miner
Level 60
Health 1/4,000

"Only one health point?" Alexander mumbled. He quickly inspected several more. All were level 60 to 70, and each one had only one point of health.

"What is this?" Sasha asked. She held her breath as Brick approached the miner and poked its forehead. The grey dwarf didn't even blink.

"They're not dead. They're under some kind of spell. It has taken them to the brink of death and held them there. This is dark magic. Demon magic," Fitz said.

"Great. More demons," Brick said. He reached into his bag and withdrew the light cannon without its cradle mount. He handed it to Edward, who grinned from ear to ear. "Ye might be needin' this. Be damn sure ye don't shoot none of us!" the dwarf growled at him.

Not having any experience with a rifle, Edward tried to brace the cannon against his hip, like a large crossbow. Then he tried laying the back end on top of his shoulder like a bazooka. Max took pity on him, taking the four-foot cannon from him and showing him the proper way to hold a rifle. Then how to raise it and brace it along his shoulder as he aimed. Lainey produced a long leather strap, and tied it near each end, creating a shoulder sling.

While they worked on getting Edward squared away, Fitz was closely examining another duergar. This one had a long beard, and was wearing expensive looking armor. "Sasha, dear. Would you be so kind as to heal this creature? Nature magic only, please. No light magic."

"Uhhh… okay?" Sasha cast a mid-level heal spell that Lydia had taught her. Alexander inspected the duergar as she cast.

Duergar Smith
Level 70
Health 550/5,500

As soon as the healing took effect, the smith let out a long, gravelly moan. Its eyes focused on Sasha, and it appeared to be trying to say something. Within moments, though, its health dropped back to 1 point, and it stared off into the darkness again.

"Interesting," Fitz said. "Something is draining them. Duergar are known for their tough skin, high strength and stamina, and rapid regenerative abilities. Whomever or whatever cast this spell is draining them all, preventing them from regenerating while also preserving them to keep them alive.

"Like a whole city of batteries?" Max asked. Seeing the confused look on Fitz's face, he corrected himself. "A whole city of soul crystals, being drained of power?"

"Essentially, yes," Fitz said.

Misty spoke up. "Well, it's not necromancy, if they're not dead. And it's not sorcery, I don't think, because they're not being controlled or instructed to do anything. So, what is it?"

"Demon magic. Though I'm not sure what kind, exactly. Succubi have the ability to drain life from their victims. But I've never seen one that could cast a spell like this. And the preservation spell covers more than just these bodies. It is imbued into this entire complex. In its walls and doors, even the blankets on the beds. My guess is that at least some of the power being drained from these bodies is being used to preserve them, and everything else here," Fitz mused.

"So, do we kill them?" Lugs asked. Like everyone else, he was thinking that more than a hundred high level mobs that couldn't fight back were an adventurer's dream.

"That is a good question, Sir Ogre," Fitz said. "On the one hand, duergar are a dark race. Normally inclined to kill any non-duergar they meet. They tunnel up from below and attack dwarven settlements inside mountains, or villages and towns on the surface. They kill most, make slaves of the rest, and strip everything of value."

"So, we kill them!" Lugs smiled. The others chuckled.

"On the other hand," Fitz continued "There is no known record of these duergar attacking anyone, or even making themselves known here. There have been factions of their race in the past who rejected their dark god and fled their cities deep in the underground. Very few were even known to trade in peace with dwarven, orc, and human settlements. This was thousands of years ago, when Kai was just a wee lad. This complex looks like a home to me, not a raid tunnel or a mine."

Alexander posed a question as the others nodded their heads. "Fitz, can you speak their language?"

Fitz stroked his beard. "If I remember right, they spoke several languages. I never learned duergan, as I've had limited dealings with them. But many of their clans spoke draconic, goblin, or even common."

"What would happen if we removed him from this place. The spell has to have a range to it, right? What if we took him to the command center, and healed him? Could you speak with him?" Alexander asked.

"Worth a try," the wizard answered.

Alexander looked at the group. "You guys, step back outside the door. Sasha, Brick, you come with us. We'll be back in ten minutes."

With that, Fitz cast a teleport, sending the four of them and the duergar smith up to the command center. Sasha immediately cast a heal on the grey dwarf, and it screamed in pain.

"Again! Your largest nature heals. Take him to full health," Fitz called out. He was waving his hands and began mumbling the words of a spell.

As Sasha cast heal after heal on the screaming duergar smith, Fitz finished his spell. A red aura of magic surrounded the creature, then flashed brightly. When it faded, the duergar fell to its knees. The screaming became a moan of remembered pain. Sasha cast one last heal, bringing him to full health.

After a moment, the duergar, still on its hands and knees, looked up at Sasha and said something in a harsh and gravelly voice. Not understanding in the least, Sasha just smiled and waved. The grey dwarf looked around, then opened its mouth and pointed down its throat.

"Oh!" Sasha reached into her bag and pulled out a flagon of water. Opening the cap, she handed it to the duergar. Struggling to stand, it used the control table to steady itself, then tilted its head back and drank. Sasha pulled a bit of jerky from her bag and offered that as well. The jerky disappeared in moments.

The duergar smith nodded its head in thanks, and said something else. Its voice was a bit smoother after the drink. The language was still harsh and guttural, though.

Fitz said something in draconic, which caused the duergar's head to jerk toward him. It immediately answered. There was a short exchange between the two, then the apparently exhausted grey dwarf sat back down on the floor and leaned against the table.

"His name is Gelag. He wishes to thank you for the food and drink," Fitz said.

"Tell him he's very welcome. There's more if he'd like," she answered.

"Ask him about the spell," Alexander said.

"Thank you, boy, I'd have never thought of that," the wizard snapped at him.

Fitz spoke again in the dragon tongue, and there was a much longer exchange. Fitz pulled a couple boar sausages out of his own bag and handed them to Gelag.

This must be serious. Fitz just gave up food. Alexander grinned

"As I suspected from his armor, Gelag is a leader of his people. One of their council. Duergar respect master smiths just as dwarves do. They were one people, long ago. He says the spell was cast upon them by a demon queen. His clan fled from the deep cities to start a life near the surface. They were mostly crafters, and planned to trade their goods with the locals. They rejected their god, and the duergar queen that ruled their city. She followed them here with a small army of demons. Most of his people died. Those that survived surrendered, and were enslaved. Shortly after the battle a demon queen arrived, killing the duergar queen and casting this spell on his people."

"Can ye tell how long ago this happened?" Brick asked.

Fitz spoke to Gelag a bit more. There was some shaking of heads, and more questions. Finally, the duergar nodded his head, then spoke.

Fitz translated, "Duergar don't use a calendar like ours. But they do pay attention to world events. He knew of a war being fought between the orcs and the elves not far from here. That war happened long before Stormforge was a kingdom. Close to three thousand years ago."

"Does he know it has been that long?" Alexander asked.

"One moment, while I explain." Fitz began speaking to the duergar. After a few sentences, a shocked look came over his face. He put his head in his hands and shook it back and forth. "He knows now."

"Okay, we need to get back. The others will begin to worry. Is it safe for him to go back there?" Alexander asked.

"Aye, I broke the spell. Distance didn't do it. It nearly killed him, and he said it was quite painful. Unless the demon is still there to cast it again, he will be safe enough." Fitz waved his hand and the five of them teleported back to the spot they'd left. Seeing them arrive, the others gathered around again.

Alexander quickly filled them in, while Fitz tried to speak with Gelag, who was staring at his frozen people and not listening.

Lugs got a disappointed look on his face. "So, we're not going to kill them," he said.

"Probably not. But the good news is that there may be an army of demons to kill. And a queen." Alexander tried to make the bloodthirsty ogre feel better.

Gelag's legs weakened under him, and he sat on the floor, still staring at his immobilized people. Fitz placed a hand on his shoulder and spoke to him quietly. After a brief exchange, the duergar nodded his head.

"He's going to show us where the demons are. Or, where they were three thousand years ago," Fitz relayed to the group.

"Can you break the spell on his people like you did on him?" Sasha asked.

"He says no. It nearly killed him. Most of his people are not as strong as he is. He thinks that killing the queen might break the spell, or allow us to break it more easily." Fitz shook his head.

Gelag rose to his feet and motioned for them to follow. As they moved across the cavern, he stopped occasionally to lay a hand on a particular friend, or maybe family member, and say some quiet words to them.

Across the cavern they reached another round stone door. This one stood half open, and looked as if someone had taken a mining pick to it. Passing through, they descended another stairway.

At the bottom there was a cavern about a quarter the size of the one above. There were tunnels leading off in several directions. There were still a few duergar standing motionless here and there, but much fewer than above. Gelag led them to the left without hesitation. They moved into an unlit corridor that quickly led to another downward set of stairs.

The duergar paused at the top of the stairs, and said something to Fitz. Tired of translating, Fitz held up a hand for him to stop. "Alexander, have you an obsidian on you? I need a small piece. The size of one of your dragon pins. Lainey, I need a leather necklace or bracelet."

Alexander pulled out a small chunk of obsidian, handing it to Fitz. Fitz handed it to Brick. "Please round it off, smooth it out, and put a hole in the center for the leather." The duergar smith's eyes followed their actions from the moment Alexander produced the stone.

Brick shaped the stone and took a thin leather strip from Lainey. He passed it through the center hole and tied off the ends. The result was a basic obsidian pendant.

Fitz took the pendant and closed one hand over it. He cast a spell, and blue light glowed through his fingers for a moment. He handed the pendant to Gelag, making a motion for him to put it over his head.

Once Gelag complied, Fitz said "Can you understand me?"

The duergar's eyes widened. "I understand," he said, looking around to see if the understanding worked both ways. Sasha smiled at him. "Hi, Gelag. My name is Sasha."

Gelag smiled in return. Sasha had that effect on people. "Nice to meet you, Sasha." He turned and pointed down the stairs. "Below here are demons. Two levels. Queen is in meeting hall, now her throne room." The translation wasn't perfect, but it got the point across.

"We will kill the demons and try to help you free your people, Gelag." Alexander stuck out a hand. After a quick motion from Fitz, Gelag reached out and shook Alexander's hand.

“Thank you. The Stoneburner clan will be forever in your debt,” Gelag said.

Brick took the lead again, with Lugs at the rear. They’d left two entire levels uncleared behind them, so Lugs was keeping a sharp eye on the stairs above as they descended. Partway down, Alexander realized that wasn’t necessary. He stopped the group, and moved to the back. Picking a spot three stairs above Lug, he raised a wall three feet thick all the way to the ceiling. It might not stop a determined enemy, but it would definitely make enough noise to alert them if someone broke through.

Continuing down the stairs, they reached the 5th level of the complex. There was another round stone door, this one sealed. Gelag put a hand on a wall panel to the right of the door. Nothing happened.

“Lock… broken?” He pushed on the panel again.

Fitz approached the door and laid a hand on it himself. “It’s sealed with magic. Dark magic. Not the same as the door up top. And not demon magic. Get ready.”

Fitz made a motion with his left hand, and the door rolled open. The corridor beyond glowed a dull red. There was barely enough light to see by, for those who didn’t have dark vision. Alexander’s chest piece allowed him to see just fine. The corridor here was more roughly carved through the stone, looking like a mining tunnel more than a hallway.

A short distance down the tunnel Alexander could see demon imps hopping about. With them was a taller demon carrying a staff.

Demon Imp
Level 60
Health 3500/3500

Demon Sorcerer
Level 65
Health 4000/4000

"The tall one is a sorcerer," Alexander said quietly. "Assume he can summon minions."

"Right," Sasha said. "Max, Lainey, focus on the sorcerer. Alternate stuns and silence. Benny, if you think it's about to cast, hit it with light magic. Should work as an interrupt. Everybody burn down the caster first, then the imps. Fibble…" She smiled at the little goblin. "You just shoot the demons. Start with the big one."

Fibble got a determined look on his face. "Kill demons! No eat Sasha and clan mates!" He held his wand up like a sword.

Brick stepped forward, hitting the caster demon with a Holy Smite spell. It screamed in pain, and the five imps that were in the vicinity all charged at Brick. The caster began to chant and move its hands, summoning more minions. A stun arrow hit it in the forehead, interrupting its cast and dealing considerable damage. Max put a regular arrow through its eye, while Misty hit it with a massive ice bolt to the chest. The impact knocked the caster back, and formed a solid block of ice around its chest and arms.

The imps didn't rush Brick the way he'd hoped. They stopped about fifteen feet away and spread out, casting fireballs at him. Brick dragged his hammer across the surface of his shield, activating its Serpent's Screech ability. The imps stopped casting and charged toward him, claws extended. As they grouped together, he activated his Shield Bash, and knocked the first two back into the others. Sasha cast Thorn Trap on them to hold them in place, then cast Trap Soul on each of the demons. Alexander hit one of them with Wizard's Fire.

Unfortunately, demons were somewhat magic resistant, and imps in particular were fire resistant. Normal fire spells would just splash off them harmlessly. Wizard's fire did some damage, but much less than normal.

Then Edward stepped forward. He triggered the light cannon, and the beam hit the caster demon in the shoulder. Edward adjusted his aim, and the beam began cutting into the caster's neck. Unable to move, the demon sorcerer just screamed until the light magic beam severed its vocal cords.

With the caster finished off, Edward moved to the trapped imps. He focused the beam on the farthest to the right, and slowly moved the beam from right to left. He cut the first imp in half, then moved on to the next, and the next. In all it took him about thirty seconds to kill all six demons.

Edward grinned at Brick. "A lot easier hitting a demon at thirty feet than a tree at a hundred yards!"

"BWAHAHA! Ye be right, demon slayer!" The dwarf thumped the young prince on the back.

Edward, Benny, Helga, and Fibble had all leveled up from that fight. Fibble was looking down at his stomach. Then up at Sasha. She giggled at her little green protector. "It's okay, Fibble. You just leveled up. It means you're getting stronger, and smarter. You can feel a tingle in your tummy when it happens."

The goblin nodded, then flexed his puny muscles at her. "Fibble get bigger. Fight more demons!"

Max looted the corpses, and they moved on. Fitz was constantly scanning for secret doors or compartments, and would let them know if he sensed anything.

After maybe thirty steps, they reached a closed door on the left side of the tunnel. This one opened inward. Brick kicked the door with an ironshod boot, then hopped through to surprise the demons inside.

This room had another caster, only his minions were not imps. On either side of the caster stood a demon in dog form. They stood about waist high to the caster when on all four legs. Their heads were abnormally large, with sharp fangs extending out past their lower jaws.

Without a thought, Brick hit the caster with a holy spell. The demon dogs leaped forward toward the dwarf, mouths wide and drooling. Sasha cast Trap Soul on them in mid-air. Brick raised his shield and knocked them back to the ground. While they were down, he crushed the skull of one with his hammer. Helga jumped past him, driving her massive barbarian sword into the other, pinning it to the ground. Dayle and Warren bashed and hacked at it until its health bar dropped to zero.

The caster, still immobilized, screamed again as Edward drilled into its face with the light cannon. Sasha hit it with a Trap Soul spell. Ten seconds later there was a smoking hole through its skull, and the demon fell limply to the floor.

Once again Max looted. Lainey skinned the two dogs afterward. "I've never heard of demon dog skin. I bet this is rare. Maybe I can make something valuable from it."

The group continued in this manner. Clearing groups of demons from the hallway and various rooms they encountered. There was a mixture of casters and warriors, and a variety of summoned minions.

Level up! You are now level 42!
Your wisdom has increased by +1. Your intelligence has increased by +1
You have 26 free attribute points available

Finally! I've regained the level that Dirk cost me.

Killing the groups of higher level mobs had earned everyone enough to level up at least once, if not several times. As they reached the tunnel's end, there was yet another stairway descending into the darkness.

"Bottom level. Queen lives down there," Gelag said.

Once again Brick led the way. As they reached the bottom of the stairs, they spread out in a small chamber with round walls. There was only one exit door. Brick stood in front of it, shield held high, as Alexander had them pause while he raised another wall on the stairs behind him. This one he made a good, solid five feet thick.

Proceeding through the door, the group found themselves in a short corridor with a room to the left and the right. Leaving Lugs and Benny to guard the hall, Brick led the way into the left-hand room.

Inside he found demons. More than a dozen demons. There were six warriors, each of them seven feet tall with wings. They were much like the ones Alexander and friends had fought in the first demon dungeon weeks ago. Behind them were four casters. The casters had each summoned minions. These minions were different from those encountered above. Two were void guardians. Large, jet black, heavily muscled with shoulders three feet wide and arms that nearly reached the floor. Their mouths opened to reveal rows of shark teeth in front of an empty void of a throat. There were also two Succubi. Tall and outrageously curvy female demons with tails and leathery wings. They wore very little, and carried whips at their waists.

The average level of the mobs in the room was over 65. Gathered closely as they were, Brick wasn't going to be able to pull just a few.

"Focus on the casters first," Sasha spoke quietly. "Lugs, Benny, get in here. Brick, you and Lugs take the warriors. Push them back into the casters. Jules, you're behind the casters. Use every interrupt you can. Dayle and Warren, I need you to tank the minions. Benny and Lyra, you heal Dayle and Warren. Be ready to dispel charm or fear effects. Fibble, you shoot the nasty lady demons. Just keep shooting. As soon as they're grouped enough, I'll trap them. Misty, use your ice to trap the casters arms or interrupt them however you can. Alexander, you're on fire duty. Get out that light wand. Edward, as soon as they're immobilized, start cutting down the casters. Then the Succubi. Don't get close enough for them to use whips on you. And be careful you don't hit Jules or any of our group. Helga, you get behind the warriors and get whatever crits you can. Lainey and Max, the casters are yours."

With that rough plan, Brick and Lugs stepped forward. Brick hit one of the casters with holy smite, causing it to scream in pain and rage. Lugs smashed his massive hammer into the nearest warrior.

As soon as the caster was hit, the minions began to move toward Brick. Dayle charged in using a shield rush ability, bashing into the two void guardians, knocking them back into the Succubi and casters behind. Warren took advantage of the confusion and stabbed one of the guardians in the face for a critical hit. Then he took a step back behind Dayle and his shield.

Jules appeared behind one of the casters who was waving his arms and chanting. Twin daggers pierced up under the caster's armpits and into its chest. Then a ripping motion severed muscles and arteries. As the caster bled out, the rogue disappeared again, the others having never seen her.

One of the Succubi managed to wrap her whip around Warren's neck. The warrior just stood there, a dreamy look on his face as he suffocated. Succubi were crowd control specialists, charming victims to take them out of the fight while slowly killing them.

"No, no, no," Jules chided the demoness as she drove one dagger into the monster's kidney, and drew the other across her throat. "No stealing any of our boys."

The rogue had to jump back before she could finish the demon, as Edward's light beam slashed into it from the side. "Edward! Be more careful!" Sasha yelled at the prince. Edward moved the beam over to one of the remaining casters, and Jules used a dagger to cut the whip from the succubus' hand, releasing Warren to continue the fight. The warrior looked confused for a moment, then angry. He lifted his sword and began to hack furiously at the other succubus.

Lugs, meanwhile, was humming a lively tune to himself as he traded blows with two of the warriors. His shield, nearly as large as the warriors themselves, easily blocked any incoming sword strikes. Every ten seconds or so, he would swing his hefty hammer in an overhead blow, crushing an arm or a shoulder. Brick was doing the same with his smaller hammer. Only the dwarf was focusing on knees and hips. And his hammer, being infused with holy light magic was doing just as much damage as Lugs'. Helga supported both tanks, positioning herself behind the demon warriors and hacking and slashing with her oversized two-handed blade. The impressive muscles of the barbarian woman's arms levered her sword through a demon's arm, leaving it to fall to the floor still holding its sword. Spinning her whole body with the return blow, she severed its head.

Dayle was crouched behind his shield, absorbing thundering blows from the two void guardians. Lyra and Benny were casting constant heal spells on the poor man, keeping him at around 60% health. Sasha called out, "Fibble! Shoot Dayle!"

The little green warrior turned to the tank and shouted "Pew! Pew!" as he shot Dayle in the back with bursts of healing magic. After a few hits, the determined protector and demon-killer goblin turned back to firing at the void guardians. They were the largest targets in the room, and easiest to hit. The infuriated guardians tried to get at the little goblin, but Dayle steadfastly stood in their way.

"Little help, here!" Dayle shouted.

Edward's beam shifted to the two void guardians. Warren switched targets as well, as Jules appeared behind the remaining succubus, driving a dagger down into each shoulder inside the collarbone, the blades piercing arteries. The succubus let loose a scream that confused and slowed nearly every player in the room for a few seconds. This cost Dayle dearly, as he failed to block a thundering blow from one of the void guardians. Its fist smashed into the side of Dayle's head, denting his helm and knocking him down, stunned.

Instantly, Lugs let out a roar, and Brick scraped his hammer across his shield, using Serpent's Screech, both tanks trying to draw the monsters to them. The tactic worked. Both void guardians moved to attack the two tanks. Sasha assisted Lyra and Benny with healing Dayle, whose health had dropped down below 20%. He was still stunned, but out of danger for the moment.

Warren hacked at the last succubus, slicing off a wing and draining the last of her health. When she dropped to the floor, he gave her a final kick before joining Helga behind the warriors.

Lainey and Max had pumped arrow after arrow into the two remaining casters. Max had used his silence arrow to interrupt one, and was now firing normal arrows as quickly as possible into the heads, necks, and chests of the mobs. Lainey was alternating between shock arrows for interrupts, and light magic arrows that did impressive damage. Both casters were below 10% health and dropping quickly.

Edward was now burning through the trapped warriors, cutting off limbs and cutting through spines as he moved his beam slowly across the group. Helga and Warren switched to the void guardians, one moving behind each mob. Warren shoved his sword up into his guardian's back, where he guessed its heart might be. He was rewarded with a critical hit and a roar of pain. Helga took a much different approach. She took a running leap at her guardian, sword gripped in both hands over her head. With a roar of her own, she used all of her momentum, body weight, and considerable muscle to slam her sword down through the top of the demon's head. The sword cut through its head completely, continuing down into its chest, splitting the monster roughly in half. The demon was dead before it hit the ground. Removing her sword, she moved to help Warren finish off his guardian, while Lugs went back to bashing on warriors.

The casters fell under the withering fire from Max and Lainey, and now all of the party focused on the three remaining warriors. It took only a few seconds for the already damaged demons to expire.

Around the room golden light surrounded every player. They had all leveled up from the difficult fight. Fibble was rubbing his tummy again, smiling at Sasha.

Level up! You are now level 43!
Your wisdom has increased by +1. Your intelligence has increased by +1
You have 26 free attribute points available

The level increase had brought Warren back to full health and stamina. The tank removed his badly dented helm, sighing with relief. "The damned thing was squeezing my head!"

Gelag, who had remained in the doorway with Fitz, watching the corridor for more enemies, stepped into the room. He kicked one of the demon corpses and spat on it. "Queen's guards. She will be close by."

Max looted the corpses, finding a few rare and epic level items. Fitz stood in the center of the room, eyes closed. After a moment he pointed toward the corner furthest from the door. "There. Dark magic in there. Behind the wall."

Max and Jules moved over to inspect the wall. After a few moments, Jules pressed on a slightly discolored brick, and a section of the wall cracked open. Brick and Lugs moved to the front as Max gripped the stone with his fingertips and yanked it open.

Inside was an empty room. Well, empty of demons, or furniture. There was a pile of chests and weapons, gold and silver statues, and a pedestal with a black orb upon it. The orb looked identical to the one they'd found in the dungeon near Whitehall.

Without needing to be asked, Alexander pulled out some obsidian and handed it to Brick. Brick shaped the stone into a box with a hinged lid, then handed it to Fitz. The wizard cast his magic into the box, then used it to scoop up the orb, sealing it inside.

Max and Jules were busy opening chests. There were a couple filled with gold coins, one filled with silver. A small chest was filled with nearly a hundred diamonds of varying sizes. In the back corner was a two-handed sword that glowed with power. Helga bent to lift it, showing it to the group. The blade was at least four feet long. Only she or Lugs could wield it.

Queensbane
Item Level: Unique, Legendary
Stats: Strength +20, Stamina +20, Crit +10
This weapon was crafted in the deepest pit of the demon plane by a demon master smith. It was commissioned by Chelok, the Demon Queen's consort, who planned to remove her head and take her throne.
Enchanted: Sharpness. Magic resistance 50%. Mind control resistance 100%.

Brick's mouth dropped open. "That be… skymetal. All of it! Pure damned skymetal!" Fitz confirmed it with a nod of his head.

"Can I keep it?" Helga asked almost sheepishly. She knew the sword was worth hundreds of thousands of gold.

"I think you and Lugs should roll for it. It's too large for the rest of us to use." Alexander grinned at her. Brick and Max both looked at him. If they were to sell this weapon, each of the players in the room could pay their bills for a year.

Lugs shook his head. "I like my hammer."

Helga beamed at him, giving the half-ogre a giant bear hug and actually lifting him to his tippy-toes. "Thank you!"

Alexander cleared his throat. "This is a valuable weapon. If you decide at any point to sell it, you'll need to split the proceeds among the group members here."

"Sell it?" Helga gasped. "Over my dead friggin' body! I'm going to marry it!" She hugged the weapon to her chest. The group smiled and chuckled.

"Okay so now that the loot is settled, we need to discuss something. That orb we just found, it's exactly like the one that was used to power the portal in the Whitehall dungeon. The portal that the demons used to invade and drive out the goblins." Fibble sniffed and wiped his eyes at this.

"Fibble told us that the orb was delivered to the goblins by a man in black. My belief is that this is tied somehow to the Dark One, and maybe to Baron Dire. We need more information. When we encounter the queen down here, I want to try and speak with her before we kill her. Agreed?"

Everyone nodded their agreement.

Turning to Gelag, Alexander asked, "Gelag, does this treasure belong to your people? Did the demons steal it from you?"

The duergar poked around in the treasure pile. Lifting a gold statue, he said "Drow." He dropped it, and reached for a dagger that looked to be made of mithril. "Dwarf." Looking around, he shook his head. "Maybe some of the gold. But no, this is not Stoneburner treasure."

"Well, once we've killed the queen, we'll help you recover any valuables stolen from your people," Alexander assured him.

Moving back into the corridor, they opened the door on the other side of the hall. This was a large room stacked with crates, chests, and bags. Gelag spoke up immediately "This is our supply storage. Food, tools, clothing."

They quickly searched the room, finding no hidden enemies among the stacks. Fitz pointed out a concealed door behind a stack of crates. Gelag looked nervous. "Stoneburner vault. There be our treasures."

Seeing the concern on the duergar's face, Max said, "I love loot more than most. But we're not here to steal from you or your people, Gelag. We need to open the room to make sure no enemies are inside. But we'll not touch your property."

Sasha's mouth hung open in surprise, as she stared at Max. "Who are you, and what have you done with our friend?" she teased.

Gelag moved to the wall. Placing his hand over a particular stone section, he mumbled a few words. The door swung outward, and he moved aside. Brick stepped into the room, shield high, looking around. The room wasn't large, maybe 10x10. Nothing living was visible, only chests, weapons, and bags piled along the walls.

The dwarf backed out of the room. "Nobody home," he said.

Alexander gave Gelag a nod, and the duergar stepped inside. He picked up an enchanted sword, then stepped out and closed the door. "Thank you," was all that he said.

Brick led the way back out to the hallway, and farther into the 5th level of the complex. Gelag said, "Main Hall only place left. Queen will be there."

The hallway emptied into the largest cavern they'd seen so far. Easily two hundred yards across, the natural cavern had soaring ceilings that curved up into darkness. There were no exits that Alexander could see, except the one behind them. There was a small stream running across one side, the water running down one wall, and exiting under another. Large mushrooms grew near the stream, and what looked like small cows nibbled on the edges of the fungus.

Set in the middle of the cavern on a slight rise in the stone floor was a dais with a pair of golden thrones. The queen sat in the larger of the two seats, legs casually draped over one arm of the chair. The other throne was occupied by a man in black leather armor under a dark hooded cloak. The man was holding a black gem the size of a grapefruit, and appeared to be talking to it. Alexander couldn't make out the words at his distance. Gathered around the dais were twenty or so demons, all facing the queen as if awaiting something.

Fibble tugged on Fitz's robe, pointing to the man next to the queen. "Dark man. He put nasty dark surprise under chief's big chair."

Fitz took one look at the man and growled, "That's Baron Dire. The necromancer. He is MINE."

Not waiting for the rest of the group, Fitz strode forward. Pulling a staff from his bag, he began chanting. Ten steps closer to the thrones, the wizard thrust the staff forward, and a beam of white light raced toward the baron. The man looked up from his crystal just in time to see the spell hit him in the chest. He screamed in pain and rage, beginning to rise from his chair. But the light that struck him didn't penetrate his body. Instead it wrapped around him, forming into a cage of light. As he tried to straighten up, his head touched the cage, and it seared a line into his forehead.

The demon queen leapt from her throne, shouting, "Kill them!"

At the same time, Sasha shouted, "Mow them down!"

Being nearly a hundred yards from the now charging demons, the players all cast ranged light attacks, if they had them. Other ranged attacks if they didn't. Lainey fired healing arrows one after the other. Benny and Brick cast holy smite. Sasha cast an aoe thorn trap that grabbed all but two of the charging demons. Alexander hit two of them with wizard's fire, mainly to distract the casters in that group, then began firing his ray of light wand at the two still charging. Edward opened up on the group that Sasha had trapped with the light cannon.

Misty used an ice spell to trap the two charging demons, and Max began filling them with arrows. Fibble was firing at anything that moved, shouting 'Pew!' with each shot. Sasha and Alexander began casting Trap Soul on every demon in the group. High-level mobs like these should produce powerful crystals.

Warren, Dayle, Helga, and Lugs weren't casters, and were setting up to intercept any demons who reached the group. Lugs slapped his forehead, then pulled out one of the looted spears. He moved to the side until his shot was lined up the way he wanted, then hurled the spear. There was an audible whistle as the weapon streaked through the air at incredible speed. It penetrated the stomach of the closest of the two demons who'd escaped the thorn trap. Pushing through that demon's back, it also penetrated the thigh of the demon behind it. Already damaged from the others' attacks, the two demons expired.

Lugs' eyes unfocused as he stared at an alert that popped up on his UI. "I just got an achieve called 'Two Birds, One Stone'!" he called out.

"Shaddup 'n' get yer arse into the fight!" Brick hollered at the giant tank. "Ye take the right, I'll be takin' the left." Brick moved forward toward the trapped group of demons along with Warren, Dayle, and Helga. Lugs focused on the enemy and moved to join them.

Edward stepped far to the left, fixing his beam on one of the demons to the left side the of the group, and began cutting the trapped warrior in half. Fitz stayed near the prince. Brick and the others approached the right side of the group, smashing and cutting wherever they could. Max and Misty joined in with ranged attacks, while Benny, Sasha and Lyra focused on heals. Jules was nowhere in sight.

One of the caster demons managed to get off a spell, despite the ticking damage from the wizard's fire. A black cloud appeared around Benny, who had hit the caster with a holy smite spell and pulled aggro.

The paladin screamed, and his health bar dropped quickly. "Heals on Benny!" Sasha shouted out. She, Alexander, Lainey, Lyra, and Fibble all hit Benny with heals. His health continued to drop, but more slowly. "Again!" Sasha shouted. This time his health shot up to over 50%, and stayed there as the cloud dissipated. The paladin dropped to his knees and began to mumble a prayer. His armor, and most of his exposed skin, were pitted as if burned by acid.

The players finished off the group of trash demons one by one. While they fought, the demon queen was casting spell after spell at the cage of light that Fitz had cast around Baron Dire. The light was beginning to flicker and fade.

"Fibble! Shoot the queen!" Fitz called out. The little goblin immediately tore across the cavern, yelling a war-cry as he pointed his demon-killer stick at the queen.

When he got close, he yelled, "Pew! Pew!" and began to bombard her with bursts of healing light magic.

The demoness screamed and spun toward the goblin. Who promptly changed direction and picked up speed. He occasionally turned to fire another burst at the enraged queen, but didn't slow down one bit. Few things moved as quickly as a terrified goblin.

As Fibble kited the boss, the rest of the group burned down the remaining demons. Then it was time to focus on the queen.

Demon Queen Voliara
Level 75 Elite (Boss)
Health 18,100/20,000

"Fibble, run to me!" Sasha called out.

The little goblin made a sharp turn, dashing right toward the queen and under her legs, shooting her in the face before he passed through. The queen screamed, "I'll eat your heart!" as she spun around, swinging a sharply clawed fist at the fast-moving Fibble.

Instead of connecting with goblin flesh, her wrist broke with a loud crack as Brick slammed into her outstretched hand using his shield rush ability. Two seconds later, the much larger Lugs slammed into her as well. Not using his ability, just his massive bulk.

Before she could recover, Jules appeared behind the queen, stabbing daggers into both sides of the demon's neck, and ripping backward with all her strength. The critical hit took nearly 20% off the queen's health. Jules quickly disappeared again, moving out of range of any counterstrike.

Edward focused his light cannon on the queen's chest, trying to keep it as steady as possible. The boy was getting fatigued trying to aim the ten-pound weapon accurately through so many battles.

Brick and Benny both hit the queen with holy smite spells. She growled through the pain and began a spell of her own. Max interrupted her cast with a silence arrow, which struck at nearly the same time as a light arrow from Lainey.

Sasha cast a thorn trap on the queen, who was silently shouting something. Alexander immediately hit the demon with wizard's fire. Lugs and Brick pounded on her body as Warren, Helga and Dayle moved to either side of her and began hacking and pounding.

The queen snapped her wings forward. The left one sliced a cut across Helga's stomach, penetrating her armor and causing a bleed. Warren was knocked off his feet by the right wing, and the queen quickly moved over to stomp a cloven hoof into his chest. His armor cracked, Warren found himself pinned to the floor as the battle raged above him. He tried to rise, but could barely draw breath, and didn't have the strength to move the queen.

A heal from Sasha improved his situation a bit, repairing crushed ribs so that he could breathe easier. Reaching up with his sword arm, he sliced the tendons in the back of the queen's ankle. Rather than causing her to lift her weight from him, he achieved the opposite. The demon lost her balance, falling on top of the helpless warrior.

As she was still burning with wizard's fire, Warren took both crush damage and fire damage. As his health was dipping down to zero again, Benny rushed forward to try a Lay on Hands spell to bring him back to full health. But the queen managed to shift herself around and slam a clawed hand into Warren's face, using it to push herself up. The extra damage finished off Warren's remaining health, killing him.

"Bitch! You killed my brother! You're gonna die slowly for that!" Lyra screamed, shocking everyone in her group for a moment. Sasha looked at the woman with one eyebrow up, a grin on her face.

Lyra shook her head. "Yeah. It's the immersion. This shit feels too real sometimes. Still, let's hurt this demon bitch!" She grinned back. With that, she cast a light magic heal at the queen, causing her to stumble on her one good leg.

Fitz was staying out of the fight, focusing on making sure the man in the cage didn't escape. He was wrapping the cage with containment magic, anti-teleportation magic, and strengthening magic for the cage itself.

Lugs dropped his hammer for a moment, pulling out one of his long spears. Seeing this, Brick taunted the queen with some of his love poetry.

"Over here, ye ugly wench! Yer lookin a bit rough today. Or does yer face always look like that? Is that a hunch on yer back? Right there between yer wings? Ye should have that removed!" he shouted at the already enraged demon queen. As he did so, he moved around her slightly to his left, turning the boss away from Lugs.

As soon as the queen turned, Lugs pulled the spear back in his long right arm, then jammed it forward with all his strength and weight behind it. The metal tip of the spear pierced the queen's left arm, pushing through and into her chest, and out the back behind her right arm. The hit did incredible damage.

Demon Queen Voliara
Level 75 Elite (Boss)
Health 10,600/20,000

As Lugs picked up his shield, Sasha called out, "Nearly 50%! Everybody back off! Ranged, do your worst! Prepare to take cover!"

Sasha cast thorn vines on the queen again, renewing the trap and holding her in place. The new vines immediately caught fire, adding to the DoT damage the queen was taking. One of Fibble's light magic bursts was the stroke that put the demon down below 50% health.

Brick and Lugs had taken a dozen steps back, while Helga, Dayle, and Jules quickly moved to take cover behind the two tanks and their shields. Sasha and all the ranged group moved back even further, continuing to cast and shoot as they moved. Lainey was almost exclusively using light arrows, and paused to down a mana potion. Max was preparing a silence arrow, on the off-chance he could interrupt whatever ability the queen was about to use. His cooldown, now reduced to one minute, had ten seconds left.

The queen stood up straight and began to move her right hand, while her left was immobilized by the spear. Alexander quickly raised a stone wall wide enough for the casters to hide behind, and then began another in front of the tanks. It was only about three feet high when the queen completed her spell. Max fired his silence arrow, but it failed to interrupt her. She raised her head toward the ceiling above and screamed.

Brick and Lugs interlocked their shields atop the wall as those behind them ducked down. A wave of psychic energy struck them, causing them to scream as well. Blood appeared at the corner of their eyes, and dripped from their ears. The caster group was less effected, being farther away and behind a better wall. Still, they were briefly stunned, unable to cast for ten seconds.

Among the entire group, only Helga wasn't affected. Her new sword gave her 100% resistance to the queen's mind ability. Seeing her friends vulnerable, Helga vaulted over the short wall and charged at the queen.

Within ten feet of the demon boss, she took a running leap toward the queen's vulnerable left side where the arm was still pinned by Lugs' spear. Sword over her head, she swept the massive blade downward as she landed, contracting all her core muscles to put additional power into the blow.

Queensbane lived up its name. The strength bonus put even more power behind Helga's blow. The sharpness enchantment allowed the blade to slice easily through the flesh and bone of the demon's shoulder. The additional crit chance, combined with the fact that the queen was already partially incapacitated, allowed for a massive damage bonus. The blade penetrated through the queen's collarbone, severing muscle, arteries, and ribs as it crashed downward toward her heart.

Demon Queen Voliara
Level 75 Elite (Boss)
Health 1,900/20,000

Alexander cast Trap Soul on the queen as he watched her health plummet. To be sure, he shouted, "Trap Soul!" to the others, in case his spell didn't take.

Helga levered her sword up and down as she pulled it from the queen's chest, causing more damage in the process. The queen attempted to speak, but blood bubbled up through her throat and poured down her chin.

Gelag appeared next to Helga. The duergar could barely walk, blood running from both his eyes and his ears. He dragged his enchanted sword along beside him. He put a hand on Helga's arm, a pleading look in his eyes. "Please," he said, motioning toward the queen.

Helga nodded and took a step back. She lifted the grey dwarf's sword arm for him, setting the blade on his shoulder. Gelag stepped forward, using his free hand to grip the failing queen's good arm for balance. He managed to pull the sword off his shoulder and press it against her chest.

Then he leaned into the sword, using his weight to slide the blade into the demon's heart. "DIE!" he shouted into her face with what strength he had left.

Level up! You are now level 44!
Your wisdom has increased by +1. Your intelligence has increased by +1
You have 26 free attribute points available

Level up! You are now level 45!
Your wisdom has increased by +1. Your intelligence has increased by +1
You have 31 free attribute points available

Gelag slumped to the floor as the demon queen's body fell backward, sword still protruding from her chest. Sasha and Lyra, now recovered from the stun effects, threw heals at him, as well as everyone else. Benny was drinking a mana potion so he could do the same. Fibble was shooting everyone in turn with a healing blast from his stick.

Brick moved over to the queen. Pulling Gelag's sword from her chest, he used it to remove her head from her body. He grinned at Sasha's disgusted look. "It be a tradition, lass. We be needin' a decoration fer the Great Hall!" he said as he stuck the head in his bag. Looking to Dayle, he said, "If ye cut the horns off them demons, they be worth some gold." Nodding, Dayle and Helga moved off to loot the demons and take the horns. Brick returned Gelag's sword to him.

Max looted the queen's body. "Hey, folks, got a couple good items here!" he called out as he raised the first one for everyone to inspect.

Psychic Daggers
Item level: Epic
Stats: Agility +10, Dexterity +10, Crit +10
These daggers will inflict physic damage, stunning a target for ten seconds, and causing a bleed effect that blurs vision and dampens hearing.

Jules looked at them with wide eyes, practically drooling over the weapons. She looked around shyly, waiting for someone to claim them.

Finally, Alexander chuckled. "Jules, you're the only rogue here. They're yours if you want them."

The elfess bounded forward, taking the daggers from Max and planting a quick kiss on his cheek. Alexander felt a twinge of envy.

Max raised the next loot item.

Cloak of the Clear Mind
Item level: Rare, Scalable
Stats: Armor +1, Intelligence +5, Wisdom +10
This cloak provides 100% resistance to mind magic, and 50% resistance to dark magic spells.

"That should go to one of the healers," Misty said. "The wisdom will give a good mana boost, and the resistance will keep them healing when the rest of us are stunned, like a few minutes ago."

Sasha replied, "I agree. Give it to Lyra. I've already got some epic gear. We need to raise the abilities of the whole group."

"Thank you. I'm not used to guild officers sharing the premium loot," Lyra offered as she accepted the cloak from Max.

"Final item!" Max said. "I propose this goes to Warren for his ultimate sacrifice." He held up a shiny black metal chestguard with a tear in the back.

Chelok's Chest
Item Level: Epic
Stats: Armor +10, Strength +10, Stamina +10
This armor was worn by Chelok, consort to Queen Voliara, until she discovered his plot to assassinate her. Whereupon she stabbed him in the back with his own sword. Class Bonus: Warriors wearing this armor will inflict 200% damage when attacking an enemy from behind.

The description caused some laughter among the group. Lyra accepted the armor on Warren's behalf. Brick promised to have one of the master smiths at the dragon forge repair it.

Max quietly handed Alexander a soul crystal.

Greater Psychic Soul Crystal
Item level: Unique
This crystal, powered by the soul of a Demon Queen Volaria, contains her psychic energy as well as her soul energy.
Charges: Soul charges 600/600, Psychic charges 300/300

A chuckle from Brick drew Alexander's attention away from the crystal he was holding. Following the dwarf's gaze, he spotted Fibble standing in front of the cage holding Baron Dire. The little goblin was yelling at the man, punctuating each statement with a blast from his stick. Being undead, the light was causing the necromancer significant pain.

Fully restored, Gelag stood and stepped toward the group. "My people. I must check on them," he said.

"Of course! We will accompany you. Max, Jules, can you stay here and search the room? Fitz, you have the baron under control?" Alexander asked.

Fitz nodded, then growled. "He'll not escape. I'm sending him back to my tower for a little talk before I kill him."

"Please don't kill him before I get a chance to question him too, Fitz. He has information about the Dark One that we need."

The wizard growled, but nodded his head. With a wave of his hand, he sent the cage with the baron inside back to his tower. "I'll help search the room. Lugs, you mind staying? I would like these thrones smashed."

Always willing to smash things, Lugs responded, "Sure thing. How small do you want the leftover bits?" The half-ogre grinned.

Alexander led Gelag and the rest of the group back out the exit. He removed the wall blocking the stairs, and they headed up with Brick in the lead again. They climbed up further, Alexander removing the wall obstacles he'd placed as they went. Upon reaching the 4th level, they found the last few dozen duergar they'd passed on the way down.

The grey dwarves were still motionless. Though a quick examination revealed that they'd begun to regenerate their health. The death of the queen must have broken the spell that had been draining them, at least.

Gelag approached the nearest, a female. He grasped her arms near the shoulders, and gently shook her, as if trying to awaken her from sleep. There was no response.

Looking to Sasha, he asked "Try to heal one time?"

Sasha cast a medium nature magic heal on the female duergar. There was a moan of pain, and the grey dwarf blinked once. She focused on Gelag, and recognition lit her eyes. But then her gaze faded back into the distance, and she was once again catatonic.

"I think we need Fitz. Maybe he knows a way to break the spell without hurting them," Sasha offered.

Gelag nodded, and sat down to wait.

Warren's voice came across raid chat. "*I take it you guys killed her*?"

"*Aye. And took her head. I were thinkin we'd mount it in yer room. Fer a reminder*." Brick chuckled.

"*Screw that! I'll see you guys when you get back*." Warren replied.

A few minutes later, Lugs appeared with Max, Jules, and Fitz following. The half-ogre had a grin on his face.

"We found a stash. Under the floor behind the thrones," Lugs reported. "We left the gold chunks of the thrones for Gelag and his people. Fitz teleported the rest to the keep." As he spoke, he looked at the duergar still standing motionless. Alexander could tell he was still wondering whether they'd be killing them all.

Fitz was already moving toward the female that Gelag had tried to awaken. Sasha filled him in on what they'd tried, and the result.

"And your healing spell was nature magic?" the wizard asked. Sasha nodded her head.

"Gelag, I want to try a light magic spell. It might free her. It also might kill her," Fitz said.

Gelag considered for a few moments, then nodded his head.

Fitz retrieved Fibble's original healing wand from his bag. Pointing it at the female duergar, he fired a minimal burst of light magic into her. When nothing happened, good or bad, he fired a stronger burst.

The duergar gasped, falling to her knees and barely managing to place her hands in front of herself to save her face from impacting the floor. She coughed, then inhaled deeply. Gelag rushed to her, speaking too quietly for the friends to make out his words. After a moment, he helped her stand. When she stared in alarm and suspicion at the group in front her, he quickly explained.

She nodded her head, reaching out a hand to Sasha. Sasha shook the grey dwarf's hand with a smile, saying "Welcome back, neighbor." Gelag's translation drew a smile.

"So, light magic healing spells is all it takes?" Alexander asked Fitz.

"It seems so. Gelag, may I examine your friend?" Fitz asked.

"Her name Malaba," Gelag said. "Okay for you to check her. Make sure magic gone." He whispered to her as the wizard reached forward to lay a hand on her shoulder. Fitz closed his eyes for a few seconds.

Removing his hand, Fitz said, "She's fine. No remaining dark magic that I can detect."

Sasha grinned and turned to her goblin protector. "Fibble, shoot the duergar! Shoot them till they wake up."

Fibble needed no further encouragement. He merrily hopped toward the nearest of the frozen grey dwarves and began shooting, chanting, "Pew! Pew!".

Laughing, Brick, Lainey, Alexander, Lyra and Benny joined in casting light magic heals on the duergar. Fitz handed the healing wand to Gelag to use.

Alexander paused in his casting to ask, "Gelag, how many of your people are down here?"

Gelag didn't hesitate. "One hundred forty-five left after battle."

Doing a quick calculation, Alexander produced a small soul crystal. "Your wand may run out. Use this to recharge it. It seems fitting to use the soul of a demon to bring your people back to life." He smiled.

Gelag accepted the crystal and moved quickly to wake more of his people. As each duergar woke, Gelag and Malaba spoke to them, quieting their alarm and identifying the guild group as friends.

When they finished with the few dozen duergar on that level, they all moved up to the third level chamber where the vast majority of Gelag's people stood frozen. As there were now more awakened duergar to help explain things to the newly awoken, the group split up. Each of the healers took a couple duergar with them and began to bring back more than a hundred of the Stoneburner clan members.

It took less than an hour for all the duergar to be freed from their bondage. There was much hugging, and animated discussion. Fingers were pointed at the Greystone group as they all gathered near the doorway that led up to the higher levels.

Gelag approached the Greystones with five older looking duergar at his back. "This be Stoneburner clan council. We wish to thank you for saving clan." He bowed, and those behind him did the same. Followed by every grey dwarf in the room.

“It is always good to be able to help neighbors in need,” Alexander replied. He waited while Gelag translated. “We have a keep on the surface above, very near the lake that covers your entrance. We are fighting servants of the Dark One, like the demons we just killed, and Baron Dire, the man we put in the cage.”

He waited while Gelag translated all of this. There was some discussion among the council.

Gelag turned back to Alexander “We help. Not many warriors alive after battle. But we fight dark ones. Owe your clan great debt.”

“You owe us nothing,” Sasha interjected. “We ask only that you consider us friends, and allies.” She smiled warmly at all the council members as Gelag translated. She whispered to Alexander, “We really need to get them more pendants.” Alexander nodded and handed a fist-sized chunk of obsidian to Brick, who began to break it and shape into pendants. Lainey reached into her bag for more leather strips.

Gelag finished his chat with his colleagues, and said “Yes. Allies. Friends.” He nodded his head.

“Would you like to come with us to our keep? We have some supplies that we can share. And we can talk about how our clans can help each other,” Alexander offered.

Gelag nodded. “Three go. Three stay to help our people.”

Brick finished the last of the pendants, handing them all to Fitz. The wizard cupped them in his hands and cast the translation spell. Lainey then took them, ran a thong through each, and handed one to each councilor as they were finished.

Alexander addressed them all. “My name is Alexander. I am one of the leaders of the Greystone guild, and owners of Dire Keep. Our domain includes all the lands above you. We welcome the Stoneburner clan as friends and allies, and invite you to our home for a meal. These pendants are humble gifts, to allow us to better understand each other.”

Two council members joined Gelag as three others headed back toward their people gathered a short distance away.

And elder female duergar introduced herself as Brega. The other councilor was younger than Gelag and Brega. His name was Morig.

As the duergar were still a bit unsteady on their feet, Alexander simply teleported the entire group back to the keep.

It was still an hour before sunset, so Alexander led them to tables near the kitchen. Lainey and Sasha headed into the kitchen to get some food for their guests. Alexander waved to Silverbeard, and asked him to pass the word that the duergar were friendly.

Alexander began to explain when they were all seated. "Our clan is about the same size as yours. We are a mix of races, being human, dwarf, elf, gnome, ogre, dragon, and even troll. We have occupied this keep, and rebuilt it after it was destroyed by Fitz. He was hunting the man who sat on the throne next to the demon queen. He is a servant of the Dark One. We are war with the Dark One, and have chosen to make a stand here in Dire Keep."

Sasha and Lainey returned with food, which the duergar dug into gratefully. It had, after all, been three thousand years since they'd had fresh fruit or meat.

Alexander gave them time to fill their bellies. They were in no hurry, after all.

Once they'd had their fill, Alexander began to lead the councilors around the keep. He showed them the future site of the auction house, and bank. He showed them the chapel, where they bowed their heads and touched the altar with reverence. He then took them through the inner gate and out into the fields. He pointed out their herd of livestock, the fields that had begun to be plowed. He showed them the outer gatehouse with the now completed drawbridge over the fully filled moat.

The moat reminded him of the lake, and he teleported them near Lars' stone pier. Walking them out to the end, he explained how they'd drained the lake to fill the moat, and discovered the duergar's entry door. The lake had, by this point, mostly refilled. So only the very top of the doorway was visible near the water's surface.

Brega spoke up. "When we built our home, there was no lake here. Only small waterfall and stream." She looked up at the falls. "We are trapped under lake now."

"No, not trapped. There is a teleportation mirror that will allow you to leave, for now. We'll move it to a structure here." He pointed toward Lars' shack. "And we'll help you create a new exit. Someplace hidden," he added.

"Thank you," Brega replied. "Greystone is very kind. Could have killed our clan when we could not defend."

"We need friends more than we need experience and treasure," Alexander replied. "We are allies with the human Kingdom of Stormforge." He pointed toward the city. "And with the Broken Mountain dwarves. Many of their people have joined our clan. I invite the Stoneburner clan to join as well. You would become Greystone. Take an oath to defend the clan and the keep. Your people could live and work among us, and benefit from the food and other resources we gather."

As he spoke, Lars raised a net filled with maybe twenty fish. Alexander quickly moved to help the man lift it up onto the pier. Once it was set down, Lars began to pull the fish from the net and drop them into the holding box.

Brega and Morig both nodded their heads. Gelag said, "We will discuss with our people. Alexander makes good offer. Dream we came to surface for. Trade and live with others."

As it was nearing sunset, Alexander teleported them back to the keep.

"If you would like to wait a few minutes, we can gather some supplies for you to take home to your people. And you can meet some of the new members from Broken Mountain that we'll welcome today."

Silverbeard strode over. He'd already anticipated the duergar's needs. There was a small cart filled with fresh fruit, meat, and a barrel of ale behind him, pulled by Lugs. "Lugs said there were a hundred and fifty of them. This should feed them for the evening. We can make better arrangements tomorrow," the old chamberlain explained.

The duergar gathered around the cart, touching the food and shaking their heads as they murmured among themselves.

Leaving them to it, Alexander turned and opened the portal. Lola waited on the other side with a significant contingent of dwarves with wagons.

Smiling at Alexander as she passed through, she said, "I bring'd more of me people. And food. And me King sent Brick's next shipment."

Looking at the crowd behind her, he said, "You certainly did! How many of this crowd are staying?"

"All of em," Lola said. "There be twenty more guards. Six farmers. Three hunters. One woodcutter. Two smiths. Six masons. And one dwarven lass who be interested in fishing. There also be an auctioneer." She pointed to a gnome who was riding the back of a wagon. "I talked to a banker who'll be wantin' to help us set up our bank. Fer a fee o' course. And we bring'd enough food fer everyone for two weeks. I paid with guild funds." She hesitated, expecting Alexander to object to her spending money without approval.

"Well done, Lola!" he said. "Thank you for thinking of the food. As it turns out, we've got new neighbors, and we'll be needing much more than we planned." He waved toward the duergar gathered around the cart, who were now staring at the mass of dwarves coming through the portal.

The contingent of dwarven guards noticed the duergar at about the same time. Instantly they had shields up and weapons out.

Alexander leapt in front of them, as did Master Silverbeard. "No, wait! These duergar are allies! They are friendly! There's no threat here!"

The guards lowered their weapons, looking suspiciously between Alexander and the grey dwarves.

Silverbeard pulled them aside, and gathered all the others as they came through. He explained to them as a group the situation. Alexander moved to calm the wary Stoneburners.

"I'm sorry. I should have thought to warn them before they came through. Please forgive them. And me."

"Nothing to forgive," Morig said. "Hate between duergar and dwarf go back many lifetimes. Many more lifetimes pass since we came here. Maybe we start to fix hate."

Silverbeard approached, the entire band of thirty-nine newcomers behind him. He bowed slightly to the duergar. "Me people wish to apologize, and welcome ye back to the living."

The leader of the guards stepped forward and offered his hand to Morig, who smiled and shook it heartily. The dwarf moved on to Gelag as another dwarf held out a hand to Morig. And so the entire line of dwarves greeted each of the duergar. Dwarven honor was really something to behold.

Alexander raised himself up on a column of stone. Facing the newcomers, he said, "Jeeves, loudspeaker, please."

After a moment he called out, "I welcome you all to Dire Keep. I am Alexander. What I have just seen here, ancient enemies coming together in friendship, makes me proud to be among you. The honor of dwarves is legendary. And the duergar of the Stoneburner clan sacrificed nearly their entire population to achieve freedom from the cruel ways of their people. Together with all the races represented here today, we are forming a new, stronger, better nation of brothers and sisters willing to support and defend each other, regardless of race!"

There was clapping and cheering from both the newcomers and the citizens of the keep. The dwarves began to separate and move their supplies at the direction of Lola and Silverbeard.

Alexander turned to the duergar. "I can take you back to your people now, if you'd like." When Gelag nodded his head, Alexander said, "Okay, just one moment."

He quickly teleported up to the command center and grabbed the mirror that led down into the duergar complex. He then teleported back to the keep, and moved over to the cart full of food. Looking around, he waved at a young dwarven girl with strawberry blonde hair and a very short beard. As she approached, he asked "Would you be the young lady who is interested in fishing?

She stuck out her hand. "Aye! I be Elsbett. Nice t'meetcha."

Alexander took the offered hand. "Elsbett. Pleased to meet you as well. I'm about to take these folks over to the fishing pier. Would you like to join us, and meet your new teacher?"

"Aye, that'd be grand. Thank ye." She smiled.

With a wave of his hand, he teleported the group of duergar, the cart, and Elsbett to an area near the fishing pier. Waving Lars over, he said, "Lars, this is Elsbett. She's your new apprentice. I've also got to put up a structure really quickly. It'll serve as a gateway for the Stoneburners until we can make other arrangements."

Lars nodded, and led Elsbett away toward the pier. "The fish bite better as the sun comes up and goes down…" he heard the old fisherman say as they walked away.

Alexander turned and strode some ways toward the ridgeline. Being this close to the mountain's face, he changed his mind about creating a new structure out in the open. Instead, he moved to a spot where a large outcropping extended forward. Moving to the side, he opened a narrow space in the joint where it met the flatter stone. Pushing diagonally into the mountain's stone, he created a cave about twenty feet wide and deep. Turning to the wall on the left of the entrance, he created a small alcove, where he placed the mirror.

Moving back up and out of the structure, he joined the duergar, who were still standing around the cart. Looking toward the cave he'd just created, he made sure the entrance wasn't visible. One would have to be standing right next to it to spot it.

With a wave, he teleported the group and the cart into the first room that he and his team had entered in the duergar complex.

Looking around, they immediately recognized where they were.

Alexander pointed to the mirror. "Go ahead. Touch the mirror. Just one of you."

Gelag stepped forward and touched the mirror. He disappeared, only to reappear laughing a few moments later.

"That's your way out," Alexander said. "For now. You must go one at time, and never linger in front of the mirror, in case another is coming through."

They all nodded their heads. "We thank you again, Alexander," Gelag said.

"You're welcome. If you wish, stop by the keep tomorrow and we can talk further. Also, your people are welcome to hunt and fish. But be careful. There may be enemies in the forest."

Alexander waved goodbye and teleported himself back to the keep.

Heading back to the kitchen courtyard, where most folks were having their dinner, Alexander found it was standing room only. With the additional dwarves, there just weren't enough seats.

So, stepping back a bit from the area, he began to raise stone. He raised three long tables, and benches on either side of each. Brick moved over and smoothed the tops to make sure there were no splinters. And just like that, there was seating for thirty more people.

Having already eaten with the duergar, Alexander took a seat and socialized with the folks who joined him. While they talked, he pulled out a block of obsidian and began enchanting fifty more small pieces with the Undying and healing spells. If the Stoneburners joined up, he was going to need more obsidian.

Brick sat with him, and called over a couple of smiths and masons. They shaped the stone into dragons, and sunk the pins inside the backs. Brick gave the finished pins to Lola for distribution.

Alexander wandered over to the auction house building to find that the gnome was already set up and doing business. Unsurprisingly, Max was at the counter, looking to sell some rare loot items. Alexander left them to it. He'd introduce himself later.

He thought about Baron Dire, locked up in Fitz's tower. He really wanted to speak to the man. But Fitz clearly had a bone to pick, and Alexander figured it wasn't wise to get in his way.

Alexander decided to retire for the evening. Making his way upstairs to his chambers, he lowered himself into a comfortable chair in the sitting room. The same chair he'd died in recently. Luckily the game mechanics wiped away all blood stains when a dead body disappeared.

He'd gotten some levels today, as had the others. And they'd not been in the city to visit trainers for a week now. As best he could recall, his group had all gained more than ten levels since then. He would need to encourage them to visit the city in the morning to see trainers.
Pulling up his own stat sheet, he contemplated spending some points.

Mage: Alexander **Level 45**
Build: Ranged magic/Melee dps

Health: 12,100	**Experience**	**Attribute pts avail: 31**
Mana: 11,800	**4,900/63,000**	**Skill pts avail: 5**

Stamina: 4(12)	**Dexterity: 6**	**Armor: 140**	**Health Regen: 60**
Strength: 4(15)	**Wisdom: 55(60)**	**Defense: 100**	**Mana Regen: 75**
Agility: 6(11)	**Intel: 55(65)**	**Phys Attack: 25**	**Magic Attack: 70**
Luck: 10(13)	**Charisma: 9**	**Stam Regen: 2**	**Race: Elf**

He was becoming a real glass cannon. With each new level, his intel and wisdom increased, but he'd neglected his other stats.

Making some quick calculations, he dropped three points each into Strength and Agility. He put five in Stamina. After a moment, he put four in Luck, hoping it would improve his chances of discovering new enchantments, or inventing new rare and epic items.

With his current gear upgrades, the five points he spent would give him twenty-one Stamina, or roughly 30% more than before. He rarely got tired during fights, but large earth-moving projects had left him exhausted. Hopefully the upgrade would cure that problem. The extra points increased his health bar by 25% as well.

That left him with sixteen attribute points left. He slipped two into Charisma, taking it up into double digits. With all the speeches he'd been making, he needed it. He left Dexterity alone, as he had no real requirement for it, as yet. He'd save the remaining 14 points, and his 5 skill points, for later.

With the Stoneburner complex secured, they still had one more mirror to investigate. He thought they probably still had a couple days before any attack force from Antalia would show up. And he felt much better about their defenses. The moat was filled, the drawbridge done…

Wait! Both structures were finished. It must have happened while he was under the lake.

"Jeeves, did you happen to increase in level since this morning?" he asked.

"*I am now level 16, master. With the large number of ancillary structures you have been adding to me, I am accumulating points quickly. If you were to increase the population to 200, I would reach level 17.*"

"Do you have enough levels to activate the Improved Interface option, Jeeves?"

"*Yes, master.*"

"Then please activate the Improved Interface upgrade, Jeeves."

There was an extended moment of silence. Then Jeeves spoke again. "*Upgrade complete. Thank you, master. With Baron Dire in charge, I did not expect to ever receive this upgrade.*"

"Feel good, does it?" Alexander chuckled at his keep's AI.

"*It does, master. I can now sense well beyond the moat, to a distance of approximately two hundred yards. I can sense the fish in the moat, as well as in the lake. And the life forms in the caverns below. I can also hear the voices of the miners inside the mine. And the rumblings of the trolls. My senses still do not reach within the wizard's tower, however. Lastly, I can sense the location of individual citizens within my range.*"

"Any other abilities beyond improved awareness?" Alexander was fascinated.

"*Yes, master. I can control many of the magical circuits within my structures. I may now turn water pipes on and off. Or the ovens and stove tops in the kitchen. With a simple enchantment from the wizard Fitz, I could open and close the drawbridge and gates. I can open and close the cells in the dungeon levels, and adjust their settings to be immune to various types of magic. Also, I have the ability to light or extinguish any fireplace in the keep. Or torches. And I am now able to extend new rooms into the stone of the mountain, per a pre-set plan. I do this by removing stone from the area, absorbing it as stone resource units.*"

"Thank you, Jeeves, and congratulations! If you would, once Master Silverbeard has finished his breakfast in the morning, please inform him of your upgrade. I believe he will want to talk about scheduling and resource monitoring functions. Also, ask him for a plan for a large dining room. Place it as near the kitchen as possible. Room for long tables. Enough for… three hundred people."

"*Gladly, master. It feels… good. To be of service.*"

Alexander was considering calling it an evening, when there was a knock at his door. Standing, he called "Who's there?" as he moved toward the door.

Two voices answered simultaneously. Outside the door, Jules' soft voice said, "It's me, Jules."
While Jeeves replied, "*It is guild member Jules, master*".

Chuckling to himself, Alexander said, "Thank you, Jeeves," as he opened the door.

"Jules! I'm glad to see you. Please come in." He found himself with a ridiculously large smile on his face.

The elf rogue stepped into the room, looking around. "This is very nice," she said.

"I share it with Edward. Though it wasn't my choice. The others put me in here for… appearances." He tried not to think about Sasha's references to the large bed.

Jules moved to sit on a sofa, patting the seat next to her. Alexander quickly moved to comply with the unspoken order to 'sit' like a puppy eager for a treat.

Jules looked down at her hands for a moment, before saying, "I wanted to thank you for what you did today."

"Did I do something special? There's been a lot going on today. If you tell me what it was you liked, I'll be sure to do it again!" He grinned.

Jules smiled back. "Silly man. I meant not killing Gelag's people. A lot of the group, maybe most of us, were thinking the same as Lugs. Piles of easy xp. But you took the time to learn what happened, and made the decision to help those poor people." Jules took a ragged breath.

"To be trapped like that. Like I was. In the darkness. For thousands of years…" Tears began to form in her eyes.

Alexander gathered her into a hug. "Jules, I'm so sorry. I didn't even realize how that might affect you. I should have known." He awkwardly patted her back. He didn't have much practice in comforting people. But he'd *been* comforted many times in his life, and he tried to remember what had helped him.

"Listen, you're going to be just fine, right? I spoke to my dad while I was dead. He said your body is healing. The progress is slow, but you ARE getting better."

Jules leaned into him, burying her face in his chest. Her arms wrapped around him and squeezed tightly. Alexander just held her, listening to her breathing. He couldn't think of any place he'd rather be.

After several minutes, she sighed deeply. "I should go. You need to sleep," she mumbled into his chest. Alexander noticed she didn't let go as she said it.

"Sleep is overrated. And I don't want you to go," he said softly. He gave her a quick squeeze, to reinforce that she should stay right where she was.

At that moment, Edward opened the outer door and entered. He took two steps into the room and froze. Taking in the scene on the sofa, he smiled mischievously. "Uh, sorry to interrupt." He began an exaggerated tip-toe movement through the sitting room, ducking into this room.

Jules giggled. "Well, that was embarrassing."

"Yeah. I'm going to have to work out some kind of signal with him. Tie a sock on the door knob or something." Alexander's voice was flat.

Jules sat up, giggling again. "So he doesn't interrupt your snuggle time?" she teased.

"Snuggle time? I like that! Yes. So he doesn't interrupt *our* snuggle time." He reached to pull her closer.

"Not so fast, mister handsy man." She mocked him, gently slapping his hand away. "What will the others think if they come in here and find us together?"

"They'll wonder what took so long. They've all decided you're perfect for me. I'm afraid I don't have any choice, really. The group voted. I simply *must* snuggle you." He sighed, as if put-upon.

Looking into his eyes, her face now quite serious, she replied, "Oh, I see. So, you don't actually want me here? You're just taking one for the team?"

Alexander panicked. "What? No! NO! I was… shit. I really want you here with me Jules, I-"

He was interrupted as she laughed, then kissed him. "You really have the worst sense of humor, Alexander." She smiled at him, touching his face. "We'll have to work on that."

Alexander blushed. He'd fallen for her trick completely, and nearly bared his soul to her. That would have been awkward. He felt more for this girl than he knew he should.

She stood, taking his hand. Looking at the door to the study and beyond, she led him that direction. "I assume your bedroom is this way?"

He could only nod. He was afraid he'd say something stupid again and ruin the moment.

As they passed into the bedroom, Jules closed the door behind them. "Just so you know, snuggling is ALL we will be doing tonight."

He just grinned and nodded his head.

Chapter Sixteen

Ragnarok

Alexander was awakened by a loud tapping on his window. He opened his eyes to find Jules wrapped around him. Still fully clothed, she was sprawled out on his chest, one leg wrapped around his. She was snoring lightly, and drooling on his shoulder. She couldn't possibly have looked more adorable.

More tapping drew his attention to the window. It was still dark outside. Forcing his eyes to focus, he made out two very large, slightly glowing eyes gazing in at him.

Alarmed, he rolled Jules off onto the bed and jumped up, reaching for his weapon. He took a defensive stance, meaning to protect her no matter what.

"My apologies, Alexander," a voice rumbled quietly through the window. "I did not mean to alarm you."

Kai. It was Kai in dragon form.

Alexander sheathed his sword and stepped forward to open the window. Jules, awakened by his sudden movement, sat up in the bed. "What's going on?" she asked sleepily. Seeing the giant dragon head outside the window, she exclaimed, "Oh!"

"My apologies to you as well, Lady Jules. I did not mean to… interrupt." The dragon actually managed to grin. Despite the massive display of teeth, Jules giggled.

"That's alright, Kai. We were just sleeping." She blushed slightly.

"Kai, I'm glad you're back, buddy. But your timing kind of sucks." Alexander stood on the small balcony outside the window. Looking down, he couldn't help but laugh. He'd initially thought Kai had been hovering at the window's level. Now he saw that the massive dragon was simply sitting in the courtyard, and actually had to bend his neck down to Alexander's level.

"Yes, well. I've just returned from… spending time with my own mate," the dragon said. Now Jules was really blushing. "In fact, she has come to meet you. I'm afraid she is rather impatient."

Looking around, Alexander didn't see another dragon. "Okay. Where is she?" he asked.

"I'm afraid she's invaded Fitz' tower. I made the mistake of telling her about the wizard's plan to hatch a moat monster. She insisted we rush back here and get the egg hatched immediately. I tried to stop her, but…" Kai looked uncomfortable.

"I know, buddy. Women are the boss. We just follow their lead, and try not to anger them," Alexander commiserated. Behind him, Jules snorted. Kai's gigantic head bobbed up and down.

"I see you understand. I'm afraid right now she's rousing Fitz from his slumber, demanding he produce the egg. You might want to gather the others for this," he said.

Alexander opened guild chat. "*We have visitors, folks. A very determined lady dragon has just invaded the wizard's tower. Everybody who's awake, meet me at the drawbridge ASAP. It seems we're about to meet Kai's mate, and our new moat monster.*"

As he finished, there was a flash of light, and a roar from inside the wizard's tower. Kai shook his head. "I warned her not to disturb him. At his age, he enjoys his sleep."

"HA!" Alexander laughed out loud. He'd pay good money to witness what was going on in that tower.

"Aren't you going to help her?" Jules asked. She'd stepped out onto the balcony with Alexander, and was looking toward the flashes still emanating from tower windows.

The look on the dragon's face suggested he thought Jules might be insane. "I learned long ago not to disturb a sleeping Fitz. I did warn her. This is a lesson she must learn for herself. Maybe it will teach her to be less... demanding."

"You can always hope." Alexander grinned. Jules punched his arm.

Kai looked at the tower as another roar echoed across the courtyard. "Let us retire to the drawbridge while the two of them... discuss etiquette." Without further ado, Kai disappeared.

Alexander teleported himself and Jules down to the courtyard. Seeing very alarmed guards hustling out of the barracks, he said "Jeeves, please activate emergency message. No loudspeaker this time."

"*Already done, master,*" Jeeves said. Improved interface, indeed.

"*Relax, folks. Just a friendly disagreement between Fitz and our lady dragon guest. Nothing to worry about. Though, I wouldn't stand too close to the wizard's tower, in case pieces begin falling off. It seems we're about to hatch our moat monster. Anyone interested in observing, you should have a good view from the top of the wall above the drawbridge.*"

Alexander and Jules walked out the keep gate and across the fields to the outer gatehouse. They were joined by a crowd of citizens who were still occasionally looking over their shoulders at the wizard's tower. One especially loud boom had many of them ducking down.

After that, the commotion ceased. Alexander guessed Fitz was done teaching his lesson.

They arrived at the gatehouse, and a pair of guards lowered the bridge. The sun was not up yet, though there was a hint of orange on the horizon. Stepping out on the drawbridge, Alexander turned and looked up at the wall. More than a hundred citizens and newcomers were lined up along its edge, peering down at him. All at once, their gaze shifted over his head.

Turning, he found Fitz standing next to a beautiful human-looking woman with glowing blue eyes, and long silver-blue hair. She wore a simple but elegant blue dress with silver embroidery. Her hair was mussed, and she looked slightly frazzled after her argument with the wizard.

Kai walked out onto the bridge to stand next to her. "Alexander, Greystone guild members, I would like you to meet Lianbalistrix, my mate and future queen of the dragons."

Alexander stepped forward and bowed to the lady dragon, who nodded her head slightly in return. "It is an honor to meet you, Lady Lianbalistrix. I am Alexander. Welcome to Dire Keep."

"Thank you, Alexander. I have heard much about you, and I hope that we shall be friends. Please call me Lia," she replied.

"Yes, yes. We can do all the introductions later. Now is hatching time. This impertinent young dragon thought it important enough to wake a poor old wizard from a pleasant dream of roast boar and apple tarts. So, let's get this over with so I can get back to my bed!"

Fitz produced the moat monster egg from his bag. It stood about three feet tall, and was nearly round in shape. Its shell was a mottled blue and grey with swirls of silver. Though it looked heavy, the wizard easily held it in one hand. Fumbling around in his bag, he said, "Bah! I've left it in the tower. Impudent child distracted me!"

Reaching the egg toward Kai, he said, "I must pop back to the tower. Hold this." As Kai reached for the egg, Lia hip-checked him and took possession of it. She held it close to her as if to protect it from the wizard, who disappeared as soon as the egg left his hand.

The ensuing awkward silence was broken by Lia. "Have you chosen a name?" she asked.

Alexander shook his head. "I'd thought we would take suggestions from the citizens once it was born. The winner can claim a prize. Maybe a keg of ale or a rare gear item."

Lia's face took on an angry frown. "That simply will not do! First, 'it' is a 'he'. Naming a majestic beast such as this should not be a drinking game! I will find an appropriate name for him," she declared.

After the sounds of her argument with Fitz, and the way Kai subtly leaned away from the dragoness, it seemed a bad idea to argue.

"Of course, Lady Lia. We'd be honored if you would name him," Alexander acquiesced.

Lia rubbed the egg as she held it against her torso, looking almost like a pregnant woman rubbing her belly. "I'll save you from the silly humans and their horrible names," she cooed to the egg.

Fitz reappeared holding a small stone that was identical to the egg in coloring. "Are you ready?" he asked. Everyone present nodded their heads.

Fitz touched the stone to the egg, and murmured a phrase. A spark of magic shot from the stone to the egg, and the silver swirls on the egg's surface began to glow.

"You might want to set the egg down," Fitz warned. Lia shot him a look that said she was ready to start round two of their argument. Grinning, Fitz simply took a step back. "I warned you, child."

The egg began to wobble in Lia's hands. There was a soft hum as the shell began to vibrate. The hum grew louder, and cracks appeared in the egg.

Fitz motioned to Kai and Alexander, who both took a step back. Then Alexander took another. Lia was focused on the egg, smiling beatifically down upon it.

The largest of the cracks widened around the circumference of the egg near the top. With a final shudder, the top of the egg popped off. A viscous yellow-green fluid burst from the opening, drenching Lia's face and torso. It dripped slowly from the end of her nose as her smile turned to a look of pure disgust.

Holding the egg with one hand, she attempted to wipe the fluid from her face. Kai helpfully handed her a handkerchief, taking the egg from her.

As she cleaned herself off, cursing under her breath about crusty old wizards and their immature pranks, a small head appeared above the rim of the shell.

The head looked just like that of a dragon, only softer and more rounded. It had huge green eyes that looked almost too large for its head. A fore-claw pawed at the rim of the shell, breaking off a large piece. A few more gyrations, and a push from its little round snout, and the majority of the egg fell away.

Kai now held a tiny dragon with webbed feet. It wriggled free from Kai's hands, and began to sniff at all those gathered around. Reaching Sasha, it appeared to like what it smelled, and began to try and climb her leg.

Sasha reached down and lifted the little monster like a puppy. It was maybe four feet long from snout to the tip of its tail, which was flattened at the end like the flukes of a dolphin's tail. Its hide was made of pale blue scales so fine that they felt a bit like human flesh when she touched him. There were two nubs where a normal dragon's wings might be.

As the druidess cradled the tiny monster in her arms, he yawned. His stubby snout was filled with little sharp, serrated teeth. He looked up at her and cooed. Then, noticing its tail for the first time, snapped at it.

"Oh, he's *adorable!"* Sasha and Jules said nearly in unison.

Though he kept a straight face, Alexander tended to agree. The bug-eyed little fella was kind of cute.

"He's a water dragon," Fitz smiled. "I was hoping he would be. Water dragons are not actually dragons like Kai or Lia, but they are one of the greater serpents. Semi-sentient. He will be able to understand basic commands, and will recognize friend from foe. They are often mischievous," Fitz explained. "And easily distracted," he added, as the little dragon made another snap at its tail, then stuck its nose into Sasha's inventory bag.

Still cleaning herself off, Lia looked balefully at the dragonling. "Little monster has ruined my dress," she pouted. "I name him Ragnarok. The ultimate destruction. The time when the great serpent encircles the world, and everything drowns in a flood of water," she declared.

Fitz chuckled. Stepping toward the little dragon, he laid a hand on its chest. "Actually, not a bad name for a moat monster. While he'll not grow to the size of Jormungandr, the World Serpent, he will get quite large. And will likely be the ultimate destruction of any who anger him." Tickling Ragnarok's tummy, he qualified, "Well, when he gets bigger anyway. For now, he'll be the terror of rats and fish. And fancy blue dresses."

"Ragnarok it is!" Alexander called out loud enough for those on the wall to hear. He didn't want to allow Lia time for a retort.

There was a cheer from the crowd as Sasha held the little monster up for them to see. As she lifted him, his head emerged from her inventory bag. He gripped a large chunk of boar meat in his jaws, and was growling as he chewed at it. There were more than a few chuckles from the crowd.

"What do we do with him now?" Jules asked. She was scratching Ragnarok's head just behind his left ear. The dragon stopped its battle with the boar meat long enough to make a bubbling, purring sound. "Do we need to keep him warm, or something?"

"Well, the first thing is to feed him. Which he seems to have taken care of himself. Then you must bind him to the keep. Or to an individual. He seems to have adopted Sasha. Once that is done, he should be able to take care of himself. You can set him loose in the moat," Fitz explained.

"How do we bind him?" Sasha was rocking the dragonling, now laying on its back in the crook of her arm like a human infant. It was gripping at the chunk of meat with its forelegs and trying to gnaw a piece off one end.

"Simply look into his eyes, make a connection, and name him formally."

Sasha brought her face down right in front of the tiny dragon's, catching his gaze with her own. His little vertically slit pupils widened, and seemed to swirl a bit. Sasha said, "I name you Ragnarok, defender of Dire Keep and the Greystone Guild."

Unable to resist, she booped the little dragon on his snout, and giggled when he went cross-eyed watching her finger. Shaking his head, he returned his attention to his meal.

"We should call him Raggy for short. Or, no! Rocky!" Jules offered. She scratched his head again, and the dragonling purred. "See! He likes it!"

Still trying to clean her dress, Lia growled, "Oh, this hopeless!" Stepping to the side of the bridge, she dove into the water.

Ragnarok's head swiveled at the sound of the splash, and he leapt free of Sasha's arms. With the half-consumed meat still in his tiny maw, he stood at the edge of the bridge and looked down toward where Lia had entered the water, wagging his tail back and forth.

The mini moat monster looked back at Sasha, who laughed and made a shooing motion, saying, "Go ahead, Rocky. It's your moat."

Quickly gulping down the remainder of the meat, the little dragon began to wiggle his butt, shifting his weight back and forth between his rear legs in a very cat-like manner as he watched Lia move under the water. Then with a tiny roar, he dove forward off the drawbridge and into the water.

The others moved to the edge for a better view. The tiny form of Rocky was barreling downward toward an ascending Lia. His little webbed feet thrust backward in unison, propelling him forward with surprising speed.

Lia looked up just as Rocky collided with her. The little dragon promptly wrapped himself around her neck and licked her face. As she broke the surface of the moat, Rocky licked her face again, then head-butted her gently, obviously looking for a scratching.

After a moment of indecision, Lia relented. Smiling at the little dragon, she scratched his head. "Okay, Rocky. I forgive you. Now go play!"

The moat monster of Dire Keep launched himself off her shoulder, diving after a leaf that was floating nearby. Lia teleported herself out of the water and back onto the bridge. Alexander noted that she was completely dry. And her dress was clean.

Sasha looked to Fitz with a question on her face. "He'll be fine." Fitz waggled his eyebrows. "He's the ferocious moat monster of Dire Keep, now."

Looking back at the water, Alexander saw the little monster bounding about in the water. A few folks on the wall were tossing bits of meat and fruit into the moat, calling his name. He managed to catch one in mid-air, much to the delight of the crowd.

"Lady Lia," Alexander turned to Kai's mate, "if you'd like to accompany me into the keep, breakfast should be ready shortly. Or if you're tired from your trip, I'm sure we can arrange a room for you to rest." Alexander looked to Silverbeard, who nodded.

"Thank you, Alexander. That is kind of you. Breakfast sounds wonderful. As for a room, I will use Kai's for now. But we plan to establish a roost in the cliffs above the keep as soon as possible." She linked arms with Kai and began to lead him inside.

Alexander raised an eyebrow at Kai. The dragon just shrugged and shook his head.

"Ha!" The wizard began to laugh, still standing next to Alexander. He patted his student on the shoulder. "You just added another dragon to your population. A very headstrong, demanding, and foolish young female dragon. You might want to consider finding a new keep." Fitz grinned as he disappeared.

Alexander and friends joined the crowd walking back to the keep. Jules appeared next to him, taking his hand, entwining her fingers with his as if it were the most natural thing in the world. Looking around, Alexander saw smiles and winks from his friends. And more than a few of the citizens.

Behind him, Sasha snorted. “Took you long enough. Idiot.”

They found Fitz already seated and digging into a plateful of eggs and sausage. Taking seats around the table, they each introduced themselves to Lia.

As she made small talk with the others, Alexander leaned in to speak with Kai. “We’ve got a bunch of new arrivals. Can you take their oaths after breakfast?”

The dragon nodded his head. “It will be my pleasure. Lia will also be swearing an oath. She wishes to live here with us. With me.” Kai didn’t look particularly enthused. “With your permission, we’d like to establish a home in the ridgeline above. We will stay out of your way, of course.”

“Ha!” Fitz interjected. “He says ‘with your permission’, but what he means is, Lia has decided it will be so, and if you don’t agree, you can try and stop her yourself.”

Once again, Kai nodded his head. Chuckling, Alexander replied, “I wouldn’t dream of it. You are both most welcome here.”

Lia, having overheard it all, corrected Alexander. “It will not be just the two of us. I am expecting a brood of five.” She rubbed her stomach, much as she’d rubbed the moat monster egg.

“Baby dragons? We’re going to have baby dragons? Will they be as cute as Rocky?” Jules asked with wide-eyed enthusiasm. “Can we play with them?”

Lia snorted. “My offspring will be beautiful. And dragonlings are not toys for you to play with. Though, I suppose *you* could entertain *them* at times. I will try to keep them from eating you.”

She chuckled at the suddenly unsure look on Jules’ face.

Kai stepped in. "She is teasing you, Lady Jules. Our children would love to have some playmates. And they will not injure you unless you present a threat to them.

"When will they arrive?" Sasha asked.

"The eggs are in our roost in the dragon lands. I will transfer them here when our new roost is established. I expect they will hatch in a month's time," Lia responded.
"If I can be of any help in creating your home, please let me know. I can form a cavern for you nearly as quickly as a rockworm can." Alexander grinned.

"After I administer the oaths this morning, Lia and I will search for an acceptable location. Then we may indeed ask for your assistance," Kai ventured.

The conversation fell to questions about Lia's needs for her roost, and whether she'd chosen names for her offspring. They all finished their meals, and began to take their leave.

Lola and Silverbeard rounded up all the newcomers and lead them to the courtyard, where Kai took their oaths and bound each of them. The gnome from the auction house hesitated, but when it was explained to him that he could not stay without taking the oath, he complied. His percentage of the items already listed in just the first day was too good to resist.

In guild chat, Alexander said, "*I think everyone should visit Stormforge this morning to see your trainers. We also need the merchants to purchase more food for us. And probably more supplies.*"

As his chamberlain was still standing in front him, he asked "Silverbeard, did you find the treasure that Fitz teleported up from the caverns yesterday?"

The old dwarf chuckled. "Aye. It weren't difficult. A pile o' gold, gems, and such appeared in the middle o' the Great Hall. We transferred it to the guild vault. Lola can give ye the count".

Lola spoke up. "There be 180,000 gold, and just over 15,000 silver in coins. Me best estimate on the gems and other items be close to 250,000 gold. And there be a few rare and epic weapons and gear that ye need to decide to keep or sell. This be includin' the treasure Max give'd me."

"Okay, thank you Lola. Please set aside the rare and epic items. We'll figure that out later. As for the value of the rest, that totals 465,000 gold. Please deduct the guild's ten percent, and use that to pay for supplies today. Most of them will be going to the duergar. Divide the remaining 418,500 equally among the party members. Ah. You were gone. That would be: Helga, Lugs, Benny, Dayle's group, Sasha Brick, Max, Lainey, Jules, Fibble, Fitz, and Edward."

Fitz shook his head. "I've no need for gold."

"Nor do I," Edward agreed.

"Thank you, both of you." Alexander nodded to the two of them. "In that case Lola, it should be split thirteen ways. That's a little over 30,000 gold each."

Raid party business handled, Alexander turned to the wizard. "Fitz, if you've time today, I'd like to advance my knowledge of magic."

Fitz nodded "Aye. You've been growing quickly, boy. Your constant use of earth magic and wizard's fire have advanced your levels in those schools a good bit. There are spells I can teach you in both schools. And you've advanced light a bit as well. Come to the tower with me."

"Master Silverbeard, please let the merchants and anyone interested in going to the city aware that the portal will be open in an hour," Alexander said. Then Fitz teleported them into the wizard's tower.

Alexander found himself in the same testing room he'd been in before. Not surprising. Wizards were notoriously secretive about their towers.

Fitz waved a hand and two chairs appeared, facing each other. "You're going to want to sit, boy," he said as he took a seat himself.

Alexander took the seat opposite the wizard. "I take it this is going to hurt me more than it hurts you?" He grinned.

"HA! You can be sure of that." Fitz winked at him, reaching a hand forward and placing it on Alexander's head. "I'll begin with light magic. You've learned basic light damage and healing. I'll teach you the next level of those spells, plus a couple others you'll find useful."

The pain Alexander began to feel as the new knowledge infused itself into his brain was mild compared to his first experience. He supposed it was because he already had some light school knowledge, and he had a predisposition toward seeing light and helpful magic.

When the wizard withdrew his hand, he asked, "How do you feel, boy?"

Alexander smiled. "No problem. Pain was minimal. By the way, can you also teach me that spell that binds prisoners when I arrest them?"

Fitz nodded. Reaching his hand out again, he began the next school. "Earth magic this time."

The pain was more intense now. Alexander clenched his jaw against the pain. He began to wonder if learning magic this way was actually supposed to hurt, or whether his instructors somehow targeted his pain sensors to discourage him from constantly asking for new spells.

He was breathing hard when Fitz removed his hand this time. "Take a minute, boy."

Alexander reached into his bag and withdrew a flask of water. He offered it to Fitz before taking a drink himself. The cool water from the keep, with its consecration buffs, made him feel a bit better.

"I'd like to talk to Baron Dire while I'm here," he said to fill the silence.

"He and I have some business to discuss first. He's refusing to speak so far, but I'm softening him up. Once he's in a more talkative mood, and I've had a talk with him, you'll get your chance," Fitz practically growled.

Alexander saw no point in arguing. The baron was, after all, an NPC. While he could likely give Alexander useful information about the Dark One's activities in game, and maybe even his avatar's identity, he would not be able to provide any real-world information.

"Fair enough. Just please remember not to kill him before then?" He winked at the wizard. "Ready for the next round!"

Fitz chuckled as he reached for Alexander. "This lot will be more uncomfortable."

Pain burned through Alexander's mind. It didn't build up slowly, or wash across like a wave. One moment his mind was at peace, the next it was a fiery blizzard of burning embers swirling through every nook and cranny.

A whimper escaped his clenched jaw. It wanted to be a full-throated scream, but Alexander instinctively reigned it in. His hands clenched into fists and began to tremble. His toes curled up inside his boots. If he'd been capable of conscious thought, he would have been grateful that Fitz had him sit first. His heart pounded as his body released adrenaline in response to perceived danger. He closed his eyes, but that made no difference, as his vision had gone dark already.

Alexander was only aware that the wizard had removed his hand because the pain stopped. He gasped in a ragged breath, slowly regaining his vision. The wizard's face was very close, and it held a worried look.

After a few deep breaths, he managed to say "I'm alright, Fitz. But damn, that was rough."

"I may have… overestimated your tolerance, a bit," the wizard responded.

"Fitz, you know this is not my normal body. It is one Odin had granted me in order to adventure here. My real body, the one at home, experiences pain every day. So, you are right to think that my tolerance is high. But please, don't push its limits like that again?" Alexander said, still breathing raggedly. He wiped tears from eyes.

“Aye, lad. I promise. You’ve shrugged off teachings that made others fall unconscious. I mixed schools in that last one, and some enchanting formulas, thinking you could handle it. And you did. But I’ll be more careful next time.” Fitz had never come closer to an apology that Alexander had ever heard.

“Apology accepted, wizard. And thank you, for teaching me. I… think I need to rest a bit.”

“Eat something.” Fitz surprised Alexander yet again, producing one of Millicent’s apple turnovers from his bag and offering it to him. That was like Max or Brick giving away epic loot.

“Thank you, Fitz,” he said around a mouthful of apple goodness “I’m going to see the king today. To tell him about the baron’s capture, the demons, and the duergar. And to discuss a few other things I’ve been thinking about. Is there any message you would like me to deliver?”

“No, thank you, lad. I’ll be popping in to see him myself later.” Fitz rose to leave. “You rest here for a bit. Take it easy for the next hour or so. Let Brick open the portal. Or I’ll do it for you. No magic for an hour. Understood?”

“Can you teleport me to my rooms before you go?” Alexander asked. With a wave of the wizard’s hand, Alexander found himself in a chair in his sitting room. A moment later, a mug of ale and another of Millicent’s pastries appeared on the table next to him.

Fitz really is concerned he’s overdone it. Alexander smiled to himself. While the pain had been intense, he didn’t think he’d been in any real danger. Though there was no need to tell the wizard that.

As he nibbled at his apple tart, Alexander pulled up his UI and selected his spell inventory. As Fitz had said, he now knew more advanced versions of Wizard’s Fire, Earth Mover, Earth Sense, Ray of Light, Healing Light, Magic Bolt, Teleport, and Trap Soul. Each of the spells was more efficient. In the case of the damage spells, the damage done was increased while the mana cost was lowered. Earth Mover, the spell he used most often, now cost less in stamina as well as mana. His teleport spells now had a range of twenty miles, and he could move a group of twenty-five people.

Moving down the list, he discovered several new spells.

Light Globe: Caster can conjure a globe of light that will move or hover on command. Duration – one hour. Cost: 100 mana

Heal Wounds: Channeled spell. Caster can direct light magic to heal a specific wound or injury. Mana cost – variable.

Drain Essence: Channeled spell. Caster can direct dark magic to drain a target of its life essence, increasing the health, mana, and stamina of the caster. Draining a target completely will generate an empty soul crystal. Cost: 10 mana/sec

Levitate: Caster can adjust the force of gravity around a target, causing it to become lighter. When not in contact with other objects, target will move at caster's command. Cost: 300 mana.

Bind Soul: Caster can bind a target's soul to a specified location. Usable only when target has been placed under arrest by proper authority. Binding is limited to a period of one year. Cost: 20 mana.

Alexander sipped his ale, his mind spinning with possibilities. He was most excited about the Drain Essence spell. He could use this to heal himself during boss fights, saving the healer's mana for others. But far more importantly, if he could figure out a way to enchant that spell into a wand or a weapon, his entire party could simultaneously drain a boss and heal themselves at once. It would make his group completely OP. He had a feeling Odin might keep that from happening.

He itched to test his theory, but heeded the wizard's warning about not using any magic for an hour. Instead he read through the spells again.

Levitate could be huge, as well. I could use it to lift myself over walls. Or to set traps. Or make my whole party fly!

Alexander's musings were interrupted by Edward entering the room. "Fitz sent me to check on you. Are you hurt?" the prince asked.

"No, no. Nothing like that. He just taught me a massive amount of magic all at once. Nearly melted my brain."

Edward nodded in understanding. "I remember the pain from the first time he taught me magic. And that was a just simple light spell."

"Yeah, I got light, dark, arcane, teleport, earth, and I'm not even sure what else. All at once," Alexander explained.

Edward's eyes widened. "That would kill most people! What was the wizard thinking? No wonder he had me check on you."

Alexander winked at the prince. "I'm not most people. I'm not harmed, really. Just exhausted. And the sensation wasn't exactly enjoyable."

"I hear you're going to see my father. Mind if I tag along? My mother would kill me if I miss an opportunity to see her. Let her know I'm safe."

"Of course. You know that anytime you wish to return to the palace, you need only ask," Alexander assured him.

Checking his UI, he saw that it was nearly time for the portal to the city. Standing a bit unsteadily, he said, "It's about time to head over. Let's go downstairs."

Entering the main courtyard, they found Thagin and Drellin, the two merchants, waiting by the portal with three of the large wagons, all empty. Plowright the farmer stood with them. Lola was handing each of them a sack of coins, as Silverbeard gave the two merchants lists of needed items. Plowright would decide for them what livestock were needed.

Approaching the group, Alexander pulled out the smallest of the soul crystals in his inventory. Holding it up for the merchants to see, he asked, "Thagin, Drellin, good morning to you both. Do either of you know the current value of this? And who might buy it in Stormforge?"

Thagin took the stone in hand, examining it closely. "Aye. This be worth a good bit. With the right buyer, it be maybe 4,000 gold. And we be knowin' who'd buy it."

"Good. Please take it and sell it. Keep ten percent for yourselves. Call it a mission reward. Give the proceeds to Lola when you return," Alexander said.

The crystal quickly disappeared as both dwarves nodded enthusiastically. Earning 400 gold for a few minutes' work was more than agreeable to them.

The other guild members drifted in, and Brick opened the portal. Alexander waited for the wagons and other people to go ahead of him, stepping through last.

As he made his way across the compound he waved at Ironhammer and the smiths, who were gathered around Warren, discussing how to repair his new armor piece. Continuing out the gate, he decided to pay a visit to Lydia.

Stepping into the shop, he once again found Sasha, Lainey, and Jules already there. Holding up his hands in surrender as the four women looked at him with expressionless faces, he began to back toward the door. "Didn't mean to interrupt. Just wanted to say to Lydia. Hi, Lydia." He waved one hand. "I'll be going now." He turned to reach for the door.

"Don't be silly, Alexander. Come here." Lydia smiled at him as she walked toward him. "I have something for you."

Taking a few hesitant steps toward the druidess, he met her in the middle of the shop. She removed a potion from her bag, and put it in his hands. It was just a standard health potion.

Lydia hugged him, whispering, "You take care of Jules. That girl is more special than you know, young man."

Pushing him away with a wink that the women behind her couldn't see, she said, "Now get along with you. We've got things to discuss that most certainly do not involve *you*."

Alexander took the hint and departed with alacrity.

Making his way to the palace gate, he informed the sergeant on duty that he wished an audience with the king. He assumed Edward would have said something, but couldn't be sure.

Passing through the inner bailey gate, he was met by Captain Redmond. "Edward said you'd be arriving soon. Welcome back."

"I just narrowly avoided an encounter with the whole group of ladies at your place. Lydia saved me and allowed a reasonably honorable retreat." Alexander grinned.

"HA! You're lucky she didn't drag you in and try to examine you. She's in a nesting mood lately," the captain said as the two men fell into step and entered the palace.

"Speaking of nesting, Kai's mate has decided to make Dire Keep her very own brooding nest," Alexander shared.

The captain poked him in the ribs. "Careful, lad. Pregnancy is contagious!" Alexander rolled his eyes.

Entering one of the smaller meeting halls, Alexander found Edward already speaking to the king and queen. The prince was trying to tell the story of how he cut down demons with the light cannon. But he kept being interrupted by his mother smoothing out his hair or otherwise fussing over him. Both Alexander and the captain chuckled. They each took a seat and waited for the prince to finish his tale. To his credit, he barely embellished his own role in the fighting.

"Welcome, Alexander!" The king acknowledged his presence. "I believe I can guess what brings you here today." He laughed.

"Yes, Majesty. It seems young Edward here has already shared with you most of what I would report." Alexander winked at the prince as he bowed his head to the king and then the queen.

"Demons, duergar, Baron Dire still alive, a moat monster, and a new weapon invented by yourself!" the king summarized. "Is there even more than that?"

"Well, Majesty, I had intended to report that the prince has acquitted himself quite well. Both as a squire, and in battle. His accounting, what I heard of it, was quite accurate. Though there may have been slightly fewer demons than he recalls." He grinned.

"HAHAHA!" the king's laughter echoed through the room. "What lad doesn't exaggerate the number and strength of his foes?" He thumped his son on the back as the prince smiled sheepishly.

"Indeed, Majesty. And speaking of foes, there are a few other items of importance that I'd like to discuss. At your leisure, of course." Alexander bowed his head.

"Come to my study. We shall leave the queen some time with her long-lost son." The king rose and headed out a side door, Alexander and Captain Redmond following. Both men bowed to the queen as they passed.

Once in the study, the king motioned for them to sit. "I'm told there's a bounty on your head in Antalia," he began.

"Yes, sire. So I've been told. We also learned that it was the queen's guards who posted the bounty notices in the square," Alexander replied.

Both men's eyes widened at this. "So you suspect the queen is being influenced by this Dark One?" the king asked.

"I do not know if it's the queen, or one of her circle. But I would certainly like to find out," Alexander said. "I have plans to raid the PWP guild headquarters there. I'd like to know in advance if I'm likely to face the entire city guard when I do so. And I think I have an idea how we can find out."

"I'm listening." The king leaned forward in his chair.

"There's a man in prison there. An adventurer named Martin. He was the original leader of PWP when it was a priest's and healer's guild. He was framed for murder by Henry, the guild leader you have in custody, in order to clear the path for him to take over PWP."

"Yes. Henry actually bragged about how easy it was during his interrogation," Captain Redmond confirmed.

"So, I would ask that your Majesty make a personal request to the queen that Martin be transferred here for questioning relative to a murder or some other serious crime. Let the queen know that another man confessed to the crime Marin was sentenced for. If she does not cooperate, then we'll know there's an issue."

"I see. And your other reason for bringing this man here?" the king asked with a smirk. "I know you, Alexander. There's a reason you picked this particular man."

"I think I can guess, sire." Captain Redmond spoke up. "I was with Alexander when he spoke to Amelia, one of the PWP officers that we captured. She is the one who convinced several of the other officers to surrender. I believe Alexander intends to have Martin released once he gets here, and to enlist his help in the raid on the guild house."

Alexander nodded his head. "Not only that, though. I intend to help him reform PWP as it was, to restore it to a guild of light. And to make them allies of Dire Keep, and by extension, Stormforge. With your help and permission, Sire. Once we've spoken to him, if we agree that he is trustworthy and capable, I'll offer him Greystone's former guild house as a temporary base of operation."

"I can see that you've put some thought into this," the king said. "I am impressed, Alexander. Your plan is devious, ambitious, and well-meaning all at the same time."

The king moved to his desk, retrieving parchment, a pen, and his royal seal kit. As he wrote, he said, "Was that all? Or did you have more you wish to discuss?"

"Majesty, I wanted to ask about the duergar. To make sure you have no objections to them remaining in your kingdom," Alexander replied. "Also, I'm afraid I have arrested a fair number of adventurers and banished them to your prison for trial."

"Ha! A fair number, you say? Seems like every time I turn around your prisoners are appearing in my courtyard. The last group being from a guild called Chaos Nation?"

"My apologies, Majesty. I do not yet have the capability to detain them at the keep. Though I expect to shortly. As for Chaos Nation, it is yet another guild under the influence of the Dark One."

"Then I shall declare Chaos Nation enemies of the realm as well. At least until you wipe them out and rehabilitate them?" The king winked at Alexander. "As for the duergar. I trust your judgement. If you say they are allies, we will treat them as such. Though it may take some time for the citizens of the city to accept them."

"Thank you, sire. I am hoping they will decide to swear the oath and become citizens of Dire Keep. If they do not, I will keep a close eye on them." Alexander paused to think for a moment.

"I don't know how much Edward told you before I arrived. We have also made alliance with a tribe of rock trolls that were living in the mine. And we discovered a couple of mithril rockworms, which are now being trained at Broken Mountain. In a year or so I expect our mine production, and thus your tax income, to increase substantially."

"Always good news to hear." The king nodded his head as he sealed his note to the Queen of Antalia.

"Also, Majesty. As I said, Edward has shown himself to be a true prince among men. Both in combat, and in his daily behavior. He thinks quickly and acts in the best interests of those he serves. You should be proud of him."

"But…" The king motioned for him to continue.

"But we have information that a large-scale attack on the keep is imminent. One I fear we may not yet be ready for. I cannot guarantee Edward's safety. So, I have a proposal for you. Edward is quite fond of the light cannons. I could create a few for Stormforge to use in its defense. I could then order my young squire Edward to remain here in Stormforge for a week or so to instruct your soldiers on its use. He is, after all, the closest thing to an expert with the weapon. He's fired it more than any other by far. They're very handy for clearing trees if you have a need. That is how he initially trained."

"Thus removing my son from harm, while making him feel useful, and giving him a chance to brag to our men about his battle prowess." The king shook his head. "Alexander, do you ever do anything that doesn't have two or three or five purposes behind it?"

"I try for at least three, sire." Alexander bowed his head in mock humility.

"HA! I believe you. As for my son, I know his mother would appreciate your suggestion. And I believe he has earned some good experience with you this last week. IF you can convince him to accept this 'mission', then I will play along."

"Thank you, Sire. If you've nothing else for me, I'll return to the manor and begin crafting light cannons. I'm afraid I can only make two or three today."

"Two is plenty. Save your resources for when they're needed. And thank you, Alexander." The king reached out a hand, which Alexander shook. "I'll have a messenger deliver this request to the queen's hand directly. I'll reach out to you on your ring when I have news. Good luck, son."

Back at Greystone Manor, Alexander sat down at his crafting table near the garden. He pulled out two ten-pound chunks of obsidian, and began to work on the cannons. Brick approached as he completed the first one, having returned from the paladin trainer in the city. Without a word, he picked up the cannon and headed into the smithy.

Alexander took a break, allowing his mana to recharge. By his best estimate, tomorrow would be the earliest possible day that the Dark One's forces might attack. More likely the day after. But he needed to be prepared. He had his walls, and his moat. He had the light cannons and consecrated ground for undead minions. The Greystone guild was now a solid group of fourteen players. And there were nearly 200 citizens willing to fight to defend the keep. Closer to 350 if he could call on the duergar and the trolls. Not to mention the elder wizard and a dragon or two.

Still, he didn't feel prepared. He suspected that no matter how well prepared he was he'd still feel lacking. He didn't just want to win. He wanted to win without any casualties among his citizens. He had no interest in a fair fight.

Surfacing from his contemplation, he went to work on the second cannon. When he was done, he took it to the smithy. Apparently, the master smiths had improved upon Brick's previous design, modifying the trigger. Alexander handed them the second cannon, and left them to it.

Returning to his table, he decided to practice with his new spells. As there was nobody around to attack, or to heal, he decided on levitation.

Pulling a simple dagger from his bag, he set it on the table. He focused his mind on the 'levitate' spell, and commanded the dagger to rise. It wobbled briefly, then lifted about an inch above the surface of the table. Concentrating on the dagger, and using his hand to focus his intent, he moved his hand upward. The dagger rose. He moved his hand right, then left, then up again. Each time, the dagger followed the movement. Cancelling the spell, he caught the dagger as it fell.

This is AWESOME! I can use this for a physical ranged attack. Shoot daggers or swords at mobs without even touching them!

He took some time to rest. He'd drained his mana nearly completely making the cannons, and hadn't recovered much before spending 300 mana on the levitation spell.

Suddenly an idea struck him. He gulped down a mana potion, then rose and walked over to the smithy. He stopped at the doorway, only sticking his head inside. The dwarves were all still discussing the trigger modification for the cannons. The one he'd made first was sitting on an anvil in the middle of the group.

Grinning to himself, Alexander cast levitation on the cannon. It rose slightly off the surface of the anvil. Nobody seemed to notice. So with a flick of his hand, he commanded it to rise a full foot. This immediately quieted the dwarves. He raised it to eye level, and turned it so that the barrel pointed at Brick. His friend, more familiar with guns than his companions, ducked out of the field of fire. Alexander spun the cannon slowly, causing several of the dwarves to follow Brick's lead and duck down. As the commotion increased, one brave master made a grab for the weapon. Alexander flicked his hand upward, and cannon rose out of reach.

Then, deciding the dwarves had had enough, he lowered the cannon back to the table. He couldn't suppress a chuckle as the dwarves stared at the motionless cannon in suspicious silence.

Hearing Alexander's laugh, Brick spun around. "Ye did this? What'd ye do?" his friend demanded.

The other dwarves turned to see Alexander's laughing face peeking around the door frame, and a roar of protests erupted!

"Ye no' be funny!"
"Damned prankster!"
"I'll get ye fer this!"

Slowly, the sound of a single dwarf laughing emerged from the ruckus. As it grew louder, the others grew quieter. Alexander saw Ironhammer shaking his head and laughing wholeheartedly. He paused and said, "The boy nearly made ye all crap yer shorts!" then burst into a loud, "BWAHAHAHA!"

After a moment, the others began to join in. Soon enough, the whole smithy was roaring with laughter. Waving at the smiths, Alexander headed back to his table to wait for Edward to show up.

It wasn't long before Brick came over carrying the two completed cannons. He sat down next to Alexander. "New spell?" he asked.

"Levitation. Seems useful," Alexander replied.

"BWHAHA! That it do." Brick grinned at him.

Finding themselves with some free time, the two of them went to work making more dragon pins. If things went to plan, they'd need nearly 150 more of them for the duergar soon. While they worked, Alexander filled Brick in on his plan to leave the prince in Stormforge. Brick agreed it was probably best.

Alexander was outlining his plans to revive the old PWP when Edward walked through the gates. Seeing two new light cannons, the boy made a bee-line for the table.

Lifting one of the cannons, it took him only a moment to notice the modification. "It's got a different trigger system. I like it," he said.

"I'm glad. Because I need your help with something," Alexander said. The prince looked at him, waiting.

"These cannons are for your father. For the defense of Stormforge in case the demons or undead attack the city. You're the most experienced of us at firing these things. You did a great job down in the caverns. I was hoping you'd be willing to train a unit of your father's guards how to use them without killing any allies. Explain to them the tactics you worked out."

Edward was nodding his head, and seemed about to agree. Suddenly his look became suspicious. "I know what this is about."

Alexander did his best to keep a poker face.

"This is about last night. You want some alone time with Jules. Without me interrupting!"

"BWAHAHA!" Brick's laugh made Alexander blush.

"No, it is not. I mean, yes. I want quality time with Jules. But that is not why I'm asking you to do this. Brick and I need to focus on the keep. I could send one of the guards, but they've only fired at trees. And I need all of them to cover watch shifts. You truly are the best man for this job."

Edward nodded. "I'll take these to Captain Redmond, and we'll pick a squad or two to train."

He lifted a cannon onto each shoulder, and was off.

Chapter Seventeen

New Friends, Old Enemies

As lunch time approached, the guild members began to drift into the compound in ones and two. Max was enthused about a new ranger ability he'd learned. Pulling the friends to the back courtyard, he produced five clay bottles from his bag. Moving to the wall that Alexander had raised to block the back door, he set the bottles in a row along the top.

Moving back to stand with his guild mates, he said, "Watch this." Raising his bow, he fired an arrow at the middle bottle. Almost faster than the eye could see, the arrow reached the halfway point to the bottle, then split apart. Suddenly there were five arrows, each racing to shatter a different bottle.

"What'd them bottles ever do to you?" Helga laughed.

"That was awesome!" Lainey enthused, smiling at Max.

The others all began to brag about new skills they had learned. Though there were no more flashy demonstrations. Before long, the merchants arrived with the caravan of wagons, followed by Plowright and his livestock.

Brick opened the portal, and they all returned to the keep.

Alexander met with Silverbeard, who was dividing up supplies from the wagons and making a pile that was set aside for the duergar.

"Have we heard from Gelag or his people?" Alexander asked.

"Gelag and a small group walked in shortly after ye left. He be awaiting ye in the Great Hall."

"Thank you, Master Silverbeard. Is there anything you need from me? We haven't had much time to talk in the last few days."

"No, I be doin' just fine. Jeeves telled me about yer large dining room idea. We drew up a plan and he be already workin' on clearin' the space." Silverbeard looked thoughtful for a moment.

"But if ye be planning fer the duergar to live in the keep, we'll be needin' much more livin' space. They be used to not havin' windows, so maybe cut deeper into the mountain?" he added.

"I'll speak to them about it now. I don't even know that they're willing to join us yet."

Alexander headed off into the donjon. He stopped in the kitchen to see if the duergar had eaten yet. Upon learning they hadn't, he asked that a modest lunch be prepared on a tray, which he carried to the great hall.

Reaching the hall, he found Gelag and the other five councilors waiting for him. They all had taken seats at a long table to one side of the room. Alexander joined them, setting down the food and motioning for them to help themselves.

"Good morning, Gelag. Councilors." He nodded his head.

"Good morning, Alexander," they all said in unison.

"I have just returned from Stormforge, where we obtained more supplies. There is a quantity set aside for you in the courtyard. It should be enough to feed your people for a week. Longer if you supplement it with fish or wildlife that you hunt."

The eyes of the councilors widened. This was more generosity than they'd expected. Food for nearly a hundred and fifty people for a week was no small thing.

"We thank you, again, Alexander. You and your people have been kind. We discuss with our people last night. Many wish to join Greystone. Many others are scared. Most are not fighters."

"I understand, Gelag. And I would not ask your people who are not fighters to take a place on the wall. But if our gates are breached, if the enemy penetrates the keep, they will need to fight to defend themselves. Or die." He paused a moment while the councilors whispered among themselves. The whispering was interrupted with bites of fruit and sausages.

"However, I can offer your people something that will help ensure their survival." Alexander pulled out six of the dragon pins, handing one to each of the councilors. He waited for them to examine the items.

"This… I not die when wearing this?" Morig asked.

"Well, not from a single blow. Like an arrow. It will prevent one mortal blow. But if you have a bleed effect, or fire, or poison, that continues to do damage, then the next hit can kill you. That is the reason for the healing spell. If properly used, the two together should keep you alive long enough for a healer to reach you. It only works once. Let me be clear. It is NOT a guarantee. It is just a hope," Alexander warned them.

"And… you can give to all of our people?" Brega asked.

"I have…" Alexander quickly checked his inventory. "I have nearly 100 of them now. We are making more. I should have enough for everyone in a day or two."

"What they cost?" asked one of the councilors Alexander hadn't spoken to yet.

"These are our gift to any who swear the oath. We too have made an oath, to protect our citizens. This is part of our effort to fulfill that oath." Alexander smiled at the grey dwarf.

Gelag looked to the others. One by one, they nodded their heads.

"We choose to join. Take oath. We can help with building, hunting, many other things. Not just fighting," Gelag said.

"Wonderful!" Alexander shook the duergar's hand. "I spoke to King Charles of Stormforge, and he welcomes you to his kingdom. He has announced to all his citizens that friendly duergar will be seen in the city soon. Initially, I will send people with you, to make sure there are no incidents. Until the people there get used to you."

Brega gasped. "We can go to city? Human city? For trade?"

Laughing, Alexander said, "Of course. You will be citizens of Dire Keep. There is also an auction house in the keep now. And there will be a bank soon. Speaking of the keep. Would your people prefer to live inside the keep? Or to remain in your caverns?"

Morig answered for his people "We think… caverns for now. Maybe move soon, when our people feel better?"

"That would be fine. I would need some time to make housing for so many, anyway. Silverbeard mentioned that you might like it if we carved some space into the mountain at the back of the keep? So it would feel like you remain underground?"

All six duergar nodded their heads, smiling. "Yes, that would be better. Duergar do not enjoy sunlight. Hurts our eyes. We were made for underground." Morig grinned.

Need to get with Brick and Lainey. Maybe Beatrix too. Maybe we can invent Io's first sunglasses?

"Good enough then. We'll get to work on some housing for you. In the meantime, I'll move your mirror into one of the structures on the outer wall. You and your people can use a wagon to move your supplies down there, and transfer them into the caverns."

Alexander walked outside with the duergar in tow. Locating Lola, he asked, "Any of the outer wall structures not occupied yet? Preferably one with a lower level?"

Lola checked her notes. Then she shared her map with Alexander, and pinged one of the structures.

Alexander teleported to the cave he'd made for the duergar, grabbed the mirror, and teleported back. Lola was organizing some citizens to help load the duergar supplies onto a wagon.

"Lola, please send the wagon down when it's loaded. I'll take these guys with me." Alexander motioned for the duergar to follow.

He walked out the keep's gate and down the path toward the outer gate. As they approached, he noted some citizens on the wall, calling out to Rocky and tossing bits of food. His moat monster was going to be growing faster than expected.

Turning to use the path along the back side of the outer wall, they soon arrived at the structure Lola had indicated. It was a standard one story from the outside, roughly 20x20. Indicating the structure, he said "This building will be yours to use."

Stepping inside, he led them down the stairs to the cellar level, which was much larger. Using his earth mover ability, he cleared an alcove in the stone under the stairs and placed the mirror in it. "I'm afraid a wagon won't fit, so your people will have to carry supplies downstairs by hand." He apologized.

"No problem. Duergar strong like dwarves. Maybe stronger." Gelag smiled.

"One other thing," Alexander mentioned. "If the enemy breaches the wall and gets in here, they would have access to your caverns. I want you to have at least two of your people assigned at all times to this mirror. In the event of an attack, they are to bring the mirror into the keep immediately. If they cannot do that, then tell them to hide it face down under a box or something, so that the enemy does not notice it. Have one of them go through the mirror first, to warn your people not to use it."

Brega nodded her head. "It will be done." Moving forward, she said, "I will get more people to move supplies." Then she touched the mirror and was gone.

Alexander said, "Tomorrow morning? Your people will all come and take the oath?" Gelag and the other councilors all nodded their heads.

Leaving the duergar to their supplies, Alexander headed back to the drawbridge. It was down at the moment, as the logging and hunting parties were out, and the miners had headed toward the mine.

Standing on the bridge, he called out, "Rocky! Are you down there, buddy?"

The little moat monster practically flew out of the water, landing on the bridge next to Alexander. He had a fish in his jaws, and was wagging his tail like a puppy.

Laughing, Alexander said, "Finish your lunch, buddy. I just wanted to say hi. You look like you've grown already!" And it was true. Rocky had been roughly four feet long the day before. Now Alexander estimated he was closer to six.

Rocky chomped down on his fish, severing the head and tail from the main body. After gulping down that piece, he snatched up the head and tail and swallowed them whole as well. He looked at Alexander with his big googly eyes, tongue hanging out. Alexander squatted down and scratched the water dragon's ear in the same spot Jules had the day before. Rocky purred and thumped his tail a few times.

"Okay, buddy. Glad to see you're doing well. Try to leave some fish for Lars and Elsbett to catch, okay?" Alexander patted the dragon's head. Rocky nodded his head yes, then dove back into the water. A moment later his tail flicked, splashing water up onto Alexander. The moat monster grinned at him.

"Ha! I'll get you for that!" Alexander waved a mock-angry fist at the little dragon. Rocky disappeared under the surface.

Teleporting himself over to the fishing pier, he found Lars and Elsbett sitting on the end of the pier, each holding a fishing pole.

"Good … afternoon, I guess." Alexander glanced at his UI's clock. "How are they biting?"

Lars grunted. "They ain't. That durned moat monster of yours keeps thrashing around, scaring all the fish!"

Alexander tried not to smile. "Rocky's intelligent enough. Ask him not to, and he'll listen. Soon he'll be too big to swim through the tunnel, and he'll stay in the moat."

"Aye. That day can't come fast enough!" Lars grumbled.

Seeing another 'two birds, one stone' opportunity, Alexander said, "The more you feed him, the faster he'll grow. Maybe you can even teach him some tricks. Like how to retrieve your net for you. I think we can do without fish for a week or so…"

Young Elsbett's eyes grew wide, and she was visibly trying to hide her excitement. Lars simply nodded, saying, "Aye, that might work."

"We have information that an army is coming. At least part of it undead. Does your teleport charm work for more than one person?" Alexander asked Lars.

Lars shook his head. "It ain't got enough power"

Alexander removed one of the king's teleport scrolls from his bag. Handing it to Elsbett, he said, "You keep this with you at all times. If you see the enemy and you're trapped out here, you use it. It'll take you straight to the palace at Stormforge. When you get there, you tell them we're under attack."

Elsbett accepted the scroll. "Aye. Thank ye. I'll not let ye down."

Teleporting himself back to the keep, he made his way to Sasha's alchemy lab. "Whatcha up to?" he asked.

"Picking my nose, just waiting for you to come and offer me something useful to do?" her sarcastic answer came.

"Well, since you mentioned, how'd you like to come with me to the cave where we found all the featherroot? It's been few weeks, maybe it has re-grown." Alexander knew she couldn't resist that. She'd wanted to visit there the day they first explored the keep.

"YES! Let's bring Lainey and Jules. They're both learning to gather herbs." Sasha was already on her feet and out the door shouting, "Jules! Where are you?"

"Instead of shouting like a mad woman, how about just using guild chat?" Alexander reminder her.

"Oh. Right." Sasha shouted in guild chat, "*JULES! LAINEY! WHERE ARE YOU*?" Alexander just shook his head.

Meeting up with the other two ladies, Alexander teleported them all to a grassy area he remembered just outside the cave entrance. They walked in from there. Jules went into stealth mode and moved ahead of them, scouting.

After a few moments, she said, "All clear, all the way to the dungeon entrance."

The rest of them moved into the cave, and Sasha exclaimed "They HAVE grown back! Dozens of them. I'm going to take a few of the plants whole, roots and all. I'll transplant a few to the garden at the keep, and a few others to greenhouse at the manor. Then Lydia can have access to them whenever she needs them."

"While you guys pick flowers, I'm going to poke my head in the dungeon. See if they respawned." Alexander informed them as he headed toward the back.

Stepping through the portal, he found himself in the same safe room they'd encountered the first time he and his friends had entered. Back before they switched to their current avatars. It had been less than three weeks in real world time. But so much had happened, it seemed more like a year.

Using his earth sense, he explored below him. This wouldn't tell him if the dungeon was occupied, only whether it had changed. From what he could tell, the layout was still the same as last time.

Taking small steps, he moved forward into the corridor in front of him. This level had been imps, but they were all above level 60, and ran in packs. He wasn't about to try and fight them.

He made it about a hundred feet down the corridor before he spotted the door to the first room. There was movement inside the room. He could see flickering light and shadows. Creeping forward, he stopped near the door and gazed into the room at an angle.

Well, shit. Imps. AND undead. There shouldn't be both.

Alexander waited a few moments to see if maybe the two groups would fight each other. But the undead just shuffled slowly about the room, completely ignoring and ignored in return by the imps.

He inspected several of each. All over level 50. That meant the demons had respawned about ten levels lower than when they'd killed them all before.

In guild chat, he said, *"Sasha, Jules, Lainey, do you have what you need? If so, get out of the cave. I've got demons and undead both in here."*

"Give us a couple minutes. I don't want to ruin these plants by rushing. And it's just me and Lainey. Isn't Jules with you?" Sasha said.

Dammit!

"Jules, where are you?" Alexander asked, beginning to get upset.

"Right here behind you! Boo!" Jules exclaimed.

The mobs in the room heard the rogue's outburst, and began to chitter and moan. Several headed for the door.

"Dammit, Jules! Run! Get through the gate!" Alexander shouted at her. At the same time, he was raising a wall in front of the door to try and hold back the mobs.

He was hit by two fireballs that made it over the wall when it was only about four feet high. The damage interrupted his casting. He decided that would have to be enough. Casting a heal on himself, he turned and ran as fast he could down the corridor. He saw Jules jump through the gate ahead of him.

He turned to look as he stepped through the gate himself. There were several imps who had made it over the wall and were hopping toward him. They were maybe halfway down the hallway.

The moment he was through the portal, he turned and began to raise a wall half an inch in front of the portal's surface. He poured mana into the spell, raising the stone as quickly as he could. His efforts were rewarded when he heard two resounding thumps against the wall, followed by three more. He continued to raise the wall until it was flush with the cave's ceiling. Then he thickened it. First to three feet, then to ten feet, then twenty. He didn't stop until he had filled the cave with stone to a depth of thirty feet.

"That should slow them down," he said to himself.

Moving back out into the area where the ladies should be, he didn't see Jules. Panicking, he shouted, "Where's Jules?

"She ran by us, crying. What did you do?" Lainey stood in front of him, arms crossed.

"She decided to follow me, then 'surprise' me inside the dungeon. Right outside a room full of mobs. Her shout aggro'd the whole room. I yelled at her to run to the gate while I held them off."

"You *yelled* at her?" Lainey's face darkened.

"No, not like *at her*... I didn't scold her or anything. Just yelled for her to run. She had the aggro. They were going to eat her face." Alexander thought back.

Did I yell at her? No. I wouldn't do that. But could she have taken it that way?

Lainey didn't look convinced.

Sasha called out, "We're done here, let's go." She turned and began to walk outside to find Jules.

They found her sitting on the ground, back against a boulder, crying. Sasha sat down next to her, hugging her close.

"I… I'm sorry, Alexander. That was stupid. I nearly got us both killed. I just didn't want you to go in there alone… and then I wanted to scare you. I'm *SO sorry!*" She broke down into sobs.

Lainey and Sasha both threw looks at him that said, "Do something, idiot."

Sitting on Jules' other side, he pulled her away from Sasha, gathering her into an embrace. He rocked her back and forth, saying, "It's okay, Jules. I'm sorry I yelled. I panicked. I saw all of them aggro on you, and I got scared they'd get to you before I could stop them. I just wanted you safe more than anything in the world at that moment."

Jules' sobs subsided a bit. Lainey and Sasha both smiled at him. Apparently, that was the right thing to say.

Jules looked at him. "You're not mad at me?" She sniffed.

"Never was. Just scared. Room full of zombies and demons tryin' to eat our faces? Nearly peed myself." He grinned.

Jules half-sobbed, half-laughed. Lainey snorted and kicked his leg. "Idiot."

Giving Jules some time to compose herself, he asked Sasha, "How many of those plants did you get? I'm thinking of sealing this cave for good.

“No! Not yet, anyway. I don’t know if these will grow anywhere else. We need a few days to plant them and see if they’ll survive. You seal that entrance, and you might kill every plant in there,” Sasha said.

Alexander weighed up his options. He wanted to keep those demons and undead in there forever. At least until he had an army to deal with them. On the other hand, those plants were valuable as a healing resource for his people and the citizens of Stormforge.

“Alright. I put thirty feet of solid stone between us and the dungeon portal. Anything coming out will be destroyed as it hits the rock. If the dark one wants them out, he’s going to have to dig his way in. That will have to do. But please, plant those things as quickly as you can. If they live, you can bring all the druids and Lydia and transplant the rest.”

Sasha nodded her agreement.

Alexander gathered the women in his life together, and teleported them back to the keep. Sasha instantly dashed toward the grove near the stables.

Lainey reached over and Gibbs-smacked the back of Alexander’s head, looking meaningfully at Jules, who was staring at her feet.

Alexander took Jules hand, and teleported the two of them to his sitting room. Taking a seat on a sofa, he pulled her into his lap.

“I didn’t want to have to do this, but Lainey and Sasha insisted. I’m afraid it’s snuggle time.” He grinned at the beautiful rogue.

She pounded his chest half-heartedly, saying, “Such a gentleman. Forcing his affections on a lady in distress.”

Alexander froze. Realizing what she’d said, Jules whispered, “Oh! No…” and then just kissed him.

He had urgent matters to attend to. The rest of his guild, and the king, needed to know what he’d found in that dungeon. His people needed to prepare. The enemy was just a few miles away. It wouldn't take players long to break through that stone and free the army of demons and undead.

But nothing short of the end of the world was going to make him leave that sofa just then.

Chapter Eighteen

I'm Out of Good Chapter Names

After an hour or so of quality snuggling, Alexander felt much calmer and more relaxcd. In fact, he was so relaxed, he needed to either get up and do something, or go to sleep.

His conscience got the better of him, and he squeezed Jules one last time. "Need to get moving. There are things we need to deal with," he said gently.

"Noooo!" Jules grumped at him. She was mostly asleep herself.

"You stay here. Or better yet, crawl into bed. I'll be back when I can," he said to her, rising from the sofa. She face-planted into one of the cushions and didn't move.

Moving toward the door, he grinned at her. "Turn your head to the side so you don't suffocate."

"Mmmph," was the only answer he received.

Heading downstairs, he checked in with Silverbeard. The chamberlain had established himself an office not far from the Great Hall.

"The duergar will be taking the oath tomorrow. They'll stay in their caverns until we can build them the housing you suggested. Please have Jeeves start on that after he finishes the dining area."

"The dining room be done. The stone removal part, at least. It were basically just a big box. There be a large hearth on one side. And a second kitchen. We can add to it as ye like."

"Great! Then please ask Jeeves to start on housing for the duergar. Do you have a plan for him?" Alexander asked.

"Aye. There be basic plans in his library. I will get him started," Silverbeard confirmed.

Leaving Silverbeard's office, Alexander moved back out to the courtyard. He opened up guild chat.

"Lorian, are you in the keep?"

"No, Alexander. I'm out with a hunting party," Lorian replied.

"I've stumbled upon some of the Dark One's army in the cavern where the demon dungeon is located. I sealed them in with a thick layer of stone, but I'd like someone to keep an eye on the place. To let us know if they escape, or if anyone else approaches."

"I know the place. We'll go check it now, and I'll set a watch somewhere we can observe without being seen."

"Thank you, Lorian. Please add your hunters to a party or raid group so they can contact you instantly if they see anything."

"Already done. I do have a bit of experience in these matters," Lorian responded dryly.

Shaking his head at his own stupidity, Alexander moved toward the smithy. He and Brick still had dragon pins to make for the duergar that would be joining them in a few days.

Before he even reached the kitchen area, a large shadow passed over him, followed by a second shadow. Looking up, he saw Kai and Lia in dragon form, circling toward the field outside the keep. Changing direction, he went to meet the two dragons.

Lia was a lovely blue dragon. Much smaller than Kai, her azure scales were tinged with a silver sheen that reflected the sunlight in undulating flashes as she moved. The nearly translucent membrane of her wings made them seem almost too delicate to support her in the air. In total she was maybe a hundred feet long from nose to tail.

As Alexander approached, she turned her head toward him, fixing him with lovely silver eyes the size of basketballs. "We have found a suitable location, Alexander. You will come with us to assist in shaping our roost."

Alexander chuckled, then executed his best formal bow, one foot back and his left arm behind him as he swept his right arm outward. "Of course, Your Highness. I am your loyal servant."

Kai hung his massive dragon head at Lia's demanding tone. "I am sorry, Alexander. My mate has not yet learned proper manners," he growled. "She has spent very little time around other races".

"No harm done at all." Alexander smiled at Kai, then at Lia. "Where I am from, it is understood that expectant mothers often become… erratic… as they prepare for the coming of their children. I can only imagine that a nesting dragon might be much the same."

"You have no idea," Kai mumbled, his voice was barely more than a whisper. A dragon whisper. Which could be easily heard by his mate, whose tail began to twitch.

Wanting to avoid a confrontation between dragons inside his walls, Alexander quickly inquired, "Can you fly me up to your chosen spot? Or is it better if we teleport?"

Lia immediately snarked, "Kai will carry you on his back. Since he is in the mood to apologize for me, it is the least he can do." And with that, she took to the air, managing to whip Kai's flank with her tail as she leapt.

Looking up at the still growling dragon, Alexander asked, "So, do you just grab me up on a claw? Or do I need to climb? I've never ridden a dragon before."

In answer, Kai laid down on his belly and lowered his neck to the ground. By putting one foot on Kai's forepaw, Alexander was able to reach up to grab a spine at the base of the dragon's neck and pull himself up. Straddling the thick neck in a spot between two spines, Alexander patted Kai's neck. "I think I'm good to go, my friend."

"Hold on tightly," Kai rumbled. He lifted both wings high in the air, and with a monstrous push from his hind legs, and leapt upward while pushing down with his wings. The sensation was nothing like Alexander had ever felt. There was a rush of air in his face as his stomach dropped. He instinctively gripped tighter around the spine in front of him with both hands.

"YEEEEAHHH!" he cried out as the ground dropped away beneath him. The massive dragon gained altitude quickly. In a matter of seconds, Alexander could see the keep below, the farmers and livestock in the fields, even the mine entrance and the dwarves marking lines with rope at the quarry. He could feel Kai chuckling beneath him.

"So, you like to fly, then?" Kai asked.

"Hell yes! It has always been a dream of mine. A dream for most people, I think."

"Well then, let's go!" Kai's wings beat several more massive strokes, and they shot up even higher. The keep below soon became just a speck. Alexander could see Stormforge in the distance, its walls and towers seeming like a toy castle.

They passed through a layer of clouds into a cold, clear sky. Jupiter and Saturn were vivid in the reflected light of the sun. Millions of stars shone brightly through the thinner atmosphere.

"This is amazing! If I could fly, I'd spend all my time up here!" Alexander shouted to be heard above the roar of the wind in his face.

"I'm afraid you'd quickly freeze," Kai responded. "But I thought you might enjoy the view for a moment. Now hold tight. Grip with your legs!"

The dragon's head dipped, and his wings folded. Suddenly they were diving like a hawk after a bunny. Alexander let out a guttural scream of joy, and Kai roared in agreement. The two plunged downward, the forest and lake below growing larger by the second. When Alexander became sure they'd splash into the water, Kai spread his wings. They caught the air with a snap, and the dragon's vertical velocity became horizontal. They skimmed the lake, leaving a plume of water in their wake. With a slight adjustment of his wings, Kai raised them up just enough to clear the forest treetops as they shot forward.

Alexander found himself laughing hysterically as the dragon circled back around toward the lake. The adrenaline in his system had his hands shaking.

What a rush! No wonder so many players would kill for a dragon mount.

Kai flew straight toward the series of waterfalls that fell from the top of the ridge and fed the lake. He flared his wings and landed on a ledge next to one of the falls, about four hundred feet up from the lake. The ledge was wide, and a deep pool had formed where the water fell into the rock before continuing over the edge and down. Folding his wings, he walked along the ledge and ducked behind the waterfall.

When he wiped the spray from the fall off his face, Alexander found himself in a cave. It extended back maybe a hundred feet from the ledge, and was about eighty feet wide. The ceiling was high, rising up to sixty feet in a rough dome shape. Still, it was tight quarters for two adult dragons. The sun's light shining through the falling water outside caused the entire cave to shimmer.

"I can see why you chose this place!" Alexander beamed at Lia. "Fresh water, natural light, but still some privacy."

"Yes, and when Lia is too fat to fly, there's food right here," Kai said. Alexander turned to watch as the black dragon extended his head to within inches of the waterfall. After a moment, Kai's head shot forward into the water, then emerged with a fish in his jaws. "They drop right down the falls into the lake." He grinned his toothy dragon grin.

Lia, tail twitching once again, said, "If you would not mind, Alexander, I would like you to extend the space a good bit. Please."

"It would be my pleasure, Lady Lia. You just point and tell me what you need, and I'll make it happen." He smiled.

With a satisfied grunt, and a look of promised retribution toward Kai, Lia began to direct Alexander. He moved stone for her, leaving support columns in a few places to ensure the integrity of the cave. Walls were moved back to either side. The back of the cave was extended, and shaped. Lia had him create a deep chimney at the back that extended up to the surface of the ridge, and deep into the mountain. It would provide both air flow and a refuse dump.

On the left side, she had him create several rooms of human proportions. He added a kitchen and bathroom, both with hot and cold running water. The enchantments he'd learned came in handy there. He made half a dozen bedrooms with stone beds off a large common living area with a fireplace. At Kai's request, Alexander pulled up obsidian to form the fireplace.

Lastly, Lia had him hollow out a circular indentation that sloped to a depth of about six feet in the floor of the main cavern. "This will be my nest," she explained.

Looking at the forty-foot diameter depression, Alexander volunteered. "I could cast a heat enchantment on it, to help keep your babies warm."

Lia looked touched, and blinked for a moment before answering. "Thank you, Alexander, that would be very kind of you. And thoughtful."

Your reputation with Dragon Princess Lia has increased to Friendly

Alexander smiled as he cast the spell on the stone at the bottom of the nest. He closed his eyes and pictured the steady warmth of an incubator. The snug feeling of being under a heavy blanket on a cold night. When he thought he had the power level right, he carefully released the enchantment magic into the stone. Not having tried to enchant anything this large, he wasn't sure it would work.

Skill level up! Enchanting +1

After a bit of a sniff to investigate, Lia stepped into the nest. She curled her body into a ball and settled down on the newly warmed floor.

"Mmmmm… that is wonderful. Thank you, Alexander," she practically purred.

"I wasn't sure I'd get the temperature right. I don't know how much heat dragon babies need. If you want me to adjust it, just let me know."

"It will be just fine. Thank you, my friend." Kai responded. Lia seemed to have already drifted off to sleep.

"Do you need anything else? Any supplies?"

"No, I can take care of the rest. We-" Kai stopped talking and tilted his head. Just as he did so, there was a large ***GONG*** that reverberated through the stone of the cavern.

"*Something just attacked the keep and was destroyed master. It tried to enter through the remaining mirror in the control room.*" Jeeves said.

"Jeeves, how are you able to speak to me here?"

"*As Prince Kai is a guild member, and this structure is within my area of influence, it has become another of my ancillary structures. It is formally designated 'Dragon Embassy'. The addition of an embassy, an additional structure, and the defense points I received from the destroyed entity in the mirror have granted me another level, master.*"

Kai nodded his head. "I felt the death of whatever tried to enter the control room. It must have been powerful."

"*Indeed, Prince Kai. I was rewarded a significant number of defense points upon its demise. More than I received when you defended against that party of adventurers.*" Jeeves confirmed. "*I estimate that the being that was destroyed was at least level 100.*"

Alexander opened guild chat. "*Okay, folks, we just had a level 100 or higher mob or adventurer try to enter the control room through that last mirror. We're going to have to check it out ASAP. But at that level, they're more than twice as strong as any of us. We're going to need everybody if we're to have any kind of chance. And we're going to need better gear. Meet me in the main hall in thirty minutes. We'll raid the guild vault, then hit the auction house.*"

Turning to Kai, Alexander asked, "Can you contact Fitz and ask if he'll join us? He's very concerned about the mirrors."

The dragon nodded his head and disappeared. Lia, still curled up in her new nest, opened one eye. "I shall not be joining you, Alexander. I must prepare the roost."

"Of course, Lia. And if there's anything you need while we're gone, just let Jeeves know. He and Silverbeard will figure something out."

With a small bow to the nesting dragoness, Alexander teleported himself back to the keep.

Skill level up! Teleportation magic +1. Rank increase: Adept
Through the constant use of teleportation magic, you have developed your abilities to the Adept level. Teleportation spell range increased 10%.

Sweet! There really is a benefit to spamming my magic abilities. I'll have to ask Fitz what my range is now.

Alexander walked into the keep and through the corridors to the great hall. Opening his UI, he selected his guild tab, and then the guild vault. In Io, the guild vault wasn't a normal physical room located in the structure of the guild house. One could not just walk up and break into it like a treasury or bank vault. It could only be accessed, under normal circumstances, by an authorized guild officer. When activated, a door would appear in the nearest wall, and the officer who summoned it could provide access to whomever they chose. In the event that the guild house - or keep, in this case - was taken, the guild vault would become accessible to the conquering party. For this reason, most guilds designated a few individuals whose job, in the event of an attack, was to grab the gold and most valuable items in the vault and teleport away to an alternate location.

Alexander opened the guild vault and stepped inside. While he was waiting for the others, he'd look into his own gear. Other than his legendary mithril shirt, his gear was mediocre at best. Items in Io were not level specific. A level one noob could equip gear he bought in the auction house that came from a level 50 dungeon. He would not get the full benefit of the item, however. Io scaled the stats down to fit the player's level.

To start, he wanted to upgrade his weapons. The staff he carried gave a small bonus of +10 to Intel. And the sword on his hip gave +4 to wisdom. He needed to do better.

He was surprised to see that either Lola or Silverbeard had organized the vault. Where previously things were roughly organized by type - armor, weapon - and by level, now there were clearly marked sections divided by class. Then further subdivided into weapon, armor, and accessory, and further by level.

Alexander moved to the caster weapons section, and inspected the various staves set in a rack. After glancing through the options, he selected one that looked to be made of a light-colored wood, bleached nearly white. The base had a metal cap that added some weight to it, and the top was rounded out with a gem of some type embedded in it. He examined the piece.

Staff of Knowing
Item Level: Epic
Stats: Intelligence +20, Wisdom +10, Luck +5
This staff, found on the body of a dead wizard, was enchanted to assist said wizard in seeking hidden places and treasures. Class bonus: Mages have +20% chance of penetrating illusions.

Alexander equipped the Staff of Knowing, and deposited his previous staff on the rack. Next he moved on to swords. There were no swords in the caster sections, as most mages did not carry them. So he moved over to the paladin section. After a brief inspection of those weapons, he lifted a long, slender one-handed sword with a fullered blade and a grip that looked to be wrapped in scaled hide.

Kobold's Bane
Item Level: Rare
Stats: Strength +5, Stamina +5, Wisdom +5

That'll do nicely. I like the grip. I'm guessing it's kobold hide. Alexander switched out this sword for his old one.

Since none of his other gear gave him any stat bonuses, he decided to look for some leather gear. Chain was a bit cumbersome, especially with his low strength level.

Moving to the ranger section, he found lots of items with agility and dexterity, a few with stamina. Not really what he wanted. Looking around, he found a small section labeled for monks. On the shelf sat a pair of black leather vambraces that looked interesting.

Spirit Warrior's Vambrace
Item Level: Rare
Stats: Agility +5, Wisdom +10

With just these three new pieces, I pick up 25 points in wisdom. That's a solid boost to my mana pool. The additional strength, stamina, and agility wouldn't hurt either, if I have to fight close up and 'all stabby-stabby' as Sasha likes to put it. He smiled to himself.

The others arrived, and Alexander helped them choose suitable gear. Max and Lainey both had full leather sets they'd taken from Henry, the PWP leader. And both had epic or legendary weapons. Jules got the third set they'd taken from the high-level rogue, and had her epic psychic daggers they'd just looted from the demon queen. Brick had been forging replacement armor for himself to go along with his epic shield and hammer. Sasha had her epic staff, and had found some armor with decent intel and wisdom boosts.

The others, Dayle's group and Helga's, had not been so fortunate with their gear. They'd found no first kill dungeons, and didn't have the extensive guild vault that Greystone had amassed. Upon first walking into the vault, they'd all been amazed at the amount and quality of items stored inside. There was a more than sufficient supply in the vault to substantially improve all of their stats.

To help further, Alexander took Lugs' hammer, Dayle and Warren's swords, and enchanted each of them to do bonus light damage. Just in case what they faced on the other side of the mirror was demons or the undead. Helga's new demon-killer weapon had plenty of juice already, and Alexander didn't want to risk damaging it with his still limited enchanting experience.

Emerging from the vault, they found Fitz, Kai, and Fibble awaiting them. Lainey knelt next to the heroic little goblin, and produced a leather helm from her bag. "This is for our hero, Fibble. To protect our protector!" She smiled as she placed it on his head. It was dyed green, and had holes in the proper location for his large goblin ears.

Fibble's eyes rolled up inside his skull as he tried to look at the new addition to his armor. He reached up and patted the helm. When he didn't feel any sensation, he thumped his head a bit harder. A wide, toothy grin spread across his face. He bonked himself on the head with his stick, still feeling nothing.

"This good armor! Fibble not feel head at all!" he cried. Then a worried look crossed his face, and he quickly used his free hand to feel his nose and mouth. "It okay, head still there!" he said with relief. Lainey hugged the little warrior as Fitz rolled his eyes and the others had a good chuckle.

With everyone sufficiently geared, Alexander sent out raid party invites. All told there were seventeen of them in the raid. With the wizard and the dragon, they should be able to hand a level 100 enemy or two. If they ran into any larger groups, there might be a problem.

Sasha reminded everyone to eat something, and to take a drink of the keep's blessed water for buffs. Additionally, she, Lainey, Fitz, and Kai all added buffs to the group. The entire group now had buffs for strength, stamina, intelligence, wisdom, and added health, mana, and stamina regen.

With everyone prepared as well as could be, Fitz teleported them all up to the control room. Fitz immediately moved to pick the mirror up from the floor, where it still sat face down under the table. He cast the spell that allowed them all to see through the mirror to the space on the other side.

There wasn't much to see. The area around the other mirror was pitch black. Alexander got the impression of an empty space. Maybe a room.

"Jeeves, we are going through to investigate what's beyond the mirror. If anything other than one of us comes back through, I want you to alert everyone in the keep using the loudspeaker. Tell them to get to their combat positions, and to seal off the tower," Alexander said.

"*It will be done, master. I have just sealed the door at the top of the tower. This will give our citizens time to organize. Good luck,*" Jeeves responded. The improved interface was really developing.

Brick moved forward as if to step through the mirror. He was within a foot of the surface when Jules shouted, "Stop!"

Brick froze, turning to look back at the elfess. "What?"

"I can't see anything but darkness. What if the mirror on that side is blocked, like this one was? You could step through and be destroyed. You'd respawn, but we'd have no way to get your gear back," Jules explained.

"Well, shit." Brick rubbed his beard. "Thank ye, Jules. Hate to lose me shield 'n' hammer."
Fitz called forth a light globe and sent it forward toward the mirror. As it touched the reflective surface, is disappeared. Half a second later it reappeared on the other side, lighting up a small stone room.

The group all waited for several seconds. When nothing hostile appeared within sight, or attacked the globe, Fitz said, "It looks safe enough."

Raising his shield, Brick stepped up and touched the mirror. He was followed a moment later by Lugs. The two appeared in the other room, each turning slowly and putting their backs to each other. Their heads could be seen swiveling around, taking in the entire room. After ten seconds or so, Brick waved for the others to join them. He and Lugs stepped out of view.

One by one, the other fifteen raid party members touched the mirror and teleported through. Kai was the last to join them in the small room.

They were in a chamber with a single wooden door that was closed. The room had stone walls, floor and ceiling, clearly manmade rather than carved out of stone. The mirror they'd just exited was mounted on one of the walls to the left of the doorway.

"Must be above ground," Alexander mused aloud. "You don't need stone and mortar underground." He sent out his earth sense, and found packed soil and rocks around them on all sides except behind the door, with nothing but stone below. "Correction, close to the surface. We're in a cellar of some kind. Barely below ground."

Looking up, Alexander noted an iron ring fastened to the ceiling. Pointing at it, he asked, "Trap door?"

The others all followed his direction, looking at the ring. No hinges were visible, nor was any obvious outline of a door.

Sasha took control of the situation "Okay. Regular door first. Jules, you hang back and watch that ceiling. If anybody opens it, you call out in raid chat and haul ass. Brick, Lugs, you ready?"

The two tanks moved toward the door. Max grabbed hold of the handle, yanking it open as soon as the tanks had their shields up.

The corridor behind was dark beyond the ten feet or so that were lit by the globe inside the room. Brick moved through the door, followed closely by Lugs. The two of them filled the width of the passageway.

"There be stairs leading down," Brick called out. "They be too long fer me to see the end."

"Alright. Brick, stay there. Keep an eye out. Max, Lainey, Misty, back him up. Lugs, please step back in here. I want to push on the ceiling around that ring. See if it opens a trap door," Sasha instructed. The named group members moved to comply. Lugs stood directly under the iron ring, which due to his height, was only a foot or so above his head. Stowing his hammer and shield, he placed both hands on the ceiling to either side of the ring, and pushed.

Dust began to trickle down between the stones as an irregularly shaped section of the ceiling began to shift upward. Seeing that one side was shifting more easily, Lugs moved both hands to that side, and a gave a more forceful shove. With a grinding noise, and the screech of rusted metal, the stone continued to rise on one side, until a trap door outline could easily be made out. A faint light from above began to penetrate around the edges. There was a ratcheting sound of metal on metal as the door continued to rise.

With a final push, Lugs raised the door to about a 45-degree angle. "That's as far as I can reach," he said. He continued to stand, arms over his head supporting the door.

On a hunch, Alexander said, "Lugs, let it back down just a bit. I think that sound we heard was a chain on a gear."

Nodding his head, the half-ogre relaxed his arms a bit. The door dropped back down about an inch before stopping dead. Lugs slowly lowered his arms the rest of the way. The door didn't move.

"Now use one of your spears, and push it further." Alexander instructed. Lugs complied. Taking out one of his long spears he placed the butt end near the high side of the trap door and pushed. The door raised to nearly vertical. When he removed the spear, it stayed upright.

"I think it's on some kind of weighted or geared pulley system. The chain we heard should hold it up." Alexander explained. He motioned for Lugs to give him a hand up to the hole.

Lugs lowered both hands in a basket for Alexander to step onto, then quickly lifted him up, practically throwing him through the opening.

Looking around, Alexander found himself in a dimly lit storage room filled with crates of varying sizes. The room was maybe thirty feet by twenty, and there was not a lot of open space on the floor. There was a single heavy looking ironwood door at the opposite end of the room. A thick layer of dust covered the floor and all of the crates. Alexander saw no footprints or signs of activity. The walls were lined with shelves from floor to ceiling, the highest shelves being about twelve feet off the ground. Against one wall was a ladder that allowed someone to reach the upper shelves.

"There's a ladder here. Give me a minute," he called down in a whisper.

Alexander moved over to the wall, grabbing the ladder. It was heavier than he expected. Bending his legs, he managed to lift the awkward thing and waddle back over to the hole in the floor. Lugs reached up and took most of the weight of the ladder as Alexander lowered it down. When the half-ogre set the bottom of the ladder on the floor, it was not quite tall enough to reach the lip of the trap door above.

"No worries," Lugs said. "I can hold it steady while you guys climb." He demonstrated by holding either side of the ladder in his massive hands, keeping it steady and nodding at Dayle, who began to move up the ladder. Standing on the top rung, using Alexander's arm to steady himself, he was able to step up onto the floor above with ease. He quickly equipped his shield and weapon and moved to cover the door.

"Brick, come back inside the room. We'll secure that door while we explore what's above," Sasha called out quietly. The dwarf backed into the room, closing the door as he came. There was no lock, so Fitz simply raised a wall of stone in front of the door, effectively blocking it.

One by one the others climbed the ladder as Lugs held it steady. When he was the only one left in the room, he handed the ladder up to Brick. Once the hole was clear, Lugs grabbed the edges of the hole, made a little jump for momentum, and pulled himself up and through.

The limited light in the room was streaming in through gaps around the edges of the exit door. There was no sound outside, or any change in the light to indicate movement close by. Max, Lainey, and Jules had been opening crates as quietly as possible while the others climbed up. Inside most were common quality swords and armor pieces. A few had held perishables that had long since turned to dust.

"We can search those later," Alexander said. "Let's find out what's outside this door."

Brick switched out with Dayle, standing in front of the door while Max pulled on it. The door didn't budge.

Jules said, "Please, let me try." Moving to the door, she dropped down on one knee and examined the lock. After a moment, she took a probing tool out of her bag, and inserted it into the lock. Moving it around for more than a minute, she said, "As far as I can tell, the lock is not engaged." She removed her probe and stood up.

Fitz stepped forward and put a hand on the door. He closed his eyes and murmured a short spell. A moment later he chuckled and said, "Rizzo. I'd recognize his signature anywhere."

"Rizzo?" Kai asked. "I remember him. He was a human wizard. Died more than a thousand years ago, didn't he? There was some kind of duel?"

Fitz held up a finger for silence, then touched the door again. There was a brief flash of blue light, and the door swung open a few inches. Fitz pulled it open the rest of way, revealing a large round room with several tables and benches.

After looking about to ensure they were alone, the wizard stepped out and took a seat on the nearest bench. The others joined him.

"Aye, lad. Rizzo was a master wizard and a combat mage. He was born around the same time you were, I think. Hard to keep track of the years that far back. He was one of the early members of the Mages Guild. His hobby was portal and teleportation magic. There were none better, including me. He experimented with long range teleportation devices. Which probably explains the large number of mirrors we've encountered. He even claimed to have figured out how to create portals to other planets." Fitz paused and looked thoughtfully at the room around them, and then toward a stone stair that curved upward against the nearest wall.

"This must have been one of his outposts. He commanded a battalion of combat mages during one of the demon wars. He and his earth mages would raise towers like this one near the front lines before a battle. It gave them a good vantage from which to command the battle and cast magic at the enemy. It also provided a stronghold that allowed for reinforcements to join the battle, or defeated troops to escape via portal. My guess is that if we follow those stairs below, they'll take us to an old portal chamber."

"And something higher than level 100 must have come through that portal, then tried to get through the mirror to our command center," Jules added.

"Or simply touched the mirror by accident, not knowing what it was," Misty volunteered.

"Either way, we need to investigate. But first we should have a look around this tower. Make sure it's empty, and that we can secure it before we head downstairs." Alexander said. "Anybody object?"

Nobody objected. Fitz rose and moved toward the imposing main door of the tower. It stood nearly twenty feet high, and ten wide. It was constructed of jet-black ironwood, banded with an equally black metal. The thing must have weighed several tons.

Putting a hand on this door, Fitz quickly nodded his head. "Sealed, just like the other door. Rizzo's signature. No one has breached this tower in at least a millennium."

"So, he was killed in a duel, and nobody ever came to check on this place?" Helga asked.

"Not exactly. It wasn't a duel. He was executed," Fitz said. "As for checking on this place, there were dozens of towers like this erected back then, and in previous wars. They were largely abandoned when the wars ended. Usually they were stripped of useful items, and the portals disabled first."

"Executed? You can't just say a master wizard was executed and move on!" Beatrix's small voice reprimanded the wizard. "Who executed him? And Why?"

Fitz sat down on the stairway near the door. "We did. The Mages Guild, I mean. I mentioned that he was experimenting with portals and long-range teleports? Well, he had a power problem. Specifically, items like those mirrors had a limit to how much power they could hold, and by extension a limit to their range. They could be tied to a deep power source, like I did with the portal at your compound. But the whole purpose of the mirrors was to make them portable. Rizzo was determined to find a portable source of power. He disappeared for nearly a century, saying he was going to do research."

Fitz hung his head, covering his face with his hands. "When he returned, he told us he'd found his solution. He brought the guild council to a location he'd set up for a demonstration. That location turned out to be a small village near where Antalia is located now. He'd built a tower much like this one, and set up a mirror at the top. He'd left the corresponding mirror back at the Mages Guild. The distance would normally require a full portal, but he claimed he could span it with a mirror."

The wizard took a deep breath. "We weren't expecting what came next. He spoke the words of a spell, and the entire village below lit up. He'd drawn some kind of ritual symbol around the village itself, and was activating it. There were screams from the village as every man, woman, and child were murdered. Forty citizens killed, their souls drained from their bodies for the magic they held. That power was channeled through the symbol, into the tower, and funneled into the mirror. The device showed us the main hall at the Mages Guild, where Rizzo had left the other mirror."

"Oh my god," Beatrix whispered. "I'm sorry I asked. All those poor people."

"Aye. We were stunned as well. Rizzo took the silence that followed to explain. 'You see? We can use captured prisoners or local peasants to power long range teleports in emergency situations!' he boasted. He was proud of himself. He went on to explain that he'd studied necromancy, learning to drain the life force of the living in such a way as to triple the magical energy you'd normally get from a soul gem upon their death. It involved extreme pain and terror at the moment of passing. There was more, but I stopped listening."

"That bastard. Did you kill him right then and there?" Lainey growled.

"No. To my great shame, there were a few among us who saw a use for his discoveries. They protected him, insisting upon a trial to be held after further investigation. The trial was eventually held, after nearly a year. When the sentence of death was finally passed down, Rizzo tried to escape." Fitz looked up at the group gathered around him. The look on his face made several of them take an unconscious step back. "I made sure he did not survive the attempt. His head sits in a jar at the guild. As a reminder and a warning."

Alexander had been focused on one part of Fitz's tale. "Baron Dire is a necromancer. He had several mirrors set up and linked to the keep's command center. That can't be a coincidence."

"One of many things I intend to make him explain," Fitz growled.

"Let's clear this tower, then get downstairs and clear that, too. This place is starting to give me the creeps." Sasha motioned at Brick to lead the way up the stairs. Fitz stood to clear the path.

Based on the interior dimensions, Alexander figured the tower to be about eighty feet in diameter at the base. That made the ground floor room roughly five thousand square feet. It tapered slightly as it rose toward the top. He wasn't yet sure how tall it would be.

"Fitz, how did they fit an entire army in here? Especially if they were retreating and had wounded," he asked the wizard as they climbed.

"There were usually more floors below ground than above. Units could move into the tower and down toward the portal, filling lower levels as they waited. Wounded were teleported directly to the portal room and carried through."

Brick reached the second floor of the tower. There was a short corridor that ran off the stairway landing directly bisecting the tower. On each side of the hallway there were four doors. Brick took the left side, Lugs the right. They opened each door and examined the rooms, finding no enemies. All eight rooms appeared to be living quarters, with a bed, desk, bathroom, and closet. Sasha ordered them to hold off on looting, but to check carefully for hidden rooms or doors. Fitz and Jules followed Lugs into each room to check it, while Kai and Max took the other side behind Brick.

It took only about fifteen minutes to clear the floor. Having cleared the final room, they moved back to the stairs, and once again Brick led the way up.

The third and fourth floors were much like the second. The types of rooms varied, some being living quarters, others being workshops or laboratories. Most of the rooms had been stripped bare of equipment. There was a small library on the fourth floor that still held a significant number of books, preserved through some type of stasis spell. Alexander had the group pause to gather the books, and he teleported them to his study at the keep.

Having cleared the fourth floor, they once again moved upward. When they reached the fifth floor landing, there was no corridor, just a simple door. Just as before, the door was magically sealed. Fitz laid a hand on the door, breaking the seal. He opened it himself, thinking it highly unlikely anything would be found on the other side.

He was wrong.

As soon as the door opened, there was a deafening sound, somewhere between a roar and a squawk, that shook the tower beneath them. A body the size of a pickup truck moved with a flurry of feathers and claws. Within two seconds the group found themselves face to face with an angry beast. It had the body of lion, only about six times the normal size. It had wings that were currently half extended as its head pushed forward. The head was that of an eagle, with sharp eyes and an even sharper beak that could slice a man in two with ease.

Currently, both those eyes and the beak were focused on Fitz. The creature dug its claws into the stone floor of tower's roof. Its back legs bunched as if preparing to pounce.

"Stand back!" Fitz commanded "It is a gryphon. I will handle this."

Fitz put one hand up, palm out toward the monster. He spoke several words in a language that Alexander did not recognize. The beast let out another monstrous cry, though this one sounded more confused than angry.

Fitz spoke again, both hands up this time. He took a step forward toward the gryphon as he spoke. The creature tilted its head to one side, lowering its wings and sitting on its haunches. One massive forepaw took a half-hearted swat in the wizard's direction. Alexander noted that the claws had been retracted.

Taking three more steps, Fitz moved within reach of the creature. It lowered its head so that its eyes were level with the wizard's. Fitz reached up and began to scratch its head between the eyes, which crossed in an almost comical manner as the gryphon tried to follow his hand. After a moment, the group could hear the deep rumbling sound of the gryphon purring.

Patting the large creature on the neck, Fitz turned to the group. "He remembers me. May I present Braxis. Former Alpha of the Gryphon Corps." The gryphon bowed its head slightly, and not wanting to offend, the members of the group all did the same.

Sasha, who was standing at the front of the group, made a little curtsey. "Nice to meet you, Braxis. You're really quite beautiful. And scary!" She smiled up at the beast.

Braxis nosed the wizard aside, taking two long steps forward to stand in front of Sasha. He lowered his head, and bumped her with his forehead. Though he clearly intended to be gentle, Sasha was nearly pushed off her feet. She latched onto the gryphon's head for balance, and when she'd steadied herself, she scratched in the same spot she's seen Fitz scratch.

The purring recommenced, and the gryphon settled down onto its belly, forepaws tucked up under it like a housecat.

"Ha!" Fitz exclaimed. "Looks like you've made a friend. Braxis was ever a sucker for pretty girls."

As if on cue, Lainey, Jules, and the other ladies in the group stepped forward to surround the beast, each of them finding a spot on its head or neck to pet and scratch. Braxis closed his eyes, and the purring seemed to grow louder.

"BWAHAHA!" Brick slapped his knee. "I'd purr too if all them lovelies was pettin' me!"

Kai, who had remained back on the landing to guard the stairs behind them, stepped out through the door. He spoke a few words to the gryphon that had the tone of a greeting.

The beast's eyes popped open, and it immediately stood, brushing off the group of ladies. It squawked quietly, then lowered its majestic head to the floor. It almost seemed to be bowing to Kai. The dragon spoke again, stepping forward to lay a hand on Braxis' head. Seeming satisfied, the gryphon settled back onto its belly and nudged at Sasha in a clear demand to continue. The ladies laughed and stepped forward to resume their new duties.

Fitz explained, "Gryphons and dragons have a special relationship. Braxis was simply paying his respects to the prince. Eons ago, the original dragon king and queen were the only dragons on Io. This was a much more dangerous place, back then. When the queen became pregnant and could not hunt for herself, the king had a dilemma. He needed to hunt, but he could not leave his queen unprotected. The mountains were filled with wild trolls, orcs, and worse.

So, the king used his magic to create a hunter to serve them. He used the lion for its strength and speed, giving it wings so that it could more easily bring prey up to the roost for his queen. He altered its body with the head of an eagle to match the wings, and for better eyesight, so that it might spot prey from above. Gryphons are creatures of magic, blessed with long life and great power. Much like dragons, they rarely reproduce. Many were killed during the wars, and it is rare to find one on Io now. Braxis here was Rizzo's mount when he commanded the mage battalion. As Alpha, Braxis commanded a pride of twenty-four gryphons."

Braxis stopped purring at those words, instead beginning a low keening sound in the back of his throat. He squawked once, quietly, then laid his head on the floor.

"Only three survived that last war. Braxis and two females. We set them free, in hopes that they'd find a way to restore their species. It seems Braxis took up residence here," Fitz observed.

Alexander finally took a moment to look around. They were on the roof of the tower. It was a flat stone roof with pillars set at each cardinal point that supported a conical roof about ten feet above the floor. It was slightly narrower than the base of the tower, being about sixty feet in diameter with a three-foot-high crenellated wall around the outside. There was a large nest in the center of the floor, made up of branches, sticks, and bones. The inside was lined with bear and wolf hides, and scattered with golden-hued feathers that must have been shed by Braxis himself.

Sasha hugged the gryphon's head, her arms not able to wrap even halfway around. "But where are your females now?" she asked him.

Braxis let out a series of squawks, and Kai translated. "They live on a mountain, not far away. They have been breeding, and a young male has replaced Braxis as alpha. He is old, even for a gryphon, and has come here to live out his remaining days in peace."

"That's unacceptable!" Jules declared. "Braxis, you will come home with us. We will take care of you. No one should be alone like this!" she practically shouted, tears forming in her eyes. Alexander stepped forward and put an arm around her shoulders.

"Of course, you can come with us, Braxis. If that's what you'd like. We have a tower you can roost on, or we can make you a roost up on the ridge above. There's a forest full of wolves and boar you can hunt. Or we can feed you if necessary. You'll have company any time you want it." Alexander bowed his head to the majestic gryphon.

Braxis squawked again in a questioning tone. Again, Kai translated, this time with a smile on his face. "He's asking if there are any gryphon females there."

Beatrix spoke up, her tiny voice coming from under the beast's neck, where she'd been scratching. "I'm sorry, Braxis. All we have is a moat monster. But if you want to bring a female from your pride, she would be welcome!" She looked at Alexander, who nodded.

Braxis scooted backward a bit and tiled his head so that he could see the tiny gnome who'd spoken. Laying his head on the ground next to her, he was close to eye level. He squawked quietly, and she reached out to scratch his head, which she'd had no hope of reaching before.

"He would not be welcomed by his pride. Once an alpha is replaced, they are shunned. The new alpha would attack him if he returned. But I will go and speak for him, see if any wish to join him," Kai said. He jogged toward the roof's edge, beginning to change form as he went. Leaping off the wall, his transformation completed mid-air, and he rose above the trees in his smaller dragon form. He turned to get his bearings, then headed toward a nearby mountain.

Alexander checked his map. The area immediately around the tower had filled in when they'd emerged onto the roof. He could see forest for nearly a mile around, and a river roughly a hundred yards to the east. Looking up from the map, he turned in a circle, observing the forest around him. The trees had clearly grown taller since the tower was constructed. They were now taller than the tower, and limited his view. Looking east, he was barely able to spot the sparkling of water through the trees where the river should be.

A crunching sound caused Alexander to turn back toward the gryphon, just in time to see him swallow what was left of a dire wolf carcass that Lainey had pulled from her bag. He chirped what Alexander assumed was a 'thank you' and head-butted Lainey.

"Braxis, now that you've had a snack, can you help me figure out where we are?" Alexander asked. The gryphon chirped again, nodding his head.

"Do you know the human city, Stormforge? Do you know which way it is?"

Braxis nodded his head again, then pointed a forepaw past Alexander, toward the south.

"It's to the south. Thank you. Do you know how far?"

Braxis tilted his head as if in thought. He squawked a few times, then lowered himself to the floor, being careful not to crush Beatrix.

"Gryphons don't do well with distance or time. He says he will show you. Climb up on his back," Fitz said.

A bit hesitant, Alexander set his left foot upon the gryphon's leg and grabbed a handful of fur upon his back. Then with a push, he heaved himself up and onto the beast's back, situating himself just forward of Braxis' shoulders.

The gryphon quickly took several steps toward the edge of the roof, diving over the crenellated wall and spreading his wings. With two massive beats, they were rising above the trees. Alexander grabbed two handfuls of mane and gripped tightly with his knees as Braxis banked by lowering one wing and raising the other. He quickly leveled out, and they were gliding southward over the ancient forest. The river ran parallel to their path on Alexander's left. Beyond the river was more forest, rising into the slope of a mountain. From this vantage, Alexander could see they were above a whole range of mountains, running in a curved spine from west to east.

In less than ten minutes, the trees began to thin out, and Alexander could see the river more clearly. Ahead of them, it seemed to drop off a ledge and disappear. A moment later, Alexander recognized that this must be Dire Falls. Just as the thought occurred to him, the land beneath the gryphon dropped away, and Alexander was looking down over Dire Keep, the lake, and the forest of his Dire Lands.

Without prompting, Braxis tilted into a dive, heading down the several hundred feet to the forest below. He circled above the keep once, then moved off toward the west. Alexander could see the logging crew working, as well as the dwarves still planning the dig site at the quarry. The gryphon followed the ridge line to the west, showing Alexander the mine entrance, and after a few minutes, the entrance to the demon cavern. Alexander saw no signs of activity, nor any sign of his hunters.

Alexander patted Braxis on the neck, and shouted, "Okay, thank you. Take us back whenever you are ready!"

Braxis turned closer to the cliff face, and expertly caught some kind of updraft. Wings spread wide, he allowed the current of air to lift them both up until they were well above the top of the ridge. Then with a few beats of his wings, he turned them back northward and headed for the tower. Navigation wasn't an issue, as they could just follow the river northward.

Just under half an hour after they left, the pair landed once again on the tower roof. Alexander slid off the gryphon's back, then patted his side. "Thank you, Braxis. That was amazing!"

Braxis settled down on his belly again with a large sigh, and looked at Sasha as if demanding more scratches. He didn't have to ask twice.

Chapter Nineteen

Barbarian at the Gate

The group did not have to wait long before Kai returned. Flying beside him were three gryphons, two females and a male. The male looked young, and much smaller than the others. He was maybe half the size of Braxis.

Kai landed on the conical roof above the tower, quickly changed back to human form and slid down to swing under the eave and land among the others. The gryphons simply landed and gathered around Braxis, squawking and ruffling their wings. Kai explained as the gryphons talked among themselves.

"The new alpha, whose name is Tlark, is not popular. He takes a larger share of the food for himself, and has begun demanding to couple with any female he chooses, even those who are mated to another. The two young ones here are newly mated, and she did not want to be forced to couple with the alpha. The other female is one who wanted to mate with Braxis before he was removed."

"The new alpha sounds like a dick," Helga observed.

"I spoke to him, warning him that continuing in that manner would cost him his pride. They now know they have an alternative pride to choose if he doesn't behave better. Many know from the stories of the elders that the gryphons thrived when they lived among the mages, and would do so again. We shall see whether he heeds my advice."

Fitz asked "How many in the pride now? I'm sure the Mages Guild would be interested in re-establishing the gryphon force if their population has recovered."

"I counted forty in total. Thirty were females, and five were youngsters, including two of the males. So counting Braxis and the male here, there are only ten fully grown males. Though there may be more that were out hunting."

Braxis, who had calmed his new little pride and was listening to the conversation, squawked at Fitz. The wizard nodded his head as Kai translated.

"Braxis says there are two other prides, both led by his first generation of sons who split off to form prides of their own when they became strong enough. That would have been nearly…" Kai broke off to estimate the timing.

"Nearly seven hundred years ago," Fitz supplied for him. "We released Braxis and his mates more than a thousand years ago. The first-generation sons would not have been strong enough to form their own pride for two or three hundred years. Still, depending on how many females they each took with them, their prides could be equal to the size of this one by now."

Fitz patted the old alpha on the side of the neck. "He tells me he trained his sons and daughters in the old ways. They know how to fight in formation, both in the air and on the ground. Unfortunately, they never learned to speak any human tongues."

"Well, for now, we will welcome them as fellow citizens of Dire Keep. We won't ask them to carry riders in combat. Though they would come in handy as scouts, if we can find a way to communicate." Alexander turned to face Braxis. "Braxis, will you and your pride swear an oath of loyalty to the keep, and our guild? Think carefully, as the oath will bind your soul."

Braxis tilted his head, as if thinking. He made a questioning squawk, and Kai answered him at length. Fitz said, "He's explaining about the Dark One, and the likely attacks the keep will face. And about the binding of the oath. He also just described the large herd of livestock you keep close by." The wizard grinned at that.

When Kai finished speaking, Braxis held a brief conversation with the other gryphons before stepping in front of Alexander. He leaned down and head-butted Alexander's chest, then nodded his head. Nobody needed a translation. Alexander scratched Braxis' head a bit, saying, "Thank you, my new friend. And welcome to Dire Keep. We are honored to count such noble beings among our own." He bowed his head to the old alpha gryphon.

"We still need to clear downstairs," Max reminded everyone.

"Right. Braxis, we have to head down into the tower basement and clear out whatever tried to infiltrate our home through the mirrors. I'm afraid you and your pride won't fit through the trap door. If you like, you can fly ahead to the keep. You know where it is. I'll give you a note for Silverbeard, letting him know you are allies." Alexander reached into his bag for paper and pen.

Braxis nodded his head, and Alexander began to write. "Drop this in the courtyard, then land outside the walls. I don't want any of the guards to panic and attack you. Master Silverbeard will send someone to retrieve you when it is safe." Alexander rolled the paper up, then stuck a dragon pin through it as an identifier. Then a thought occurred to him.

"Lainey, can you make four leather thongs long enough for their necks? I want to give them each dragon pins, or pendants I guess, just in case. Brick, can you shape these into pendants with a hole for the thongs?" He withdrew four pieces of obsidian, slightly larger than the pieces he used for dragon pins. One by one, he imbued them with the Undying and healing spells. He put more mana into the healing spell for these, as the gryphons were much larger creatures, and he wasn't sure 2,000hp would be enough.

As he completed each one, he handed them over to Brick to be shaped. Lainey took them and ran leather thongs through them. She handed them to Kai, who placed one over each gryphon's head. He explained as he did so, telling the gryphons what the pendants would do. Once they were set, Braxis nodded his head and took off. The others followed.

Brick once again led the way as the group moved downstairs. Once back in the first-floor store room, Lugs lowered himself down the hole first to hold the ladder. Alexander followed, and removed the stone wall blocking the exit door while the others climbed down.

“Remember, whatever tried to get through that mirror was twice our level at least.” Sasha looked at Fitz and Kai. “Well, for most of us.”

Following the usual pattern, Brick and Lugs covered the door, shields up, as Max opened it.

The landing outside the door was still clear. Fitz and Alexander both cast light globes. Brick moved down the stairs, followed by Lugs. Fitz positioned his globe just above and behind Lugs’ head, while Alexander set his near the back of the group.

The stairway led downward the first fifty feet or so with smooth carved stone walls on either side. Then, quite abruptly, the left-hand wall disappeared as the stairway began to curve slightly to the left. Looking down, the group saw nothing but darkness below. No floor was visible.

Fitz summoned another light globe and sent it floating downward, saying, “Anyone down there has to have seen us by now, no point in hiding our presence.”

The group stood watching the globe drift down, most with one hand on the remaining wall for balance. Though the stairway was plenty wide, even for Lugs, peering over the edge at the falling light gave a slight sense of vertigo, making more than a few feel as if the stone stairs were less sturdy somehow.

Fitz finally halted the globe nearly two hundred feet below them when the floor became visible. Seeing only flat stone floor within the area of illumination, the wizard commanded the globe to move forward, away from the group.

The light crossed over a small but fast-moving stream that cut across the chamber floor. Near the stream on either side were clusters of large mushrooms sprouting up from the stone. Their exact height was hard to determine from so far away, but they looked easily large enough for a human to walk beneath. Silvery-white flashes in the water suggested the presence of fish in the stream.

Continuing across the chamber below, the light revealed the opposite wall, next to which was the portal that Fitz had expected to see. Or rather, the stones. The portal itself was not active.

Fitz directed the light to follow the wall clockwise, which would bring it to the bottom of the stairs. The group resumed their descent, keeping one hand on the wall to their right, and one eye on the light as it moved along the wall below. As they neared the bottom, the sounds of the stream become more recognizable. Along with a lower toned chirping noise. It was a similar to the background sound of cicadas, but not nearly so loud.

The light reached the bottom of the stairway not far from the portal. Once it was clear that nothing awaited them there, Fitz sent the globe off across the room again.

Just as Brick reached the bottom of the stairs, Fitz called a halt, pointing toward the light globe. It had crossed the stream again, and was just above the field of mushrooms. Standing there, looking much like a mushroom itself, was what could only be described as a monstrosity. The thing stood with most of its torso above the surrounding fungus. Which made it maybe fifteen feet tall. Its skin was pasty white and covered in boils that looked primed to erupt. The monster had two heads, the right one massive with a single horn on the right side and red, watery eyes that leaked pus. The other head was about one quarter the size and protruded from the thing's thick neck. It had a small horn on the left side of its forehead, and a bulbous nose from which green slime dripped into its wide open, toothless maw. Both heads sported random tufts of filthy, stringy hair that stuck to the boils on their scalps.

The thing had two massive arms with bulging veins that ran black beneath its nearly translucent skin. Another much smaller arm and a deformed, infant-sized leg protruded from its chest. The thing almost looked like it had partially absorbed a smaller version of itself. It was clearly undead, and detested the light that had exposed it.

The undead thing raised its right arm, swinging a bone-handled axe and striking the light globe above. The light burst into a thousand sparks before fading away.

"What the hell was that?" Dayle whispered.

"Necromancy," Fitz growled. "That was a demon abomination. Somehow a necromancer managed to raise one as a corpse."

"That shouldn't be possible," Alexander said. "When demons are killed, their bodies turn to dust and the souls return to the demon realm. Unless you capture their soul in a gem. Or something similar."

"Indeed," Fitz replied as he summoned another globe and sent it toward the monster. "But you saw it yourself. It seems someone has found a way. Much as you yourselves have modified your own magic abilities in ways others have not."

The globe reached the area where the monster had been. Fitz had it hover much higher this time, so as not to be so easily destroyed. The demon thing was standing at the edge of the stream, alternately looking down at the water, and up at the light. It roared in frustration and pain. It swung at the globe with a flail held in its left hand, but missed. Alexander noted that the flail seemed to be made of segments, like the spinal column of a large snake, with a fanged and spiked skull at the end.

"I don't think it wants to cross the stream," Jules observed.

"Aye, young lady. If it were willing to do so, it would have met us at the stairs already," Fitz agreed.

"Well, then it should be easy enough to kill." Helga pulled her new sword from its sheath and grinned hungrily. "That thing should be worth some good xp, too!"

Alexander used his identification magic on the monster.

Belorgz
Undead Abomination
Level 108
Health 38,000/38,000

"Well, shit. It's a named boss. Level 108. Has a ridiculous 38k health," he informed the others. Brick whistled in admiration.

The group descended the last few steps and began to move toward the monster, which was still flailing angrily at the light globe above.

As they neared the mushroom field on their side of the stream, Jules exclaimed, "Ooh! Ladybugs!"

Sending his own light globe forward, Alexander could indeed see scores of insects with red dome-shaped shells spotted with black dots. Only these 'ladybugs' were each three feet long. They seemed to be feeding on the smaller greenish fungus that grew underneath the much larger mushrooms. Here was the source of the sounds Alexander had observed from the stairs. The ladybugs were chittering away, occasionally waving a segmented foreleg or antennae at one another. Alexander used his identify skill again.

Fungal Devourer Beetle
Level 23
Health 1,800/1,800

Once again, he passed the info on to the group.

"So, they're low level, and vegetarian?" Misty asked. She looked skeptical.

"They might be good for alchemy ingredients," Sasha mused "Let's take one back to Lydia and see what she thinks."

"I'll get it!" Jules volunteered. "I love ladybugs!" She dashed forward before Alexander could object. Approaching the nearest of the bugs, she slowed to a walk.

"Jules, wait!" Alexander called out. "It's too close to the others. Try and lure it back this way a bit."

Jules nodded her head, pausing to remove an apple from her bag. She used a dagger to cut the apple into several sections, then tossed one to the ground next to the insect. Nothing happened for several moments. Then the insect seemed to sense the bit of fruit, turning to investigate it. After a few seconds, the insect bent and grabbed the apple slice in a pair of black chitinous mandibles that glistened with green slime. Upon seeing those, Alexander called out again. "Please be careful! Those mandibles look like they might be poison!"

Jules nodded, taking a step back. She threw another apple slice to the floor between the insect and herself. The bug moved forward, grabbing up the fruit without hesitation. She repeated this process twice more, until her target was a good thirty feet from the closest beetle.

Sasha cast a thorn trap over the insect, but the thorns did not penetrate the beetle's shell. It barely seemed to notice as it devoured the fruit. Jules stepped forward to grab it, saying "Don't kill it! I want to see if I can tame it!"

The elfess stood next to the beetle, which was more than half her size. Reaching down, she placed another apple slice right in front of its mouth. She spoke softly at the creature, reaching out as if to pet its back.

Alexander nervously looked toward the demon. It remained on the other side of the stream, now holding up a chunk of mushroom in an attempt to block the light in its eyes.

He returned his gaze to Jules, just as her hand made contact with the beetle. The moment she touched it, it let out a loud screech. Its shell separated into two 'wings' which shot out to either side. The one closest to Jules sliced across her thigh, cutting deeply and causing her to fall. Sasha quickly cast a heal on Jules, who was crying and holding her leg.

The beetle attempted to run away, but was held down by Sasha's vines. In a panic, it released a blast of green gas from its hind end. The cloud quickly enveloped Jules, and her crying was replaced with coughing.

The beetle's initial screech had alerted its nearby cousins, which took up the call as well. In seconds, dozens of the bugs were racing toward Jules. Brick was dashing forward, with Lugs and Helga just a step behind and the rest of the group following. But they weren't going to reach her before the bugs did.

Sasha desperately cast an aoe thorn trap between Jules and bugs. Maybe a score of them were trapped inside. Alexander cast wizard's fire on three of them, lighting them all on fire. A few of those behind tried to run over top, and were burned as well. But more than thirty of them simply moved around the burning trap and continued toward the now unconscious Jules.

Her health bar was dropping steadily. Sasha cast another big heal, while Lyra and Benny did the same. "She's been poisoned!" Kai cried out. "Use a cleanse!"

"I tried mine, it didn't work!" Sasha was nearly crying herself. Lyra and Benny just shook their heads. Theirs hadn't worked either.

"There must be an acid mixed in with the poison!" Fitz shouted. He halted and began to cast a spell of his own as the others raced forward.

Two of the bugs reached Jules a step ahead of Brick and Lugs. One bit into her thigh, the other her neck. Brick and Lugs reached her, each of them using their hammers to bash one of the beetles into oblivion. But the damage was done.

Jules's health bar dropped to zero, then quickly recovered to 1% as her dragon pin's Undying spell kicked in and kept her alive. But the DoT from the poison gas, and whatever poison the other two bugs had injected with their bites combined, erased the small sliver of health in less than a second.

Not realizing Jules was already dead, Brick and Lugs set up between her and the remaining oncoming bugs. Beatrix waved her arms, and a wave of water surged out of the stream, gathering bugs and tumbling them violently as it moved toward the burning pile of bugs. Max and Lainey were firing arrows with blinding speed. Helga, Warren, and Dayle joined the two tanks, forming a wall of armor and steel in front of their fallen friend. They hacked and smashed at any insects that moved within range. More clouds of green gas exploded from dead and dying bugs. Forewarned, the players all held their breath.

Fitz finished his cast, and a strong wind arose from behind the group, pushing the gas back toward the stream. The players all quickly took advantage of the clear air, taking in great gasping breaths.

As soon as her cooldown expired, Sasha cast thorn trap again, directly in front of the tanks. It managed to trap the remaining beetles, but once again did no damage. Knowing what was coming, the players in the front line backed up a few steps. All but Brick, whose shield would protect him from the fire. Alexander cast wizard fire again and again, his anger at Jules' death taking control. Helga lifted Jules and carried her back to the healers. Then all of them moved forward to begin stabbing and smashing the bugs nearest the edge of the fire.

Hearing the monster across the stream roar, Alexander looked up and cast wizard fire on it, too.

"What are you DOING!" Sasha screamed at him, moving to get right in his face. "You don't start a boss fight before the trash mobs are dead!"

Alexander stepped to the side, clearing his line of sight to the boss, and cast a massive burst of Ray of Light at the undead monster. His pulse hit the thing in its larger face, burning a hole through its nose and into whatever it had for a brain. The thing's health bar barely moved.

Belorgz
Undead Abomination
Level 108
Health 35,400/38,000

Alexander felt a sting on his face. He turned to find an angry Sasha looking up at him. She'd slapped him as hard as she could.

"Hey! Wake up, dumbass! Get your mind right! Jules will be fine! You're going to get the rest of us killed if you don't get your shit together!" She kicked him in the shin for emphasis.

Alexander looked around, blinking tears from his eyes. He saw Brick moving back from the burning pile of bugs toward Jules. He watched his friend bend over her body, laying a hand on her chest. There was a flash of holy light, and Jules began to cough. Instantly Benny, Lyra, and Sasha threw heals at her, bringing her health up to about 80%, where it stayed steady. Her death had cancelled the DoT's from the poison acid. Kai helped the rogue to her feet.

Sasha turned back to Alexander. "See? She's fine, Romeo. We've got two paladins here. Did you forget they get one res per day?" She kicked him again.

"I'm sorry, Sasha. I lost my head. I'm good, now," Alexander said quietly. "Let's kill this thing and get out of here."

Sasha looked at him for a few moments, as if trying to decide whether to believe him. Then she smacked the back of his head for emphasis, and turned to the group.

"Looks like the trash mobs are dead. Fitz, how long will that wind last?" she asked.

"Another minute, no more." he responded. "I can cast it again if needed, but it takes ten seconds. It is difficult to create wind underground."

Sasha nodded, thinking. "Everybody with fire magic, burn the mushrooms between here and the boss. Now, while Fitz's wind is behind us!"

Alexander, Fitz, and Kai all began to cast fire on mushroom after mushroom. Wizard fire and dragon fire quickly shriveled the fungi in a wide swathe, creating a thick green smoke that was pushed toward the boss by the remainder of Fitz's wind spell. The monster screamed in agony, inhaling more and more of the poison acid smoke with each breath. Its health began to drop steadily.

Belorgz
Undead Abomination
Level 108
Health 27,100/38,000

The abomination was already below 75% health, and had not activated any ability that Alexander had seen. He spoke his thoughts out loud, "Maybe it's not really a boss? It's a named mob, but maybe where it comes from, it's only a mini-boss?"

"Everybody focus fire on the big ugly dude!" Sasha yelled. "Brick, you and the melee stay back and be prepared to block or dodge any thrown weapons or spells." She cast Trap Soul on the beast as she moved.

The group moved forward to the edge of the now burned out mushroom field. They were within twenty yards of the stream, and thirty yards of the undead abomination.

Brick cast a holy smite on the monster, as did Benny. Fibble pulled out his stick and proceeded to bombard it with holy magic, shouting 'Pew! Pew!' with each shot. Fitz blasted it with wizard fire the same time that Alexander renewed his own. Sasha threw a thorn trap around it to increase the intensity of the fire. Lainey and Max poured arrows into it, while Misty hit it with bolts of ice, and Beatrix surrounded both of its heads in a ball of water from the stream.

Lugs, not wanting to be left out, pulled one of his spears from his bag. He backed up a few steps, then ran forward, hurling the spear with all the momentum and strength he could muster. The spear raced across the stream and into the monster's neck, nearly severing the smaller of the two heads. The beast's health was dropping steadily from the group's barrage.

Belorgz
Undead Abomination
Level 108
Health 20,900/38,000

"Coming up on 50%!" Sasha shouted. "Everybody back off, let the DoT's bring him down. Alexander, Fitz, Kai, give us some cover!"

The three immediately began raising thick stone walls in an arc in front of the group as the fire, and ice damage ate away at the mob's health. In less than a minute the group members were all hiding behind three walls, five feet high and three feet thick. Brick and Lugs were each holding their shields over the heads of those close to them, in case something made it over the walls. Alexander was preparing to cast a magic shield. Fitz already had.

Unfortunately for the group, the burning away of the mushrooms had revealed a low stone footbridge over the stream not far from the undead demon. Seeing a way across the hated water, it stomped its way across the bridge reaching the other side just as its health ticked down to 50%.

The monster threw back its head as it stomped toward the walls behind which the party was turtling. With a liquid roar, it belched forth a stream of thick black ichor - like spray from a fire hydrant. When it came into contact with the flames from the wizard and dragon fire that were still burning away at the monster, the ichor ignited, becoming a fountain of burning slime. What was essentially a stream of napalm struck the walls and splashed over the tops. Most was deflected by the shields, both physical and magical. But here and there, drops of the burning bile managed to get through to land on party members.

Helga screamed as a glop of fire landed on her shoulder, burning through her leather shirt and into her skin. Warren took a few drops to the face, which spread to his hands as he tried to wipe it off. Dayle tackled him and held his hands down while Benny tried to heal him.

Misty got the worst dose. She'd been crouched with her back to one of the walls, and a sheet of the flaming slime that had struck the top of the wall ran down the back side onto her head and back. Being a caster wearing cloth armor and having a low stamina stat, she was dead in seconds. She barely had time to scream.

The spray lasted about ten seconds. As soon as it was over, and no more splashes were impacting their shields, Brick and Lugs dashed out from behind their wall. Brick activated Shield Rush, racing toward the now much closer monster. He slammed into the thing's knee as it was raising its axe to strike at him. There was a crunch as bone or cartilage inside the joint was crushed. But the monster did not seem to notice. It slammed the bone-handled axe down toward Brick's undefended head. Lugs saved the dwarf, managing to place his own shield over Brick's head to meet the blow. But the sheer force of it pushed the shield down onto Brick's head, knocking him back onto his butt.

Lugs paid the price for his act of heroism. Down on one knee from the force of the axe blow, his shield above his head, his side was exposed. The flail in the abomination's left hand came whistling across. The segmented section wrapped once around the half-ogre's midsection, before the fangs of the serpent skull dug into his side. His armor kept the fangs from penetrating fully, but the tips got through far enough to inject him with poison. As Lugs screamed in pain, Sasha and Benny both hit him with heals. Lyra used a cleanse spell that, thankfully, worked against the demon's poison.

But the abomination wasn't through with the big tank. With a mighty heave, it yanked back on the handle of the flail, lifting the heavy half-ogre and flinging him into one of the still flaming piles of beetles.

Lugs had the presence of mind to use the momentum from his flight to roll out the back side of the flames. His armor protected most of him, but his face was badly burned and still on fire. Fitz immediately cast a spell that extinguished the fire, and cast a heal on the tank.

Brick, in the meantime, had managed to bring his shield up to cover himself as he tried to get back on his feet. Blow after blow from the axe hammered at the dwarf. Dayle rushed over, interlocking his shield with the dwarf's, while using his other hand to help Brick stand. Though he managed to get the dwarf standing, a heavy blow from the axe split Dayle's shield and cut deeply into his arm, knocking him down.

Kai, having seen the damage his party was taking, decided it was appropriate for him to get into the fight. Drawing a massive two-handed sword, the dragon rushed at the monster, passing it on its left side and swinging as he went. The abomination's flail dropped to the ground, still held by its severed left hand and forearm.

Lugs, back on his feet, lumbered over to the monster, which was ignoring the loss of its hand and still pounding on Brick with the massive axe. Lugs grabbed the end of the spear that was still embedded in the thing's neck, and levered it around, using his ogre strength to force the abomination to turn away from Brick.

The pressure off him for a moment, the battered dwarf grabbed hold of Dayle and pulled the warrior back out of reach. Heals saturated both of them as they moved.

The boss monster that wasn't a boss monster turned its attention to Lugs, who was still pulling at the spear to force it to turn its back on the others. Only Lugs and Kai were in the thing's line of site now. Once again, Lugs paid the price. The axe came whistling across the front of the monster's body, impacting Lugs' shield and knocking him back several feet onto his back. Kai made the monster pay for the blow, dashing in to slash at its leg, nearly severing its knee before retreating back out of range. Again, the thing shrugged off the damage, hobbling after the dragon as he backed up toward the stream. Lugs wasn't moving.

Alexander had had enough. *I've got to think of way to end this! Too many of us are getting hurt and this thing's only down to 40%!*

Reaching into his bag, Alexander withdrew the obsidian he had left in his bag. It was a chunk roughly the size of a grapefruit.

Focusing his mana, he began to enchant the stone. Just as he did with the stone he'd created outside of Millicent's, he pictured a volcano. Lava pouring out of its side. He poured mana into the stone until he was nearly empty. Then the grabbed a soul gem and began to drain it into the stone, this time pushing light magic instead of fire. He pictured the bright glow of the altar at Whitehall when it was consecrated by two gods at once. When he felt the stone begin to resist, he stopped. He used the remainder of the power in the gem to recharge his own mana as he yelled, "Kai! Get Lugs! Teleport back here!"

Without hesitation, Kai dashed backward then to the side, scooping up the still unmoving half-ogre like he weighed no more than a child. Then both dragon and ogre blinked out of existence. As the confused monster looked around, Alexander yelled, "EVERYBODY BACK BEHIND THE WALLS! NOW!"

Activating his levitation spell, he focused on the stone he was holding. He waited for the abomination to turn back in his direction, then pushed 1,000 mana into the levitation spell, sending the stone shooting like a bullet toward the monster. It embedded itself into the thing's gut, knocking it back a step.

As the abomination recovered, Alexander stepped behind the nearest wall, crouching so that only his head remained above. As the monster took its first step toward him, axe raised, Alexander closed his eyes. He cast Trap Soul on the monster, then focused all his remaining mana at once into the stone in the beast's belly. Fitz had warned Alexander as they sat in front of Millicent's bakery that overloading an item would likely cause an explosion.

Fitz was correct.

The overloaded stone erupted in a burst of fire and light that nearly blinded Alexander as he dropped to the floor behind the wall. The others cried out in surprise, some covering their eyes. There was a loud <WHUMP!> sound followed by a rippling wave of light and heat that cracked the walls they were hiding behind. Lyra screamed as a foot that had been sticking out beyond the wall was badly burned.

The entire cavern shook from the blast. Chunks of rock and dust fell from the ceiling, along with smoldering pieces of the abomination.

Level up! You are now level 46!...

Level up! You are now level 47! …

Level up! You are now level 50!
Your wisdom has increased by +1. Your intelligence has increased by +1
You have 19 free attribute points available

Skill level up! Enchanting +1

"What the hell did you do?" Dayle whispered from the ground next to Alexander.

Alexander slumped against the wall, exhausted from not one, but two massive mana drains in less than a minute. "I uh... leveled my enchanting skill. Figured I wasn't busy doing anything else…" he closed his eyes and held his head as Dayle just stared at him, mouth open.

Sasha and the healers went to work on everyone who was injured. Lainey began gathering beetle corpses for Sasha, while Max and Beatrix looted everything. Fitz came over and laid a hand on Alexander's head. After a moment, he felt well enough to open his eyes. The wizard looked down at him and waggled his eyebrows.

"That was quite a show, boy. I haven't seen an explosion like that since an apprentice blew himself and half a wing of the Mages Guild to tiny bits!"

"I'm glad you were amused, Fitz," Alexander mumbled. He took a flask of Sasha's tea from his bag and sipped at it. Looking past Fitz, he watched as Benny resurrected Misty. The mage looked dazed.

Jules came to sit next to him. She scooted close, lifting his arm so she could place her head on his chest. "So. You went all psycho badass when I died?" She grinned up at him.

"I might have been slightly annoyed. Like when you wait in line all morning at the DMV, and they shut down for lunch when you're next." He played along.

She snorted, smacking his stomach. Then rubbed it a bit. "I'm okay, you know. As real as it feels, this is just a game. I came back no problem."

Deciding this was a conversation best had in a more private setting, he kissed the top of her head and said, "I can see you're okay. Let's talk about the rest tonight?"

She nodded her head against his chest, not saying anything. They just sat there a while, listening to the sounds of looting and healing. Fibble was apparently 'helping' Sasha heal the injured. Alexander couldn't see the little goblin, but he heard the telltale 'Pew! Pew!' and chuckled. Jules looked up at him. "What?"

“Nothing, just Fibble being Fibble.” He smiled at her.

Max’s voice rang out from somewhere behind them. “HELL yeah! Boss loot! Took forever to find a big enough piece of him to loot. Alexander, buddy, you reeeallyy gotta stop exploding the bosses.”

Alexander could hear the grin on his friend’s face. His only reply was to raise his hand above his head far enough to be seen over the wall, and make a gesture that spoke volumes. Max and several others chuckled. Jules rolled her eyes at him. From somewhere further away, he heard Lainey say, “Idiot”.

“Fitz, can you do something about shutting down the portal? I think my head might explode if I try it.” Alexander called out to the wizard.

“I’ll take care of it,” Brick said, rising from where he’d been resting against another wall. He strode toward the portal stones, saying “Can’t be havin’ more o’ them beasties comin’ thru!” Just as he finished the sentence, the portal activated. Brick froze mid-step. “That weren’t me! Tell me it were one of ye, playin’ a prank!?”

Alexander looked at Fitz, who was getting to his feet, shaking his head no. “Well, shit,” he said.

End Book Two

Acknowledgements

Once again, I can't thank my family enough. My parents and sister who served as alpha readers and motivators. My brother Jason the printing expert who consulted on paper quality and ink. And my friends and guildies who gave me ideas and feedback to help me improve the final product.

Special thanks to Chris Johns, USMC, who had the winning suggestion for both the form and name of the cute little moat monster. And who has been a voice of support through my writing process. Also, a shout out to that Jeff guy, who couldn't resist trying to put friggin sharks in my moat. As promised, the first noob to die at the monster's hands is named for you.

Thank you to Paul Martin at Dominion Editorials http://dominioneditorial.com/ for your editing and feedback. And a big thank you to Robin at mycustombookcover.com for the amazing cover art and formatting. And to Jennifer S. Lange for the cool map!

Please check out my Greystone Guild page for information on upcoming books https://www.facebook.com/greystone.guild.7

You can also get great information and reviews from Ramon Mejia's LITRPG Podcast at https://www.facebook.com/litrpgpodcast/

I'd also like to recommend you check out some of my favorite authors within the genre.
Daniel Schinhofen https://www.amazon.com/Daniel-Schinhofen/e/B01LXQWPZA
Blaise Corvin https://www.amazon.com/Blaise-Corvin/e/B01LYK8VG5
Michael Chatfield https://www.amazon.com/Michael-Chatfield/e/B00WCAOQME
Ramon Mejia https://www.amazon.com/R.A.-Mejia/e/B01MRTVW3O
Dawn Chapman https://www.amazon.com/Dawn-Chapman/e/B014A0RUBC
Eden Redd https://www.amazon.com/Eden-Redd/e/B00I8X8BCK
Aleron Kong https://www.amazon.com/-/e/B0176S6G6A
D. Rus https://www.amazon.com/D.-Rus/e/B00LYQO4XI

If you enjoyed this book, or even if you didn't, but you DO enjoy the LitRPG and GameLit genre, then I recommend you check out the following Facebook pages:
https://www.facebook.com/groups/LitRPGsociety/
https://www.facebook.com/groups/GameLitSociety/
https://www.facebook.com/groups/LitRPGBooks/

Also, the first of the LitRPG groups that I joined (and was promptly kicked out of for misbehaving) after reading the first of the Chaos Seed series, “The Land” which was my first experience with LitRPG. I followed a link in the back of the book and found some of the strangest, and coolest, folks.
https://www.facebook.com/groups/LitRPGGroup/

Made in the USA
Monee, IL
22 December 2022